DEVIL'S

BOOK TWO OF
THE BLACK ROAD

SIMON BESTWICK

Proudly Published by Snowbooks in 2016

Copyright © 2016 Simon Bestwick

British Library Cataloguing in Publication Data
A catalogue record for this book is available from the
British Library.

Hardback | 978-1-909679-90-0
Paperback | 978-1-909679-91-7
Ebook | 978-1-909679-87-0

Printed in Denmark by Nørhaven

For Vicky Morris,
A true friend.

ACKNOWLEDGEMENTS

Emma Barnes at Snowbooks for her patience and general loveliness, and my amazing editor Tik Dalton. Thanks again to Anna Torborg, for opening the door. I'm hugely grateful to you for letting me start – and continue – along the Black Road.

Jim McLeod, Paul Holmes, Anthony Watson, Peter Watkinson, Gareth Hughes and Matt Fryer for their advance reviews, and Peter Tennant at *Black Static* for a great combined review and interview.

Michael Wilson and Dan Howarth at This Is Horror; Ray Cluley; Mark West; Keith Brooke at Infinity Plus; James Bennett; Paul Finch; Rosanne Rabinowitz; Andy Angel; Thana Niveau; Mark Allen Gunnells; Anthony Watson again; Graeme Reynolds; Jay Faulkner; Jenny Barber and Cate Gardner, for hosting the *Hell's Ditch* Blog Tour.

All who attended the online and meatspace launch events for *Hell's Ditch*.

The music of Ladytron (*Best of 00-10*, *Witching Hour*, *Velocifero*), Christopher Franke (*Babylon 5* and *Babylon 5: Messages From Earth*) and, as always, Dark Sanctuary (*Exaudi Vocem Meam Part 1* and *Royaume Melancolique*) provided the soundscape that *Devil's Highway* took shape to.

Priya Sharma and 'Lord' John Llewellyn Probert both for being good friends and for giving me the benefit of their medical knowledge with regards to head trauma. Whatever I've got right is thanks to them – any inaccuracies are my fault.

Former Royal Marine Commando and marksman Peter Sharp for casting a military eye over the Battle of Ashwood Fort and for sharing his knowledge of weaponry – not least regarding the 'Charlie G' – and physics. And to his daughter, Jeannie Alderdice, for putting us in touch. (The same rule applies here with regard to any mistakes.)

My heartfelt thanks to you all.

Last and most, thanks go once again to my wife, Cate Gardner, for reading a very rough first draft and for believing in me even when I don't. Thank you, my love.

PREVIOUSLY

Twenty years after the nuclear attack, Helen Damnation came back from the dead.

For nearly four years she'd lived like an animal, after the defeat of the last rebellion against the tyrannical Reapers. But eventually her past caught up with her, and so did the vengeful ghosts of her husband Frank and daughter Belinda. They demand a soul in payment for their deaths – either hers, or that of the traitor who betrayed their base, the Refuge, to the Reapers: Tereus Winterborn, now Reaper Commander of Regional Command Zone 7.

Helen spent the next year tracking down other surviving rebels and seeking new allies among the tribesfolk of the Wastelands. Then at last she returned to the city of Manchester, Winterborn's seat of power. Danny Morwyn, one of a rag-tag band of urban youths rescued from the streets by her old mentor, Darrow, helped her evade the Reapers.

Danny brought Helen to meet with Darrow – and with Alannah Vale, a one-time intelligence officer for the rebels. Alannah was still traumatised from her torture by Colonel Jarrett, an officer in the feared elite unit, the Jennywrens, but

Helen badly needed her aid to discover the location of Project Tindalos, a new secret weapon being developed by Winterborn's chief scientist, Dr Mordake. Helen had been warned that Tindalos could potentially destroy all surviving life on earth.

Next, Helen and Danny entered the empty district known as Deadsbury, in search of its sole inhabitant, Gevaudan Shoal. Gevaudan, the last of the genetically-modified Grendelwolves, used as the Reapers' shock troops until they finally turned on their creators, wanted only to be left alone. He'd found a safe haven in Winterborn's territory, and a steady supply of the Goliath serum he needed to survive, by dangling the promise of future cooperation in front of the Reaper Commander, but he had no intention of fighting again, for either side.

But something about Helen's determination impressed Gevaudan, and when she was captured by her old enemy Jarrett, the Grendelwolf ended his self-imposed isolation to rescue her. Meanwhile Danny, Alannah and Darrow had discovered Project Tindalos' location: a Reaper base in the Wastelands called Hobsdyke. With the city perimeter sealed, Darrow was forced to attempt an uprising to give Helen, Gevaudan, Danny and Alannah to escape. He succeeded, but only he and a handful of his fighters survived.

At Hobsdyke, Helen and the others joined forces with Wakefield of the Fox Tribe and her warriors, but the base was empty except for the dead. They found, however, an entrance to a cavern system under Graspen Hill, where the base stood; there, they encountered near-indestructible, semi-human creatures that had once been the base's personnel – the Styr – and the grotesquely transfigured Dr Mordake.

Project Tindalos was an attempt to use the ancient ritual technology of a lost civilisation, the North Sea Culture, to awaken latent powers in the human mind; powers Mordake had hoped could undo the devastation of the War, and restore his dead wife, Liz, to him.

But the powers Mordake had sought to awaken had been implanted in humanity's ancestors by mysterious entities called the Night Wolves, venerated as gods by the North Sea Culture. Unable to survive in our world, the Night Wolves had influenced the development of the human race, implanting abilities that would enable their resurrection. The Styr, created by the partial success of Project Tindalos, existed to bring about the rebirth of the Night Wolves.

Helen and her allies managed to foil the materialisation of one of the Night Wolves. The resulting explosion caused the cavern system to collapse, destroying most of the Hobsdyke base and apparently killing Mordake.

*

In the months that followed, Helen's alliance against the Reapers has grown. In a hard-fought campaign over the bitter winter, they've seized territory from the Reapers to create their own sphere of influence, controlled from their secret base at Ashwood Fort.

News of the uprising has spread beyond RCZ7 to the Reapers' other Command Zones; now, there are rumblings of discontent across the British Isles. If he's ever to rule a reunified Britain, Winterborn must find a way to crush the rebellion before it can grow.

DEVIL'S HIGHWAY

BOOK TWO OF
THE BLACK ROAD

PROLOGUE

The heart of winter, and all the world was snow.

In the howling force-ten gale, it piled inch-thick on the landcruiser's plating; the wipers fought in vain to clear the windscreen and the headlights' glow, alone in the night, showed only a whirling white vortex ahead.

"Christ," moaned Walters. It was pretty enough to watch; that was what made it dangerous. The swirling patterns hypnotised you, your mind wandered – and out here, that was enough. Their fuel was dwindling, and if the 'cruiser's boiler went cold, so would they. "The hell did this come from?"

Patel scowled, shook his head. "Fucking MetSec. Couldn't predict steam rising off me piss."

"Fuck-all chance of *that* right now. Where *are* we?"

Patel adjusted the radio. "Sunray from Delta Oscar Four, do you copy? Over."

Static was their only answer. Somewhere in it Walters thought he heard voices, but couldn't make out any words.

He glowered at Patel. "Join the Jennywrens, you said. Better pay, you said. Thanks a fucking bunch for that one."

"There," said Patel. "There's a road, going up."

"So?"

"High ground. We make for it, try for a signal. It's our best chance."

"Not much of one." Even so, Walters steered the 'cruiser up the worn track.

*

"This is Delta Oscar Four. Any REAP Command personnel receiving, please respond."

The static squealed and hissed. Patel scowled and threw down the mic.

Outside was only darkness, half-hidden by flurrying white; no light but their own. And any other lights would probably be those of tribesfolk or rebels: as lethal as the cold, but more painful.

Snow thickened on the windscreen; the boiler's pressure gauge sank another notch. Walters' teeth chattered. He huddled in his seat for warmth. Tired.

Patel's head was nodding, his eyelids drooping shut. Walters closed his eyes.

"Delta Oscar Four, do you receive? Acknowledge. Over."

Walters grunted, blinking. Patel sat up straight, rubbing his eyes.

"I say again. Delta Oscar Four, do you receive? Acknowledge. Over."

An ugly voice. Grating, harsh, almost metallic. But a voice all the same. "Get it for Christ's sake," said Walters.

Patel grabbed the radio mic. "Delta Oscar Four here. Over."

"What's your status?"

Patel glanced at Walters. "We're a GenRen patrol – out on recon when this storm blew up. Unable to establish contact with unit and our location is unknown."

"Is your compass functional?"

On the dashboard, the compass needle swung and spun. "Not very."

"All right. Stay on the line. We're triangulating your signal now."

"Understood." Patel licked his lips. "Who am I talking to?"

"A friend," said the voice. "That's all I'll say for now. Never know who's listening. Now: hit your transmit button every ten seconds till told otherwise. Copy?"

"Understood." Patel looked at Walters. He counted to ten, pressed *transmit*, held it down, released it. "What d'you reck?"

"Long-range fieldbase." Walters fumbled out a pack of Monarchs, took one, offered another to Patel. "Somewhere out in bandit country. Not gonna risk giving owt about *that* away to the rebels, are they?"

Cigarette smoke filled the cabin. Patel pressed *transmit* again. "Wouldn't break radio silence for two stragglers, though, would they?"

"Maybe not ordinary Reapers, but GenRen, like us? Base like that'd have to be a GenRen op too."

"Even so."

"Is that ten?"

"Dunno." Patel pressed *transmit* again.

"Delta Oscar Four?" said the voice.

"We're here."

"We've triangulated your signal and have your position."

"Where are we?"

"Can't tell you, I'm afraid. Because then if I guide you here, and the wrong people are listening, they'll find us. For the same reason, I can't give you my ident."

"Secret base," said Walters. "Told you."

"What I *can* do is direct you to us from where you are now. In the meantime, just call me Ned."

Patel looked at Walters. "No call sign, no details, and we're driving blind. Could be a trap."

Walters' teeth chattered. "Got a better plan?"

Patel picked up the mic.

"Okay, Ned," he said. "Standing by."

*

An hour later, Walters thought Patel could be right. Fuel was running low, and the 'cruiser's boiler pressure starting to inexorably dip. And all either of them had seen, so far, beyond the white and whirling snow, were odd glimpses of ruins and twisted woodland.

But then the wind dropped, and the buildings loomed out of the night. Little stone cottages, shops, a church. A village of some kind – empty, abandoned, by the look of it. What got him most about it was how well-preserved it all was: most of the houses still had their roofs, even glass in their windows. Walters had only the haziest memories of the world before the War, but he remembered places like this, just about.

As they passed the church, a light flashed: high above them, on a hill.

"Delta Oscar Four, I can see your lights," said Ned. "You should have us in visual range by now."

"That's affirmative," Patel said. "Can see a light shining on higher ground."

"That's us. Carry on out of the village, and you'll find the road to the base."

"Understood."

The village's buildings fell away from them, and the full fury of the snowstorm surged across the exposed ground to buffet the landcruiser.

"We're nearly out," said Walters. The boiler pressure was almost at the redline as he forced the 'cruiser up the hill. The headlights were dimming too; the battery was failing. He focused on the light above them: the beam shone out over the hill's brow.

"Just a little further," said the voice. "You're nearly there, Delta Oscar Four. Nearly there."

And in that moment, the light went out.

"Ned?" Patel said. "Ned, you still there? Ned!"

But the only sound was static.

"The fuck just happened?" Patel asked.

4

"Maybe the generator blew a gasket or something. Long as they've got walls, heat and shelter, I couldn't give two shits."

The landcruiser's innards groaned and clanked. "Come on," snarled Walters. "Come fucking *on*."

"There," said Patel.

A pair of gates stood open in a chain-link fence, but no-one came to close them when Walters steered the landcruiser through. Patel climbed out and blundered through the snow to drag them shut; Walters spat curses as the cold air rushed into the cabin and the engine sputtered.

He peered out through the windscreen. Everything was dark. There were cracks in the ground. A watchtower loomed above them nearby. The light that guided them in must have come from there, but now it was dark and looked empty. There were buildings, nearby, blurred silhouettes in the snow; Walters shone a torch at the nearest. A prefab hut, used to build barracks in a hundred compounds like this one, but lightless, with soot smudged round the empty holes that had been windows and doors.

Patel climbed back in, yanked the door shut. "Seen the state of the place?" said Walters.

"Looks a bit fucked."

"It's burnt out. A fucking ruin."

"Maybe something deep cover? Secret base, you said it yourself."

"Yeah, or maybe something else."

"Like what?"

"I dunno."

Rebels. Tribesfolk. Ferals. Or worse. They both knew that out in the Wastelands, whatever pockets of life clung on to existence usually had to find harsh and often twisted ways to do it.

"There," said Patel. Walters looked and saw another light, shining through the billows of snow.

"Not much choice, is there?" he said.

"Not really."

"On guard, then."

Both men reached under the dashboard and unclipped the Sterling submachine guns secured there. Jennywrens always went heavily armed; as well as their revolvers and the Sterlings, there were two automatic rifles in the back of the cruiser's cabin.

Walters cocked the Sterling. Then, with the last of the boiler's steam, he steered the landcruiser towards the light.

The ground tilted underneath them, sloping down towards somewhere in what Walters guessed was the middle of the compound. But they were heading away from that: the light was coming from a small hut on the compound's edge, near the fence. It still had windows and a door, and the glow that shone from it promised comfort, shelter and warmth. A stubby metal chimney jutted from the hut roof, leaking pale smoke.

"Let's go," said Walters. He shouldered his rifle and swept it to and fro across the compound, backing up steadily after Patel as they neared the hut. Patel's rifle was slung across his back, the submachine gun ready for close combat. The air smelt of woodsmoke.

Walters flung the door wide; Patel dived through, rolled and came up on one knee, the SMG at his shoulder. "Clear. Get in and shut the door."

Walters slammed the door and bolted it. The hut's warmth was near-tropical after the cold outside. Lanterns hung from the ceiling, emitting the glow they'd seen. There was a double bunk against one wall and a couple of chairs against the other. Walters slumped gratefully into one. "Proper little home from home. Where the bloody hell is he?"

Patel propped his rifle against the wall and went to the far end. There was a pot-bellied iron stove, neatly-chopped wood piled up beside it, and a table bearing a heavy radio set with earphones and a small metal box. "Dunno. But he didn't call from here."

"Eh?"

Patel motioned to the radio set; now Walters saw the bullet holes in the casing. "This hasn't worked in weeks, or months," Patel said.

"Well, *that* has." Walters nodded at the stove, then the lanterns. "Them, too."

"Yeah. I know." Patel studied the metal box. "Bloody hell."

"What?"

"Have a look."

The box was a plain thing of dull grey metal, tightly sealed. Resting on top of it was a clean white paper envelope, which read, in neat but spidery block caps:

FOR THE PERSONAL ATTENTION OF
COMMANDER TEREUS WINTERBORN.

"What is it? A bomb?"

"Doubt it." Patel prodded the box. Walters yelped. "Whatever it is, think we're best off letting them find out back at the Tower."

The wind howled outside. "The fuck's going on, Saeed?" Walters asked.

"Pete?"

"Yeah?"

"Reck we should sleep in shifts."

"With you on that."

And so their watch began.

*

The Black Road winds on, endless, through ruins and dust, although the dust is one with the night. All that separates road from wilderness are the cobbles of white bone that mark its edges. Above, below, before, behind, there's only the dark. And no hope of any end to it; nothing to do except go on.

So on she walks, tattered coat flapping round her, gun weighing heavy in her hand.

Cold light flickers in the distance, limning the City's broken towers.

This isn't fair, isn't right. *We give you a season*, Frank said. *We return in the spring.* But it's still winter: months to go till she walks the Black Road again, or meets the ghosts it hides.

And as if the thought had summoned them, they appear. Two figures, one tall, one tiny. Pale blurs in the darkness up ahead. Frank. Belinda. The husband and child she lost. Lost because –

She doesn't want to think of how they died, or why. What she wants is to stop walking: to turn and run. Her ghosts are hungry, and wait to feed. But on the Black Road, there is only one way to go.

The pale shapes turn away, dissolve back into the eternal night. It isn't time yet. This is just a reminder. But it means something, even if she doesn't know what: on the Black Road, signs are hard to read.

She looks ahead, to the City. And beyond it something rises, dark and hunched, like a huge dog climbing to its feet. A dog, or perhaps a wolf. A long head turns towards her, and two vast pale eyes, like lamps in the night, pin her in their glare.

*

Helen woke, gasping. The room's dark was thick around her: she struggled upright and fumbled for her bedside lantern. Light spread and filled the room. Shadows danced on the walls.

Steady breaths, in and out, till her heart slowed.

Outside the room there were sounds: muffled conversation, footsteps, laughter and a distant song. Even in the dead of night, Ashwood Fort was never wholly still. It had been strange, at first, after being alone for so long. Now it was a comfort.

She went to the window. Wind howled; a thin, sharp draught sliced in through a crack in the glass. Helen lifted the curtain, peered outside.

Waves of snow washed across the landscape, shining in the light from the Fort. The world beyond was hidden. She kept watching, though, and remembered other dreams – if dreams *were* only dreams on the Black Road.

Tindalos, she thought. *The wolves are running.*

Only a dream. She told herself that: only a dream.

But still she was glad of the snow. If it hadn't been there, she'd have seen a long way. Maybe all the way to that huge shaggy head, and the glow of its lamplike eyes.

"Wakey-wakey, you cunt." Patel shook Walters awake. "Anyone told you, you snore like a fucked pig?"

"Lots of times." Walters yawned and sat up. "How would you know, anyway?"

"Thought it was your mother at the time."

"Fuck off." Thin chill light shone through the window, bright enough to make Walters wince. "Time is it?"

"0800. Getting light out, and the storm's dropped. Reck we should get moving."

"No-one came to look in on us, then?"

"Nobody," said Patel. He had the gunmetal box and the envelope in one hand, his Sterling in the other. "And you know what? I don't mind that at all."

"Me neither." Walters picked up his rifle, creaked open the hut door.

Everything was white, except the remaining huts, which were charred and blackened. Walters went across the compound. The cracks in the floor grew wider and more jagged, and he saw they radiated from a gaping hole in the compound's centre. The ground underfoot suddenly felt fragile and unsteady; Walters backed away towards the landcruiser.

"Come on, you lazy sod, give us a hand with this." Patel re-emerged from the hut with an armful of wood, dumping it in the 'cruiser's flatbed.

They stocked up on fuel and set the furnace going, eyeing the white stillness around them until the boiler pressure rose high enough for them to drive. Walters stopped at the main gates, ran out and pulled them wide. That was when he saw the sign.

"Fuck me," he said, and ran back to the 'cruiser.

"Let's go," he said, "and I mean fucking *now*."

"Shouldn't we try and work our position out?"

"I just have." Walters pointed.

Patel looked, then went still. "You're bloody joking."

"Some fucker might be, but I'm not. Now *come on*."

The radio crackled. "Delta Oscar Four," said the voice they'd called Ned. "Are you sure you've got to go so soon?" Its metallic, grating quality increased: at the same time, it started laughing. It hurt to hear it. "Wouldn't you rather stay for breakfast?"

"Drive," Patel shouted.

As they rolled out through the gates, the voice sounded again. "Fly back to your nest in the Tower, little Jennywrens," it said. "While you still can. Fly away. Fly away."

The landcruiser hurtled down the hill. Patel was staring back at the base, but Walters kept his eyes on the road. It was a long and dangerous way home, and anyway he never wanted to see that place again. Not the hut or the burned-out barracks, not the watchtower or the fence, and not the gates with the rusted plaque that read *HOBSDYKE*.

PART ONE
CATCHMAN

1.

THE DEVIL'S HIGHWAY

18TH MARCH, ATTACK PLUS TWENTY-ONE YEARS

High earth banks stood each side of the road, shored up with clapboard and wire netting, topped with brambles and coarse grass and speckled brightly where wildflowers bloomed to scent the air.

Not that Danny Morwyn smelt them; his suit and mask shut them out. He smelt plastic and old sweat, heard his own breath rasping. Among the other speckles of colour, almost right in front of him, pitted and porous, was a yellow-white nub of bone.

The road below was a Devil's Highway; he was lying on a grave.

The revolver on Danny's hip dug into his side; he shifted position. Beside him was a hand-held radio, a flare-pistol, and a Lanchester submachine gun. Inside a zipped pocket on the suit, something else poked into him; a small effigy made of twigs, cloth, dried mud and hair. He was never sure who it was meant to be, but it was something, a kind of prayer, like the candle he'd lit in the shrine back at the Fort. A prayer to the dead, the parents he'd never known: *get me through this*.

Movement to his side; another monkey-suited shape wriggled through the dirt to press against him. He knew who it was, even before he glimpsed the blue eyes and reddish hair. "Flaps."

"Lover." Flaps squinnied over the bank. "Still nowt?"

"Soon as there is, old Creeping Death'll let us know. Everyone in position?"

"Mine are." Flaps's fingers drummed on the barrel of her Sterling. "Not them I'm worried about."

"My lot'll be fine."

Flaps snorted, bumped her hip against his. "Can't have a laugh with you any more."

Danny looked away. He needed to focus now. They both did.

The Devil's Highway was a flat, smooth, tarmac ribbon, empty as the sky. Green grass, yellow dandelions, white daisies and violet bluebells twitched and shivered in the breeze.

The handset crackled. "Ranger One to Central, do you receive?"

A deep, rumbling baritone, rich and low. Danny snatched up the handset. "Central receiving. Over."

"I have visual contact. Nine landcruisers with .50 cals, troopers in back. Estimate one minute from my position. Over."

"Copy that. You know what to do."

A sardonic note entered the voice. "I do seem to vaguely remember. Ranger One out."

"They're coming," Danny said.

"I heard." Flaps knocked two stones together, three times,fast. The same sound came back in answer, three or four times, from each side of the road. Flaps pulled the bolt back on her Sterling, sighting down the barrel.

Danny cocked the Lanchester, propped it on the earth bank ready to fire, his right hand around the grip. He raised the flare pistol with his left, thumbing back the hammer.

Further down the Devil's Highway, Gevaudan Shoal watched the landcruisers approach with yellow, wolflike eyes, through the sights of his Bren gun.

The first 'cruiser passed so close he saw the Reapers' faces through the face-panels of their suits. Some could have been no more than fourteen. The first signs of puberty made you an adult now. *Young men marching.* Young women, too.

But Danny, Flaps and the rest were no older. There'd be dead on either side; Gevaudan had tried to go without choosing one, and ultimately the price had been too bitter to be borne.

Gevaudan waited, watched, and kept his hand on the gun.

*

Reaper Twemlow huddled in the last but one landcruiser's flatbed, wishing again for his desk at the Tower.

Inside his suit, he sweated. Tried to tell himself it was only the heat. He was thirsty too, ached to pull off the headgear and gulp water, but doing that before the all-clear would be suicide.

"You doing all right?" said another trooper. A scarred brown face, greying dark hair, an old Thompson gun at his side. "Twemlow, right? I'm Ahmad. First time out here?"

"Yeah."

"Where were you before?"

"AdminSec."

Ahmad grinned. "You a swot then?"

"My Mum was a teacher," Twemlow said. "you know — before. Taught me to read and write."

"Lucky," Ahmad said. "Not enough like you to go 'round. The fuck'd you end up here?"

"Fucked if I know."

"Pissed someone off?"

"Just kept me head down and worked."

"Sometimes that's enough," Ahmad grunted. "AgriSec, me. Nice little billet. Then someone remembered I had combat experience." He nodded at Twemlow's Sten gun. "Any good with that?"

Twemlow snorted. "Haven't fired one since fucking basic."

"Keep your head down, don't panic. Anything happens, just stay with me, Kay?"

"Thanks," Twemlow managed at last.

Ahmad grinned. "It's a bugger round here – you're boxed in. But you've seen how we're tooled up. It'll be fine."

Someone up ahead shouted. Twemlow turned. A thin white ribbon of smoke twisted in the air above the road, hanging from a point of red fire that sailed upward then fell, dying, towards the ground.

"Shit!" he heard Ahmad saying. "Get down –"

*

Gevaudan sighted on the rear landcruiser and fired; a short, efficient burst that knocked the machine gunner back off the flatbed. His second burst stitched across the boiler. Steam sprayed from the holes; the landcruiser shuddered to a halt.

The Reapers left in the flatbed scrambled for the heavy machine gun: a longer burst from the Bren cut them down.

Guns thundered up ahead – Danny and the rest. The other 'cruisers' .50 cals chuntered in reply. Bullets chopped the ground inches from Gevaudan's head; the machine gun in the last but one 'cruiser was raking the earth banks, while the other troopers started to de-bus. Gevaudan brought the Bren about, and fired back.

*

The flare whistled up. As Danny grabbed the Lanchester, the rebels either side of the road opened fire; the lead cruiser surged forward, the .50 cal firing up at Danny. The ground in front of him exploded in a shower of dirt.

"Fuck!"

Sprays of grit and soil marched away from him as the gun traversed. Flaps aimed her Sterling over the bank, firing down at the landcruisers. Danny scrambled back up alongside her.

A hole appeared in the lead 'cruiser's windscreen, white cracks racing outward. The driver pitched forward and the vehicle slewed; the co-driver grabbed at the wheel, trying to steer, but another hole starred the glass and he slumped too. Scopes' work; she was up the road, on higher ground. With her rifle, at this range, she hardly had to try.

The machine-gun was coming around: Danny took aim at the gunner, but the back of the Reaper's head bloomed open like a flower and he fell backwards. *Fuck sake, Scopes, leave some for the rest of us.* As if in answer, steam jetted from the landcruiser's boiler as two rounds punched holes in it. Danny opened fire on the Reapers in the flatbed as they hopped out.

*

Ahmad had hold of Twemlow's shoulder, pushing him down. Two other Reapers bailed over the side as the .50 cal thundered, spent casings spewing from the breech as the bolt chopped back and forth.

"Head down, keep moving," shouted Ahmad. "And w –"

And then the air was full of bullets – buzzing and cracking past them, sparking off the metal. The man on the .50 cal collapsed, still clutching the gun; the muzzle jerked up and shot the sky. Ahmad grunted, went sprawling across Twemlow.

*

The open flatbeds let the Reapers fire back and bail out fast, but gave them no protection with the rebels shooting at them from above. With the front and rear cruisers disabled, they couldn't go forward or back, so their best bet was to rake the embankments and hope to get a few grenades over.

Danny fired another burst. No mercy, no let-up; don't give them time to hit back. "Smokers!" he yelled.

A dozen grenades flew over the embankments onto the road, hissing smoke. More dirt sprayed from the bank-tops as the .50 cals swept about, but the Reapers were blind now.

Beside Danny and Flaps was a rope, one end bolted to the ground. Flaps threw it over the side and shinned down; Danny followed.

*

The machine gun hammered on; brass cases spilled down on them, bounced off Twemlow's faceplate. "Fuck," Ahmad shouted.

The .50 cal cut out. There was still gunfire, but it wasn't hitting the 'cruiser any more. Twemlow stayed down all the same.

"Fuck." This time Ahmad spat it through his teeth. He rolled off Twemlow, clutching his shoulder. Blood oozed through his fingers.

The flatbed was awash in blood and bullet casings. The .50 cal had jammed; the ammunition belt had kinked and the bullets fed in at the wrong angle. The machine gunner hung head down over the flatbed, a line of exit holes in his back. Twemlow scrambled to Ahmad's side, stuck a dressing over the wound to staunch the bleeding and reseal his suit.

The bushes atop the earth bank moved. A huge dark shape rose, a weapon in its arms. Twemlow fumbled for his Sten, but the dark thing was already moving, jumping from the bank to the road.

*

Bullets zipped and whined, cracked and buzzed. Danny hit the ground, rolled, saw Flaps dart away and vanish in the smoke. Danny unslung the Lanchester, ran after her. Two other shapes ran at him; Reapers. One saw him, shouted; their guns rose. Danny fired, zig-zagging the barrel in a capture burst; the Lanchester's brass butt-plate hammered back against his hip-bone. One dropped, his legs collapsing under him; the other fell and writhed, coughing blood. Danny leapt over them, ran on. No time to stop and think.

*

Twemlow saw the Reapers scramble from the rear landcruiser as the dark thing approached. One cried out and raised his pistol; the dark thing cut both men down with a single burst from the Bren gun it carried like a toy.

It was tall, and all in black – a long black coat flapped around it, long black hair blowing back from its pale, high-cheekboned face. The eyes were yellow, feral; if Twemlow hadn't already known, those would have told him.

"Grendelwolf!" It came out as a scream; the yellow eyes flicked towards him.

Twemlow threw himself down among the blood and cartridge cases as the landcruiser roared forward. The Grendelwolf's Bren gun chattered, bullets spanging off the 'cruiser.

Fucker's going for the boiler. If they stopped, they were dead. Twemlow poked his Sten over the flatbed. Go for the head; it was the only way that even stood a chance.

Behind them, the Grendelwolf was closing in, stepping over the Reapers it had killed. *Bastard.* Twemlow fired; the yellow eyes found him again, and the Bren gun came about.

The driver cried out; the landcruiser swerved. Twemlow turned to see a stalled landcruiser blocking the road. The driver tried to overtake, but there wasn't room and the nearside wheels hit the foot of the embankment. Twemlow grabbed at a stanchion as the landcruiser flew, turning over as it went; then it crashed back down on the road, its boiler bursting in a welter of white steam.

*

Ahead, another landcruiser: windscreen shattered, driver and co-driver dead in their seats, machine-gunner firing at the embankment down the road. Danny saw four, five rebels down on the ground; he shot the gunner in the back, knocking her sprawling across the flatbed. Another Reaper scrambled up, firing a Sten; Danny threw himself sideways, fired back.

The Lanchester spat two rounds and died: a misfire or a jam. The Reaper came back up, aiming. Danny let go of the Lanchester and rolled, scrabbling for the revolver at his hip as bullets kicked up chunks of tarmac. He fired twice, ran round the front of the cruiser, leapt for the flatbed. The Reaper turned, the Sten coming up; Danny fired three times and he fell back over the side.

Movement to his left; the machine-gunner, still alive, a Browning automatic in her hand. Danny turned – but he was too slow, she had him, this time he was dead.

The Browning flashed; the bullet plucked the shoulder of his suit. But she was squeezing off another shot, and this time she wouldn't miss. He started dropping to one knee, but he was still too slow; he wouldn't make it. Then pain twisted the Reaper's face and her arm spasmed. The Browning's muzzle flicked sideways, and the bullet sang harmlessly away.

Danny's knee hit the flatbed and he brought his gun to bear. Her teeth were bloody, gritted: she tried to aim a third shot.

Like his first time: everything had run slowly then, too. The plainclothes Reaper agent running at him, gun in hand; Danny aiming two-handed, like Darrow had said, and squeezing off two shots.

Danny squeezed the trigger, felt it cave; the hammer rose and fell.

The Enfield bucked and the Reaper's suit burst open at the throat. Blood sprayed down her suit; behind her visor she gagged and choked, and the Browning slipped from her hand.

Danny pulled the trigger again: the memory of that first kill, perhaps, or out of mercy. No point, either way; the hammer clicked on spent brass.

Danny broke the revolver open, spilling empty casings onto the flatbed, then thrust a speedloader into the hungry chamber mouths, snapped the weapon shut. He crawled to the Reaper, swept her gun away. He could hear her choking. Horrible fucking sound. He could barely see her face now: the face-plate was fogged with breath, spittle and blood.

Danny pulled a patch from a pouch on his suit, slapped it over the tear at the shoulder to reseal it.

The Lanchester's bolt was fully forward, not stuck half-way. He pulled it back and a bullet fell into the blood, dirt and empty casings on the ground. Danny aimed at the road, fired a short burst.

When he turned back to the Reaper, she was still and silent; behind the bloody face-plate her eyes stared and didn't blink. Danny covered them with a rag from the flatbed floor.

A shape loomed out of the smoke and swung towards him; the muzzle of a Bren gun was an inch from Danny's face.

Gevaudan breathed out and lowered the weapon. "Sorry, Danny."

"Cheers." The smoke was clearing. Bodies everywhere, but most of the rad-suits were in Reaper colours. Odd bursts and single shots rang out: mopping-up. Sounded better than *finishing off anyone we didn't kill.*

Gevaudan looked tired: Danny had always thought that was impossible. "*Next to a battle lost,*" he muttered, "*the saddest sight is a battle won.*"

"What?" asked Danny.

Another burst rang out. Gevaudan glanced back down the road. "Doesn't matter."

Danny shrugged. Sometimes the Grendelwolf was just bloody weird.

*

Under the landcruiser, Twemlow huddled in one corner of the flatbed, staring at the gap between it and the roadway. Feet ran back and forth; bodies strewed the ground. The rebel dead were dragged away now; dead Reapers were stripped of their suits, weapons and anything else of possible use, and left lying in the road.

"Bastards," he moaned, teeth chattering. "Sick fucking –"

"No, they're not," Ahmad said, tightening the dressing on his wound. "They can use the suits and boots, same as they can landcruisers, guns and anything else. Now keep it stum and —"

A pair of booted feet appeared under the flatbed. Twemlow fumbled for the Sten gun, but their owner fell into a crouch beside the cruiser and spoke: "Family man. *Family man.*"

Ahmad grabbed Twemlow's arm. "Easy."

The rebel crawled under the flatbed, dug something out of his rad-suit pocket. "Get this to Colonel Jarrett. At the Tower." He disengaged the .50 cal from its buckled mount, pushed it and the ammo belt out onto the road. "Giz your gun."

"What?" said Twemlow.

"Just you. Keep the other."

"Do it," said Ahmad.

Twemlow handed over the Sten. "Look happy, you twat," the rebel said. "Your lucky day."

*

"Move 'em out, lads," Danny called. "And for fuck sake, Harp, put your fucking mask back on."

"Gah." Harp scowled, fumbling the mask back into place. He was stocky, with greasy dark blond hair and a wide flat face. He was a tribesman, too — Wakefield's lot, the Foxes — and hated the suits and headgear. Danny wasn't keen on them either, but he'd seen what a creeping dose did, and that was worse.

"A good day's work?" Gevaudan said, watching the functional landcruisers rolling past.

"We're still alive," said Danny. It came out sharper than he'd meant; sometimes Gevaudan seemed to forget how much easier it was to die if you weren't him.

"Most of us, anyway," said Flaps. She squatted beside a Reaper corpse, then wandered over to another.

That stung, but Danny knew she didn't mean owt by it. "Lish," he called up to the embankment, "what's the damage?"

"Three dead," she answered. "Five minor injuries, two serious. Need to get them back to the Fort now."

"Do it," Danny said. He turned back to Gevaudan, shrugged. "We've got more guns and 'cruisers now, and they've got less. That's good and all."

"Fewer men, too," said Gevaudan.

Danny saw them in the road at the edge of his vision; he didn't look because he knew who'd be there. Nadgers, Ashton, Nikki, Hinge, Thursday: fuckers kept popping up. Wasn't even like he'd killed them, or even like it'd been his fault they'd died. Darrow, Helen, Gevaudan – they'd all told him that. Still felt like it was, though.

"Better them than us."

Gevaudan looked down the road to the abandoned landcruisers. "You're just leaving those?"

"They're both too fucked to move. We got the others, anyway."

"I'll try to do less damage next time."

A hacking, gagging sound; Danny looked round to see a big lad about his own age doubled over by one of the landcruisers, mask off, throwing up. A smaller, wirier lad rubbed his back. "Fucking hell, Mackie, get your mask back on."

"Soz." Mackie spat bile and straightened up, blinking big, moist eyes. "Just not used to it."

"Yeah," said the smaller one, as Mackie fitted his mask back into place. "We're used to scavving for arms caches."

"Sorry, Cov," Danny said. "Needed the bodies."

"Huh." Cov glanced at the corpses on the road. "You got 'em an' all."

"Look at this." Flaps crouched by another dead Reaper. His suit, boots and weapons were gone, but the uniform underneath remained. "The shoulder flashes."

Danny crossed and knelt beside her. Below the standard Reclamation and Protection Command one was the coloured flash for the Reaper's Command Section. "CiviSec?" said Danny.

"Same as the rest," said Flaps. "CiviSec, AgriSec, AdminSec."

"Street patrollers, farm overseers and office workers," said Gevaudan. "On a long-range patrol into enemy territory. No GenRen?"

"No," called Flaps, inspecting another corpse. "Not even CorSec."

Gevaudan raised an eyebrow. "Perhaps they're running out of Jennywrens."

Danny grinned. "If only."

"But no CorSec either? They're the next best thing."

"Next worst," called Flaps. She stood, making for the upturned landcruiser.

"Leave it," Danny said. "We'd best skate."

"Shit," said Flaps.

"What?"

"They're a decoy," she said. "Bait." Flaps pointed to the receding convoy. "They need to strip the lot for bleepers. Lead the Reapers straight to the front door."

"Already gonna," said Danny. "Couple miles to get clear, then strip-check the lot."

"They gotta know we'd do that, though," said Flaps. "So why?"

"Hoping to get lucky, perhaps," said Gevaudan. "I'm sure we'll find out in time." He turned to go.

"You can come to ours." Flaps nodded to the embankment, where her crew waited. "Danny is."

"Preparing another joint report?"

Danny's face got hot behind his mask. "Dead important to make sure we co-ordinate and that."

"That's what they call it these days?"

"We don't get much time together." Him and Flaps were an open secret, but no-one based out of the Fort was meant to stay at the fieldbase for a second longer than they had to.

"You're lucky," said Flaps. "Your bit's back at the Fort. See her all the time."

"Helen," said Gevaudan, "Is not my *bit*."

Flaps grinned and raised an eyebrow.

"Anyway," said Danny, "you come back to the field-base, they won't freak out so much. Not like the Reaper're gonna catch you."

Gevaudan studied them both, then shook his head. "All right, children. I'll join you. I assume you still have that old guitar?"

"Might have," said Flaps.

Gevaudan sighed. "I thought so."

"Cheers, Creeping Death," said Danny.

Gevaudan shook his head. "Youth of today. No respect for their elders." He studied the bodies on the Devil's Highway, its banks of bone-filled earth. "Understandably, perhaps."

He climbed up the embankment. "He's weird," said Flaps.

"I know," said Danny, a bit defensively.

"But he's okay."

Danny grinned back at her. "Yeah. He is." He unzipped the pocket on his suit, pulled out the remains of the doll. It had been crushed to dust and splinters; he let them fall to the road. "Come on."

They climbed up after Gevaudan to their 'cruiser; it hissed and clanked away into the distance and briefly, there was stillness. Then the crows and ravens came to peck at the dead, rats crawled down from the embankment, and Twemlow crawled out into the road, clutching Ahmad's Thompson gun.

"Fucking hell," said Ahmad as Twemlow helped him stand. The other landcruiser's tyres were in ribbons, its boiler riddled and bled out. "Looks like we're walking."

Twemlow studied the package they'd been given. "What d'you reck this is?"

"Probably more than your life's worth to find out." Ahmad started walking, nursing his bad arm. "Just let's concentrate on getting back to the Tower with it."

ARMOURY, ASHWOOD FORT

"Helen!"

She reached for the .38 that wasn't there, then relaxed when she saw who it was. "Alannah."

Alannah smiled, looked as though she might offer a hug by way of greeting, clapped Helen on the shoulder instead. "You look like death on a stick."

"Love you too."

Looking at Alannah now, it was hard to picture how she'd been: ragged and stinking, ghost-white from five years underground. She was still pale now, but wiry and lithe from daily running, her silver hair brushed smooth and gathered back. She wore a white linen shirt, leather waistcoat, leggings and boots. Only one thing hadn't changed – the haunted, shadowed look in her eyes.

On her hip she wore a heavy First World War revolver, the kind that would knock a man flat even with a flesh wound. In another, hidden holster she carried a .22 pistol and in each boot was a short, heavy-bladed knife, with another sheathed on her left forearm. Technically, weapons weren't supposed to be carried inside the Fort except in an emergency – which was why the pouch on Helen's coverall was empty – but Alannah refused to go anywhere unarmed. The Reapers had taken her once; they never would again.

"What you up to?" she asked.

Helen jerked her head at the steps leading down to the armoury. "Zaq's got something to show me, apparently."

"Has she now?" Alannah grinned. "That'll make Gevaudan jealous."

"Oh, put a sock in it." Helen started down the steps. "Want to join me, so I don't have to face Zaq alone?"

"I heard that," a voice called up the stairs.

Fuck, Helen mouthed, while Alannah bit her lip to muffle laughter. Finally she nodded and waved Helen ahead down the stairs.

The armoury was hot, close and dark; Zaq always had a furnace on the go. There were a couple of electric lights, which Zaq had lobbied hard and loudly for and finally been given on condition they were only used when absolutely necessary. As a result, the only light most of the time was the gridded orange glow from the furnace.

"Zaq?"

"Over here." One of the lights clicked on; the armourer put her hands on her hips and glowered at them. She wasn't a tall woman – about five-four in her socks, five-six in her heavy boots – but generally managed to look bigger. She was trim-built and black-clad, with a round, pretty face and black hair with a silver streak, and there were hardened fighters who'd declared they'd rather take on a squad of fully-armed Jennywrens single-handed than share a confined space with an angry Zaq.

Zaq balled her gloved hands into fists and put them on her hips.

"You, um…" Helen cleared her throat. "You wanted to see me?"

"Wanted? No. Thought I better had? Yes. Here." Zaq snatched something from one of the work-tables and lobbed it in Helen's direction.

She caught it. "Okay," she said. "And?"

Zaq snorted and folded her arms.

"Zaq, what? Just looks like a bog-standard Sten gun to me."

"Bog standard? I'll have you know that's a damn sight better quality than most of the original ones ever were. Also it's compatible with Sterling and Lanchester magazines and has a grooved bolt like the Sterling so it's self-cleaning."

Helen turned the submachine gun over in her hands. "You mean this is a brand new one? Made from scratch?"

"No, Helen, I fucking carved it out of a giant mushroom I grew down here. Yes, of course I built it myself. Not that difficult. Just needed the metal."

Helen shouldered the gun, cocked and dry-fired it. "It been tested yet?"

"Fired a few practice rounds, but it needs a field trial." Zaq put her hands on her hips again; she could tell Helen was impressed. "You might like these, too," she said, motioning to the worktable.

Helen came over and looked.

"What you've got there is the Mark 1a," said Zaq. "That's the 1b –" she pointed to another weapon, identical to the one Helen held except that the magazine pointed downwards instead of sticking out to the side. "Here's the Mark 2 – or the Stenchester, I call it." The Mark 2 had a wooden stock, like Danny's Lanchester. "Saves on metal. Takes longer to produce, of course, but I'm looking at designing a mould so we can make it from wood-chip composite. And this is the Mark 3." She held up what looked like a Mark 1b gun that had been chopped down to about two feet in length. "The Sten pistol. I call it the Stemp. Selective fire, so if there's a shortage of handguns it'll come in handy. Or you can use it as a machine pistol. A bugger to control, of course, but very useful for close-quarters stuff."

Zaq was actually beaming; it reminded Helen of her mum at the school gate when she'd been little. *Mum.* Helen looked away, hefted the gun. It balanced well, aimed naturally. "Not bad."

Zaq's smile became a scowl."Not bad?"

"I mean, it's excellent. This is great, Zaq."

"Yeah." the other woman took the Stemp back. "First new guns made since the War, I reckon." She sighed. "Be nice if I could make something a bit less lethal, but needs must. Anyway, thought you'd want to see. Now you have, so you can bugger off."

Helen waited till they were back in the corridor above and several yards on from the entrance before speaking. "Christ Almighty," she said. "I always feel like I've been beaten up when I talk to her."

Alannah's smile vanished. "Don't. Please."

"I'm sorry." Helen touched her arm; Alannah flinched away. "Are you —"

"No, of course I'm not okay. None of us are." Alannah breathed out. "You never did get it, did you? What that bitch Jarrett did —" She pressed a fingertip to her forehead. "It *stays.*"

"I'm sorry," Helen said again.

Alannah smiled. "It's okay. My problem, not yours." She hugged herself, fingers drumming on her arms.

Helen knew the signs. "Danny not back yet?"

"He'll be along later. Gone to the fieldbase to debrief Flaps." Alannah's mouth tightened at the name.

Helen half-smiled. "Alannah, *you* shut things down with *him.*"

"I'm old enough to be his mum. Or his gran."

"Then you don't get to be jealous. But it's okay to be worried about him."

"I'm not."

Helen frowned. "When are they coming back?"

"Tomorrow."

"For fuck sake. Danny knows where we are."

"He says they're co-ordinating."

"Like bloody rabbits," muttered Helen.

"Gevaudan's staying over as well."

"Seriously?"

"Something about it being more secure."

Helen shook her head. "The Reapers just need to capture one of them and –"

"I know. I know. I'll have Darrow talk to him when he gets back." Alannah looked away. "Come on. Let's get in."

*

Helen ate, then washed and climbed into her bed. She was asleep at once, and without dreams.

She woke near dark, and lit the candle by her bed; its light spread across the room.

"Hello, Helen."

Frank spoke just as the spreading light reached the chair in the corner. Belinda knelt beside him, head against his knee. "Hello, Mummy."

Their hair was bleached and dead, their chalk-white skin cracked and dry. Their eyes were clots of blackish-red, and their grins showed rows of needle teeth.

"Frank," Helen said. "Belinda."

Frank stroked Belinda's hair. His hand looked like a bird's claw. Talons instead of nails.

"We promised you a season," he said. "Now it's done."

Helen glanced at the bedside table, where her revolver lay beside the candle.

Belinda giggled. "Silly Mummy."

"Silly Helen," smiled Frank. "You can't kill the dead." The smile faded. "The same deal as before. Give us Winterborn, or we take you."

"I'm working on it."

"Time's passing, Helen," Frank said. "And it's not on your side."

"Tick-tock, Mummy," Belinda said. "Tick-tock, tick-tock."

"We're hungry, Helen," said Frank. "And the Wolf is waking."

Belinda tittered; Helen couldn't look at her child any more. "Leave me alone," she said.

Frank tittered. "Don't worry, Helen. We won't hurt you." Their smiles vanished. "But something will."

And the room was empty. All around, the Fort was silent stone. Like a tomb to bury her in.

REAP HOBSDYKE
19TH MARCH, ATTACK PLUS TWENTY-ONE
0400 HOURS

Above the empty village, on the hill, the gate in the mesh-wire fence creaked to and fro. No bird sang; no fox or wild dog barked. Not even a rat's scuttling broke the hush.

Beyond the gate, the ruined complex: the burned-out huts, the new-built shack, the gaping hole in the compound floor and what stood beside it. It was robed and hooded, in a soft, loose, grey robe. At last it moved, and slow, gritting footsteps echoed across the compound.

Its sleeves were joined, overlapping; when it reached the gate they separated, but the sleeve hung down over its hands. It didn't touch the gates, but when it extended an arm they swung wide.

The Walker's sleeves joined together again, and it stepped out through the gate, onto the road down Graspen Hill.

2.

THE TOWER
19TH MARCH, ATTACK PLUS TWENTY-ONE
0410 HOURS

A clock was ticking.

The Ops Room filled the Tower's twenty-fourth floor. Individual rooms had been knocked together into a single open space, filled with monitors, radio sets and charts of Regional Command Zone 7's various sectors. The entire RCZ was controlled from here; now and then, a section of it was dedicated to running a specific op, but not today.

Today was quiet; so quiet, the murmur of voices and comms chatter so low, that the loudest sound was the clock's ticking. Jarrett shook her head: it was too loud, too sharp. "Colonel Thorpe?"

"Ma'am?"

"Still waiting for those reports."

"I'll chase them up, ma'am."

"Do so. Also, increase perimeter security in Sectors Forty-Four through Forty-Nine and detail Jennywren Units One and Twelve to enter Sector Forty-One. Usual punitive measures: find somebody, make them hurt. Then –"

Something pattered on the floor, then on her head. Jarrett touched her hair; there was dirt there, grit. She looked up; more fell in her eyes and mouth.

She gagged, coughed, spat; when she looked round, Thorpe was backing away. The other Reapers, too; getting up and shuffling back. There was nothing in their faces, as if they'd been playing parts they'd lost the will to maintain.

The Ops Room's light dimmed; the other Reapers vanished into the dark. The light shrank around her; a pale, lonely island. More dirt fell on her, pattered on the floor. Looking up, Jarrett saw a gallery above the Ops Room. Where had that come from? People stood there, looking down.

"Who are you?" Jarrett shouted. "The hell do you think you're doing?"

"Nicola?" Jarrett went still. "How could you, love? How *could* you?"

More earth fell. This time it wasn't a light rain: it was a shovel-load of clods and soil. Jarrett threw her hands up to protect her eyes, spat out dirt and looked up again.

The gallery brightened. She'd been right about the voice. She couldn't have been, she knew, but there was no mistaking Mum's kind, round face, the wart on her chin, the grey hair. But Mum's face wasn't kind any more: it was blank and emotionless, as Thorpe's and the others' had been. Beside her were Dad, and little Mandy, and next to Mandy, Tom – sweet Tom, whom Jarrett would have married – all still, all blank-faced.

Dad shook his head. He raised a shovel, upturned it. Earth rained down on her.

Mandy was crying; tears ran down her face.

"Mandy!" Jarrett called. There had to be a way up there, she'd take the child in her arms, she'd –

"I *hate* you," Mandy shouted. Beside her Jarrett saw a plastic seaside spade, sticking out of a pile of earth. She heaved a shovelful over the railing onto Jarrett.

Now Tom spoke. "You disgust me." He picked up a shovel too. "I never want to see you again," he said, and tipped more dirt over the rail.

"Stop it," Jarrett screamed. She never screamed. Losing control was weakness. But nonetheless, she had.

Her hand went to her hip-holster. Could she really do that? Fire on those she loved, even if they were dead? But it didn't matter; the holster was empty.

Around her was only the dark; the light was a narrow rectangular bar, her body's length and width. She could no longer see her family. She must escape; she'd have to risk the dark. But when she tried to run, the dark hit her in the face.

Jarrett reached out and touched a wall of cold damp earth. She spun, reaching out all around her. But in each direction, the story was the same.

More dirt fell on her, then more still. She heard the shovels working: when she looked up she saw them all again, their faces white, blank, implacable.

Then the masks fell and they began to laugh. Until the dirt rose up around her and she began to flail and scream. She slipped and fell and couldn't rise; the dirt rained down and they laughed and laughed.

And there was another face among them, laughing with the rest. Long and pale, red hair, grey eyes. Helen Damnation.

Then the earth fell in Jarrett's face; it was in her eyes, her nose, her mouth. She couldn't breathe, and –

*

Jarrett lurched upright with a cry, scrubbing at her mouth and eyes.

She hit the bedside light, grabbed and cocked her Browning and swept it across the room.

Nothing. Cool sheets beneath her; clean, dry air. Just her familiar quarters, empty but for her.

Jarrett made her way to the adjoining room, legs shaking, and sat at the desk by the window, pistol close at hand.

In front of her were the latest reports, a pen in front of her, and a small ceramic jar; she shook two white pills from it, swallowed them dry and started reading.

A column on the Devil's Highway, massacred by the rebels. Two survivors: one of them with a message. It was included with the other papers, still sealed; Jarrett opened it, and read.

Target Alpha still based at the Fort. Never leaves. No new info on the Fort's location.

She heard that laughter again, saw that hated face laughing down at her as the dirt rained down. The wound in Jarrett's soul that festered and wouldn't heal.

Jarrett looked up, saw herself in the window: half-dressed, wild-haired, pale, gaunt, red-eyed. Jarrett went into the bathroom, washed herself and cleaned her face. The pills were working; she wouldn't sleep again, wouldn't dream.

She donned her uniform, bound her hair, stood to attention and studied herself in the mirror. The black leather tunic and trousers were spotless, the blue shoulder-flashes straight (still strange not to see the white flashes of GenRen any more), bronze rank-badge polished to a shine. Clean, ordered, but she felt her hands trembling.

Deep breath. Still. Steady. Calm.

When she studied at her hands, they were still again.

Jarrett took a deep breath, and went out to pace the corridors. A few hours of that, before she descended to the Ops Room.

Hobsdyke Village

0750 hours

The cool morning was bright and clear, Spring's first flowers coming into bloom to scent the air.

Hobsdyke village's long-empty houses of stone sat quiet in the sun. Their empty gardens ran wild, their painted front doors peeling, but most still had their windows and roof-slates.

And there was still life; small unseen things scuttled in the undergrowth and birds twittered in the eaves of houses and the trees on the village green.

As it came along the High Street, the Walker was tempted to pause: in this world, here was a scene to linger over. But it had a mission; it had dawdled on its way down the hill, relishing its return to the light and open air. It wouldn't do to delay further, not at this stage; it had a long journey ahead of it.

Besides, as the Walker passed, the birds' twitter faded and the hedgerow and undergrowth grew still: the village was a held breath, waiting for it to pass.

The hooded head turned left, than right; it made to move on, then stopped beside a garden wall. A blue tit perched on it. It didn't sing or fly away, even when a shrouded arm reached for it; only perched motionless, staring up with beady eyes.

The Walker's sleeve slipped back from a pale grimy hand. One extended finger and stroked the blue plumage with the gentlest of touches.

The bird cheeped once, then was silent. The Walker withdrew its hand. A weary, mournful sigh escaped; it turned away and walked on. Behind it, on the wall, bird lay still, bright feathers ruffled by the wind, bead-like eyes glazing as it cooled.

The Tower
0800 hours

Jarrett walked into the Ops Room and there was Tom in a Reaper uniform, snapping to attention and saluting. She blinked, and a young Reaper stared back at her. She didn't know how she could have taken him for Tom; there was virtually no resemblance at all.

They acted their part; so must she. Jarrett returned the salute and walked on.

From one desk, Mum glanced sidelong at her; on another, Mandy sat cross-legged in front of Dad. Mandy waved; Dad looked up and saluted. Jarrett blinked: just another Reaper, with a computer terminal on his desk.

"Ma'am?" She nearly jumped. She must act normal. She was watched. No-one could know. But surely they couldn't miss the Commander's Adjutant coming apart before their eyes?

"Colonel." She returned Thorpe's salute. "Anything new?"

"Just one thing, ma'am." Thorpe passed her a folded note. "Just received from REAP Thurley. Your eyes only."

Jarrett opened it and read, smiled. *All will be well, all will be well, all manner of things shall be well.* It would take so little. One death, and she would live again.

Jarrett pocketed the note and clicked her fingers at a communications tech. "Get me Kellett at REAP Base Thurley. Now."

*

From his office window, Winterborn could see all the way to the Pennines, if he chose. But not today; today his focus was narrower, closer.

"There," he breathed; he put the tiny screwdriver aside and took the jeweller's glass from his eye, blinking hard. Before him was a silver box, four or five inches square. Till recently, it had been dull and tarnished; it had taken hours of patient cleaning and polishing to bring it to its former shine. After that, his thoughts had turned to improving other aspects of it. It had been a way to calm his mind through the long winter nights and their endless roll-call of rebel gains.

He eased the lid open; now would be the test. Bright, tinkling chimes sounded, the beginning of a tune. Winterborn leant back and closed his eyes. The music woke some distant memory of warmth. There'd been words that had gone with it: *I dreamt I dwelt in marble halls…* And then, it stopped.

Winterborn breathed out through his nose, opened his eyes and stared at the box, fists clenched. Sometimes it was simpler just to smash what wouldn't obey your will. He was still considering whether to do so when the intercom buzzed.

"Yes?"

"Colonel Jarrett," said a voice.

Winterborn sighed. "Show her in."

Jarrett entered; her uniform gleamed, her hair was brushed and tied back and she stood straight and neat, but the sickness was there underneath. It had always been festering there, but it didn't stop her doing her job; it might even help her to.

"Reporting as ordered, Commander."

Winterborn motioned to the chair before his desk. "Sit, Jarrett."

She obeyed and waited. Her eyes were bloodshot, he noted.

"I've been hearing a great deal from the other Regional Commanders," said Winterborn. "Word of our little problem has spread."

"I thought we clamped down on it pretty hard. A brief insurrection, crushed almost instantly. Some resistance as we push into the Wastelands."

"There isn't a Commander in the British Isles without agents in the other Commands, Jarrett. Should Britain ever actually reunify, we'll all be potential rivals for the top spot. The main problem, however, is that word has spread *beyond* the REAP Command structure."

"To the civilian population?"

Winterborn nodded. "And it's giving them *ideas*. The spectre of rebellion is haunting the other Commanders. And they aren't happy."

"And," said Jarrett, "it's all our fault."

"We failed to nip it in the bud."

"Their inspiration comes from the rebels in the Wasteland," Jarrett said. "They're proof we can be defied with impunity. Demonstrate that we can't, and the rest of the country falls back into line in weeks. Take out their Fort, their central command, and –"

"The rebel-held areas are still mostly uncharted and accessible only via the Devil's Highways," said Winterborn. "Which, as your decoy column established, the rebels also control. We'd have to retake the Wastelands sector by sector. It would take months, they'd fight us every step of the way; ample time to abandon their base and relocate if it was endangered.

Meanwhile, resistance keeps growing in the other Command Zones. So forgive me if I don't share your optimism."

"Four Jennywren battalions, in small to medium pursuit cruisers, could get up the Devil's Highway like a ferret up a drainpipe. Smash through anything in their way. One all-out, targeted, high-speed assault. Surround them before they can evacuate, bring in a support column with heavy weapons and finish the job. Game over."

"Your agent with the rebels?"

"Still stationed at one of the Wasteland field-bases."

"So they only get to the Fort if they're picked up by a transport from it, scanned for bugs and blindfolded for the rest of the journey."

"They know it's a weakness," said Jarrett. "Even when Darrow evacuated what was left of the city crews in the winter, they were blindfolded on the approach to the Fort."

"Yes, Colonel, I remember reading the report. So, what's changed? I assume something has."

"Just got word from REAP Thurley, sir. The CATCH program is now operational."

"My fondness for an ace-in-the-hole has never been a secret," said Winterborn, "but the CATCH program's antecedents…"

"The technology is now controllable," said Jarrett. "And can be targeted. We can use it to go straight to Helen herself, wherever she is."

"I'm sure that's what Dr Kellett said. Nothing would be more certain to gain your support."

"I wouldn't say that, sir," said Jarrett. "The prospect of killing the bitch myself would be far more appealing."

"I won't deny that without Helen our current problem would lose a great deal of momentum, but –"

"Helen never leaves the Fort, sir. So if we find her –"

Winterborn nodded slowly. "And your four GenRen battalions?"

"Put on standby as soon as Kellett informed me, sir."

"Hm." Winterborn pondered.

"Phase One of Operation Harvest only risks one life," Jarrett pointed out. "An individual who to all intents and purposes is already dead."

"And worth little enough when alive," said Winterborn. At last, he nodded. "All right, Jarrett. Go ahead."

"Dr Kellett's standing by at REAP Thurley," said Jarrett. "Given the circumstances, I thought you might like to give the command personally."

"How well you know me," smiled Winterborn.

REAP Thurley
0830 HOURS

Kellett looked up from his desk; outside the window the gleaming band of the river blurred into the marshes spread on either side, born when the river had burst its banks after the War.

Closer to was what remained of Thurley: gutted, roofless houses and jagged stumps of wall, half-lost in standing water, reeds and a layer of pale mist. A high fence with watchtowers and a gate cut across the marsh and the road to the base. REAP Thurley stood on higher ground, above the ruins: blocks of low-rise flats now ringed with wire, machine-gun nests perched on their rooftops.

Kellett looked back down to his desk and the crumpled, water-damaged photos on it. More or less irreplaceable now: photographic equipment was hard to come by, and used only sparingly.

Real children, ironically, could have been procured with far more ease. But Thurley was a PeriSec base, using clearance crews to drain the marsh; the CATCH programme inhabited part of one small block, barely tolerated by the commandant, Major Watkins. Watkins was of a boringly rigid moral persuasion, and would not have approved. So for now, Kellett made do.

The intercom buzzed.

Kellett swore, swept the pictures into a drawer and fastened his trousers. He was a scrawny man with greying hair, mud-coloured eyes, a crumpled, monkeyish face and prim, puckered mouth. "REAP Thurley," he said. "CATCH Program."

"Dr Kellett." A. Kellett had only heard the thin, cold voice issuing from the speaker once or twice before, outside of official broadcasts; each time it had been enough to make his testicles shrivel.

"Commander," he said.

"Colonel Jarrett tells me that you can find me the rebel base, Doctor," Winterborn said. "Is this true, or has she been... misinfomed?"

"No, sir," said Kellett. "I believe –"

"I don't care what you *believe*, Kellett." Kellett licked his lips. Winterborn's tone was gently teasing; that meant he could turn in an instant. "Will it work? Yes, or no?"

"Yes, sir." Kellett kept his voice level. He'd worked long and hard on this, taken it from a clump of barely-legible notes to a fully-functioning programme in two months. "It will."

"Let's hope so, Doctor. Very well. Proceed."

"Yes, Commander –" But the line was dead.

Kellett took a few seconds to compose himself, then pushed another button on the intercom.

"Yes, Doctor?"

"Major Watkins." Kellett was smiling now. "I've received orders from Commander Winterborn."

"So have I. Well?"

"Open the main gate," said Kellett. "And have your men stand clear. They don't want to get in its way."

"I'll tell them," said Watkins. It came out clipped and tight; Kellett could almost see his disgusted grimace, and bit his knuckle to avoid giggling. The line went dead.

Kellett pushed a third button. "Yes, sir?" said a voice.

"We're ready," he said. "Move the subject into position."

"Sir."

Kellett took a small metal box from a drawer and went to the window. As he watched, the Reapers guarding the main gate pulled it wide. He looked down at the box he held. It was featureless, except for a metal cover, which he flicked back. Underneath was a red button; Kellett stroked it with his thumb

A landcruiser rolled into view across the forecourt, stopped before it reached the gates. Four Reapers sat in the flatbed, around a shapeless object swaddled in tarpaulin, about the size of a man curled into a foetal position. They got out, carrying it, and set it down between the 'cruiser and the open gates. Kellett saw two of them wipe their hands as they ran back to the landcruiser, as if they felt unclean.

The landcruiser drove back into the base complex. The wind blew in across the marsh, flapped the tarpaulin wrapping the thing on the ground. The guards on the gate tried not to look at it.

Kellett smirked, then pushed the red button. There was a faint buzz; nothing more.

The bundle on the ground rocked and swayed; something moved inside. The tarpaulin stretched, then tore. A hand emerged, groping at the air; then another forced itself through the gap, stretching it wider, and something climbed out: man-like, but hunched like a beast. The sentries at the gates had already stepped back; Kellett smirked again as the thing started across the forecourt and they retreated further. They loathed him, despised him, whispered beside his back – but they feared him, too, and that was enough.

The thing stumbled through the gates, then stopped and straightened, its head swivelling side to side. And then it strode with military precision through the marshy ruins of Thurley, knee-deep, then thigh-deep in the stagnant water, till it vanished in the mist.

GAFFER'S WOOD
0900 HOURS

In the pine wood beyond Hobsdyke, no bird sang, no animal disturbed its peace. But there was movement in the trees as the Walker passed through them, and voices, whispering.

Others had heard those voices, passing through Gaffer's Wood, but few had emerged again. The wise and the lucky ones had turned back to find another way. The rest had stayed to listen longer, and followed the voices to a fate none beyond the wood knew.

But the Walker walked undisturbed. The voices didn't threaten or seduce it; instead they whispered blessings. And on it walked through Gaffer's Wood, and the pines were hushed once more.

Ashwood Fort
1100 hours

Alannah closed her eyes, breathed deep, trying to picture the hillside in the quiet dawn. She sat on a dais against the room's back wall, facing the door. Between it and her were ranks of radio operators with headsets, microphones and notepads. From the listening posts in the Wastelands and the cities, every Reaper transmission they could intercept came here.

"Alannah?" She started, blinked, opened her eyes. She still wasn't fully adjusted to the noise in the Intelligence Centre. After five years hiding in dark and silence, she'd taught herself to love the light again – each morning, rain or shine, she went running outside – but losing the silence had been harder.

"Sorry," said Hei.

"What is it?"

"We pick something up," he said. Hei had a slight accent; his family had spoken in Cantonese among themselves, trying to keep both cultures alive. They'd been fishermen on the coast, he'd told Alannah, till a Reaper coastal patrol sank his father's boat for being in the wrong place at the wrong time. His mother, already sick, had died not long after, and he'd decided to find and join the rebels. Also, his parents had named him 'Hei' because it meant hope. That was the sum total of what Alannah knew about him after three months: he'd told her all of it one night, working late, but that had been the only time he'd opened up. He was friendly, bright and efficient, but other than that one occasion, absolutely private.

"It was in Scramble Code 3," said Hei. "They still don't know we crack it."

"What have you got?"

"Said they activating something called the Catch Programme. Also, 'The Catchman is en route to target'."

Alannah shook her head. "Catch Programme? Don't recognise that one."

"Me neither," said Hei. "But if they were using Code 3…"

Alannah nodded. "Have Records check up on it. And keep listening. Meantime, flag up 'Catch' and 'Catchman'. Anything with those in, I want to see it."

"Understood."

Hei walked away. Alannah breathed deep, willing the hubbub to fade.

3.

The bright stream chuckled down the hill's green slopes. A cracked tarmac road wound down beside it and ran into the distance. From this angle, leaning on the stone bridge's parapet, Helen could almost see the world they'd lost: unspoilt, undamaged, one where the War and the Reapers had never been.

But barbed-wire and fire-trenches marred the hillside; beyond them were stumps and craters where the woods had been cut down to keep the approaches clear, so no enemy could approach unseen. And whatever might remain unspoilt was just out of reach, beyond the wire and the trenches, beyond the safety of the Fort. It called to Helen, but she had to stay. Security.

A faint cry from behind her made Helen look up the hill towards the Fort. The original wooden palisade had been replaced by an outer wall of crudely mortared rubble, fifty feet high and crenellated, machine guns poking over the parapets. One of the lookouts there was pointing.

Helen looked down again: there were more hills in the distance and where the woods had been, the land shelved down, but otherwise the surrounding terrain was flat, ensuring a clear view. Down the road, a lone dot was approaching the Fort.

Helen peered through her binoculars, and the dot became a landcruiser. The only occupant was the driver: tall, massive-shouldered, long black hair blowing back from a white face.

The road went past the stone bridge; Helen need only wait. She smiled and lowered the binoculars, studying her booted feet, the grass, the stream, till the landcruiser's hiss and clank reached her.

"Waiting for me?" Gevaudan said. His coat was dusty and hung around him like broken rook-wings, but he sat straight, long white hands resting almost delicately on the steering wheel. A faint smile touched the full mouth; the yellow wolf's eyes held her. "I'm touched."

"I've been saying that since I met you. I'm just enjoying the scenery."

Gevaudan eyed the wall. "Yes, it does have a certain *je ne sais quoi*."

"What?"

"I don't know what."

"Then why did you say it?"

Gevaudan looked at her; Helen grinned. "Nearly had you there."

"Your sense of humour will be the death of one of us," said Gevaudan. "So you were just killing time?"

"They don't let me out to kill Reapers any more."

"I seem to have mislaid my calendar," Gevaudan said, "but isn't there a full Council meeting today?"

"Is there?"

"If memory serves, it was due to convene fifteen minutes ago."

"Really? Mind like a sieve, that's me."

Gevaudan was quiet for a moment. "It's important to you, this one," he said. "Isn't it?"

"I'm that easy to read?"

"The devil on your back isn't hard to spot."

"What?"

A slight smile touched Gevaudan's lips. "And yet you're here. Not important enough for you to be there on time?"

"Too important," she said. Gevaudan raised an eyebrow. "You should have been an interrogator."

"We all have our gifts."

Helen sighed. "I didn't want to go in on my own. Okay?"

"Then you won't." Gevaudan gestured to the passenger seat; Helen climbed aboard. "But you'd have saved a great deal of time if you'd just come out and said so."

"Where'd have been the fun in that?"

*

Across the corridor from the Intelligence Centre was the War Room. It was much the same size, but emptier, with a circle of desks and chairs arranged in the centre.

Alannah stood; she had the silence now, at least, but every eye in the room was on her. There were friendly faces, at least: Wakefield from the Fox Tribe, and Darrow, of course. She and Roger went back a long way.

"We now have listening posts throughout the Wastelands," she said, "and in every major city in RCZ 7, including Manchester."

Darrow raised an eyebrow.

"Just one cell," she explained. "Five people, two transmitters, picking up what they can. It's just a fraction of the traffic from the Tower, but we can build on it."

"We may be in a position to do so soon," Darrow said. He smiled. "Depending on of a proposal I have to make."

Alannah cleared her throat. "We've also broken a Reaper scrambler code used for high security transmissions. They have four – we're close to breaking a second."

Wakefield grinned and clapped, then stopped, flushing red. Alannah hid a smile and carried on. "But in the long term, we're going to need eyes and ears inside REAP Command itself. We had a decent network during the Civil Emergency, but we lost a lot of them, especially after the Refuge fell. Some, however, are still alive. We're trying to contact them and get them back onside. They wouldn't want their superiors to know about their past, after all."

That got a few chuckles.

"It's still early days. We have three 'other ranks' Reapers in the Tower. They don't have much access to sensitive information, but it'll be easier for them to slip out of the Tower when necessary to pick up or carry messages. Obviously what we need are high-level contacts – officers, and in particular senior ones. So far, I've managed to reactivate one high-level contact so far, codename Honey Badger."

A few more chuckles. Alannah shrugged. "I had to call them something. Honey Badger's an officer in AdminSec. No involvement in planning or operations, but access to records. Better than nothing. It's a beginning. Trust me, there'll be more."

No-one said anything in reply. Alannah coughed. "One more piece of good news," she added. "Despite Winterborn's best efforts, I can confirm that word about the December Uprising's definitely spread outside RCZ7, and that the other commanders have all been experiencing their share of civil unrest. We're still trying to make contact with any potential allies in the other Command Zones. We're going to need them, unless we want to knock out Winterborn just to find ourselves taking on all the other Commands in Britain."

*

Gevaudan followed Helen down the iron staircase to the sub-basement, booted feet clanking on each step. It was well-lit, walls glaring white, but cold, rank air blew from it like a chill breath. She hated this place, he knew, but went nonetheless. That was Helen: she might fear, but it didn't stop her.

At the foot of the staircase was an iron door fastened by a wheel, flanked by armed guards. But their business wasn't here: the staircase led down one level more.

Whoever had owned the Fort in its previous life had obviously foreseen the War, although apparently they'd had no chance to take advantage of it. Below the Fort's basement was a blast shelter, built on two levels. For the leadership council, it was the deepest level of their headquarters; for Helen, the deepest of her nightmares.

Behind another iron door was the lowest level, housing the Intelligence Centre and the War Room. At the end of that corridor was another door still, tightly shut. Helen turned away from it, stopped outside the War Room. The guards waved them through. The delegates inside fell silent, looked up.

"Sorry I'm late," she said.

"Good of you to grace us with your presence," said Darrow.

"Darrow," said Gevaudan, as he sat beside him. Darrow nodded back, his face unreadable. Helen pulled back a chair and sat down.

The Tower
1515 hours

Winterborn was silent; he gazed out of the window, over the city.

Jarrett's hands clenched and unclenched on her knees. Wheels were turning at last, machinery months in the making creaking into use, and she wanted to see it do its job. And she could feel the speed wearing off, weight creeping into her limbs and eyelids. She needed to drop a couple more pills, notch herself back up again.

She cleared her throat. "Commander?"

Winterborn blinked, then turned to her. There was nothing in his face: absence, emptiness. He blinked again, and his eyes registered her. "Yes, Colonel?"

"Do you need me for anything else?"

"Need?" he said.

"Anything else we need to discuss. Now that the Catchman's been activated…"

"Now that the Catchman's been activated, you want to be with Kellett, so you can watch Helen die. Correct?"

Jarrett licked her lips. "I wouldn't put it quite like that, sir."

"Who am I to judge, Colonel? We all have our kinks." Winterborn opened his desk drawer. "Run along and play, Jarrett. Have fun."

"Sir." Jarrett saluted. Winterborn didn't respond. She turned and marched to the office door; her spine tingled between her shoulder-blades, the very point a bullet might strike. As she left, she heard two or three tinkling chimes sound before the closing door cut them off. As she stepped into the lift, she took the little jar from her pocket, shook two pills into her hand, swallowed them dry.

CHADBOURNE TOWN
SECTOR 32, THE WASTELANDS
15.30 HOURS

The town of Chadbourne had stood undisturbed for twenty years and might for twenty more. In its shopping precinct, a paved arcade of shop-fronts with flats above them, the signs in the cracked windows were faded and weeds sprouted between paving stones. Ivy crawled up the sides of buildings, corners were choked with dust and in the dust lay bones: mostly human, largely intact. Even twenty years after the War, nothing that came here lived long enough to get out again, so the bones went unscavenged; both beasts and humans knew to avoid it by now, so on most days the town's peace went undisturbed, the only sound the wind blowing down the precinct. But today, footsteps crunched in the powdered grit that carpeted the ground; today, the Catchman walked.

Two hungers stirred the red mire of its brain: the familiar one for meat and blood and bone cracking in its jaws, and another that was more an ache.

The Catchman's red, teeming mind could grasp no more: there was only a dim understanding that at the end of that path it walked it might find the ache's cause and end it.

The Catchman stopped and straightened: its other brain now spoke. Not red, this part, but silver, steel: a cold bright thing of gears and cogs. The steel brain had guided it thus far: now it chattered, clicked, stirred and listened. The call it sought was distant, faint, but present: wheels spun, gears shifted, dials clicked. Readings were taken: bearings, co-ordinates. The steel brain compared them to the previous set: it clicked precisely as they matched. Then the machine brain stilled itself, and sank beneath the red of the Catchman's other mind.

There was only the red mind now, and the hungers that gnawed it: and so the Catchman walked on.

REAP THURLEY

Kellett crossed the Ops Room below his office and studied the map on the wall. One red pin marked the location of REAP Thurley; a second one, the outer limits of the Thurley Marsh. Now he found the circle that appeared beside the name Chadbourne, pushed a third pin into place, and ran his fingertip from one pin to the next, tracing a clear, near-straight line into the Wastelands.

4.

Crybb swung down from the coach on his crutches, gulping the cool fresh air. His big, thick shoulders heaved him forward. He kept hard and lean; body and mind. That's why he was here: still serving the Hawk tribe, one leg or no. Hard muscle: all of him was, even now.

The old coach was by an orchard on a hill. Below it, heather and moor; above, a ruined stone house, walls black from old fire.

Crybb limped into the trees, propped his crutches against one, undid his breeches, pissed. He fastened up, grabbed the crutches, nodded once at the low earth mound nearby. There'd been bodies in the coach. Not much more than bones, but you respected the dead.

53

He limped back, stepping over the cable that snaked from the grass and ran up another tree's trunk. Crybb squinnied up into the branches; he could hardly see the aerial among them, and he knew it was there. Safe. Crybb climbed back into the coach.

"Anything?"

"Nowt but chatter," Breck said, scratching notes on his pad. "One from the Fort – flag up owt with the word 'Catch' in it."

"Catch?"

"Catch programme, Catchman – catch a bloody cold, all I know."

Crybb snorted, peered out the foxed and grimy window to the heath below. "There," he said.

"What?"

"Sure I saw something."

"Can't see owt," said Breck. "You're getting old."

"Piss off."

Breck shrugged and put his headphones back on. Crybb kept looking. A bird flapped from the undergrowth. Maybe that was what he'd seen, hopping in the brush before flight. Either way, the heath was still now.

*

In the brush, the Catchman lay, claws hooked into the earth. Even its red brain understood that the squared-off thing up ahead was not nature's work: too straight, too regular. Man had made it: but inside, there was warm flesh. The red brain throbbed and sang: the Catchman licked its lips. A thin drool fell from its chin, its breath hissed in and out through its gridded teeth.

In the red mire, the machine mind stirred: gleaming silver steel. The coach was an obstacle: the Catchman could circumvent it, or go through it by force. Either would be effective: one would be faster.

The machine mind whirred and clicked: the faster option would sate the red brain's thirst. The red brain was a dog on the machine mind's leash: gratified, it would do the machine mind's will more gladly.

The machine mind issued its command and sank once more beneath the red brain's mire: all that remained was ravening need.

ASHWOOD FORT
1645 HOURS

"Any other business?" Alannah said.

Darrow raised a hand. Her stomach tightened; *don't, Roger, please.* Her past was faded, tattered, like rotten cloth. The tighter she held it, the faster it came apart, but this one scrap she couldn't lose.

Darrow stood; a little slow, a little stiff. That had only come on him in the last few months. Loss, not age, had done it; when he'd escaped from Manchester after the December Uprising, Darrow had left most of the children he'd recruited and raised behind him, dead. Something had died in him then, burned away.

He looked around the circle; his eyes lingered only twice, on Alannah and on Helen. "We've made real gains," he said, "so our next step must be to capitalise on them. The listening post in Manchester is a vital new asset, but it stands alone, and unsupported. A number of cities in RCZ7 still have crews – cadres of young fighters set up by survivors of the Refuge. But not in Manchester. We lost almost everything we had there and in several other cities back in December." Darrow folded his arms. "We need crews in all the cities – Manchester most of all. The people we need are there – orphans, ferals. Given a home, a family, a purpose, they'll fight for us. All that's required is someone to recruit them."

"Let me guess," Alannah said. "You?"

"I have the experience," said Darrow.

"Which is why every Reaper station in Manchester has your face on its wall," said Helen. "You have something else, too: the location of the Fort."

Darrow smiled. "It's in safe keeping."

"The Reapers are very good at making people talk," said Alannah. "I have experience of that."

"But you didn't," said Darrow. "Talk, I mean."

"Somebody got to me in time." Despite herself, Alannah glanced at Helen.

"They wouldn't take me alive," said Darrow.

"You can't guarantee that. If you go back, Roger, you'll be found and you'll be caught."

"I've been in and out of Manchester three times in the last month."

"What?"

Darrow pinched the bridge of his nose. "I worked out some potential infiltration routes; it was time to test them. While I was there, I scoped out potential bolt-holes and started recruiting a central cadre to act as cell leaders. The Reapers never even knew I was there."

"That'll change," said Helen.

"The foundations are already laid," Darrow said. "I need a few experienced fighters, possibly some of the crew members who escaped in December. With those, I can return to Manchester permanently."

Alannah felt the floor drop away. "Permanently?"

"This work is vital. If we're to stand a chance next time, we need not only a listening post, but a fighting force inside the capital."

Helen opened her mouth; Alannah raised a hand. "Two separate votes," she said. "The first on establishing a new crew network in Manchester. The second will be on who takes charge. I don't think it should be you."

A dour smile pulled at the corner of Darrow's mouth. He knew Alannah had half a dozen good reasons, but behind them all was the one she couldn't say: *Not you too.*

"Agreed?" she said. "Then let's vote. First motion: re-establishing crew networks in cities without them, starting with Manchester. For?"

Darrow raised a hand; so did the others. Alannah was the last to raise hers.

"Motion carried by unanimous vote," she said at last. "The second motion: leadership of the Manchester operation. We can appoint General Darrow to the role, or review suitable candidates for the post. Those in favour of General Darrow?"

Darrow raised his hand, but it stood alone. *General*: he just looked like a tired old man. She breathed out in relief. Darrow's mouth tightened; his fists knotted on the table.

"Those for the selection of alternative candidates?"

Alannah raised her hand; so did Helen, Wakefield and Gevaudan, then all the others but Darrow himself.

"I see." Darrow's lips were pressed together. "The nays have it."

Alannah felt weak with relief, but didn't dare meet his eyes. Instead she stared at the printed agenda before her; the words were as meaningless as a forgotten tongue. At last she looked up again. "The motion falls," she said. "All right – if there's no other business, then –"

"There is something," said Helen.

Darrow leant back in his chair. "I think I can guess what."

Helen glared at him, looked at Alannah. Alannah nodded; Helen stood.

*

Working a crowd had never been Helen's strength. Persuading people, one on one, yes; if you got a feel for who someone was, what they wanted, you could work out how to ask for what *you* wanted, in a way they couldn't refuse. *You can always get them to die for you, can't you?* Alannah had said once in a bitter moment; it had hurt because of its truth. But different people wanted different things; there wasn't one argument to persuade them all.

Some fights you went into with a grim hollow in your gut, knowing you'd lost before you'd begun. But nonetheless, you fought.

She clasped her hands behind her back. "Everything we do in RCZ7 is directed from here. The bulk of our forces not deployed in the Wastelands are here. It's the nerve centre of our intelligence network, it's where the different groups that make up the resistance meet. The heart, the brain, the centre of the fight against the Reapers is here. It's our stronghold," she took a deep breath, "and our weakness."

There were snorts and mutterings; across the table, Darrow raised a sardonic eyebrow. *Bastard.* She made herself look from face to face. She'd have preferred to look at the ceiling or the floor, or focus on the ones that might understand her: Wakefield, Alannah – Gevaudan, maybe, most of all. But she had to reach the whole room.

"We're well-defended," she said over the mutterings. "But not well-defended enough to withstand an all-out Reaper assault."

"We have to base ourselves somewhere," Darrow said. "We have to direct operations, communicate with our forces, gather information – and quickly, decisively."

"Fox Tribe moves around," said Wakefield. "Camp to camp, never stopping. Harder to find."

"And, with respect," said Darrow, "the Reapers drove your tribe – and the others in the Wasteland – to the very point of extinction. As Helen says, the Fort is well-defended. Moreover, in order to even try an attack, they'd have to find us first," Darrow said.

"Yes, I know. It's our best defence. As it was with the Refuge."

"The Refuge." Darrow sighed. "I was waiting for that."

"Well, you can't deny it. The Refuge's biggest strength was that the Reapers couldn't find it. It was well-hidden. Underground. The only problem was that when the Reapers found it, they were able to destroy the entire rebellion."

"I was there," said Darrow. "Remember?" His face shadowed. "I know what it is to lose people I care for. Do you really think I don't care about our safety? That I don't want us to *win* this time?"

"Roger, I've never doubted that of you."

"Nevertheless, *you* can't deny there are past issues here that may be colouring your judgement."

"That's unfair."

"Is it?"

"If we lose the Fort, we lose the whole war. We're one intelligence failure, one traitor, away from that."

"And you have a solution?"

"Yes. We disperse our command structure among a series of strongholds, spread across the Wastelands. It would take multiple intelligence failures to make them all vulnerable to attack."

"They'd also weaken our defensive forces by spreading them more thinly," said Darrow, "so that the Reapers could mount a successful attack with a smaller force."

"The Reapers don't have the people or firepower for multiple long-range strikes into the Wastelands against four or five bases. But they *do* have the numbers for one such strike. If we blew up the Tower tomorrow, killed Winterborn, it still wouldn't be over. The Reapers don't have a single weak point that would finish them at one blow. But right now, we do. Just as we did then."

"We'd have to find the potential sites," said Darrow, "then develop them into strongholds, all while keeping their locations secret. It would be a huge operation, and we need all our resources to press home our advantage against the Reapers. We cannot afford to lose momentum."

Wouldn't anyone else speak up, for or against? "And what if I'm right?" Helen said. "What if we can't hold out? With nowhere to evacuate to, we'd be split up, hunted down and wiped out. Multiple bases give us fallback options."

Darrow leant forward. "Helen, I cannot exaggerate the importance of morale right now. Yes, we're still outnumbered, but nowhere near as badly as we were. Our numbers are growing. We're gaining support: people are actually leaving Reaper territory to come to us. Even after what happened in December, there are people in Manchester willing to fight with us. Why? Because they believe we can win. Because they've seen the Reapers driven back. They've seen us win the Grendelwolf to our side when Winterborn couldn't."

Gevaudan raised an eyebrow. "And there I was thinking that that I'd made up my own mind. Did you slip something in my coffee, Helen?"

There was laughter at that. Even Helen couldn't keep her face straight. Nor could Darrow, but he soon sobered again. "I'm talking about what people see," he said. "What they think. Despite the rout in December, we've come back stronger. We've taken territory, we've inflicted defeats on them: people are seeing us landing blows on the Reapers. If we lose that momentum, it'll look as though they're turning the tide."

"If they can find the Fort, they actually *will* be."

Darrow took a deep breath. "Helen, I know what you went through: I still have nightmares about that day, and you suffered far worse than I did. But that was then, and this is now. I suggest, respectfully, that your judgement is coloured by your experiences," he looked down, "and your guilt."

"Guilt?" Helen's control slipped. "You really want to talk about guilt, Roger? Let's talk about guilt."

"That's enough," snapped Alannah. "Do either of you have anything else to say?"

Helen took deep breaths. "No."

Darrow sank back in his chair. "No."

"Then we'll vote," said Alannah. "Those in favour of Helen's proposal?"

*

Gevaudan's hand rose; so did Wakefield's. Helen's too, of course. Her grey eyes darted round the table. Alannah looked down before she could meet them.

"Three in favour," said Alannah. "Those in favour of maintaining the present arrangement?"

Darrow's hand went up; then two others. After a moment, Alannah raised hers too, not meeting Helen's eyes. She'd uprooted herself once; she couldn't again. She needed a place to call home. "The motion falls," she said. "If there's no other business, I bring this meeting to a close."

Helen jumped up and strode to the door. "Helen," began Alannah – but the door was already swinging shut behind her.

LISTENING POST 23
1656 HOURS

Crybb woke; his breath was short, skin clammy. "Breck!" he barked, scrabbling for his crutches, groping for his Sten. "Breck!"

"Wha – ? What?" The younger man pulled his headphones off. "What?"

Crybb stood; he had no answer, just a feeling. Danger. He looked out of the window; something burst from the long grass nearby, running for the coach.

"There!" He pulled back the Sten's bolt, but too late. Metal screamed: the coach door was torn off its hinges and something leapt through.

A man's shape, but not a man. Sweet mother, the *smile* that stretched its face –

Crybb shouted at Breck, but it fell upon the boy. Its claws grabbed and tore; Breck's body flew one way, his head the other. And then the thing was looking straight at Crybb.

It ran at him: Crybb pulled the trigger. The Sten bucked and stuttered; at that range, he couldn't miss. The thing twitched and jerked as the bullets hit it, but didn't stop.

And the Sten fell silent, emptied; Crybb pulled the trigger and nothing happened. He reached for his revolver, but the thing leapt. Its claws gouged his shoulders; the right one crunched in a starburst of pain. And above him a fanged grin that wasn't possible yawned into a screaming laugh and fell towards his face –

*

The red brain was as close to peace as it could ever come. The Catchman tore at the kills: wrenched limbs from sockets, cracked the ribcages open to reach the soft meats within.

In the red mire, the machine mind waited: the red brain was a dog on a leash, still half-wild and ravening. There was a time for the cracked whip: a time, too, to give it free rein.

At length, the machine reared from the bloodmire: it roused the Catchman from the kills. It let it gather some pieces of flesh for the long march ahead, then urged it out into the gathering night: it listened, scented, calculated range and course.

No change: the bearing remained constant. The machine mind gave its instructions, then sank again beneath the red: the Catchman walked on towards its prey.

5.

Outside the War Room, someone called her name: "*He*-len." Low, crooning.

She knew who it was, and wanted to pretend she hadn't heard. But she'd always faced the ghosts; it was, she supposed, the least she owed them.

The steel door at the corridor's end swung open, and there stood Belinda and Frank. They smiled and waved. "Why not you come and join us, Helen?" Frank called. "Hide in the earth. You have before."

Frank laughed. Helen turned away. A cold breath blew down the corridor. A cave system honeycombed the inside of the hill, so the shelter's builders had installed an airtight door for access. So far it had gone unused; at some point it would be explored, but not by Helen. The shelter was bad enough – she'd hated anywhere underground ever since the Refuge – but the thought of those other depths was the worst of all.

But the whole of the Fort felt a prison to her now; not a stronghold but a trap to hold her fast for the kill. She strode through the checkpoints, up the staircases to the ground floor, and made for the canteen. Her quarters would have been too silent; better to be alone in a crowd. When she smelt cooking meat and gravy, she realised she was hungry anyway.

"What is it today, Vi?" she asked.

The chef grinned. "Cottage pie."

"I'll risk it."

Helen found a table and sat down. The pie wasn't bad: real carrots and potatoes, grown in the fields near the Fort where the cesspits' contents were emptied every few days. No way of knowing what the meat was, but she'd probably eaten worse. She looked up; Darrow came in, looked away from her and nodded to a small figure with spiky black hair.

Danny. Then Alannah came in and she and Danny went still, looking at one another. Helen thought Danny said something, but couldn't tell what, or if Alannah mumbled a reply before dodging past him after Darrow, who smiled at her and touched her arm.

Helen looked down again, but a shadow fell across her table. "May I?"

"If you must."

Gevaudan sat. "Are you all right?"

"Fine," she parted her teeth long enough to say.

"You don't sound it."

"No?" Helen stabbed her fork into her cottage pie's remains. "Maybe that's because these fucking idiots just voted to make us a sitting target. The Reapers find us and *that's it. Game over. Lights out.*"

The wolf-yellow eyes glanced away. Helen looked, saw a pair of young fighters stare down at their food-bowls. "We're well-hidden," Gevaudan said. "Alannah's taken thorough precautions. And we are well-defended."

"Glad you think so," she snapped. "But you don't *get* it, Gevaudan. It's all right for you. You can fight your way out.

Practically bounce bullets off your chest, you're fucking indestructible. But the rest of us? One person fucks up, says something they shouldn't, sleeps with the wrong person –"

Gevaudan frowned. "Sleeps with?"

"Forget it." Helen tried to make herself eat, and couldn't. "It's a house of cards," she said. "One mistake and it all falls down. They've learned nothing from before. *Nothing*."

His long white hand moved towards her. "Helen –"

"Forget it." She glared at the next table; its occupants looked away from her even faster than they had him. "I don't need my hand held. I need something these bloody idiots won't do. That, and I need to be alone. Okay?"

Gevaudan lowered his eyes. "Very well." He got up and walked away.

"Wonderful work, Helen." Frank now sat opposite her. Beside him, Belinda rested her chin and hands on the table's edge, giggling. Frank drummed his fingers on the table. They clicked; his nails were yellow and pointed. "You've driven him away too. It's a gift, isn't it? You did it to me, to her –" he tapped Belinda's head "– even to Percy."

"Shut up about him."

"It's true."

"Shut up." She tried not to move her lips. If she wasn't careful, whispers would start behind her back: she was shredding, couldn't hack it any more. Just another victim of the Refuge.

"You *did* die there, Helen," said Frank.

"I've enough on my plate without you making me look like a casualty in front of everyone."

"You don't need my help for *that*. You drive us all away, in the end. Your coldness, your selfishness –"

"Stop it."

"That's who you are, Helen. Cold, selfish, unable to trust –"

"Sing another fucking song, Frank."

He chuckled. "I'll see you later." Then he was gone; other raised voices washed in.

"Aw, come on, Gev –" *Gev?*

"Gevaudan," the Grendelwolf growled. Half a dozen youngsters surrounded him. Helen almost laughed: the killing machine who'd singlehandedly made Deadsbury a no-go zone now couldn't even scare children.

"Gevaudan, *please*," said another child. "Come on. You always do."

"I'm not in the mood."

"Please," said another still. "*Please*." Some of them were urban, some tribal. One pulled a chair behind Gevaudan and tapped on it.

Finally he sighed. "All right." The kids whooped; laughter rippled across the canteen. "Where's the guitar?"

Vi rolled her eyes and retrieved a battered wooden guitar from behind the counter. A youngster ran to Gevaudan with it.

Gevaudan sat and picked at the strings. "Apologies to anyone hoping to enjoy their meal in peace." More laughter. The Grendelwolf was no longer human, with Christ knew how much blood on his hands, should make your skin ripple cold and your blood chill, but he drew them to him, didn't drive them away. Frank wasn't there to say it, but Helen heard it just the same. That was ghostlighting for you: even when your dead weren't with you, they were there.

"This song," he said. "is, like me, very old." Laughter. "Much older, in fact. Hundreds of years." He looked up, into Helen's eyes, for a second before glancing away as if the contact had stung, and began to play.

"Lay still my fond shepherd and don't you rise yet,
It's a fine dewy morning and besides, my love, it is wet…"

The canteen stilled; it always did. Despite his size and appearance, there was a delicacy to the Grendelwolf, most of all when he played. His fingers were nimble and precise on the frets and strings; his voice deep and rich, yet soft. And the song, Helen realised, was a love song, and through it all the one face he never looked at was hers. Her throat tightened; her eyes stung.

"Oh the lark in the morning she rises from her nest
And she mounts in the air with the dew on her breast

And like the pretty ploughboy she'll whistle and sing
And at night she will return to her own nest again…"

She'd had a dream about Gevaudan: he'd come at her, scarred and glowering, and somewhere a voice had whispered *he will destroy you*. But sometimes, even on the Black Road, a dream was just a dream. And the song made her think of meadows and fields, the world outside the Fort, that she'd seen only distantly, from the walls or the hillside, since the winter.

"Helen."

"Roger." She looked away.

Darrow sighed. "I know you're angry with me."

"You don't miss much."

He sat opposite her. "I wanted to talk."

Easier to be angry than trying to puzzle out her feelings for the Grendelwolf. "Well?"

"None of this is personal, you know."

"No?"

"I think you're wrong. That simple. I *am* allowed to."

"Right." She looked down at the cooling remains of her meal. "Not like you blame me for the people you lost."

"I don't, Helen." She looked at him. Darrow took a deep breath. "Yes, you persuaded me to help you deal with Project Tindalos. Yes, because of that, people died. But you're not to blame."

"Bullshit."

"No." Darrow showed no anger; he just, she realised, looked desperately tired. "I tried to name them all, you know."

"Who?"

"The children. The ones who died last winter. Do you know something, Helen? I couldn't. Oh, I could name some – Nadgers, Thursday, Lelly, Pipe, Telo… but there were so many more I couldn't. Age, perhaps. I don't know. But you were right, Helen. What you destroyed at Hobsdyke – what we did had to be done. But even so – the price."

"You aren't young any more," said Helen, "if you ever were to start with."

He smiled. "You haven't lost your charm."

"You don't miss what you never had." A pause. "Look, Roger – it wasn't personal for me either, voting against you."

"I know that. There were entirely valid arguments against it being me."

"Apart from anything else, did you think even for a second what it would do to Alannah? You're practically all she has left."

"She's doing better than she thinks. She's come a long way in the last few months."

"Maybe, but losing you would hit her hard."

"It still has to be done."

"I don't dispute that, but did it have to be you?"

"Yes."

"You really can't forgive yourself, can you?"

"Can either of us?"

1812 HOURS

Gevaudan walked through the dusk, to the cottage near the Fort.

Once he could have seen for miles, but then the walls had gone up. Still, there was a blue sky above, and the stream that rose from a spring nearby ran by the cottage; this close to the source, it still ran clear.

His home stood by itself on a small island of untrampled grass, ringed by a fence. The one thing, along with the Goliath serum, that he'd asked in exchange for his help: a place of his own, quiet and private. He'd lived in Deadsbury for years, with the whole dead town as a home; he hadn't needed or wanted anything so spacious any more, but he couldn't have faced living in the village, among the crowded smoky dwellings and stench of the cesspits and middens, or in the Fort.

The rebel leaders had readily agreed; the cottage had been there when they'd found the Fort, but the arrangement suited them also. They might warm to his occasional musical performances, but few would actually visit the Grendelwolf in his lair. Or want to sleep in the neighbouring bunk.

Helen would have lectured him that even the village was a paradise compared to the conditions in the cities. She'd have been right, of course, but –

His front door was ajar.

There was a spare key beneath the worn old WELCOME mat outside, but Gevaudan didn't get many visitors. He went through into the kitchen, then out into the garden, approaching the small figure kneeling by the cairn. "Hello, Flaps."

She flicked hair from her eyes and grinned. "Yo." The smile faded. "Soz."

"What for?"

"Should've asked if it was okay." She'd laid a fresh stone on the cairn. Like Gevuadan's own, larger heap, it hid a heap of white-painted pebbles, each bearing a lost loved one's name. Whenever the grief weighed heavy, you added another rock to the cairn. Flaps spent most of her time in the Wastelands these days, but whenever she came to the Fort she always called by.

"Of course it is." He crouched beside her. "I know what this is like, remember?"

"Yeah." She looked away. "Thanks."

She'd probably been ghostlighting, but she if she wanted to tell she would. When she said nothing more, Gevaudan climbed the ladder propped against the wall to the look-out point above. After about a minute, Flaps climbed up and leant on the parapet beside him, although she moved aside rather than let her shoulder brush against his. Wolf and wildcat: by now they knew each other well enough, sharing the space with the comradeship of fellow carnivores.

Flaps watched him, blue eyes narrowed. "You all right?"

He could have lied, chose not to. "I don't know." He couldn't put it into words: an unease, a discomfort, a sense of *something* wrong. He would have liked to put it down to the business with Helen – it smarted to be on the receiving end of her anger, to be pushed away – it would have been simpler and easier. But no, this was something else, something more.

"Same," said Flaps. She folded her arms, leant on the parapet. "Summat's coming. Dunno what, but there's summat not right."

Gevaudan nodded. For a while they looked in silence over the parapet – down the hillside, past the church, the village and the sprawl of cruder shelters around it, to the cut-down woods beyond the outer wall and the jagged red glow where the sun died behind the hills.

Something fluttered overhead; seconds later it fluttered back again. A bat, hunting the insects that swarmed above the middens and cesspits. They flew back and forth, repeating the same endless arcs and sweeps in the darkening air. Patterns: men and women were slaves to them, too.

"Gotta go," said Flaps. "Field-base is waiting."

Gevaudan nodded. "Be careful."

"You too."

She climbed back down; Gevaudan watched her go. He looked back towards the hills and the dying sun, while the bat flew back and forth around his head.

THE FLATS
SECTOR 21, THE WASTELANDS
1912 HOURS

The Catchman crawled through mud: the red brain took a simple, tactile pleasure from the cold wet slippery clay.

In the distance were noises: the Catchman crouched between the banks of the mud creek. It peered over the bank, through the dark.

More grunts and mutters: a dozen men and women with rifles and submachine guns picked their way across the mud flats, slipping and sliding as they went.

The machine rose, calculating: wait and let them pass, or kill them and avoid delay? But before it could decide, one of the moving figures pointed towards it: a shout echoed across the flats.

The decision was made: *attack*. The machine stilled itself and sank again: the Catchman bounded from the creek and towards the patrol.

They fired: the red brain dimly felt the bullets' sting. But that was all: and then it was upon them.

REAP Thurley
1930 hours

"Excellent progress," said Kellett. "All right. Initiating shutdown and hibernation mode."

"What?" Jarrett stood, hands on her hips. "I thought you said this thing didn't get tired."

"It doesn't." Kellett bit off a chunk of smoked meat.

"And that nothing could kill it." In her pocket, her fingers closed around the pill jar. She let it go: not yet.

"Virtually nothing, Colonel." Kellett chewed slowly; light from the monitors glimmered on his spectacles. "But it's never been tested under field conditions before. So it makes sense to shut down, hibernate and run a diagnostic. We'll reactivate it in the morning and continue from there. Apart from anything else, it'll do us good to be rested too." He looked at her and smiled. "After all, you and your men want to be ready to move as soon as we know we're going, don't you?"

His smirk made Jarrett want to smash his face in, or shoot it. But he was right – which was even worse. She didn't want to wait, not now. Not for a second longer than she had to. "All right," she said. "Shut it down. But I want it going again at first light."

Intelligence Centre, ashwood fort
2102 hours

The centre was hushed, only half a dozen operators at their desk; Alannah rubbed her eyes, then focused on the report again.

Someone coughed, softly, nearby. She looked up, and there he was. *Stephen*, she thought – but of course, it wasn't. Stephen was dead; it was Danny. That should have dimmed the ache, made her heart beat the less, but it didn't. The jagged black hair, pale pinched face, puppy dog eyes, the way he looked at her; it was Stephen and it was something else all its own.

He was a man now, by today's lights – an officer, a fighter, even a veteran – but Alannah only saw a boy. Before the War, he'd still have been in school, getting his first girlfriend. (Actually that credited him with a little too much innocence; he'd probably be on his fifth.) Something fell away from him when he saw her, all the armour he'd built up, just as it threatened to fall away from her.

He shuffled towards her, reddening as a couple of the listeners glanced at him; one hid a smirk behind his hand.

"Get to work," Alannah called. They all looked down, including Danny, as he reached the dais. He wore army boots, dogskin trousers, a linen shirt; the belstaff jacket Gevaudan had given him hung open.

"Yo."

"Danny."

He looked around, then climbed up on the dais. "You doing all right?"

She leant back in her chair. "Yeah."

"You're lookin' all right."

"I am," she said. "All right, I mean."

"You still runnin' and that?"

She smiled. "Ten times round the inner wall every morning."

He grinned back, turning redder still. "Well, that's good," he said. "Good for you, I mean."

"Yes," she said, "it is. It's done me a lot of good."

"Can see that. Make up for when you were –"

"Yeah."

"Anyway –" Danny glanced up, then down again. Every time she thought he couldn't go redder, he deepened another shade.

"What about you?" she asked.

"Me? All right."

"Keeping busy?"

"Yeah. Plenty to do. You know."

"And – you're being careful?"

"Obviously."

"That's good. Are you still with –"

"Flaps?"

"That's right. Flaps."

"Still together," he said. "You know. Lot in common."

Like age. "I'm sure she's a very nice girl," said Alannah, then muttered, before she could stop herself, "if you like that sort of thing."

"What?" He was frowning now, the flush fading.

After a moment, he folded his arms. "Anyway," he said. "Better skate."

"Oh. Okay." Why had she said that? It was her who'd ended things between them, before they'd even really begun. And it'd just been puppy love for him. God knew why, she was old enough to be his mother or his gran, and she'd been living in a hole in the ground for five years. But it had been there – shy and awkward, saying the wrong thing half the time, but it had been there. And it could have been hers, but she'd turned him away. She'd no right to complain if he'd sought comfort elsewhere.

But it had been said, and words were bullets: easily fired, but impossible to recall, much less to reverse the damage they did.

"I'm sorry," she said as he turned away.

He turned back, but wouldn't meet her eyes. "S'okay." He nodded at the papers on her desk. "What you got?"

"These?" She sighed. "Reports. They come in thicker and faster than I can look at them, so I work late." Alannah glanced at the one she'd been reading. "Actually, this one might be for you. Or maybe your – Flaps."

Danny folded his arms. "How d'you mean?"

"One of our patrols in the Wastelands. Lost contact with them last night."

"Whereabouts?"

"We had a field report around 1900, but nothing since. That was from the mud flats in Sector 21."

"I know them."

"Might be a comms failure."

"Or not. Like some Jennywrens on the sniff?"

Alannah shrugged. "They want the Fort. A long-range recon patrol would be the logical way to try and find it."

"I'll get hold of Flaps," he said. "Get her to sweep north at first light. I'll take some of mine out same time, sweep south. Anyone's out there, we'll find 'em quicker."

"Okay." She hoped she sounded neutral. Whenever he left the Fort he was in the firing line, just like Darrow would be. Was that why she was looking at Danny again, to have someone to hang onto if Darrow died?

"Anyroad," he said, "I'll see you when I see you. So – see you."

"Danny –" but he'd already turned away. "Bye," she said to his back.

HELEN'S QUARTERS, ASHWOOD FORT
1138 HOURS

Fingers shaking, Helen lit the bedside candle; the dream faded as the light crept across the floor. It hadn't been the Black Road; beyond that, she remembered only jumbled blurs and snatches. Blood, screams, gunfire. And something else, with grinning fangs and eyes of glass.

That image didn't fade; in fact she saw it again whenever she blinked. She fumbled for the revolver.

"That's really not going to help," said Frank.

He sat in the corner chair, watching her, Belinda snuggled in his lap. "Shhh," he said, a finger to his lips. "Only just got baby to sleep. It's coming for you, Helen. It's going to find you soon, and when it does…" He giggled, baring his needle teeth. "You'll wish you'd stayed in your grave."

Alannah nodded forward, snapped awake again. Just about. Her eyes felt weighted, kept sliding shut; their heaviness kept tipping her head forward, threatening to send her sprawling across her desk. Best call it a night. Try and catch up in the morning.

Someone tapped at the door of the centre. Alannah grunted, blinked, sat up; Helen stood there. "Sorry," she said. "Couldn't sleep."

"Can't anyone sleep around here but me?"

"Why? Who else?"

"Danny?"

"Oh. Love's young dream?"

"Piss off." Helen said nothing. Alannah breathed out. "Sorry. Forget it. Lot to deal with right now."

"No, I'm sorry. That was cruel of me. Start again?"

"Do I have to want anything? Can't I just be looking in?"

"Yes, and Winterborn's tied up outside the gate with an apple in his mouth," said Alannah. "Never try and look innocent, Helen. You're crap at it."

"Believe it or not, it's true. So what's the problem?"

Alannah told her about the missing patrol, then picked up another report. "And then there's this."

Helen took the flimsy from her. "Listening Post 23?"

"Gone dead."

"Once is happenstance, twice is coincidence," said Helen.

"Yeah. It's the third time I'm worried about. I do *not* want the first bloody warning of a Reaper attack to be them knocking on the door. And don't say it."

"What?"

"This is not your cue to say 'I told you so.'"

"I wasn't going to. So you've got Danny and Flaps sweeping Sector 21 for the missing patrol? What about the listening post?"

Alannah shrugged. "You know what it's like in the Wastelands – atmospherics, interference, and it's not as if the equipment's still under warranty. Sometimes we lose contact for a bit. But never this long – there's been nothing since last night."

"And now this patrol."

"Twice is still only coincidence."

"But it still needs checking out," said Helen. She tapped the flimsy. "What the hell. I'll do it."

"Are you mad?"

Helen raised her eyebrows "Is that a trick question?"

"What were you saying about one security breach?"

"Look, you're not the only one who doesn't want to sit around waiting for them to show. Anyway, I've been cooped up here since Christmas. If I don't stretch my legs I'll end up running round the Fort naked biting the heads off live rats or something."

"Anything to boost morale." Alannah forced a smile. "Probably nothing, right?"

"Right," said Helen. She pointed to the wall chart. "I'll set off at first light, same as Danny. And I'll be careful, take care of myself, and keep in regular contact. Okay?"

"Not particularly."

"I'll pick you some flowers or something."

THE FLATS
20TH MARCH, ATTACK PLUS TWENTY-ONE YEARS
0003 HOURS

The cold night wind blew across the chill mud flats; a wild cat padded over them, slitted eyes searching the dark for prey. It slowed as it neared a patch of churned mud; crouched there, blinking; arched its spine, the hairs on its back bristling up. Then it hissed, darting off into the night.

Beneath the ground, the Catchman slept, curled like a foetus in the earth's embrace. The mire of the red brain swirled slow and thick in bloody dreams; the steel machine lay quiet, its gears stilled, waiting for the signal that woke them again. Silent, still, and waiting for the dawn.

6.

Grey predawn light showed through the ground mist and made the mud-flats dully gleam. In one place the ground heaved and split; a clawed hand tore free to greet the air.

Slathered in mud, the Catchman dragged itself from hiding, then stood and began to walk. Mud clung and sucked at its feet: it strode on, straight-backed.

Objects jutted from the mud: broken brick walls. Low ridges covered in slates: *roofs*. A broken, rusted hull of metal: *car*. A man, his arm raised high, on a four-legged beast: *horse*.

The Catchman stopped before this: a horse's shape, a man's, but not alive. The Catchman touched it: cold, hard. The Catchman rapped on it: metal. The Catchman studied it.

Something in its head: something that was neither the red brain nor the steel. A woman, holding it: it reaching out to hold her. Soft skin: warm flesh. Grip tear bite – *No*. No: there'd been no hunger, no killing. A woman: a child.

The red mire heaved, turbulent: the machine stirred, rose. It asserted control: the red brain quieted.

The machine scanned, listened: the bearing remained constant.

The Catchman walked on.

ASHWOOD FORT
0410 HOURS

The gates swung wide and Helen drove out into the clear morning air. The sky was still mostly dark, but clear; the air was cool and fresh.

Even now, a day could still be beautiful; this might be one of them.

She let the landcruiser idle outside the gate for a moment. The familiar view had altered; the road ahead sprang into sudden relief. Not part of the vista any more; a destination.

"Oi," called Danny from the landcruiser behind. Half a dozen others followed him. "We going or what?"

"Sorry," said Helen. In the driver's seat beside Danny, Harp grinned.

A moment later, the landcruisers rolled on down the hill.

THE FLATS
0500 HOURS

The mud no longer slowed the Catchman: the river was narrower here, the flats harder and drier.

Up ahead was a low regular shape: it cocked its head to study it. A long stone structure, supported on pillars: the word *arches* bobbed up in the red mire, then sank again.

The arches were very low now: their topmost curve rose only a few feet above the level of the silt. The Catchman stopped and studied them: scraps of memory whirled amid all the red. It tried to catch and study them: it could not. Another word surfaced for an instant: *viaduct*.

The machine mind stirred once more: the red mire calmed. And then it stirred, and scanned –

The machine went still: around it, the red brain half-woke, uncertain. This was new: the machine mind was never still, except when submerged. When it rose above the surface, gleaming and bright, it listened: it calculated, and at last commanded. Every instant of its waking time was so spent: then it sank again and the beast forgot it once more. But now – for a split-second – the machine was still.

And then it was in motion once more, but still did not command: instead it scanned again. And then a third time.

The machine calculated: the bearing had changed. And each reading had been slightly different from the last: the target was in motion.

The Catchman studied the half-buried viaduct: from higher ground it might calculate the bearing more accurately.

The machine mind gave commands. The Catchman's claws sank into the bricks like hammered nails: its boots fought for traction on the surface. It climbed to the parapet, swung over: it stood on the rusted rails and scanned again.

LISTENING POST 23
0509 HOURS

The grey twilight was turning silver. Helen killed the landcruiser's lights, picked up the Sterling from the seat beside her and ran up the hill to the ruined farmhouse, then lay down and crawled behind some stonework.

She looked down at the orchard and the coach. No sound, and no movement. Something lay among the grass and bluebells near the coach; a rusted metal door. The torn hinges gleamed;

the metal had been freshly broken. The doorway gaped, open to the wind.

They could still be inside, but Helen already knew they weren't – not alive, anyway. She was tempted to contact Alannah. But yesterday had shown that her judgement was in doubt; a false alarm would only confirm her opponents' view.

Helen cocked the Sterling and moved out from behind the wall.

The Flats
0512 hours

Mist hung over the mud as they rode. Four 'cruisers in all: two from the Fort with Danny's team, two from the field-base with Flaps'.

Flaps' team had found what was left of the missing patrol and a set of tracks leading north across the Flats. Other teams from the Fort were still sweeping south, but Danny's group had joined with hers to follow the trail.

Harp was in the landcruiser behind; beside him was Lish, the unit medic. She was willowy and milk-white with pure red hair, redder even than Helen's. From some religious lot out in the Wastelands who'd finally agreed to join up with the rebels. Danny'd heard she couldn't volunteer fast enough – her old folks had about to marry her off to some bloke she didn't want. Some of the religious mobs were bloody weird. Funny: Lish had been scared shitless of Harp when they first met – she'd been brought up to believe the tribesfolk were pagan baby-eaters – but now they were best mates. She was quiet, but she got the job done.

Danny sat next to Flaps in her 'cruiser, her thigh pressed to his. They both wore thick dogskins, but he could feel the heat of her skin through them, and remembered how it felt – hot, smooth, soft.

A few months ago he'd have put his hand on her thigh, but not any more. He was in charge now. If he fucked up, it wasn't just him who'd pay. *Mind on the job. Use your head, not your rogers.*

"Up there!" Flaps pointed; Danny looked. The river here was narrower, and over it was a bridge – a long line of arches linked together and low to the ground. Someone stood on top.

Danny peered through his binocs at it. A helmet of some kind covered most of the thing's head. He thought it wore come sort of coverall, but it was slathered in half-dried mud – mud and something else, half-coagulated red and dried black. The object in its hands was pale, except for the red holes torn in it, but you could see what it was; the hand and fingers were still uneaten.

"All right," Danny took the radio mic. "Everybody," he said, "out now."

Danny climbed out, cocking the Lanchester. "We move in," he said. "Quick and low. Get up on it before it knows we're there."

"Gotcha," said Flaps.

The two groups moved in across the mud. Nearing the viaduct, Danny could hear the thing grunting, and the crunching, tearing sounds as it fed.

"Fuck," Flaps whispered, and the thing froze. There was a sort of slurping sound; a thick wet tongue licking lips clean. And then it turned.

The dull metal helm covered the top half of its head. It had round metal grilles where its ears should have been, a triangular one where for a nose. Its eyes were perfectly round lenses, like goggles or a gas-mask.

The bottom half of the face looked pallid, mealy, the skin rubbery and loose. At first Danny couldn't see the mouth; it was a slit, like a knife-cut. But then it stretched into a grin that peeled open like a wound: wet, red, wider than anything human was capable of and filled with serrated, triangular teeth.

And as Danny swung the Lanchester towards it, it leapt down among them.

7.

Helen fell prone in the grass ten yards from the coach, watched it down the barrel of the Sterling. She already knew, though, that the place was too still; whatever had been here was gone.

Helen knew, too, what she'd find. She crept to the door and aimed the Sterling down the aisle, just in case she was wrong.

The first body was almost directly in front of her, by a shattered radio set; the legs remained, but everything from the waist up was a mangled plug of flesh and broken bone.

Helen skirted the corpse. The worn, rotten carpet was sticky underfoot. Her foot caught something; she looked down and saw a severed head. From what she could see of the face, the boy could have been no more than fifteen.

Blood dried black on the walls; there was a buzzing of flies and a reek both sweet and sour. Narrow rods of weak light dappled the interior from the bullet holes punched in the ceiling. The holes were fresh, else they'd have been patched. A Sten gun lay in the aisle, crushed like clay.

Further up the aisle was what remained of the second corpse, more mutilated than the first. She made out part of a face; the rest was just pieces.

Movement at the end of the aisle; she dropped to one knee, grimacing as blood seeped through her coverall. The sound became a skitter of paws; a rat. She backed down the aisle, trying not to gag; in the warm weather, the remains were already festering.

Helen stumbled outside. She coughed and spat, thinking she was about to vomit, but she didn't. She ran up the hill, towards the landcruiser.

The Flats

The grey thing landed in a crouch not ten feet away. Danny shouldered the Lanchester; beside him, Flaps braced her Sterling against her hip and aimed at it.

The thing rose to its feet. It made no move, just stood there grinning at them. Fuck, just that grin was reason enough; Danny sighted down the Lanchester at it.

Before, it'd looked more animal than human. But now it stood straight, head turning to and fro, blank glass eyes sweeping back and forth across them. Nothing in them at all. Not human, not even animal: a *machine*.

"What now?" Flaps hissed.

"Fucked if I know," said Danny. "That's a fucking arm it was eating."

"I noticed," said Flaps.

"The patrol?"

"They hadn't been shot or owt," she said. "Just torn to bits and…"

"Bits missing," Danny said. "Right?"

"Right."

The thing turned to Danny and grinned.

84

"Kill it!" he shouted, and fired.

Flaps fired too, and all the others with their Stens and Tommies. The grey thing jerked and flailed about, but didn't fall. A mate of Danny's had kicked a wasp's nest once; they'd boiled out, stinging. His mate'd flailed about like that, yelling in pain, swatting them aside. But they just hurt him; weren't gonna kill him.

The grey thing straightened up, grinning still. It raised a hand and slowly wagged a finger: *naughty, naughty, very naughty.*

"Fuck," Danny said.

A fighter stepped forward, fired a burst into the thing's head point-blank. It stumbled, head snapping sideways; for a moment it seemed about to fall. But it wasn't; it was crouching. And then it leapt.

The man who'd fired screamed. Once. Then the thing was rising, flinging the torn bits of him aside.

Danny and Flaps fired together, but it didn't even notice. It slashed at the fighters nearest it; one leapt out of range, but its claws caught the other in the stomach and tore her open; she fell to her knees with a scream. Lish ran to her, caught her as she fell back.

It stood, grinning mouth wide and dripping. Danny backed off, keeping his gun on it. It wouldn't fucking work, but he didn't have owt else.

It straightened and its gaze swept back and forth across them. Its gaze lingered on Lish for a second; the medic stepped back, and Harp moved in front of her, Thompson gun raised. It studied him, claws flexing; Harp tensed, bracing for the attack. And then it spun away and ran at Flaps.

Danny raised the Lanchester, but Flaps had already jumped aside, rolling clear. He fired a burst and thought he hit it, but it didn't slow. It hared back over the flats, towards their landcruisers and then past them. It was following the line of its own footprints, he realised; back the way it'd come.

"The fuck?" said Flaps.

"No clue," said Danny. "But get after it."

"Are you mad?"

"You want it running loose?" he said, running for the landcruisers.

"Fucking hell," he heard Flaps mutter as she ran after him.

REAP THURLEY
0530 HOURS

Kellett spun round as the Ops Room door swung open. "The hell do you think you're – oh. Colonel."

"Quite." Jarrett back-heeled the door shut. "Someone get me a drink. Hot."

"Tyler?" said Kellett.

A young Reaper snapped to attention and saluted, flushing red. "Tea or coffee, ma'am?"

"Actual coffee?"

"No, ma'am. Monarch brand."

"Then make it tea," she said. "I've seen what that crap's made out of. Carry on."

"Yes, ma'am."

Tyler scuttled off. Kellett chuckled. "Enjoy your work, don't you, Colonel?"

"What's our status?"

Kellett gestured to the chart. "We *were* doing fine. Monitoring the Catchman's progress." Kellett pointed to the pins one by one. "That Catchman rechecks the signal's bearing regularly. Whenever it does, we get an update on its location. As you can see, it's been moving on a constant course."

"Straight line into the Wastelands," Jarrett said, moving closer. "What's the problem?"

"The last reading." Kellett pointed again; Jarrett saw the pin he indicated was actually further back along the original line. "It's changed course."

Anger. Jarrett saw Winterborn's cold stone-angel's face. "You told me that this thing didn't run. It's supposed to be an unstoppable fucking killing machine, Kellett."

"It is." Kellett's voice rose slightly – anger, or fear? Jarrett moved in close on him to be sure; he backed away, looked down. "It's still following the signal. It's just that the source of the signal's moved."

"Helen."

"That's right."

"Your tea, ma'am."

"Thank you, Tyler." Jarrett washed down a couple more speed pills with the first gulp of tea. "From the Fort?" she asked Kellett.

"Only if that's where she was to begin with. You told me she never leaves the place."

There was a whining note in Kellett's voice; Jarrett's fists clenched at her sides. "So we don't know where the Fort is. But it's still homing in on her?"

"Yes."

Calm and warmth flooded through Jarrett. Take Helen away, the rest would sort itself. Finding the Fort would be simple after destroying the bitch. She nodded to the monitor screens on the wall. "Can you give us visual? Through its eyes, I mean?"

"Yes."

"Then do so," said Jarrett. "I want to see it. I want to be sure."

And it would be the next best thing to doing the job herself.

INTELLIGENCE CENTRE
0535 HOURS

"We lost it," Danny said.

"On the Flats?" said Alannah. "How did you manage that?"

"It's fast," he said. "And the sun's still not up."

Alannah breathed out ."Never mind that now. Important thing is you're okay."

"No we're fucking not. Tenner's dead. Stock's still alive, but the fucking thing had half her guts out. She's not gonna make it."

"Let Nestor be the judge of that, Danny. Get her on a landcruiser back here now."

"Okay. We'll carry on the sweep. See if we can find out where the fuck it's hiding."

"Right," she said. All she could see was his face – and that other face he'd described, glass-eyed and grinning. That and the damage it had done. "Be careful, for Christ's sake."

"Always am. Out."

"Wait. One thing."

"What?"

"You said it was heading back the way it had come?"

"Yeah, it was. It could have had the lot of us. We shot fuck out of it and it didn't do *nothing*. But then it sort of stopped. Sort of looking to and fro – trying to spot something."

"And it changed course," muttered Alannah.

"What?"

"Nothing. Thanks, Danny."

The line went dead. Alannah stood. Her legs felt weak: relief, realising how close Danny had come. She crossed to a map on the wall, grabbing a pencil. The listening post was *here*. The viaduct *there*. She drew a line on the map, connecting them. And the missing patrol's last known location? She marked that too. It wasn't anywhere on the line she'd drawn, but they'd have kept moving eastward after that. She traced the line the rest of the sweep would have followed, drew a cross when it, too, met the line.

"A straight line," she muttered. And she could see the direction that line was going in, too. Had it continued uninterrupted, it would have continued to the Fort.

But it hadn't; it was retracing its steps. Why? Not because Danny's team had outfought it.

She understood something – nearly did, anyway. The solution was in front of her, somewhere. It had been looking for something. What?

And had it been looking with its eyes?

The solution was here, she knew it. In a second, the pieces would have come together, but then Hei called her name.

"What?"

He held out a slip of paper. "Picked up something else about the Catchman," he said.

Alannah took it, read. And click: the pieces came together. "Christ," she said.

"What is it?"

She didn't look up at Hei as she headed back to her desk. "Get me Helen, Hei. Now. Right this second. *Now.*"

LISTENING POST 23

Helen loaded the last of the weapons and equipment into the landcruiser, took a shovel from the back. Best to bury what was left of the bodies quickly; once the sun was up, the heat would make the problem worse. Might have been easier to burn the coach, but it was a good location – you didn't throw one of those away because you didn't like the mess.

The radio crackled. "Helen? Osprey. Come in, Helen. Helen, come in *now!*"

Alannah's voice: she hadn't heard it with an edge like that for a long time. Had the stress of the job got to her? No; something else here. Helen took the mic. "Hello, Osprey."

"Helen, where are you? Where are you right now?"

"Still at the listening post," she said. "Just about to –"

"Forget that. Helen, you need to get out of there right now."

"What?"

Alannah told her about Danny's encounter with the creature. "We've been picking up chatter from the Reapers," Alannah said. "About something called the Catch Programme or the Catchman. Mean anything?"

"Nothing. What are they?"

"Still unknown. But I think this thing Danny and Flaps ran into is the Catchman they've been on about. Its movements co-ordinate with what we've got from Reaper transmissions. Including the latest."

"What do you mean?"

"Transmission from one of *their* listening posts, to REAP Thurley: *Catchman has altered course. New vector: a reversal of original path. Malfunction eliminated as possibility. Conclusion: Target Alpha has relocated.*"

"Target Alpha?" said Helen.

"It's homing in on something," said Alannah. "It was heading straight for the Fort, but now it's going back the way it came. So whatever it's homing in on —"

"Has moved," said Helen, "Me. Right?"

"I don't understand *how*, though — someone planted a bug on you?"

"If the Reapers had an agent at the Fort," Helen said, "they'd already be there."

"I don't see how else they could track you."

"So what do we do now?"

"Find out what it's homing in on," said Alannah. "Transmitter could be in your clothes, on one of your weapons…"

"Or in *me*," said Helen. "Something in my food, maybe." Vi in the canteen, slipping trackers in the cottage pie? She shook her head: ridiculous.

"Helen?"

"Keep monitoring their comms for this CATCH thing," she said. "Let's see if we can find out what we're up against."

"What about you?"

"I'm going to give it something to follow."

8.

In the cottage garden, Gevaudan sat back in a chair. Five, ten minutes, and the sun would be up; he was an early riser and enjoyed watching the dawn. The Fort was still quiet, this early; now and then an engine growled or there were muffled voices, but most of the time it was so quiet he could hear a fox barking on a distant hill. Even those sounds faded now, as he let himself drift.

It wasn't Deadsbury, but it would do. Besides, he didn't want that level of silence again. The isolation had turned him inward to his festering bitterness and loss; when Helen and Danny had first arrived he'd almost killed them. Luckily, enough had remained of the man he'd been that he hadn't.

Deadsbury had changed him, and the Fort had changed him again – he hoped into something better. Perhaps that faint,

91

distracting babble helped anchor him, connecting him again to the what passed for humanity now.

He missed music. He couldn't remember when he'd last heard any that he hadn't made himself. In Deadsbury he'd had a collection of instruments; now only a guitar or two. He missed the other instruments too: each had reminded him of a different loved one. Michaela, Gloria, David, Gideon, his parents. But the guitar reminded him of Jo. Always Jo.

A hand rested on his shoulder; it was Jo's touch. Gevaudan would recognise it anywhere, even twenty years on. He reached up to touch her hand, but there was nothing there.

Ghostlighting; he hadn't had that since Helen had come into his life. Helen had brought change with her, in blood and pain. Did it mean anything, for Jo to be here again? Coincidence, or a harbinger of some new upheaval?

"Gevaudan?"

"Jo –?" He turned.

"Who?" said Alannah.

Gevaudan turned away. "What do you want?"

"Bad time?"

He breathed out. "No." He turned back to face her, and Alannah stepped back. He didn't take it personally; even if she hadn't fought against his kind before they'd turned on the Reapers, no-one was really at ease with a Grendelwolf. They didn't quite look, or move, like humans; in most cases, the brain tried to make sense of them, failed and recoiled. "I was…" He hesitated, but chose honesty. "I was ghostlighting," he said.

"You can –"

"I lost a lot when the Reapers changed me," Gevaudan said, "but I'm still human in that respect, at least."

"Right." She looked down. Perhaps she was reassessing him, for better or worse. "Look, Gevaudan –"

"What is it?"

"Helen's in danger," said Alannah.

"The magic words," Gevaudan sighed. He strode towards the cottage.

Alannah followed him in. Gevaudan shrugged off the long coat; chances were that it would only hamper him. He opened a locked cupboard and took out two revolvers. "Tell me what you know," he said. "I'm listening."

Helen ran the flat of her knife-blade over the cloth bindings, then tested the seams with the point of her knife. Nothing. No lumps or irregularities: as far as she could make out, they were clear.

"Thank fuck for that," she muttered, and wrapped the first of her bindings around her groin and buttocks again. It was cold on top of the hill; the wind puckered her skin into goosepimples. She wrapped the other cloth around her chest, binding her breasts flat, then turned her attention to her coveralls next.

The coveralls had multiple pouches, most of them designed to be waterproof. The perfect place to stow something. She opened them, turned them inside out, tested the linings with her knife again. Still nothing.

Next she went through the contents of the pockets. Three grenades – hard to see how *they* could have been bugged. There was also a survival kit – a piece of leather that when unfolded contained fishing hooks and twenty feet of line, plus needles, thread, a compass, flint and tinder. She fingered the contents. The compass might have had something fitted in it, perhaps. She tossed it away.

A rifle, a Sterling, her revolver, the knife itself. The knife had been cut from a solid block; she unwound the leather strip wound about the handle, found nothing.

Now the guns. Strip them.

A bead of sweat ran over her temple. If the Catchman was tracking her, the distance she'd put between them in the landcruiser would only buy her so much time. But everything had to be checked. Calmly, methodically, she dismantled the automatic rifle.

"Helen? This is Osprey. Please acknowledge."

Helen picked up the radio mic. "I'm here, Alannah."

Alannah breathed out. "It's altered course again."

Helen nodded. A knot tightened in her belly, but she'd expected this. "Heading where?"

"On its current bearing, it's about an hour from Hawksmoor Fen."

Helen looked up. The sun was up now, bright in the blue sky, the air warm; as she'd suspected, a beautiful day. To the north, lakes – valleys, before the floods that had followed the War – shone like mirror-glass, and the islands – former hills – that dotted them were sprinkled with white and yellow and blue. To the west and south, hills and moors, similarly bedecked.

All was bright, except for the low ground directly below Helen to the east; it was draped in ragged white mist through which dull glints of fenwater showed. "Want to guess where I am now?"

"Christ. You get anywhere finding the tracker?"

"No." Helen started fitting the rifle back together. "Could be in the landcruiser, maybe."

"And how'd they know which landcruiser you picked?"

"Maybe they didn't," she said. "They want the Fort."

"So it's just a coincidence?"

"They happen," Helen said, disassembling the Sterling. "Either this thing had a bug we missed, or a Reaper agent in the Wastelands planted one. Either way, I'm ditching it."

"Helen, you can't keep ahead of this thing on foot."

"If it's tracking the 'cruiser, I won't need to."

"And if it's not?"

"Then things will get interesting."

Alannah sighed. "Where will you go?"

"If it follows me, I'll try and lose it on the Fen." Helen looked beyond the mists to where another, heavily wooded, hillside rose. "Failing that, there's the reservoir."

"Well, hang in there. Help's coming."

"I told you not to put anyone else in the firing line."

"It's Gevaudan. He was pretty insistent when he heard."

"I bet he was." As Alannah would have known he would be before telling him. And she'd once accused Helen of manipulating people? "Fine," she said at last. "I'd better move."

"Okay." A pause. "Luck, Helen."

Helen tossed the mic into the flatbed. Less than an hour. How much less? She needed to get clear of the 'cruiser. But first, her equipment. She fitted the Sterling back together, then started on the .38. Hard to see how anyone could have planted a tracker there as it hardly ever left her side – but that would make it all the better a way for the Catchman to find her.

She found nothing, and reassembled the revolver. Then she pouched it, slung the Sterling across her back, picked up the rifle and started down towards the fen.

COLONEL WEARING'S QUARTERS, THE TOWER
0630 HOURS

Colonel Leonora Wearing sat on the edge of her bed, studying the folded note pushed under her door.

She turned it over and over in her hands. No idea who had delivered it, of course, but that wasn't important; she'd no doubt who it was ultimately from. Her stomach felt hollow.

She wanted to burn it, shred it, destroy without looking. She could do that, of course, but it would kill her. Alannah Vale had made it clear; *you spy, or you die.*

Wearing unfolded the note. Above the fold were a few lines of nearly printed block capitals; indecipherable gibberish to any reader, unless you had the cipher. Below the fold the note was blank. Wearing took a pencil and began transposing. She'd memorised the code; the safest place to write anything was in your head.

Information required: all references to CATCH programme or Catchman. Maximum urgency. Do not delay.

It didn't end 'or else', but might as well have. Wearing sat in silence for a minute, then carefully tore the note up, stuffed it in her mouth, chewed and swallowed. She grimaced, then stood and slipped out of her quarters.

HAWKSMOOR FEN
0700 HOURS

Each breath scorched her lungs; the cold mist clung to her face like riverweeds. The Sterling bounced against her back, the revolver against her hip; the rifle was in her hands.

The ground was too treacherous for running. Visibility was poor, the mist a damp grey veil. The ground was streaked with mud and still water, beds of reeds; at its most solid, it was a spongy turf.

There were low huts to her right: fen-folk, making their living off fish, frogs and waterfowl. They were friendlies, but she kept clear. This thing wanted her, and there seemed to be no killing it. With luck she'd find a way, but if not she'd at least lead it clear of anyone else. Enough people had already died for her.

The path ahead forked three ways. No means of telling in the thickening mist which might save or kill her.

There was a noise behind her and she turned, aiming into the murk, finger on the trigger. Something moved in the dark, a quick lithe shadow in the mist. Helen sighted down the rifle, but it was already gone.

She turned and ran straight ahead; the path was broadest and seemed more solid than the rest.

Her guns' weight dragged at her. Blood pounded in her ears, and the sawing of her breath. Penned up in the Fort too long; she'd gone to seed. She should have gone running, like Alannah.

The ground slipped and slithered under her; she almost fell, threw her arms out for balance. The ground was mud. She looked behind her, saw nothing, gripped her rifle tight. It was wet, slippery: sweat or condensation.

Ahead was a structure: a wooden platform. Beyond it, water stretched from side to side and out ahead. If there was land beyond, she couldn't make it out.

She aimed the rifle into the mist; nothing, not yet. Looked around again. On the landing stage was an iron bell, a leather thong hanging from the clapper. She pulled it; the bell's clang echoed in the wet air.

"What the bloody hell do you want?" Helen spun as the voice boomed out, the rifle at her shoulder.

"Over here, you blind bat." A lantern gleamed. "And watch where you're pointing that bloody thing." She saw there was a hut on stilts beside the platform. A broad, hunched figure stood at its door, the light gleaming off its head.

"I need to get across," she said.

"Fine," he said, "I'll take thee shortly."

"Now," said Helen.

"Well, if it's *urgent*…" The man leant forward; the lantern-light revealed his face. He was her age or a little older, with a shaved head and bulging eyes, a broken nose, a jowled, double-chinned face and protruding lips. Big belly, big shoulders and a great thick neck. "Tha'll make it worth my while, then?"

"Whatever you want," she said. "I haven't much, but…"

His eyes gleamed. "That rifle?"

"You want it? It's yours. But we go, *now*."

The man waddled across the landing stage and started hauling a coracle out from under it. Helen looked back into the mist, the rifle aimed. "Come on then, if you're coming," he called.

Helen climbed down. The boat rocked in the water; when she got in, it lurched and she nearly fell. The boatman laughed. "Happens t' best of us," he said, "if tha's not used to it. Now sit thee down, for Christ's sake, else tha'll go in headfirst when I start."

"Okay," Helen sat, shoving the rifle over to him. "Now, *please*."

"All right, all right." The boatman cast off and pushed them clear of the stage. "They call me Frog."

"Helen." Close to, he wasn't as fat as he'd looked; under a thick sheepskin coat were layers of clothing, for protection against the cold and damp. The big arms and shoulders worked: the boat slid across the water.

The landing stage vanished; there was only the flat dull water and the mist. Something splashed; Helen started.

"Watch it, love," snapped Frog. "Tha'll have us over." He laughed. "Not scared, art tha? Big, tough lass like thee?"

Helen peered past him into the mist. Another splash: bigger, louder. She flicked the Sterling's safety catch to 'F'.

"Take it easy, will tha?" said Frog. "I know every bloody beast in the fens and I'll tell thee now, there's nowt –"

A loud, hissing screech rang out in the mist. No beast in the Wastelands had a cry like that. Yet at the same time it *was* familiar.

Frog licked his lips. His bulbous eyes met hers. Helen looked at the pole in his hands. Frog looked too, then blinked. "Oh. Aye." He pushed down; the boat sped on.

Frog poled faster, forehead glistening. "Nearly there."

Helen looked over her shoulder. Through the mist, she saw a low, broad shadow; the fen's far bank, a dozen yards away.

A splash came from behind; something big and heavy floundered through the water. "Christ," muttered Frog. "What the bloody hell– ?"

Helen pulled back the Sterling's bolt. Behind Frog, in the mist, was another shadow; smaller, man-shaped, and wading fast towards the boat –

"Get down," she shouted. When she aimed the Sterling, Frog moved faster than she'd expected, diving to the floor of the boat. Water splashed over the gunwales. Helen fired. Her burst flew high, and the dark shape lunged; Helen aimed low and fired half a dozen short bursts at its centre.

Frog cursed and yelped. The boat rocked, and Helen grabbed the gunwale with her free hand to avoid going over. She looked up, steadying the gun. The dark shape was gone.

Was that it? After what it had done on the Flats and at the listening post, had she dropped it with a burst in the dark? A lucky shot, perhaps. Even the Catchman must have a weak spot.

"Hellchrist." Frog sat up. "I'll tell thee, lass, th'art paying extra for –"

Hands lunged out of the mist and caught his shoulders, claws tearing through his clothes into the flesh. Helen was still lifting the Sterling when they heaved the whole bulk of him over the side. The boat's stern was pulled under as he went; stagnant water flooded aboard.

Frog screamed once; it ended in a gurgle as blood or water drowned it. The thrashing in the water stilled, and the fen was still.

The boat had partially righted herself, but water was still pouring in. Helen looked for something to bale it out with, found nothing.

A shadow rose, waist-deep in the fenwater. Frog? No – too thin. Helen fired; the shadow rocked, then lunged forward. If she hit it, it had no effect. And then the Sterling was empty, and the Catchman climbed aboard the sinking boat.

Helen crouched. Her enemy was still just a shadow; all she could see was the glint of its steel helm and the faint ghostlight that lit its eyes. It let out that hissing screech again; its breath reeked of old blood, spoiled meat, hot metal and decay.

She had three grenades, each in a separate pouch; she got one open, flinging the Sterling at the Catchman's face. When it flinched aside, she pulled the grenade's pin.

One, two…

The Catchman was about to spring; Helen dropped the grenade and fell back over the side.

She hit the water, went straight under; she struck out in a breast stroke, aiming down towards the bottom.

A dim flash from above, then a dull thump and the water heaved and slammed into her. Shockwave. Air rushed out of her. Silver bubbles. She stopped herself breathing again just in time, forcing her boots into the ooze to find solid ground. Had to stand. She forced her legs straight; they shook. Then her back.

She stood. For a second she couldn't breathe, as if the shock had made her forget how. Then the cold air rushed into her lungs. It burned them.

Frog, the boat – gone. But the Catchman – Helen blundered towards the bank's dark shoulder, fighting the water's weight, the suck of the mud.

The water fell to her thighs, then her knees. Her heart thudded; her lungs burned. The mud, the water, her wet clothes all slowed her. The Catchman. The Catchman.

Whatever it was, the thing was fast enough at the best of times. But now the water was at her shins, and now her ankles; she fell to her hands and knees, heart still thudding, arms and legs limp, the bones like mud themselves, and crawled the last few yards to dry land. She lay there gasping.

Something splashed behind her; Helen rolled onto her back, stared into the mist. In it was a shadow: man-shaped but not a man, wading towards the bank.

Helen rolled back over and forced herself to all-fours. Then her knees. Then at last she stood. Her legs wobbled; her bones were pulp. She put one foot in front of the other, each a little further up slope. Now faster. Faster. The fear kicked in; the adrenaline snapped everything into focus, driving pain, fatigue and tiredness back, and she ran.

9.

WOODS NEAR HAWKSMOOR RESERVOIR
20TH MARCH, ATTACK PLUS TWENTY-ONE YEARS
0720 HOURS

The mist thinned as Helen stumbled up the hill, and finally she broke free of the white-out into warm sunlight, scraps of blue sky showing through a mesh of branches. The air was clearer, the smell of the fen giving way to the fresh scent of pine as she stumbled into the trees.

She glanced back, glimpsed the Catchman coming out of the mist. She gritted her teeth, ran harder; every second was precious now.

She'd set a grenade off practically in its face; Danny and his squad had shot it point-blank with submachine guns, and still it came on, apparently unharmed. She had two more grenades and her .38; after that she'd be down to a knife and bare hands. But anything could die. She just had to live long enough to learn how.

In the meantime there was only the hill, the trees, the burning in her lungs and the aching in her legs as she ran. The running was everything now: every foot of distance she could buy was vital.

She reached a narrow path between high earth banks. From behind her came the Catchman's hissing screech. Up ahead she saw the skyline. She was near the top of the hill – but to the limits of her endurance, too. She focused on a single tree; when she'd reached it, she could stop. When she drew abreast of it, she chose another, and ran on.

The earth banks gave way to a drystone wall. Helen dropped to one knee, took out the two grenades and the survival kit, unravelling the fishing line.

Quickly – she heard branches snapping as the Catchman came. She wedged a grenade into the wall on either side, then tied one end of the line around a thick root that wormed free of the earth on one side. She looped the line through the first grenade's ring-pull, then pulled it taut across the path and repeated the process with the other grenade before knotting the far end around a tree trunk.

The Catchman screeched; its footsteps thundered. Helen swayed, legs throbbing, and stumbled on.

*

The machine was silent: they were so close upon the prey the red brain needed no guidance. Its hunger and its kill-need drove it – and, most of all, there was the ever-growing pain the target's existence caused. The pain grew worse as it came closer, but that didn't drive the beast away; if anything caused it pain, its response was to destroy. The beast could find the target unaided now.

The path rose: the trees cleared. Stone walls: pale sky up ahead. Then something caught at its legs and it flew forward. Snarling, it thrashed, kicking to break free of the strands that held it.

The machine mind rose: something was different, perhaps a threat. There was a smell: burning.

The machine needed only seconds to calculate, and its conclusion was a single word: *fuse*.

And in that second, the grenades exploded.

*

Helen was just over the crest of the hill when she heard the blast. She looked back; smoke billowed skyward, black against the blue. She laughed and began stumbling down. She knew she was flagging, she was sodden and cold, her limbs heavy and stiff.

In front of her were the Hawksmoor Reservoirs. She wove past the smaller of the two: sheer grassy sides sloped down two hundred feet to the stagnant, weed-filled water at the bottom.

At the far end of the smaller reservoir was a low, square stone building with dull glass windows and a wooden door. Helen made towards it. Whether or not she'd killed the beast, she'd reached the limits of her strength.

*

In the woods, upon the path, the Catchman's pieces lay.

The shrapnel had torn off both legs and an arm, blasted away its face and torn its chest and belly open, this was death. The red brain raged and screamed: terror, pain and fury, a mad beast pounding the walls of its cage.

The machine clicked and calculated, the beast, in its terror and wrath, barely sensed it. But other things moved in the red, rising like the consciousness that had faintly shone before: memories.

There was a woman, smiling, and a feeling – or the *memory* of one – that was neither anger, hunger nor fear: it was something neither beast nor machine could name. A hand reached out to stroke the woman's face, the hand was the Catchman's, and yet was not: it was human. A child held its arms out, smiling, the same hands reached down to pick it up. The beast's fear grew: here was something it did not understand. Its fear became rage, screamed loud across the red mire to drown the pain of dying.

The machine ignored the fragments, they were of no import. Other memories flickered too, equally irrelevant to the machine and perplexing to the beast, but these were different memories: a cavern beneath a hill, lit by fire. In was an altar, and on that altar were heads, sacrifices to what was worshipped here.

Other shapes stood, knelt and chanted, their faces were hidden, and even the Catchman's beast-brain knew that was good. "*Angana sor varalakh kai torja. Angana sor varalakh cha voran.*" The chanting reached a crescendo. All awareness blotted out in a white flare of pain that swept away all memories, human or not, and left the beast screaming, as torn nerves and muscles awoke. Something reached from its shattered body, sought out its fragments – and then, with a wrenching convulsion, flung what had been torn asunder back together. Shattered bone grated on shattered bone, torn flesh was pressed to torn flesh. Bone and flesh ran like water. Then it solidified again. The beast's shrieks changed from agony to exultation, it was whole.

It stood and flexed newly healed limbs, threw back its head and howled. The machine sank again beneath the red mire, leaving the beast to its hunger and need: they would complete the task.

*

Helen ran to the stone building. A rusting, faded sign: *Pump House*. A flight of steps led from a mossed-over concrete wall to a short walkway with rusted iron rails. She stumbled across it to a heavy wooden door. She flung herself against it, twisting the handle; for a moment she thought it wouldn't open, but it last the door swung inward.

The building reeked of damp brick and urine. The lower floor consisted of two bare rooms with one window and a winding metal staircase. Helen drew the revolver and climbed.

Upstairs were two bare rooms, one with some sort of control panel, smashed and broken. They were more brightly-lit than the lower storey, though; there were two windows, front and back, although they were almost opaque with grime and moss.

Helen went to the one overlooking the reservoir. Directly below the building was a bell-mouth overflow – a raised concrete circle, inside which was flight after flight of concrete steps ringing a gaping stone throat.

Beyond that, Hawksmoor Reservoir. It was roughly rectangular in shape, with high, sloping banks thick with grass, and edged brick walls. To her right, a gaping fissure split the banks.

Mum and Dad had brought Helen here before the War, or somewhere like it. A hot summer, when water supplies were low. The reservoir had been almost emptied by the drought, exposing the ruins of a village drowned to supply water to cities that were now ash.

At this end of the reservoir the water was still deep, the remains of the buildings still permanently submerged. Towards the far end, ruined houses and a broken church tower rose from the green, weed-thick shallows. The water lolled sluggishly, sparkling in the sun.

Helen crept to the other window, keeping low, and slipped her revolver from its pouch. She flipped out the cylinder; gun and bullets were both dry, ready for use. She snapped the cylinder shut, peered through the cracked window's film of dirt and moss.

The Catchman came out of the trees. It didn't seem injured at all. It stood, hunched and snarling then straightened, head swivelling from side to side. Like a machine. Then it strode forward, along the reservoir's bank.

Before, the Catchman had been a shadow, even in the boat. But now Helen could see her enemy – and, so doing, knew it for what it was.

INTELLIGENCE CENTRE, ASHWOOD FORT
0740 HOURS

Hei ran up to Alannah's desk. "Kingfisher, Scramble Four."

Kingfisher: their listening post in Manchester. "Put them on." Alannah grabbed her headphones. "Have a stenographer listen in."

She picked up the microphone. "Osprey."

"Osprey." The voice on the other end was clipped and taut. "Honey Badger's come through. We have the file on the CATCH programme. Ten minute window before it has to go back. Ready?"

Alannah looked up. Hei nodded. "Go," she said.

"The CATCH programme's a new weapons system, developed at REAP Thurley, under Dr Martyn Kellett. Basically, they take some poor bastard and operate on them, turn them into something they can send out to hunt whoever they want dead."

"The Catchman?"

"Yup. And it says here CATCH is an acronym. Stands for Cybernetically Augmented Targeted Combat Humanoid."

"Cybernetics?" said Alannah. "They had nothing like this before the War, and you're lucky if you find a working laptop these days. How the hell –"

"Yup," said Kingfisher. "But according to the file, it isn't strictly speaking cybernetic."

"What?"

"Back in the winter, a couple of Jennywrens got lost in the Wastelands during a major storm. They made contact with someone who guided them to a REAP base. Thing was, turned out the base had been empty for months. But there was a file, addressed to Winterborn."

Alannah felt cold. "What was the base called?"

"Hobsdyke."

HAWKSMOOR RESERVOIR
0745 HOURS

Helen ducked as the Catchman's head turned towards her, heart thumping.

106

She was surprised Danny had missed it, but then he'd have seen only the helmeted head and grinning teeth. And hadn't it been caked in mud and blood? The fen had washed that coating off, revealing the dull grey hide beneath; that, and the long black talons on its fingers, identified it to her. *Styr.* One of the creatures she'd faced at Hobsdyke – or some variation of it, at least.

She moved close to the window, listening.

INTELLIGENCE CENTRE, ASHWOOD FORT

"The notes pertained to a Project Tindalos," Kingfisher said. "Not much about it in the CATCH file, but what there is sounds barking mad, quite frankly."

"It was," said Alannah. "And they used it to create the Catchman?"

"Correct. A more limited range of use, it says, but controllable."

"I'm sure they think so," Alannah said.

RUINS OF VISITOR'S CENTRE, HAWKSMOOR RESERVOIR
0750 HOURS

When the reservoir at Hawksmoor had been breached during the War, the floodwaters had surged through the valley, sweeping trees, houses, people and cars away in its wake. Their remains were half-buried in accumulated silt, now thickly overgrown with grass and young trees. The road to the old visitor's centre beside the reservoir was still intact, though; a fast-pursuit landcruiser had done the rest.

Gevaudan stopped beside the centre's ruins. A stream ran past him, trickling from the base of the rift in the reservoir's high, rearing banks.

Gevaudan climbed the slope beside the rift to the footpath above. The open, empty space of the main reservoir gaped below him, the drowned village on its stagnant floor.

He looked from right to left, across the hills that rose around the reservoir, to the pump house at the far end.

THE PUMP HOUSE, HAWKSMOOR RESERVOIR
0752 HOURS

Brittle grass crunched and snapped underfoot, and in the still air Helen heard the Catchman's breathing – loud, rasping and hoarse – as it closed in. It was close; just outside.

She listened for footsteps on the walkway, but none came. However it was homing in on her, perhaps her signal was too close to pinpoint, a blur of white noise. She crouched, clutching the .38 till her knuckles ached, teeth gritted so they wouldn't chatter. Shaking. A few months ago she'd been in a succession of firefights, the Reapers had taken her prisoner and beaten her bloody, and she'd gone straight on from that to face what they'd created at Hobsdyke. But now, one soaking and a bit of a run and she was close to collapse.

She took deep breaths, in and out; steadied herself. Outside, it was quiet. Maybe the Catchman had gone; it might be circling the reservoir to try and get a fix on her. Or it might still be below, waiting.

Another deep breath; Helen slowly raised her head and peered over the sill through the grimy window. As she did, a steel helmet rose into view; two round glass lenses lit by a pale, flickering light stared into her eyes. Breath gusted from the metal grille over its nose, misting the window. Below that a red and white grin stretched impossibly wide across its face.

For a second time stopped, didn't exist, and there was just the damp brick room and the Catchman's face grinning through the window.

The grin widened further still; the Catchman screeched, the glass rattling in its frame. Helen flung herself backwards as a clawed hand smashed through the window; a moment later the rest of the Catchman followed.

*

The screech echoed out across Hawksmoor. Gevaudan looked to the pump house.

The sound he'd heard hadn't been human, but the voice that cried out in terror and rage a moment later was. And he knew whose.

*

Helen reeled clear of the staircase, nearly colliding with the back window overlooking the bell-mouth. She turned to run for the door, but something dropped from above to land in a crouch between the exit and her.

She fired as the Catchman came at her, knowing it would do nothing, and ran for the window.

*

Four shots rang and echoed across the reservoir; for a second, Gevaudan was still. Then he leapt across the breach, landed in a crouch, and ran along the bank towards the pump house.

*

Helen smashed through the window, arms over her eyes. For a second she hung half-in, half-out – the Catchman's clawed hands would seize her, drag her back inside – but then she squirmed free, landing on the bell-mouth's concrete sill.

She slid, started to roll down the steps, but caught a jagged railing with her left hand. Rough metal gouged her palm, but she hung on and got back on her feet.

The Catchman's face appeared in the window. Two rounds left in the Smith & Wesson; those and the knife were all she had left.

She edge around the bell-mouth, away from the window. The shaft gaped below her like a hungry throat. What was at the bottom? Concrete or water, the fall would most likely kill her either way, but it might be a cleaner death. Behind her, now, was the dam; that fall might do the job, too.

The Catchman crouched on the opposite side, grinning. Then it leapt, clearing the shaft to land two or three steps below her.

Helen kept edging around the bell-mouth as the Catchman climbed up towards her, its pale, dim eyes never leaving hers. It hissed, shook its head from side to side, then wagged one clawed, blood-encrusted finger to and fro.

Its grin stretched, gaped; Helen backed away, till the pump-house wall was at her back.

Nowhere left to go.

Grinning, it came for her.

10.

As he reached the end of the reservoir, Gevaudan saw Helen scramble out through the pump house window, and the thing that followed her. He saw her nearly fall, regain her balance; saw her pursuer leap over the shaft to land beside her. She looked paler than ever; drained and close to falling.

Gevaudan rounded the corner of the reservoir, charging towards the pump house, knowing as he did that there was no time. Helen was backed up against a wall, and the Catchman was close enough to touch. In a second, it would be upon her.

Helen pulled back the Smith & Wesson's hammer with her thumb: a crisp triple click sounded in the still air. The Catchman cocked its head, eyes glinting.

Two rounds left. Even if she'd guessed right, there was no guarantee of success. But she was a good shot; she at least had a chance.

As the Catchman lunged, time ran both fast and slow. It came at her as if through water, while her hands had perfect speed and fluency.

At Hobsdyke, the Styr's mouths and eyes had been their only weak spots, the only way to inflict a killing wound. Helen levelled the gun and aimed, lining up the front and rear sights on the Catchman's left eye.

She squeezed the trigger. The .38 kicked in her hand and glass splintered; the Catchman reared back, screeching. Helen aimed again and shot out its other eye.

The Catchman pitched sideways, caromed off the steps below and fell, still screeching, into the blackness of the overflow shaft, the howl trailing away to end with a dull thud of impact.

"Helen!"

She looked up, leaning on the cracked railing around the overflow, and saw Gevaudan clambering onto the bell-mouth, fine black hair blowing back from his face, the yellow wolf's eyes full of – Relief? Concern? Care? She pushed the revolver back into its pouch and fastened it. The railing shifted in her grip; it was broken, cracked. A long steel shard hung loose; she twisted it and it came free. Helen stared at it. Nothing seemed quite real.

*

"Helen," Gevaudan called; she looked close to falling. He caught her arm and she almost pulled free; then recognition dawned. "Gevaudan?"

"Are you all right?"

"Think so." She laughed weakly. "Out of action too long. Forgot what it's like."

Gevaudan smiled. "You seem to have made out all right." He nodded to the shaft. "I suppose it's like riding a bicycle. You never lose the –" he stopped.

"Gevaudan?"

Grendelwolves were faster than humans, stronger, their reflexes quicker; their sight and hearing were keener too. In the shaft's darkness, Gevaudan saw movement, and heard the scuffle and scrape of something climbing up the stone.

"It isn't dead," he said.

"What?"

"There's a landcruiser by the old visitor's centre," he said, "back the way I came. Take it. Get out of here."

"It'll follow me," Helen said.

Gevaudan shook his head. "This ends here."

"Gevaudan, you don't understand what it is."

"They call it a Catchman," he said. Down in the shaft, its eyes shone.

"Yes, but you don't understand what it *is*–"

The Catchman saw him and hissed, scuttling spiderlike around the inside of the pipe.

"Move," Gevaudan shouted, and jumped as it scrambled up the steps towards Helen. They crashed down onto the steps. Gevaudan grabbed a railing, as Helen had; the Catchman seized his leg. He writhed and kicked, and fell back down the steps again.

The Catchman got up. Helen was reloading her revolver. Gevaudan, his back against the railings, prepared to leap again. But the Catchman's rage overrode its programming: instead of Helen, it hurled itself at him.

It slammed into him, claws tearing at his shoulders, seeking his throat. The collision drove him backwards, and he felt the railing crack. Gevaudan fell backwards, but caught hold of the Catchman as he did, dragging it after him over the side of the bell-mouth.

The water flew up to meet them. The Catchman's grip broke on impact and they plunged away from one another through thick green water and clinging weed. Gevaudan crashed into stonework; bones cracked.

He spun away, stunned and sinking, sodden clothes pulling him down into the silt of what had been Hawksmoor's High Street.

Thin, weak shafts of pale light reached down; all else was silty dark.

Gevaudan could feel the cracked bones – ribs, mostly – knitting back together under his skin. He released the breath he'd been holding. The skin of his throat horripilated; then there were sharp, stinging pains as if the skin had been cut – it felt as though it had been slit in three or four places, either side of his Adam's apple. A moment later the cold water washed into the bloodless wounds, and he no longer struggled for breath.

A pale film slid sideways across his eyes. For a moment, he couldn't see properly; then his vision cleared. The gloom lifted; the reservoir's depths were murky and green. Around him were windowless, doorless, roofless houses, the cracked column of a war memorial. Thick green weed billowed in the water like drowned women's hair.

Something gleamed in the water, but when he looked he saw nothing, other than the submerged houses. Gevaudan moved towards them, and fish scattered from one house's doorway; a moment later, something with pale, luminous eyes burst from it.

Clawed hands seized him; Gevaudan bellowed, stagnant water flooding his mouth. His own claws slashed across its face, dark blood clouding the water. He drove a kick into its chest, sending it spinning back, but the water was deepest here, harder to fight in. Gevaudan struck out away from the pump house, towards the shallows at end of the reservoir. Glancing back, he saw the Catchman's eyes shining through the water as it followed.

Light gleamed through the water. He fought towards it, found his footing and stood up, bursting free of the water among the grey stone walls. The light exploded in his eyes; he couldn't see. He coughed, gulped for breath, then sucked in clean cold air as his lungs started working again. As the gill-slits in his neck closed, he blinked and his vision cleared; the nictitating membranes in his eyes retracted and the glare faded as his vision readjusted.

The water heaved and bubbled. The Catchman rose, grinning. As it surged towards him, raising a bow wave of stagnant water; he summoned the Fury.

The Catchman lunged at Gevaudan; he leapt aside from the blow and struck its throat. His claws punched through its skin, his fingers driving into the raw flesh. He sought the jawbone, gripped hold and pulled. It came loose with a gristly pop; the Catchman howled. Gevaudan wrenched; flesh and skin tore, bone snapped, and with a final convulsive heave he ripped the lower half of the Catchman's face away. The Catchman tried to scream without a mouth; Gevaudan caught its arm, twisted, wrenched again. The joint dislocated with pops and cracks. He pulled harder, raked the skin with his talons; the arm tore free and he flung it aside.

Bleeding, the Catchman wove in the water, then lurched towards him with its surviving arm. Gevaudan flew at it, raking, tearing, twisting, thumping, hauling. The other arm flew free, then a leg. He ripped open its belly, clawed at its guts and dragged them out. The Styr's hides had been impenetrable to his claws, but this wasn't. He didn't think about that. Didn't think on what he was doing. The thing had to die – or if he couldn't kill it, he'd break and tear it apart so it couldn't harm –

The Catchman fell back into the water, staining it red. Gevaudan stumbled back, breathing hard as the Fury ebbed out of him. The water bubbled and heaved. There was movement under it. Something broke the surface – the Catchman's hand, the clawed fingers twitching as it moved. Suddenly it halted, flexed hard.

And the water exploded as the Catchman stood.

It spread its arms – unmarked, intact – as if for Gevaudan's inspection, and grinned, the smile stretching across its face, literally from ear to ear. Or would have been, if it had had ears.

Gevaudan looked up towards the bell-mouth, towards the tiny figure far above. "Go," he shouted up at her. "Get away!"

She shouted something back – his name. A warning, he realised, in the instant before the Catchman smashed into him and they both crashed backwards into the water.

*

Helen blinked, straightened up. The water was a white thrashing blur.

Go. Get away. She shook her head. Too many dead for her as it was. She edged around the bell-mouth, fast as she dared, clambered over the wall. Her legs wobbled. No. Steady. Keep going. There was something. Something she'd forgotten – one more thing left to try. It had worked at Hobsdyke – not on the Styr themselves, but on what they'd served, and its death had killed them too.

She'd have to be quick; against the Catchman, even Gevaudan wouldn't last long. But at the same time, she had to get it right. One detail, and they'd both be dead.

She drew the knife. In her other hand, she still clutched the shard from the railing. She tested the point; sharp. She pressed it to the knife-blade, bore down and drew it down, carving the upright of a symbol. Then the cross-piece.

At first glance the symbol might have resembled a Christian crucifix, but it wasn't; viewed more closely, the shape, the angle, the proportions were all subtly different. Helen had first seen it in a church, though; the one in Hobsdyke village.

The cross was carved. Helen took a deep breath, threw the shard aside, then sheathed the knife and ran, veering down the embankment towards the shallows.

*

Gevaudan blinked blood from his eyes. The wounds in his face were closing, slowly; the one in his side was deeper, but would heal without permanent damage, given time. However, the Catchman didn't seem likely to grant him that.

He'd pinned the beast up against the wall of a half-submerged cottage, using his weight to trap his arms; it couldn't claw or slash him any more, and he was able to keep his face out of range of its teeth. But that would only last so long; even he could tire, especially when he was weakened after using the Fury. And as far as he could see, the Catchman never would, any more than it could die.

He looked up; Helen was running down the embankment, heading towards this end of the reservoir. Did she mean to fight with him – die with him? He hoped not. There were hills beyond the reservoir, where she might evade the Catchman for a time. But why bother? If it could die, Gevaudan couldn't see how. All flight did was delay the inevitable –

The Catchman's body bucked and heaved; Gevaudan was flung backwards, crashing down into the water. He climbed up, backed away as the Catchman closed. He looked left to right; nowhere much to run, and the end result was the same. The best he could hope was that in its rage it would devote itself first to killing him, buy Helen the time to get clear.

Behind him was the church; its wooden doors were long gone. Gevaudan waded backward towards the entrance, backing into the dank black cavern the flooded building had become.

Grinning, the Catchman followed.

*

Helen's lungs burned. She was shaking. Any minute now, she'd fall. And she planned to fight the Catchman with a knife? She could almost hear Frank's mocking voice.

Put that way, it sounded foolish. But if she was right, it wouldn't be a long fight; one blow would end it. And if she was wrong, then it wouldn't matter, because things had always been going to end that way.

Helen veered down the slope towards the water. Her sight was blurred, but she could see the Catchman entering the church. She splashed into the water, fell. Rose. She was close to falling again. But she staggered on.

Dim light dappled the thigh-deep water, rippled in patterns on the ceiling. It slanted through the empty church windows, fell on the Catchman's red grin and flashed off the lenses of its eyes.

Even they were unbroken now, Gevaudan realised as he backed up, wincing at the pain from the wound in his side. It was still bleeding, flowing warmly down his thigh into the water. Whatever damage was done to the Catchman, it healed, even faster than him.

He had to smile; there'd been times he'd felt like a cheat, with his strength and speed and all the other gifts, unwanted though they'd been, that his nature conferred on him. Had he, once or twice, mused on how it would be to fight an enemy as strong as him or stronger? On balance, he decided he'd preferred having an unfair advantage. Although it hardly seemed to matter now.

The Catchman's hands rose; the black talons flexed. Its grin gaped into a baying, laughing howl; that hissing screech blasted out of it, and it strode towards him to end it.

*

Helen reached the church door, peered round it. Gevaudan crouched ready to meet the attack, black hair plastered to his face, teeth gritted as the Catchman advanced.

The church was a hollow shell – any furnishings were long gone – and the splashing as it moved echoed from the ceiling. Helen edged around the door and started towards it, trying to make no sound. The floor was thick with ooze. She pulled out the knife, gripped it tight. If she could sneak up on it unawares, she might do it. If – if – she was right.

When Gevaudan saw her, his eyes widened; he looked away almost at once, but the Catchman went still. It turned, swivelling to face her with its grin. It looked back at Gevaudan, then her.

Decisions, decisions.

Helen dropped into a fighting crouch. She swayed, nearly fell. *Perfect.* The Catchman turned the rest of the way to face her.

"Come on, then," she said. "Come on!"

"Helen," said Gevaudan. The Catchman flapped a clawed hand, as if batting him away.

"Come at me!" she shouted, and the Catchman screeched.

Gevaudan leapt as it shot towards her, but fell short and crashed into the water. Didn't matter anyway. It was just her and the knife and the beast, those claws, that grin, as it bounded towards her. As it closed the last few feet, Helen stepped forward into its embrace.

*

Gevaudan, rising from the water, shouted as he saw the Catchman claim her. She cried out once; its screech blasted and echoed from the church's ceiling, and then they crashed into the water and went under. Gevaudan floundered towards where they'd been. The water seethed and churned, turning pink.

He reached under the water, and something grabbed his arm. He pulled back, and Helen burst out of the water.

"Helen! Are you – where is it?"

She sagged against him, leaning on his arm. "I got the bastard," she said. "I got it."

*

The red brain screamed. The primal terror of the dark was on it, as one by one the lights went out: brute biology, so long held at bay, reasserted itself. *Death comes for all*: the foreign phrase echoed in it, though it barely grasped at the meaning.

The steel brain clacked and chattered: again and again it assessed and calculated. And each time the answer was the same: there was nothing to be done. It was only a part, as the red brain was only a part: after shrugging off so much damage, a single blow had cancelled out the force that held all the parts together.

The red mire curdled and blackened, clotted and still: the silver machine seized up, jammed and fell silent. As the Catchman fell asunder, a flurry of memories flew up like the silver bubbles of a drowning's man's last breath: a woman's kiss, a child's smile. Sorrow and happiness: loss and joy. The man the CATCH programme had taken knew something close to peace: then he was dead, and all torment at an end.

*

By the time they dragged what was left of the Catchman onto the bank, it was little more than an empty skin. The grey leathery hide, the claws, the teeth anchored in the thick membranes of its mouth; those remained, along with the steel helm and its now-cracked glass lenses. Everything else, the substance within, had poured out of it into the waters of the reservoir.

The knife was still locked in the hide, buried to the hilt. Helen pulled it free, and on the third try, got it back in its sheath. Then she kicked the thing's remains over onto its back, glared down at its collapsed face.

"Still here," she said. "I'm still fucking here, Frank."

Her legs gave out; Gevaudan caught her as she fell.

REAP THURLEY
0810 HOURS

"It's confirmed, sir," said Tyler. He looked from Kellett to Jarrett and back again, shrank back before the looks on their faces. "I'm sorry, ma'am. We've checked and rechecked. The signal's gone. It's dead."

Kellett was brick-red; humiliated at the failure, wondered Jarrett, or about to rage against reality? Either way, Tyler would be on the receiving end of it. "Thank you, Tyler," she said. "Carry on."

She turned away from them both and studied the chart, the arc of the Catchman's journey. Thurley to Hawksmoor.

Kellett moved to her side. She caught a smell of sour sweat and grimaced, turning slightly away. "It's possible it achieved its objective," he said. "It might have killed her before –"

"It didn't," said Jarrett. "She killed it."

"Winterborn will kill us," said Kellett. "Won't he?"

"Why?"

"Because we've failed."

"He might kill you," said Jarrett. "But I think I still have a couple of lives left." She looked at Kellett for nearly a minute, enjoying his fear, before saying: "But we haven't failed yet."

"What?"

Jarrett nodded at the chart, arms folded. "Killing Helen was always a secondary objective. The primary one was to locate the Fort, because she'd be there. Her death would have been a bonus, nothing more."

"But we don't know where the Fort is, either." Kellett said it through his teeth. "She left the place. For the first bloody time in months, she left it."

"But she was still there at the start," said Jarrett. "Look." She pointed to the narrow loop where the Catchman had doubled back, then the arc where its course had veered towards Hawksmoor. "Up until then, it maintained a constant bearing. Yes?"

"Yes." Kellett licked his lips. "But we've no idea how far it still had to go…"

"Doesn't matter." There was a wooden yardstick on the shelf below the chart; Jarrett snatched it up and positioned it to fit against the line of the Catchman's original course. "There," she said.

"Where?" Kellett moved in closer.

"There's a village, see? Ashwood. It's on a hill, too – that makes sense. High ground. It's surrounded by non-Reaper controlled territory for miles, well-placed to access the Devil's Highways. Perfect. That's the place."

"What if it's further afield?"

Jarrett shook her head, not taking her eyes from the chart. "The Catchman was moving back towards the listening post it took out before. Helen would have gone to investigate it." She smiled. "A touch of cabin fever, maybe. Either way, she couldn't have done that if she was further out. No." Jarrett tapped the map. "This is our Fort. Ashwood."

Kellett began to smile.

"Pack your bags, Doctor. And the rest of your toy soldiers. Tyler?"

"Ma'am?"

"Contact the Tower and inform Commander Winterborn that Phase One of Operation Harvest is complete. Phase Two is underway."

HILL ROAD

0825 HOURS

A volley of cracks and snaps woke Helen. She opened her eyes, saw high thick hedges skimming by.

Left untended for years, they'd grown wild, branches spreading till they almost met in the middle of the road; landcruisers still shattered them en masse as they traversed the narrow hill roads.

The 'cruiser bounced; the tarmac was badly cracked, the road surface uneven, bulging in places where thick roots wormed underneath. She glanced across at Gevaudan; beyond him, she could see the flooded valleys she'd sighted before, their lakes still shining in the sun.

"Ah," Gevaudan glanced at her. He chewed as he spoke; she saw a chunk of dried meat in one hand. "You're back with us. I'd keep your head down, if I were you."

"Right." Helen hunched down. Her teeth chattered. There was a blanket around her, and underneath... "Where are my clothes?"

"In the back. How are you feeling?"

"Exhausted." She touched her forehead. "And like I'm burning up."

"Rest for now," he said. "The immediate crisis seems to be –"

The radio crackled. "Helen, Gevaudan, this is Osprey, do you copy?"

"We're here," said Gevaudan.

"Just started getting reports in," Alannah said. "Reaper attacks."

"Where?" said Helen.

"Everywhere. All along the perimeter of the territory we control. Nothing heavy, though, nothing in force."

"Diversionary raids?" said Gevaudan.

"That's what I was thinking."

"They were tracking the Catchman," said Helen. "That was always their plan – use me to find the Fort."

"You think they might have managed to?"

"It was going in a straight line until I started moving," said Helen. "That might have been enough."

"Oh Christ," said Alannah. Helen heard the fear in her voice.

"Keep it together," Helen said. "And make sure the Devil's Highways are watched. That's where the main attack's going to come."

She looked at Gevaudan and he at her; neither spoke. Finally he turned back to the road, and the landcruiser gathered speed.

THE BATTLETRUCK
0830 HOURS

Jarrett climbed the ladder to the machine gun nest atop the battletruck.

The wind blew her hair back. She spat out into the slipstream; a glob of red blew back down the road. The inside of her mouth was raw, bloody, from where she'd constantly chewed at it.

Ahead of the truck, a vanguard of pursuit 'cruisers led the way; behind was a phalanx of small and medium 'cruisers moving at speed. Each one loaded to capacity with men and women from GenRen – Genetic Renewal division. Jarrett's old division. The elite. The ones who went into the harshest, most dangerous conditions, the cleansers of the Wasteland, trained to show no mercy or pity in order to do what had to be done.

She looked up the road again and smiled; here, with these people, it felt as if she'd come home.

Life was simple again: complete the mission. Do or die. End the rebellion. And kill Helen Damnation, if possible, with her own bare hands.

PART TWO
SEEK AND DESTROY

1.

Flaps climbed onto the flat concrete roof, sprinting to the lookout post in the corner. "What we got?"

"There!" Sud bounced up and down. A skinny little Pakistani boy, he was the youngest there – thirteen, he claimed, but Flaps didn't believe it. "See?"

"Pack it in," Beak cuffed him round the ear. She was in her twenties: short blonde hair, a long square-chinned face, a broken nose. She passed Flaps her binoculars and pointed. "There."

FB-11 was an old tile factory standing by a torn chicken-wire fence, beside a river flowing between thirty-foot sandstone banks. From the roof, there was a panoramic view of the Wastelands: the ruined towns, the scorch-marks and craters where the bombs had fallen, and the Devil's Highway, coming over a hill in the distance and carrying on to carve a high-banked scar across the land.

Flaps looked towards the Highway through the binocs. "'Kin 'ell." She steadied herself. "Get me Osprey on Scramble Two."

Newt held the mic out to her. "Ready to go." He was a skinny kid, older than Sud but about the same size, with crooked teeth and a pair of crude spectacles that made his eyes look massive. Flaps nodded and took the mic from him.

"Crow to Osprey, do you receive?"

The reply was almost instant: Scramble Two was reserved for alerts. "Osprey."

"Reapers," said Flaps. "Coming up the Devil's Highway. Speed they're going, I'd guess they're fast pursuit 'cruisers."

"Stand by."

A new voice, a woman's. "This is Osprey Actual."

Alannah. "Go ahead," said Flaps. Fucking great. Alannah was always weird with Flaps. Course, Flaps knew why: she'd seen how Alannah looked at Danny when she thought no-one else saw. There'd nearly been something between them, before Danny'd got with her. Fuck knew why, Alannah could've been his nan, and she'd looked like a rat that'd drowned two weeks ago back then. But you never knew what folk would jump for. Didn't matter anyway – Danny was hers – but there was more important shit to sort.

"How many?" said Alannah.

"A *lot*," she said. "But looks like mostly small and medium 'cruisers – fast pursuit types, like I said."

"Can you get a closer look?" said Alannah. "See what we're dealing with?"

"On it," she said.

"Do *not* engage. Observe and report only for now."

The 'cruisers were coming over the hill, no end to them in sight. "Wilco, Osprey."

Flaps tossed the mic aside. When she turned, she saw a line of figures standing on the roof. For a moment she thought they were some of the field-base personnel, but then she saw their faces. Telo and Lelly, both shot to pieces in a ruined house in Northern Moor – and Heath, Frill, Tobe, Steen... she knew them all, they were all dead. Only she remained of Scary Mary

Tolland's crew. Then they were gone; Flaps blinked, and ran for the skylight.

ASHWOOD FORT
0920 HOURS

The landcruiser barrelled up the hill towards the gates; Helen saw the guns on the battlements twitch towards them, then away. They were expected; already the main gates were opening.

Gevaudan drove up through Ashwood village – stone cottages and a street full of long-empty shops, now populated by rebel fighters and their families. A scattering of new dwellings built from felled trees or mortared rubble filled the gap between the village and the square turret of St Martin de Porres' Church halfway up the hill. A reek of sewage; the river was foul where it flowed through here.

Behind the church was the second wall; its gate, too, swung open. Beyond that was the Fort itself: a former mill, converted into offices before the War, then left, like the village, standing empty till the rebels had come to claim it. A low shelter built from planks and sandbags girdled it, with wooden sawhorses wreathed in barbed wire to plug the gap. They were pulled away as the landcruiser approached.

Gevaudan climbed out, ran round to help Helen as she stepped down, still clutching the blanket around her. "I'm fine," she snapped, wincing as she stood. Her feet were bare and the grass was brittle and sharp.

A group of people came out through the main door as they approached; in the lead, Darrow and Wakefield. All of them seemed to be talking at once; Helen could only make out a blur of sound.

"Quiet!" She held up a hand. "First things first. Get me some dry clothes. I'm not walking around like this. And that includes boots." She looked at Gevaudan. "You got my gun?"

He patted his waistband. "Quite safe."

"Good." Darrow opened his mouth to speak. "Come on, let's get inside." She strode past them; the others followed.

"I want all non-essential personnel cleared out of the village, and off the upper slopes too," she said. "They need to be out of the firing line if the Reapers break through. Move them into the Fort for now – or evacuate them if you can."

"Evacuate where?" said Darrow.

"How the hell should I know?" said Helen. "This is exactly what I warned you about."

"Crazy ginger!" Wakefield ran up, holding a coverall, a pair of boots and chest and loin bindings.

"Thanks." Helen turned sideways into a small office, jerked a thumb at the two people in it. "Out."

They took one look at her, then at Gevaudan, Darrow and Wakefield, and left without another word. Helen dropped the clothes on the desk, she flung off the blanket and had to suppress a smile, despite everything, as she reached for the coverall, to see Gevaudan look away.

"Wheel out any long-range weapons we've got – see if there's any space on the outer walls for them. The more of a pasting we can give them before they get in close, the better. I want lookouts posted on the Fort roof and church tower. Also –" she grabbed the first of the bindings and wrapped it around herself as she talked "– any bottles or containers we can spare, get them filled with stream water. If we get penned up in here, we'll need it."

COMMANDER'S OFFICE
THE TOWER
0930 HOURS

Winterborn stroked the music box, turning it this way and then that on its desk to see the light gleam off the silver. He toyed with the lid, lifted it and let it drop, then lifted it again. Felt the tension of the mechanism; lift it a little higher and the music would start to play. A faint smile touched his lips, then faded; he let the lid fall back. He didn't need that now.

He pushed the music box away from him, stood. The window: he went there, looked out across the city to the sunlit hills beyond. Enough navel-gazing; enough of the past. This was the world. This was his domain.

The wild unruly world. Smoke curled up from fires and hovels. The shantytown by the Irk was a black stain among the ruins. Far below, they snapped and fought and struggled to live – lives without worth or meaning, any one of them interchangeable with a hundred others. No great loss if any of them ended. Their only value was as mortar and brick with which to build a new world.

Order. Beautiful order. He would still the chaos, make it calm. Stable. Safe.

He smiled. Safe for him. Nothing would endanger him; he would never again be threatened with harm. One day. It would come; all he did, every choice, every move, was to that end. He'd make it happen.

At his sides, his fingers moved; when he realised they were still gently stroking, as though the music box was still there, he clenched them into fists.

INTELLIGENCE CENTRE, ASHWOOD FORT
0932 HOURS

Helen strode in through the door. "Alannah?"

"Helen." The other woman watched her, frowning. "You okay? You don't look –"

"I'll cope," she said. "You got any of those pills?"

"What pills?"

"You know the ones. Keep you going."

"I don't know if that's a good idea."

Helen held out a hand; Alannah shook a couple into her palm. She knocked them back and swallowed them dry. "Ugh," she said. "Okay. What have we got?"

"Reapers."

"We knew *that*."

"A lot of them," said Alannah. "It's an attack in force. Several battalions, by the look."

"Heading this way?"

"Up the Devil's Highway," said Alannah. "Kind of hard to be sure at this stage, but the Reapers wouldn't commit a force that size without knowing exactly where they were aiming." She picked up the mic. "Rook One, do you receive?"

THE DEVIL'S HIGHWAY
0938 HOURS

"Yo," said Flaps. Beside her, Newt wriggled out of the straps holding the radio set to his back, huffing for breath, face sweaty and red.

"You have Osprey Actual, and Phoenix," Alannah's voice said. "What are we looking at so far?"

"At least two battalions' strength, maybe more. And it's the real deal this time."

"What do you mean?" said Helen.

"They're not sending us admin types," said Flaps. "Seeing a lot of white shoulder-flashes out there. Looks like they're GenRen. Nearly the whole fucking lot – might be a few CorSec in there too."

"Okay," said Helen. "Any heavy weapons? Cannon, ballista, catapults?"

Flaps peered over the embankment, where the landcruisers shot past, plumes of dust swirling up in their wake. The rest of her team were lined up along it, doing the same. Sud, as usual, was sticking his head up too far; Beak grabbed him and pulled him back. "Keep your fucking head down."

Flaps coughed as the dust caught the back of her throat; her eyes watered. "Nowt like that," she said at last. "All small and medium 'cruisers. 'Cept one."

"Which one?"

"'Bout the size of a heavy 'cruiser, but the trailer's smaller. Just some sort of cabin on the back, with a gun-nest on top."

"And a plough on the front," said Alannah. "Right?"

"Right. What is it?"

"A battletruck," said Helen. "I didn't think they had any of those left. They're mobile command centres. That's where whoever's in charge will be."

"Want us to get it?"

"No," said Alannah. "They're built to handle most things short of artillery. Speaking of which, what kind of weapons are we looking at?"

"All I'm seeing is rifles and SMGs. Heaviest gear there're .50 cals. Hang on!"

"What?" said Helen.

"Giz them fucking binocs," Flaps muttered to Newt, and squinnied through them, fumbling for the mic. "Okay – got summat else. Not guns, but – I dunno who they are, some sort of special ops mob."

Intelligence Centre, ashwood fort
0940 hours

"Say again?" said Helen. Her stomach tightened again. She was wrong. It couldn't be that. It would be something else.

"Weird-looking fuckers. Just sat in the back of some of the cruisers. Don't even move. They've got suits on – dunno what kind though. Kind of grey colour. Helmets, too, but – shit, that's fucking weird. No breathing gear. Nowt like that."

"Helmets?" said Helen.

"Yeah, metal helmets. Faces look weird and all. All grey."

Helen looked up at Alannah; the other woman stared back at her. "Catchmen," Helen said.

"What?"

"How –" Her voice felt strangled; she swallowed and tried again. "How many?" she said.

"Er…" A moment's pause. "Yeah, think that was the lot of them?"

"Flaps?" she had to keep her voice level. "How many?"

"I make it about two hundred," Flaps said. "Give or take. So, what do you want us to do?"

"Do?" Helen heard Alannah whisper. "There's nothing to do. We're dead."

2.

Helen gripped the edge of Alannah's desk. There were times she didn't want to be right, and this was one. The past was here, the past was back, the past was about to replay. The Jennywrens would reap without pity, every man, woman and child. The Refuge, all over again.

"Phoenix? Osprey?" said Flaps' voice. "Do you receive? Repeat, what are your orders? We could hit 'em from here. Thin 'em down before they reach you."

Alannah touched her arm. "Helen?"

Helen blinked, straightened up. "Negative. Repeat, negative, do not engage. You won't stand a chance."

"But they're coming straight for you," Flaps said.

"I know that." Helen took deep breaths, and some of her panic ebbed away. The Reapers weren't here, yet; Ashwood hadn't fallen, yet. There was still time to prepare; defences, weapons, tactics. Old patterns could be broken; they weren't doomed to repetition without end. If she didn't believe that, or at least hope it, why bother to fight at all?

So she wouldn't panic. She'd look for the first move she could make, then the next. Like when she'd fled the Catchman through the woods at Hawksmoor – focus on making it to the next tree, and then the next.

"All right, Rook One," she said. "Keep a count and await further orders."

"Roger that."

Helen breathed out, looked up at Alannah. "The War Room," she said, and strode to the door.

THE DEVIL'S HIGHWAY
0945 HOURS

"Sud, Beak, Newt," said Flaps, "Stay up here. Keep counting and keep 'em up to date at the Fort."

"Gotcha," nodded Beak.

Sud grinned. "Ace!"

"Shut up and keep your head down."

Newt just looked pale and scared; poor little twat just wanted to be anywhere else. Bit like a lad Flaps'd known in Darrow's old crew – Nadgers, that's what he'd been called. Dead now.

"You'll be all right," Flaps told him. "Right. Rest of you, with me."

Danny ran with her towards the landcruisers. "What's going on?"

"Waiting for the support columns," she said. "They're our job. Dunno 'bout yours."

From the road, Danny heard the Reaper landcruisers sweep past, seemingly without end.

The battletruck's front cabin was roomy. Up ahead of Kellett were two large, well-upholstered seats for the driver and co-driver. A short aisle led from them to the rear of the cabin; there were two more seats on either side of that, into one of which Kellett was wedged.

His only company was the drivers; he wouldn't have much to say to the likes of them at the best of times, and even if he had he wasn't about to distract the people responsible for keeping this hurtling behemoth on the road. The highway unspooled ahead, the high embankments sliding endlessly past; it was almost hypnotic, but he wasn't fooled. A moment's inattention and the battletruck could flip.

Kellett gripped the arms of his seat. He did not enjoy powerlessness; hated his fate to be in another's hands in this way. His brilliance didn't matter; an idiot's error could snuff it out.

"Doctor." Jarrett entered at the rear of the cabin and brushed past him to the drivers' seats, leaning between them. "Increase our speed."

"What?" Kellett shut his mouth and flinched back as Jarrett glared at him. Careful, he reminded himself; she may be a stepping stone to bigger and brighter things, she may not have half your brains, but she's dangerous nonetheless.

The driver glanced back at Jarrett. "With respect, ma'am..."

"I believe I gave you an order, Sergeant."

"Yes, ma'am."

The battletruck's engines rumbled louder. Jarrett stopped, passing Kellett. "Nervous, Doctor?"

He licked his lips. He could hardly lie to her – she could see his fear – but he wouldn't admit it.

"You think I'm obsessive," she said. "Willing to sacrifice us all in pursuit of my goals. Yes?"

Again, he didn't answer.

Jarrett sighed and crouched beside his seat, bringing her face close to his, almost as if to kiss. Her breath was hot, and faintly sour. "It's an entirely practical consideration, Doctor," she said. "Every minute it takes us to reach Ashwood gives Helen another minute to prepare for our arrival. Every minute she has to prepare improves the odds in her favour, and that can't be allowed."

Jarrett breathed out, straightened; she slumped into a chair on the opposite side of the aisle, staring out through the windscreen. "It's taken me a great deal of effort to get this opportunity," she said at last. "I'm not about to squander it." She rose, peered between the driver and co-driver at the speedometer. "Good," she said. "Maintain."

Kellett swallowed hard, and closed his eyes.

*

In the shadow of an embankment by the Devil's Highway, the Walker made its quiet, steady way; with its long trailing robe, it seemed to glide over the uneven ground.

The robe's hem was ragged, snagging as it did on the brambles that infested the ground by the embankment, swarming through the grass and bracken like so many spiny snakes. But it was never fouled for long; slow the Walker's passing may have been, but it was also inexorable, and the garment was pulled after it.

And then the Walker stumbled. It swayed, arms spreading out for balance, then looked down. It crouched, pulled back the brambles with its hands; if the thorns hurt it, it gave no sign.

Beneath the shroud of thorns, half-buried in the accumulated earth, were bricks and spars of plastic, splintered gems of glass. It ran its fingers over them, then turned to look across the nearby ground.

Patterns revealed themselves to the Walker. That was often the way. There were regular outlines beneath the undergrowth, invisible until you looked and realised they were there. The square outlines of what had been houses, the long open space of a street to separate the rows. A town had been here once; smashed flat in the War's blast and grown over.

Interesting…

And irrelevant.

The Walker let the brambles fall back into place, stood. It listened; there were engines, far off but growing closer. It turned and clambered up the embankment, hunching low at the top to peer over without being seen.

It watched the landcruisers come; the small, fast outriders, the roaring, lumbering beast of the battletruck, and then the host of others that followed. It looked along the line of them, all down the Devil's Highway, and saw no end to their numbers.

The Walker nodded to itself, and climbed back down.

And then it walked on.

THE WAR ROOM
0948 HOURS

"Speed," said Helen.

"I already gave you some."

"No." But she could feel the pills kicking in; there was a sudden fierce energy in her, to move and talk and act and do. Anger, too; she'd have to watch that. "I mean for Jarrett. Her first priority's going to be to get here. And fast, so we don't have time to evacuate or prepare." She stared down at the map. "That means the Devil's Highways. Only way to move fast overland. Remind me – how many do we have out here?"

"Three," Alannah said. "The biggest is where Flaps is based. It's wider than the others – 'cruisers can go two, maybe three abreast."

"Which means they can move faster, in a block. So that'll be the main route."

"The other two are still usable, though. It's the support columns we've got to worry about."

"That and holding here."

"No evacuation?"

"Where would we go, Alannah?"

Alannah let out a long breath. It sounded close to a sob.

141

"Get hold of Nestor," Helen said. "Tell him to clear anyone he can out of sick bay. See if he can move some patients up on the roof if things get crowded. And round up some extra bodies to help him out. He's going to be busy."

"Right."

"We also need to to divide up the field personnel. Some to the Highways, pull the rest back here."

"What about Danny?"

Alannah's eyes were wide. Helen smiled. "We'll pull his unit back," she said.

"Thank you."

Helen shrugged. "I need someone I can trust here." She took a deep breath. "Okay. Put me through to Flaps."

THE DEVIL'S HIGHWAY
0950 HOURS

"Flaps!" shouted Newt. "Phoenix, for you."

"Right." Flaps rubbed her hands dry on her trousers, took the mic. "Yo, Phoenix."

"Okay, Rook One. Here are your orders."

Flaps licked her lips.

"We've two more Devil's Highways in the area. Yours will probably be the main one, but the others need watching too. Assign field commanders to cover them, but you're in overall charge."

"Copy."

"They're travelling light, to get here fast and cut us off. Heavy 'cruisers are too slow for that, but they'll need them for their heavy weapons."

"Right," said Flaps.

"So there'll be support columns," said Helen. "Artillery, reinforcements, ammo, provisions. *They're* your job. Whatever comes down that road, you hold the line."

"Will you pull your sodding head in, Sud?" she heard Beak say; the boy was watching the main column's dwindling dust.

"Copy," Flaps peered up the road. "You got a lot coming your way, though. You gonna be able to hold 'em off?"

"We'll bloody have to," said Helen. "Start gathering your troops. Any units in Zones One through Six need pulling back to the Fort – oh, and is Danny still with you?"

Flaps glanced down the slope at him. "Yeah."

"Him and his unit too."

"Right." Fucking Alannah.

"Deploy the rest as you see fit," said Helen. "That's all."

*

Danny watched Flaps scramble down the slope to him. "What we doing?"

"*I'm* sorting out twatting the fucking Reapers when they come up the road," she told him.

"What about me?"

"You're fucking off back to the Fort. Mummy wants her little soldier."

"Fuck's that supposed to mean?"

"Work it out yourself. Now go on, fuck off. Got work to do."

She turned on her heel and stalked back up the embankment. Fucking hell. Danny slung the Lanchester over his back. "Right," he yelled. "Move out, you lot. Back to the Fort."

He looked back once as they drove away, but she still had her back to him.

THE WAR ROOM, ASHWOOD FORT
0952 HOURS

Helen handed back the mic. "Right. That's done."

"Sit down before you fall down," said Alannah, pulling back a chair. "You've had a rough day."

Helen flapped a hand, pacing. Her heart thumped; the pills. "It's barely bloody started."

"Ladies." Gevaudan swept in.

"All freshened up, I see," said Alannah. "Do you ever wear anything *but* black?"

"I wear what suits my mood."

"You *always* wear black."

"When I'm in the mood for a Hawaiian shirt, I'll let you know."

"Can we focus here?" said Helen.

"I'm focused." Alannah pulled up her own chair. "What do you want to know?"

"The Catchmen," said Helen. "What are they, exactly?"

Alannah relayed what she'd found. "They're related to the Styr from Hobsdyke, but they're actually harder to kill."

"We noticed," said Gevaudan.

"The helmets they wear have spikes on the inside at selected locations – where they go in, the spikes destroy the parts of the brain related to cognitive functions, so only the animal part's left."

"Surely that would defeat the object?" said Gevaudan. "Tindalos was designed to activate latent abilities in the brain. Why then destroy them?"

Alannah shook her head. "From what we can make out, the Night Wolves' substance is activated by some sort of neural stimulus, but it permeates the entire body. The helmet only kills the higher brain functions, at the exact moment the changes kick in – those, and the parts of the brain enabling the Styr to reach out and telepathically influence others. You're left with a beast, and a crude mechanical brain – very crude, very basic, not much more than a guidance system – to control it. Physically, the creature is similar to the Styr – incredibly strong, very hard to kill – but as you can see, there are major differences, too. It still possesses psi abilities, but they're focused on controlling its own physiology. No matter how much damage you do, it keeps pulling itself back together. It can even survive damage that would kill a Styr."

"I know," said Helen. "I shot its eyes out and it kept coming. And it could still see."

"The only thing that can kill it is the same thing that would kill a fully-formed Night Wolf," said Alannah. "An iron or steel weapon, engraved with a Hobsdyke Cross. That's it. Nothing else."

"I'd be interested to learn how they did it," said Gevaudan. "I didn't think they had anyone left to carry on that kind of work."

"None of the original Tindalos personnel survived," said Alannah, "but they had some notes."

"Even so. There are refinements here that Mordake never got close to."

Alannah shrugged. "They gave the notes to another scientist, and told him to develop them. A Dr Kellett."

"Kellett?" said Gevaudan.

Helen looked at him. "You okay?" The Grendelwolf had gone still.

"It doesn't matter," he said. "So, as well as the Jennywrens, the Catchman are coming. We'll need weapons. Iron or steel. Knives, arrowheads, bullets. How long do we have?"

"An hour," said Alannah. "Maybe two."

"Zaq always keeps her furnace lit," said Gevaudan. "It's just how quickly she can work."

"Whatever you both need." Helen grabbed a notepad from Alannah's desk, quickly sketching the Hobsdyke Cross. "Don't forget this."

"I won't." Gevaudan slipped the sketch into his pocket. "It'll need carving on each bullet."

"Leave that with you?"

"Of course."

Helen frowned; something wasn't quite right. "You sure you're okay?"

"I'm fine." Gevaudan swept out.

"Somehow," Helen said, "I doubt that. Did you get hold of Nestor?"

"He was a bit preoccupied. One of Danny's squad – Stock? The Catchman damn near disembowelled her. He's been working flat out to keep her alive."

"Did he manage?"

"He thinks so. Bit of luck, she'll pull through."

"Good. Let's hope he keeps that up."

"Helen?"

"Yeah?"

"Something there hit a nerve," Alannah said. "With Gevaudan, I mean. Soon as he heard the name Kellett. Want me to check up on that?"

"What for?"

Alannah shrugged. "We want to be sure we can rely on him."

"If he hasn't convinced you by now," said Helen, "he never will."

THE FLATS
0955 HOURS

Cov tapped Mackie on the shoulder. "Off we go."

Mackie grinned slackly and hopped out of the 'cruiser after Cov.

The flat grey mud was almost smooth, except for what lay up ahead. From the plain of dull silt, dotted with nubs of brick or concrete and scrubs of grass, jutted a row of slate-roofed brick houses with cobbled ginnels between them.

Cov ran down one of these, stopping at a wooden back gate. "Three, four... here." He kicked the gate of one house; his foot went straight through the soft, rotten wood.

"Fuck!" He flailed, nearly fell. Mackie grabbed him under the arms. "Cheers mate," Cov muttered, pulling his leg free.

Mackie grabbed the top of the door and pulled down; the hinges tore out of the crumbling wood and he tossed the door aside.

Across a plain concrete back yard was the house's back wall; up against this was a small brick outhouse with a sloped roof, wooden door, and the flaky remains of a coat of white paint. Two men could have fitted inside, pressed face to face.

A rusted padlock held the door shut. Cov gave it an experimental kick, but it was less rotten than the gate and held firm.

"Wanna do the honours?" he said.

Mackie grinned. "No probs. Like helping out."

"I know, mate."

Mackie pulled a hatchet from his belt and smashed through the lock's hasp. The door and jamb had warped solid; Mackie drove the hatchet blade between them and forced the door wide. "There you go."

In the outhouse were long thick bundles, wrapped in tarp and fastened with old rope, and a stack of ammo crates. Cov laid a bundle on the concrete, cut the rope and unwrapped it.

"Fucking beauty," he said. Eight automatic rifles, two dozen magazines.

They carried the cache's contents back to the landcruiser. As they loaded the last of them aboard, the radio crackled. "General Alert." Cov knew the voice: Flaps. "Repeat, all units: General Alert."

"What?" said Mackie.

"Shurrup," said Cov.

"All units report as follows. Zones One through Six – rendezvous points for return to Fort. Ten through Fifteen Field-Base Three. Sixteen through Twenty-One – Field-Base Twenty. All other units – Field-Base Eleven, *fucking now*." There was a pause. "The Reapers are coming."

3.

THE BATTLETRUCK
20TH MARCH, ATTACK PLUS TWENTY-ONE YEARS
1000 HOURS
T MINUS 90

When they got to where they were going, the battletruck's armoured pod would be a combined war room and comms centre. Until then, the map table, along with all but two of the radio sets and a bunch of monitors and other equipment serving fuck alone knew what purpose, were stacked against one wall and the pod filled with nearly a hundred Reapers, who sat jammed in rows with a narrow gap between them to permit movement.

Patel was at the very back, squashed into a corner where the space bottlenecked. In the narrow nook at the back were two radio sets with their operators; opposite him were the five snipers.

The pod reeked of sweat, flatulence, and cigarettes smoked down to the nub. Patel had already smoked so many of them the inside of his mouth felt raw, but he tugged the pack of Monarchs from his pocket anyway. Six left. He pulled one out, lit up and leant back, sucking the smoke in deep. He blew it out and opened his eyes, and found himself looking right at the snipers.

Fuck. They stared back at him, stony-faced. Three men, two women, their scoped bolt-action rifles propped beside them. In the middle was a stocky, fortyish man with a hard leathery face and black hair greying at the temples. He had a sergeant's stripes and hard grey eyes that didn't blink. The name-tag on his uniform read HARPER.

The sandy-haired lad next to him, youngest of the group, half-smiled back at Patel; he couldn't have been more than sixteen, with bulbous blue eyes. Scrawny, too; Patel'd seen more meat on a rabbit's foreleg. But the boy must have had something, else he wouldn't be a sniper. GREENE, according to his uniform. Greene by name and green by –

Patel realised Harper was still looking at him – well, not *at*. More like *through*. The sergeant had other things on his mind. Thousand yard stare; Patel might as well not have existed. And that was fine by him; he'd heard of this one. Word was he'd served with Jarrett herself, one of her right-hand men. Patel didn't want to be on the radar of anyone like that.

The lance-corporal on the other side of Harper, though – she *was* staring at Patel, and it didn't look too friendly. Her name was White, which was funny, since she was black – Patel stopped himself from smiling just in time. Last thing you wanted to do was let this lot think you were taking the piss. Weird lot, snipers, at the best of times.

The last two weren't any more appealing. The woman on the end was early twenties, with short-cropped hair the colour of muddy water and a round pale freckly face. She looked sullen and hard, arms folded. Her eyes stood out; they were blue-green. Patel hadn't seen that shade before. She saw him looking at her and he glanced down.

The fifth sniper sniggered. First time Patel had heard one of the weird fuckers make a sound. "Think you've got an admirer, Juliet."

The woman didn't answer.

Patel peered out from under his lowered brows at the fifth one, who was slim and milk-pale with crow-black hair and bright blue eyes. Pretty boy, but Patel doubted anyone ever took the piss; there was a cruel hook to Pretty Boy's smile, a needling tone in his voice. The woman hadn't moved, but he could almost see the air around her darken.

"Oh, go on, Jules," Pretty Boy said. "Live a little, eh?"

The woman's jaw clenched; Patel saw a muscle jump in her cheek.

"What's up with you?" said Pretty Boy. "You getting scared? Or excited? Bet you've got wet knickers either way." He sniggered. The woman's hands clenched and unclenched. Pretty Boy reached out, trickled a finger down her arm. "How's about I take your mind off th—"

The woman snapped at last, pulling away from him, raising a fist. "Fuck *off*."

"Carson," said Harper, not looking at her.

Carson subsided, turning away from Pretty Boy, who laughed.

"And you, Fox," said Harper.

Pretty Boy — Fox — scowled.

Carson's face was red; her eyes darted right and caught Patel's. "The fuck are you looking at?"

Patel looked down at the floor.

A trooper pushed his way down the middle of the pod to the radio sets at the end. "Signal for Central Command," he said, handing a sheet of paper to one of the sparks. "Personal attention of Commander Winterborn."

Patel remembered the hut at Hobsdyke as the Sparks started sending; the fire and the wind and snow outside, the box and the letter on top. He hugged himself; he felt cold.

LISTENING POST 2
1003 HOURS
T MINUS 87

Colby stood beneath the rusted pylon, breathing clean air.

She did it whenever she could, even though she was meant to stay undercover. The pylon stood beside the Devil's Highway, right enough, but the low, flat moors spread out for miles in any direction; she'd see any Reapers long before they got here. That, or hear them.

Besides, she'd spent her years in the city, in shit and filth, ruins and death, and she knew she hadn't many more to go. She limped in both legs now, coughed her guts up most mornings and the yellow cast her skin had gained meant nothing good. No, not long, and until the end she'd do her job and fight – but in the meantime, while there was air like this to breathe and such sights to see, she'd take some joy in them. Might have more years left in her if she'd lived here since the War.

The pylon creaked above; a crow cawed and settled in the nest it had built. You couldn't see the aerial; they'd done a good job hiding it.

"Colby!" The voice barked out of the ground. "We got something!"

She sighed and limped back under the pylon; there was a crack in the ground where a section of turf had lifted up on the trapdoor underneath. Colby pushed it wide, waved Swan back and climbed down into the dug-out. "What we got, then?

He handed her the slip of paper he'd scribbled on. Colby pursed her lips. "Keep listening," she said, and moved to the other radio set.

COMMANDER'S OFFICE, THE TOWER
1004 HOURS
T MINUS 86

The buzz of the intercom snapped Winterborn out of his reverie. He turned from the window and the view of the distant hills, strode to his desk. "Winterborn."

"Ops Room, Commander."

"Yes, Thorpe?"

"Message from Colonel Jarrett. ETA at rebel HQ, Ashwood, approximately eighty-five minutes."

"Very good, Colonel. Keep me informed."

Winterborn flicked the intercom off, sat behind his desk and waited.

THE WAR ROOM, ASHWOOD FORT
T MINUS 85

"Alannah?" Hei ran in, a flimsy in one hand. "Listening Post 2. Intercepted a transmission to the Tower."

Alannah unfolded it and read:

For the Personal Attention of Commander Tereus Winterborn
ETA at rebel HQ, Ashwood, approximately eighty-five minutes.
Col. N Jarrett.

Jarrett.

The room spun; the floor softened underfoot, threatened to swallow her. Her legs weren't working. Helen caught her. "Easy," she said. "Alannah?"

She tried to speak, couldn't. The Intelligence Centre was barely even there; it was a shadow or a ghost. Instead she was in a dark, cold room with damp concrete walls and floor stained brown with blood. It stank of vomit and shit and stale piss, and the acrid odour of fear. She was naked in it, and pain covered her – from blows, burns, electrodes. And through it all, that same cold nasal voice with its estuarine accent:

I don't have the power in this room, Alannah. You do. I do this because I don't have any choice. I do what I've got to. All of us in here do. We're just parts in a machine. But you're what drives it. You're the one with the choice. Do you know how much power you have, Alannah? You have so much power you can stop all this with a word. All you have to say is yes. That you'll talk. And then this stops. The whole machine shuts down. You see, Alannah? The only one making you suffer is you.

"Jarrett," said Helen. "Right?" She took the flimsy from her, looked at it. "Right," she said, then looked up at Hei. "That's all," she said. "Return to your post." She steered Alannah to a chair, helped her sit, filled a cup of water from a jug. "Here. Drink."

"Jarrett," said Alannah. "She's coming. *Here.*"

"Yes. That's right." Helen gripped the arms of Alannah's chair, brought her face close in. "So what are you going to do about it?"

"What the fuck do you *want* me to do about it?" Alannah tried to break away, but Helen's grip tightened, her arms the bars of a cage. Alannah felt her arms quiver slightly, in the grip of the speed.

"Your job," she said. "I need you if we want to win."

"We can't," said Alannah. "We can't win. This is *Jarrett.*"

"And she's lost before. She'd be dead, if I'd been a better shot, or finished the bastard job. She'll win if we let her win. Not otherwise." Helen took Alannah's face in her hands. "I need you for this." She grinned. "Look at it this way – if we can win, Winterborn'll kill the bitch even if we don't."

Alannah smiled back. "Okay," she said.

"Yeah?"

"Yeah."

"Right, then." Helen stepped back. "You're in charge of intelligence and communications. Gather intelligence, and maintain communications. I want any and all Reaper chatter, especially updates on Jarrett's ETA. I want to know if we've more time than we thought, or less. And get in contact with the Wasteland forces. We've got to be on top of this."

Alannah stood up. "You always were good at this." Helen's smile faded a bit at that, the echo of reproach: *you use others, get them to die for you.* "It'll get done," said Alannah.

Helen followed her back across the corridor to the Intelligence Centre. "You got some personal communicators I can use?"

"What for? We need you here."

"Have you got one?"

Alannah sighed and took a small handset from a drawer. "Only short-range."

"I'm not going far."

"The War Room is –"

"The fight'll be here," said Helen. "At Ashwood. We'll stand or fall by our defences. So I'll check them myself." That and she wouldn't be underground, with the hill pressing in on her, ready to fall in. The Fort felt enough like a death-trap as it was. "Got any more of these?"

"How many ears do you have?"

"I'm going to need to hand a couple out."

Alannah sighed and handed over three more. "Careful with them, for Christ's sake. Rarer than hen's teeth these days."

"You know you can rely on me."

"Yes," said Alannah. "I do, which is why I'm worried."

"Thanks for the vote of confidence," Helen said. "You need me –" she held up the communicator "– I'll be right here. Good luck."

THE ARMOURY, ASHWOOD FORT
1010 HOURS
T MINUS 80

"Zaq?"

"Whatever it is, the answer's no." Zaq glared up at Gevaudan, hands on hips, as he descended the stairs. "What the hell's this?"

"Scrap iron," Gevaudan said, and set the wooden barrel down.

"And what am I supposed to do with it?"

"I can think of a few suggestions, but the correct answer is 'make bullets'."

"Bullets?" Zaq picked a long, slightly rusted nail out of the barrel. "This is *iron*." She dropped it back in. "You make bullets from lead."

"Not this time," said Gevaudan. "And we need them within the hour."

"An *hour*? Are you fucking mad?"

"You have to find a way."

"It needs melting down, casting into bullets, then fitting into cases." Zaq waggled her leather-gloved fingers. "How many pairs of hands do you see?"

"You'll get whatever help you need," said Gevaudan. "It's a priority. One more thing." He unfolded the sketch. "This has to be carved on each and every one."

"Are you taking the —"

"I'm not," he assured her.

"The Reapers are gonna be here in an hour. *Last* thing you need is anything fancy."

"It's not just the Reapers," said Gevaudan. "There's something worse than them. It might even be worse than me."

Not many people could lock stares with him for long, though Zaq did better than most. "Do I need to stick a broom up my arse and sweep the floor as I go?"

"Only if that gives you some sort of pleasure."

Zaq glared. "Rifle or pistol rounds?"

"Rifle as a priority," said Gevaudan. "Second priority, pistol rounds for submachine guns, and arrowheads."

"What are they for?" Zaq asked.

"To stop what's coming," he told her. "Nothing else will."

"Right," she said. "You'll have what you need. Now if there's nothing else, bugger off and let me do my job."

"Your wish is my command." Gevaudan gave a mock bow and courtly wave, then turned away before she saw him smile.

VILLAGE SQUARE, ASHWOOD
1020 HOURS
T MINUS 70

"Wakefield!"

"Hoy, crazy ginger!"

Helen had to smile; she caught the little Fox warrior's upraised hand, then pointed towards the outer wall. "With me. Walk."

"What?" Wakefield frowned, striding along with her.

"The Reapers are going to be here soon." Wakefield's sharp, avian face was pinched in a frown. Helen knew the word to say, and said it. "Jennywrens."

"Jennywrens!" Wakefield spat on the ground; there was no name more hated by the Wasteland tribes.

"Right," said Helen. She spat too: blood on the ground. She'd chewed the inside of her mouth bloody. "When they get here, they're going to want us all dead."

"Course," snorted Wakefield. "Jennywrens. They only ever kill. Do we run?"

Helen shook her head. "We fight."

"Good. Run from them enough."

"To kill us," said Helen, "they've got to get through that." She pointed at the wall, steered Wakefield to the steps leading to the battlements.

"The longer the wall holds," she said, "the more they're going to need the support columns they're sending from Manchester. We've got people in the Wastelands who'll do anything they can to stop that help getting through. Without that help, we can beat them. So every minute you keep them out is another chance for us. Understand?"

Wakefield shrugged. "You want me to hold the wall."

Helen had to smile. "Yeah."

Wakefield grinned back at her. "Always good, killing Jennywrens."

Helen wasn't going to argue the point. "Here," she said, handing over the communicator. "You need help, push that button when you want to speak. Let go of it to listen. You can contact Alannah with that directly – she'll get you whatever you need. Can you do that?"

Wakefield grinned wider. "Oh yes, crazy ginger."

She skipped the rest of the way up the steps. Helen shook her head; Wakefield's sheer speed and energy left her feeling old half the time.

Behind her, laughter: she turned and saw Frank standing a few steps down, Belinda in his arms. "Not long now," he said. "You know this place can't hold. It'll fall, and then…"

Belinda giggled.

"You'll never get Winterborn," said Helen. "If I don't kill him, you'll never have him too."

"We don't care," said Frank. "You don't get it, do you, Helen? We're just bloody hungry. And we've waited too long."

"Landcruisers!" a voice shouted from above. Helen turned, ran towards the battlements. She didn't look back.

A lookout pointed at the road. Helen grabbed a pair of binocs, sighted through them. In the lead vehicle's passenger seat she saw a pale face topped with spiky black hair, the leather collar of a belstaff jacket tight around its throat. Danny.

Good news for Alannah, at least. Though if the Fort fell, his chances might have been better in the Wastelands.

Helen turned and ran for the steps.

He saw her running in as his 'cruiser pulled rolled through the gate. "Danny." She jumped aboard, pointing up towards the church. "Keep going."

"Well, go on then," he told the driver. Helen hung onto the 'cruiser's side as they went. She was pale, a fever-shine on her eyes.

"Wakefield's got the first wall," she shouted over the wind. "I want you on Wall Two. Everything between the walls is yours."

"Hang on, what?"

"I've ordered the village cleared. Do whatever you have to to stop the Reapers getting as far as the wall. If they Reapers break through the first wall, you turn this into a killing ground."

They pulled in beside the church. Helen jumped down. Danny climbed after. She handed him a communicator. "Use that to keep in touch. Anything you need, ask Alannah."

"That'll be interesting." Danny felt a stab of guilt at the joke, thinking of Flaps.

She swatted him, light, on the shoulder. "Keep your mind on the job," she said, and ran off.

"Fuckin' hell." Danny turned and stared down the slope, then turned to his driver. "You," he said, "find Scopes, get her here, *now*."

She nodded, jumped out, ran. Danny fumbled with the communicator, switched it on, then pressed transmit. "Yo? Alannah? Danny here."

Alannah tried not to smile. "The correct call sign is Osprey Actual, Harrier."

"Whatever. You there?"

"You're talking to me, aren't you?" All she could see was his face, the big dark earnest eyes in the pale skin, the hedgehog brush of spiky hair. For all the fighting he'd done, still so young, so vulnerable to harm. Stephen, but not Stephen; it wasn't just for that. It was him; Danny himself.

I shouldn't have cut off. I should have at least tried. Kissed him. What harm would it would have done? So he's young and I'm not – what does all that matter now? She wanted to hold him close; keep him safe, take comfort from his warmth. Tell him it hadn't been him, but her. But there wasn't the time now. That chance had gone.

If we live, maybe then. That's a reason to win, if you need it.

"Hello?" he said. "You still there?"

"Right here," she said. "What do you need?"

"Explosives," he said. "Owt you've got. And remote detonators." She could hear the grin in his voice. "Send the village fucking skyward if those twats get in."

"Gotcha. Anything else?"

"All for now."

"Be –" *careful*, she'd meant to say, but then the line went dead. Alannah breathed out, scribbled a requisition on a pad. "Runner!"

The group of young fighters sat at a dragged-in table jumped up and moved. One got to her desk first. Alannah gave her the note. "Armoury. Give this to Zaq."

The runner blanched – no-one liked to beard that particular dragon – but she took the note and ran.

"Wakefield for you," called Hei. "Also, we have updates from the Wastelands."

"On my desk," she said. "Put Wakefield through."

"Helen." She turned at the War Room door to see Gevaudan sprinting towards her. "Found all the iron I could. Zaq's at work on the bullets."

"How long before we have any?"

"As fast as she could, she said."

"We need them faster. We need them *now*. Go back there and sit on them. When you've got some, split them between Danny and Wakefield – inner and outer walls."

Gevaudan nodded. "As you wish." For a moment she thought he was going to say something else, but then he was sprinting back down the corridor.

Helen went in through the door. Additional staff were setting up – radio operators, runners – but the War Room's central table was still empty, except for one grey-haired figure, slumped behind a desk.

"Darrow." Helen pulled back a chair and sat beside him. "How you doing?"

He took a deep breath. "Not particularly well."

She didn't speak; what was there to say? There was no pride in being proven right like this. She'd seen her mentor wear many faces, but not this one: broken, beaten. It was like seeing a mountain crack.

"I'm sorry," he said at last. "I thought your judgement was blurred, but it wasn't."

Stop fucking whining, she wanted to say. *We've got a battle to fight. Get to your post or fuck off.* But that was the speed talking; patience was the first casualty of the energy it gave. "It was a tough call," she said. "There *were* risks with what I said. You were right about those."

"But the danger we're in isn't due to those risks. Is it?"

"Roger, we'd still be up shit creek now even if the vote had gone my way yesterday." Helen saw him half-smile, half-wince at the profanity. "You said it yourself, it would have taken time."

"You'd been saying it for months, Helen. I should have listened. My opinion carries weight; if I'd voted with you, others would have followed."

"Oh, get over yourself."

Darrow gave a short laugh. "But it's true. There was someone at that table whose judgement was flawed. Me."

"It's done, Roger. You don't have to –"

"I do. You were right. I was angry with you. All the deaths. The children. I knew them, raised them, and in the end I sacrificed them for you."

Helen looked down.

"You *were* right. I said that, and I meant it. But in a way, that only made it worse."

"I know that," she said. "They're on me. Same as at the Refuge –"

"No." Darrow's voice was sharp; she looked up. His eyes were reddened, but hard and clear. "You cannot blame yourself for that. Tereus Winterborn is responsible for what he did. No-one else."

"But I –"

"No. You cannot, must not, blame yourself for that. Especially not now."

Laughter; Helen saw Frank sitting in a chair across the desk. He clapped, slowly. "Good luck with that," he said.

Just ghostlighting. He wasn't there. Helen turned back to Darrow. "Old friend," she said, "I need someone I can trust."

"But you can't find anyone, so you've come to me?"

"Don't talk bollocks. If I can't trust you, who can I?"

"What do you need?"

"Wakefield's commanding the outer wall defences. Danny's on the inner. If that goes, the last line of defence will be the Fort itself. I need someone to take charge of that."

"Me?"

"No, Roger. I want you to brew the tea."

Darrow laughed. "One lump or two?"

Helen handed him the communicator. "Whatever you need
—"

"Ask Alannah?"

"Yes. Think you can handle that?"

Darrow nodded, stood. "Thank you."

"Thank *you*." Helen stood too, went out fast. Thank God
that was over. Another minute and she'd have snapped at him.
And she needed Darrow whole for this.

St Martin de Porres Church, ashwood
1035 hours
T minus 55

Scopes ran towards Danny, Trex huffing and puffing behind
her.

They were both fast, but her most of all. He'd heard that was
how they warmed up of a morning, running back and forth in
full kit. Didn't surprise Danny. Scopes was a weird one and no
mistake, always had been – stick-thin and near-silent, greasy-
haired and pop-eyed. But she could fucking shoot. So could
Trex, it'd turned out when they'd given the tribesman a rifle.
They made a good team. Danny had no idea if the teamwork
extended to the sleeping sack; some things you were better not
knowing.

They each had a tommy gun, a pistol and a scoped rifle – two
rifles, in Scopes' case. Danny had insisted she carry a scoped
L1A1, reasoning that their best shots should be first in line for
the automatic rifles, but, Scopes had made it clear that she'd had
her Lee-Enfield .303 since she was ten, and anyone who wanted
it could take it off her corpse.

"You rang?" she said.

Danny nodded, jerked a thumb at the church. "The tower.
Reapers get through, I need a good pair of eyes up there."

"And rifles to slow 'em down?" Trex grinned. He had a
young face, despite the grey hair.

Danny nodded. "Go for officers and comms first off. Hang on!" They stopped, turned back. "We got something else."

Danny told them about the Catchmen. "We're knocking up some special ammo to deal with the fuckers – I'm ordering some for youse two. You see them, you drop 'em."

"How will we know them?" asked Scopes.

"You'll know them."

Scopes pondered that for a second, then shrugged; she and Trex ran to the church.

WALL ONE, ASHWOOD FORT
1040 HOURS
T MINUS 50

On the battlements, the tribesfolk knelt in their groups: Crow with Crow, Cat with Cat, Fox with Fox, each murmuring their prayers.

"Fox's Spirit, run with us,"

said Wakefield with the others.

"Make us quick and cunning and brave,
Bring us victory, slay our enemies,
If we die, carry our souls."

At the end, they barked three times. The Crows cawed; the Cats yowled. Then the prayers were done, and they rose.

Wakefield looked over the battlements. Down the hill, engineers hacked the ground with shovels and hoes. Dug a hole, stuck in a landmine. Smoothed the earth over then dug again. They threw wood and straw in the fire-ditches, and barrels seeping pitch.

Blue sky, hot sun; green, flower-spackled hills. Maybe they'd been wrong. Blood, battle, war – they didn't belong on a day like this.

But Wakefield knew they did. They belonged on any day they chose.

Along the wall, the defenders took up positions. A girl Wakefield hadn't seen before stood looking down. Eyes wide and shiny. Wakefield knew the look.

Wakefield touched her arm. The girl blinked at her. Big brown eyes, black hair, smooth black skin. Pretty. "Easy," Wakefield said. "Everyone scared. Ride it. Not let it ride you."

"I was in Manchester," the girl said.

"So?"

The girl sort-of smiled. "When the Jennywrens went for the city crews," she said. "My crew all died. 'Cept me." A shrug. "Now they're here again."

Brittle, tight, but holding. "Whose crew?" Wakefield said. She knew about the crews. Danny had told her, Scopes too. Crews were tribes. Family. To be the last – the lonely of it hurt her head.

"Ashton's," said the girl.

"Then make them proud," Wakefield said. "They watch. They wait. Your name?"

"Filly," said the girl, back now straight.

"Fil-ly." Wakefield tasted it, found she liked it. "Stay close to me."

"I will," Filly said. Her eyes on Wakefield's, not leaving.

Wakefield's face was hot. She looked out to the hills, watched the road. Nothing yet. She almost wished the Reapers here.

COMMANDER'S OFFICE, THE TOWER
1050 HOURS
T MINUS 40

Leaning back in his chair, eyes closed, Winterborn listened as the music box's last few chimes slowed and faded out.

He opened his eyes, released a long and shaky breath.
Time.

He touched his fingers to the box's lid, pushed down till he heard it click. Then he stood, smoothed back his hair and left for the Ops Room.

4.

THE BATTLETRUCK
20TH MARCH, ATTACK PLUS TWENTY-ONE YEARS
1051 HOURS
T MINUS 39

The embankments fell away; empty moors on either side, trees twisted by the wind. Low hills in the distance; a dark sea's frozen waves. A weed-cracked pre-War tarmac road, with a rusting sign listing long-dead towns long emptied or destroyed. On the dashboard, Jarrett saw the rad-counter's needle dip out of the red.

Uncontaminated territory. She could live out here; she had the training. Find an abandoned cottage, claim some little piece of this unblighted corner of the world. She'd bother none and none would bother her.

Jarrett snorted. Sooner or later someone always did, and besides, how could she live alone? There had to be order, to justify all she'd done; with no work, no duty, she'd scream herself to madness in a week. She shook two more speed pills into her hand and dry-swallowed them. There were maybe half a dozen left. They'd have to be enough.

"Bogeys, dead ahead," the driver called.

Jarrett looked through the windscreen. Ahead, beyond the vanguard: half a dozen landcruisers, already veering off-road onto the moor. She saw a clenched fist painted on the side of one in red. "Rebels," she said. "Instruct vanguard to pursue. Seek and destroy."

"Yes, ma'am."

Kellett coughed. "Is that wise, Colonel? If there are hostiles up ahead... "

The vanguard peeled off the road.

"One, the rebels are falling back to their Fort," said Jarrett. "Two, we'd roll over them in seconds. Three, this means fewer to mop up later. Four, a quick, easy victory will boost morale, fire them up for what's ahead."

Kellett smiled weakly, flinched as she leant in.

"And five, Doctor – don't ever question an order of mine."

Off on the moors, guns fired.

*

The rebels were firing on them; Walters ducked as bullets zipped overhead, then again as his 'cruiser's .50 cal swept around to aim over the cab.

"Fire!" someone yelled. The .50 cal thundered; so did all the others in the vanguard.

The men and women in the rebel 'cruisers' flatbeds were swept back and smashed, as if by a huge arm. They dropped: broken, bloody rags. A cruiser's boiler burst, then another; a cabin's windows exploded in a shower of glass, and it swerved, flipped. The .50 cals fell silent; then the 'cruiser pulled up. "Debus!" the sergeant shouted.

Walters baled out and ran in, rifle in his hands. A bloody figure squeezed out of a 'cruiser's cabin, bare-headed. Saw him, swung a Sten his way. Walters dropped to one knee, fired twice from the shoulder; the woman slammed back into the 'cruiser and went down. Shots and bursts rang out. Walters ran to the cabin, aimed in. The other driver was in his seat, head flung back, throat torn out. His eyes bulged, and he made a choking sound. Walters shot him in the head.

"Don't waste ammo," the sergeant said. "He was fucked anyway."

"Just thought –"

"Don't think. And don't piss around with mercy shots. You need every round out here. Let 'em die slow. Let 'em hurt. You're GenRen. They start something, we finish it – good and hard so no-one starts again."

But they still kept starting. "Right, sarge."

"On your way."

Walters ran back to his 'cruiser.

Ops Room, the tower

1100 hours

T minus 30

It all went quiet when he entered, the chatter fading, then rising again in his wake as he passed. Winterborn went straight to Thorpe. "Report, Colonel."

Thorpe snapped to attention, a greasy sheen of sweat on his forehead. "Colonel Jarrett's making good time, sir. ETA still on schedule. They're set to reach Ashwood in thirty."

"And the support column?"

"Also en route, ETA one hour."

Thirty minutes till the rope went around Helen's neck; then in an hour, the drop. Winterborn smiled. "Thank you, Colonel. Carry on."

"Fuck me," said Mackie.

"You're not wrong," said Cov.

He halted outside the gate; the concrete yard was already full of landcruisers. The fighters in them smoked, cleaning weapons and rubbing dust into their faces. Tribesfolk, city kids like him and Mackie, others he couldn't place.

"Got guns!" shouted Mackie. "Help us out."

Half a dozen volunteers helped shift the rifles and explosives into the building, stacking them in a small room on the ground floor.

"Hey, you two."

"Yo Jazz."

Jazz grinned back. She was Cov's age, but taller, with brown skin and short black hair. "Been having fun?"

"Heads up!" someone shouted. Flaps marched past. Jazz pointed to the door. Cov nodded and they followed Flaps out, Mackie ambling along in their wake.

In the yard, Flaps jumped up on a landcruiser and yelled "Oi!" The yard went quiet: her voice could break glass.

More fighters poured out of the building, jostling Cov, Jazz and Mackie up against the fence. Cov climbed up on a flatbed, nodded to the occupants, and did a quick head count of the yard: looked like about two hundred souls. You didn't see that many in one place, not often.

"Right," said Flaps. "Reapers are going after the Fort. Yes, they know where it is. No, never fucking mind now. Main force isn't our job. There's another column coming up. Heavy 'cruisers, nice big slow targets. Even you twats can't miss 'em."

That got a weak laugh.

"Ammo. Explosives. Artillery. All that shit. So we're not letting that get through. There's a place called Bowkitt three miles west of here – what's left of it, anyway. A burned town.

Devil's Highway goes straight through. Lots of cover, high spots for obbo. So that's where we batter the cunts. We've got more people in bands further on up, 'case owt gets through, but that's for mopping up. And the more wreckage we leave on the road, the harder it is for the next lot to get through. So I don't want one Reaper cunt getting past us. Clear?"

"Yes."

"Can't fucking hear you!"

"Yes!"

"Right then. That's it. Move out."

Cov hopped down and squeezed through the crowd, towing Mackie after him. It wasn't till they were back in their 'cruiser that he realised he hadn't said bye to Jazz.

WEST OF FIELD-BASE 11

1110 HOURS

T MINUS 20

Flaps' heart thumped; her breathing was ragged and quick. Fuck it fuck it fuck it.

Not like she hadn't twatted Reapers before now. She gripped the Sterling. No, it wasn't. But this would be bigger and harder – the Jennywrens again, like back in the winter, and they'd keep coming and coming. They wouldn't stop till she was dead, till they all were. And she was in charge. One fuck-up and –

"You'll be fine."

"Fuck." Flaps jumped in her seat: the speaker was next to her, hanging onto the side of the 'cruiser as it went.

"Eh?" Her driver looked at her. "You okay, boss?"

"Fine. Watch the fucking road." Flaps turned back to the woman looking in through the window. Bone-thin and pale, cropped black hair: Scary Mary.

Ghostlighting. Fucking hell, the dead picked their times.

"It's okay," Mary said. Smiled. "Just came to wish you luck."

Flaps breathed out. "Scared," she said – mouthed it, so no-one else would know.

"I'd be worried if you weren't."

"Not just for me." Flaps whispered it into the slipstream blowing past the 'cruiser. "I mean – case I fuck this up."

"You won't, Flaps." Mary reached in through the window, touched her cheek. "You're my best. Always were. My best girl."

She let go of the 'cruiser, fell backwards. Flaps looked back, but there was only the dirt road and the other landcruisers following her. She wound up the window, blinked till her eyes didn't sting.

BOWKITT

1120 HOURS

T MINUS 10

Dust billowed up as the 'cruisers pulled in. Flaps jumped out, looking around. Most of the houses this side of the Highway were shells without roofs; a lot of them were just a few bits of wall, the odd chimney.

Across the road, though –

"Goll!"

"Yo." Goll was a big, straw-haired farmboy, labouring on AgriSec farmland till it had changed hands in the winter. Smarter than he looked, and tough.

"Take half our units and set up on the other side of the road."

Goll nodded, turned away and started barking orders. Flaps looked around. "Mackie! Cov!"

Mackie ambled up, Cov darting around him. "Yo, Flaps."

She pointed. "Over there, see?"

"What'm I looking at?"

"Highest point around here. Big square building, dome on top."

"Right."

"You and head-the-ball here get over there. I want you in the dome on look-out. Take a comm set."

Cov looked half-pissed off and half-glad. "Right."

"Keep me and the Fort up to date and show us where to twat 'em." Flaps stepped in, tapped his chest. "You do *not* fucking get into it with them. Two of you won't last a minute and you're no fucking use dead. Right?"

"Okay."

"Right. Now sling it."

OUTSKIRTS OF BOWKITT
1123 HOURS
T MINUS 7

The Walker had steered clear of the road. Partly because the ruins called to it – some part of it liked to walk in the dust and ash of a fallen world – and partly from an instinct it couldn't name.

It saw now the instinct had been right. Over the road, tiny stick figures ran back and forth; shouts and cries echoed. Some climbed down the embankments onto the Devil's Highway.

More engines growled closer to; The Walker stepped behind a shattered wall, watched landcruisers pull up. Men and women with red fists painted on their uniforms poured up the embankments, taking up positions with rifles and submachine guns, Brens and general purpose machine guns. Another landcruiser wove down a rubble-littered street towards the looming shell of a big, domed building with a gaping hole in the frontage. A sign over its door said PUBLIC LIBRARY. The 'cruiser drove in through the hole. The engine cut out; running footsteps echoed inside.

The Walker cocked its head; it heard a hiss and clank, very faint, of more engines. Still distant, but drawing near.

It turned and walked on.

THE DEVIL'S HIGHWAY
1125 HOURS
T MINUS 5

"Spread out more," Flaps shouted. "No bunching up. GPMG teams, anti-armour teams – rest of you in groups of five with small arms and grenades, one Bren gun each. Jazz?"

"Road's mined back there. Remote detonation, like you wanted."

"Right. You go on my mark, not before. Not till I tell you."

Sud and Beak were in the next group; the boy was shivering, the stock of his Sten tucked into his shoulder. Beak reached out, put a hand on his, then her arm around her shoulders. Flaps saw her lips move, but couldn't hear the words. Just saw Sud nod, and grow stiller. Beak patted him on the back and sighted down her SLR.

There were coiled ropes, each with one end pinned to the ground; Flaps flicked one over, climbing down. "Now get your arse down here and bury the rest of the mines."

ST MARTIN DE PORRES CHURCH, ASHWOOD
1126 HOURS
T MINUS 4

"Osprey to Phoenix. Osprey to Phoenix. Helen? *Helen?*"

Helen ignored Alannah's voice and leant on the pew in front. The wood was still smooth and varnished; there were still a few believers who kept the place clean.

A cross above the altar. What must it be like, to have that faith? A hope like that? She swallowed hard, tasted blood. Alannah's voice crackled from the communicator again: summoning her back below, into her grave.

"Praying, Helen?"

Frank leant against a pillar nearby, arms folded, smirking at her.

"Hello, Mummy," Belinda said, her head popping up over the back of the pew ahead. Helen recoiled.

"Getting religious in your old age?" Frank stepped away from the pillar. "Holy ground won't save you from us." He grinned wider. "Or anything else."

BOWKITT LIBRARY
1128 HOURS
T MINUS 2

Feathers, bones and bird-shit; the reek in the library dome made Cov gag. He peered through a glassless window with his binocs, down the highway; in the distance were a column of low black blurs.

"Crow's Nest to Rook One, come in."

"Rook One." A young voice, thin and sharp. Newt.

"In position."

"Copy that."

The fighters on the Highway were running for the ropes and climbing up. It was a dirt road here, and they'd smoothed the earth back over the mines; Reapers wouldn't see fuck-all till they went sky-high. The fighters all climbed back, 'cept one: small and wiry with bright red hair.

THE DEVIL'S HIGHWAY
1129 HOURS
T MINUS 1

Above, they were shouting her name. Flaps didn't listen, smoothing earth over the last mine. Simple movements. Calming. Nearly done.

"Flaps. *Flaps.*"

She looked up. Mary crouched opposite her. "That's enough. It's not just your life now."

Flaps breathed out, nodded.

Mary's face softened. "Go on then. Move."

Flaps climbed up, pulled the rope back when she reached the top. Below, the road was empty. She spread herself prone on the embankment and pulled back the Sterling's bolt.

WALL ONE, ASHWOOD FORT

1130 HOURS

T

"Reapers!"

A lookout, pointing to the road. Wakefield grabbed her binocs, focused. Small 'cruisers first, then a beast on wheels, and many more following.

She swallowed; it stuck in her throat. "The bell," she said. "Ring the bell. They're here."

5.

THE BATTLETRUCK

20TH MARCH, ATTACK PLUS TWENTY-ONE YEARS
1130 HOURS

There it was, dead ahead; a hillside slashed with wire and trenches, high walls a-bristle with guns.

"There," said Jarrett. She hadn't really believed, not really, not till now. "There it is."

"Orders, ma'am?" said the driver.

Jarrett breathed deep. Her heart hammered. "Patch me through to all vehicles."

Jarrett took the dashboard mic, pushed the transmit button down. "This is the Colonel. We have visual on the Fort. Prepare to –"

She stopped, blinked. It couldn't be. A dream. But no, it was true.

The Fort's gates were open.

The battletruck could tear through the fences, ram through the gate. Inside, keep on going, all the way to the Fort. To

176

Helen. Kill her. No siege; the support column wouldn't even matter. It would be over. Helen, dead.

Helen, dead. The prize was there, in front of her, waiting to be taken – not later, after a siege, but *now*.

"All units," she said. "Maximum speed, straight up the hill. We're going in."

St Martin de Porres Church

"Mummy's scared. Isn't she, Daddy?"

"She should be." Frank leant close, breath rank on Helen's face. "The Refuge, Helen, all over again. And just like then, it's all… your … fault."

The floor was gone; she was falling, lost. And then the bell rang.

Helen jumped up.

The church was empty. She pulled the communicator from her belt. "Phoenix to Opsrey Actual."

"Where the *fuck* have you been?" Alannah shouted. "They're here, Helen. Heading straight for Wall One. Get back here, *now*."

Helen was shaking, teeth gritted – those bloody pills. Jarrett going straight for the jugular, gambling on smashing through. Her tomb beneath the ground, waiting for her. "Not yet. Going to the walls."

"No!"

"Keep me posted."

She shoved the communicator in her belt, grabbed the Sterling, ran.

Wakefield looked down at the wire and the trenches, stopped. Something stuck out from under the battlements. Two somethings. Took her a second to realise what.

"Gates open!" She yelled. "Who left fucking gates open?" She ran across the parapet to the opposing well, shouted down into the courtyard. "Gates shut! Shut fucking gates now!"

Fighters ran, got behind the gates, started pushing them to. Wakefield spun back to the wall defences. "Load heavy weapons, wait my order. Archers!"

A dozen men and women snapped to attention. Crow tribe – all had guns, but kept their bows as well. Wakefield had fought them, carried scars where one had nearly killed her. Fuckers, but good shots. "Nock and draw!"

Below, the 'cruisers came. An arrowhead of small light ones. Behind them, the beast-cruiser – battletruck, Helen called it. The sight of it made Wakefield cold – she'd fought wild dog-packs, Reapers in 'cruisers, but this? Nothing else she'd ever seen move got big as this. A mine blew under it, rocking it, then another, but on it came.

The Crows stood, flame-tipped arrows ready. "Light them up!" she shouted, watched the arrows arc and fall, tips of flame dropping. Muzzles flashed below; she ducked as a bullet cracked past her, and one of the archers didn't drop fast enough, was knocked back, lay still and bleeding.

Whoomf and *whoomf* and *whoomf* from below. Wakefield scuttled to the parapet, watched the trenches roar into flame.

A dull thud and thunderclap, a spew of smoke and earth, and a landcruiser flew upwards. Bodies and pieces of bodies and pieces of it flew loose and it smashed down in tangled steel, screeching steam. Others veered to avoid it.

And then the Reaper guns hammered in reply, the top of the parapet exploding in splinters and dust. As Wakefield hit the ground, she heard screams from the courtyard, the thunder of rounds hammering into the gates' wood.

THE BATTLETRUCK

The battletruck rocked and shuddered from the mines it had struck, but rolled on; the underside was armoured. Smoke billowed in the cabin where something burned; the co-driver unbelted, grabbed an extinguisher and sprayed.

Outside, two more mines blew; another landcruiser flipped airward and another still swerved sideways and stopped, wheels gone, crew sprawled dead across seats and flatbed.

"Keep firing!" Jarrett shouted. "Concentrate on the gates, don't let them close."

Dust and stone blew from the stonework about the gates. Jarrett saw a body fall. "Grenade launchers, mortars, something! Stop them closing."

A few of the landcruisers had mortars. Shells whistled but fell short, exploding near the gates. The .50 cals hammered them, but the bullets weren't punching through into the men and women behind it – or if they were, not enough of them.

"You miscalculated," said Tom – suddenly he was beside her, whispering in her ear. "Too far a range, not enough firepower – and they're going too fast for an accurate shot. Oh, and –" Another landcruiser hit a mine. "Oops," he giggled, and was gone.

Jarrett looked ahead; the gates swung to.

WALL ONE

The Brens , GPMGs and .50 cals on the battlements chattered and crashed. Wakefield squinnied over the parapet. Bodies fell from the oncoming landcruisers – but still they came. Slower now, though, on the steep slope. Some small and fast – others big and slow, jammed with Reapers, beetleblack in their leather.

"Artillery!" shouted Wakefield. "Aim for the big ones." More Reapers died here, less Reapers coming over the walls.

Cannon swivelled, trebuchets creaked, ballista took aim. "Wait till they're through the mines," said Wakefield.

Footsteps clattered; Wakefield turned. "Helen!"

The crazy ginger grinned, fell to crouch beside her. "How we doing?"

Best not to tell her of the gates. "About to hit them."

A wet thump of impact, a soft spray of blood; a Bren gunner choked and fell back, throat blown out. Filly ran in, grabbed the Bren and fired, glanced back. "Good girl," said Wakefield. A quick bright smile, then Filly turned back and fired again.

Helen snatched the dead man's helmet, put it on, peeped over. "There," she said, pointing.

"Battletruck?"

"Their command centre," she said. "Jarrett'll be on board."

"Jarrett." Jennywren Jarrett – oh, Wakefield knew her name. She'd had brothers once, a sister. Then, the Jennywrens. Foxes running from their places, driven, forced to fight with Crows for land. Behind them, the echo of a name – leader of slayers, butcher of children: *Jarrett*. "Ballista!"

"Here," shouted the boy crewing it: he was small and fat, but he knew his weapon. Wouldn't miss.

"Battletruck," said Wakefield. "Aim there. Kill it."

"The windows," Helen said. "Best chance."

The boy nodded.

The battletruck forged free of the minefield, smoke billowing from underneath.

Fingers on triggers, hands on levers, knives on ropes.

"Fire!"

THE BATTLETRUCK

Up on the battlements, two of three puffs of smoke; then the crump of the shots and the projectiles whistling in. And more; the sky dimmed for a second as rocks and bolts hailed down. A medium landcruiser to the left vanished, swiped away by a fusillade of shrapnel. Then the driver came out and Jarrett looked up to see the ballista bolt sailing down.

The driver tried to turn the wheel, but there was no time. The bolt hit the windscreen and smashed straight through. He grunted once, jerked: then the bolt erupted through the back of the seat, coated and dripping.

Kellett screamed.

"Shut up!" yelled Jarrett. Guns thundered; she scrambled towards the wheel. Muzzle flashes danced along the battlements as the co-driver ran to grab the wheel; bullets punched and sparked off metal, shattered the dashboard. The top of the co-driver's head blew apart in a spray of dark matter. Kellett screamed again, then a third time as Jarrett heaved the co-driver's corpse out of the way, onto him.

She lunged across the cabin, grabbed the wheel. Half the window gone, the other crazed and splintered. The battle truck crashed across one of the fire trenches and the hot dry gulp of air she sucked in almost scorched her lungs. Screams as a medium 'cruiser tipped into the fire; a dull bang as the boiler exploded. And the weapons on the parapet crashed again; the cabin's ceiling thumped and dented inwards, a sharp barbed point sticking through.

Smoke filled the cabin. "Get the extinguisher!" she screamed. The dashboard, broken and shattered; she could barely steer. And this was the battletruck; what was happening to the rest?

Jarrett screamed in rage, grabbed the mic. Was it still working? "Abort!" she shouted. "Break off!"

Did they hear? Did they know? Christ knew. She swung the wheel right, hoping she didn't flip the truck or have whatever was left of her force plough into it. She aimed down the slope and hit the pedal. Back over the fire-trench, then the minefield, down to where the land shelved down, to where the woods had been, knowing she was crying, had bitten her mouth bloody in her rage.

"Reload!" shouted Wakefield. "Ready to fire again!"

Landcruisers smashed and scattered in the minefield, blackened and gutted in the fire-trenches, skewered and pulverised beyond them below the wall. Beetleblacks crawled from them.

"Machine guns!" she shouted. Throat hurting from the screaming and the dust, from the smoke. "Get them!"

Brens and GPMGs tilted down and fired. The air stank with it; Wakefield's ears hummed. She saw Helen run to the wall, fire a burst from her Sterling. Crazy ginger.

Over the burst of gunfire, a voice, from the communicator on Helen's hip: "Helen? Helen!"

APPROACH TO ASHWOOD FORT
1150 HOURS

Walters lay, face in earth and crushed grass. The smell of it; fresh, sweet. Then the ground beside him exploded into spraying dirt.

He rolled away, yelping, crashed into the front end of a landcruiser. He scrambled behind it. Not his. Blown in half, this one: still had bits of the crew stuck to it.

Rifle, Sterling, helmet – all gone. He could see his 'cruiser, flipped over on its back and squashed half-flat by the trebuchet load that had hit it. Bullets ripped up a line of earth that swept towards him, and he ducked. Bullets spanged off the wrecked 'cruiser.

Shouts, screams, feet thudding on the earth, landcruiser engines. It took him a second to realise they were heading away. He twisted about, looked down: 'cruisers were weaving back down the hill, followed by Reapers on foot. A dull thunderclap of soil and smoke flung a landcruiser skyward, the back wheels gone, the top half of a man landing by it, smoking, on fire, still screaming.

The bullets stopped hitting Walters' position. He looked; another group of men were trying to break downhill. Have to move, now. These cunts took no prisoners. He got up, running, pulling his Browning from its holster. Fuck knew what good that'd do, but it helped somehow.

Screams behind him; half the Reapers he'd seen running near him went down. The fire-trench came up to meet him. The fear that he wouldn't clear it, or be hit but not killed when he tried to jump – he'd fall in and burn. Not that. Not that. Anything but fucking that.

He reached the trench and jumped, screaming. The flames soared up and licked around him and he screamed again – then hit the ground on the other side, rolling. Lost the pistol. Scrabbled for it – his good-luck charm. Don't waste time, you're in the open, the guns are thundering.

Gunfire. He looked. Four Reapers running towards the fire-trench. One spun, hit, fell screaming to the ground. No-one stopped or went back. Three jumped, one fell short. The flames whitened where he fell and Walters heard him scream, glimpsed a burning shape rear up and flail. The wounded man still screamed, till a scythe of bullets swept down, sliced across the earth and him and the burning man in the trench, and both fell silent.

The other two ran towards him. One had a corporal's stripes. "Get fucking up, you twat," he screamed at Walters. "Move!"

Walters got up and moved. Over the next fire-trench, then the next, towards the retreating landcruisers. Whistling overhead – shells and shrapnel, rocks and ballista bolts flew down, smashed into the vehicles. A ballista bolt smashed one cruiser's boiler and there was a shriek of steam; the men running past it shrieked too, falling, faces boiled off the bone.

"Keep going!" roared the corporal. "Watch the ground!"

The minefield was ahead, scarred with blackened craters, pieces of vehicles, women, men. The corporal went for the craters, where the mines had been. Walters followed, tried to step only where he did.

The other Reaper with them – a girl, young – ran a few yards to the right. Not all the ground there was blackened and torn; she ran across green grass and Walters opened his mouth to shout, but the mine blew and she sailed upwards, screaming, crashed back down. No legs. One arm gone, elbow down. Guts hanging out, coughing blood. Staring at him. He tried to aim the Browning, but his fingers were thick, not working right. A shot, and her head snapped; when it lolled back her left eye was gone. Just a hole left.

"Move!" roared the corporal. His gun still smoked. Walters ran after him, towards the last few landcruisers zigzagging out of the minefield towards where the ground shelved away. One slowed down. The corporal ran, jumped aboard, held out a hand. Grey hair, a hard, rough face. "Come on!"

Walters ran up; the corporal grabbed his hand. Others grabbed him too and pulled him aboard. He fell on the flatbed, heaving for breath.

WALL ONE

"Artillery!" yelled Wakefield. "Reload! Fire at will!"

The trebuchets' arms were cranked to readiness, fresh loads were thrust into the guns and the ballista ropes were drawn back. Then the guns boomed, the loads were released, and one more payload sailed over the wall, hurtling down the slopes towards the remaining landcruisers.

APPROACH TO ASHWOOD FORT

Walters rolled onto his back, still gasping. He glimpsed faces – black, white, brown, yellow – grimed with smoke and dirt, all grinning.

The corporal leant over him. "You all right, lad?"

A whistle in the air, a dimming of the light; then a shuddering thud of impact rocked the cruiser. Hot wetness doused Walters. The corporal fell backward against the edge of the flatbed: his head and left arm were gone, only pulped red flesh and splintered bone left, thin sprays of blood hissing out. Walters heard himself scream.

Warm wetness round him, on his hands. He looked around; the other men in the flatbed were dead too, all six of them. They'd been sitting or kneeling; he'd been the only one lying down. A trebuchet load, he guessed – rock and metal fragments flung down in a hail. Chunks were embedded in the flatbed, the back of the cabin, even the boiler, which was seeping steam. But still the landcruiser plunged on down, weaving, engine groaning as the driver fought to get more speed out of it.

Behind, the scarred and burning slopes receded, black smoke pouring up, strewn with wreckage and pieces of the dead.

The Battletruck

1155 hours

The truck crashed and thundered down the slope, almost overturning. Kellett screamed and wailed behind, but Jarrett kept it under control and brought it about, finally bringing it to rest at the bottom of the steep shelf where the woods had been.

"Fucking hell." She pushed herself clear of the smoking, sparking dashboard and strode back through the cabin, throwing the door to the pod wide. "Everybody out! De-bus, now!"

Doors swung open, troops bailing out. "Majid!" she barked.

"Yes, ma'am." The captain saluted.

"Covering fire for the rest of our people falling back. And make sure the rest of the column comes straight here."

"Ma'am."

"And get a couple of engineers in. Fix up the damage to the battletruck's cabin."

"Ma'am."

"Oh, and the medics. Two corpses in there. Go on, move it."

Majid saluted again, strode out.

"Colonel?"

She turned: Kellett. "Yes, Doctor?"

He gestured to the equipment stacked against the wall. Already the base staff were setting up the chart table and the remaining radio sets, but they ignored the monitors and other equipment he'd brought from Thurley. "With your permission?"

"Fine. Yes – but not here. There should be some portakabins. You can requisition one of those with my authority. Get your little toy soldiers ready, Doctor, but they're not to be deployed without my say so."

Kellett smirked, blinking. "Of course not."

Jarrett turned away from the sight of him; it made her hands feel covered in slime.

CATCH CENTRAL

Outside the commandeered portakabin, the generator kicked into life; Kellett smirked, watching the lights and gauges on the panels in front of him blink on. He flicked a series of switches, watched another panel connected to the rest. A series of small lights, each with a button beside it.

One by one, they lit up, till they were all aglow. Kellett pushed one of the buttons at random, and watched the picture on the monitor: a Catchman, sitting and gazing straight ahead, at the end of a row of other Catchmen. Another button showed much the same view from a different angle – and another, and another, and another.

He found a control on a different panel, and pushed that. "Come to Daddy, boys and girls," he said.

"Set up look-outs," said Jarrett, pointing to the chart. "Here, here, here – regular intervals all along this line. Also, organise a raiding force."

"Raiding force, ma'am?" Majid licked his lips, hesitated.

"Speak freely, Captain."

"With respect, ma'am, the Fort's too well-defended to take with a foot assault, or even with landcruisers. We need artillery to –"

"I know, Captain. That or some other – advantage. The artillery's en route, but I want them reacting, not acting. We don't give them time to take the offensive. See to it, and send in Lieutenant Wong on your way out."

"Understood, ma'am."

Lieutenant Wong approached. Young: no more than twenty, slender and hesitant. "Reporting, Colonel?"

"You know what to do," said Jarrett. "You've the best digging equipment we can spare. We need that wall. How long?"

Wong flinched from Jarrett's glare. "Days, normally."

"We haven't got days."

"Please, Colonel – I said normally. We may have an advantage."

"What advantage?"

"I was able to review some old reports about this area. There's a cave system that we think runs under the hill. And a spring here in the camp – which may emerge from the cave system. Simply a case of getting that far and then finding our way."

"Good, Lieutenant. *Very* good. Very well, then. Proceed."

Wakefield shivered. Sudden cold. The sunlight had gone, dimmed down. She looked up. The air above was thick with smoke and dust.

"Down there!" called Filly.

Wakefield looked. Movement in among some of the wrecked landcruisers. Shapes stirring, rising, standing. Not Reapers – not normal Reaper uniform. Dull grey. She'd seen it before, but the faces were different – steel helmets, masks, grinning mouths.

"Open fire," she shouted, and the .50 cals thundered into life. The grey men jerked and stumbled in the hailing bullets, but didn't fall; instead, they turned and steadily walked back down the hill, towards the Reaper lines.

"What…?" she said. She looked at Helen. "Styr?" she said.

"Not quite." Helen shook her head. "Catchmen. An army of them."

6.

Yelps and cries from outside; Jarrett scowled, straightened up from the chart table, strode to the side-door and flung it wide.

Reapers – Jennywrens, battle-hardened men and women – leapt out of the way of the leaden-grey shapes that marched through the camp towards Kellett's portakabin. Several dozen already stood outside, at attention, gazing ahead.

Jarrett saw Lieutenant Benbow from the rocketry detachments gawping at the sight; then again, Benbow gawped a lot. Bespectacled, watery-eyed, thin and gangling, he was in his thirties and balding but still managed to look like an overgrown teenager. But he was one of the few people even remotely competent with the crude rockets they had available. The squat sergeant next to him – Mitchell was her name, Jarrett recalled, an old hand and a solid one – saw Jarrett looking and tugged Benbow's sleeve. Benbow blinked, flushed and hurried on.

Kellett stood in the portakabin's doorway, smiling and licking his lips at her people as they recoiled from the things he'd made, watching as the new arrivals joined the rest, falling into formation with them. He turned to her smiled, executed a mocking little bow. Jarrett pressed her lips together, turned and went back inside.

CATCH CENTRAL

Kellett turned from the Catchmen massing outside, shut the cabin door, sank into his swivel chair. He stroked controls, licked his lips; a deep breath, a smile, and he reached for the intercom. "CATCH Central to Mower Actual."

"Mower Actual," said Jarrett. "What do you want, Doctor?"

"The Catchmen are ready. When and where would you like them deployed?"

A long breath; a sigh. "Do you suffer from deafness, Dr Kellett? I thought I made it clear that your – creatures – were only to be deployed as and when I instructed."

"I assumed you'd want –"

"Assumption is the mother of all fuck-ups, Dr Kellett, This is a GenRen operation, so stand by. *If* I need you, I'll let you know."

The line went dead.

"Fuck you," spat Kellett. Saliva dotted the control panel. He wiped it, then his mouth; calmer, he sat back. "All right, Colonel. We'll wait."

THE BATTLETRUCK

"What's the news re the rocket detachment?"

"They survived, ma'am. Well to the rear of the column, so they never got close enough for the rebel artillery to be a problem."

Jarrett sat, studying the hastily drawn map before her. "And we've nothing else that can hit them from here?"

"No ma'am. .50 cals and mortars only – we had to travel light, no heavy weapons –"

"Yes, I know." She tapped the chart with her pointer. "How accurate does Lieutenant Benbow think his rockets are?"

Majid shrugged. "You know what those flying tin cans are like. Bit of luck, a third of them might hit the target."

"Well, if they're all we've got..." Jarrett chewed her lip. "All right. Get them set up. And send Harper and his team through."

PERIMETER OF REAPER CAMP

"Set the rest of them up along there," called Benbow, blinking behind his glasses. His team moved to prop the rockets up on their stands: lumpen iron things with a wooden stick on the end, like the bottle rockets he just about remembered from before the War. They were mounted on the slight incline below the perimeter fencing. More or less invisible to the enemy, with any luck.

Benbow clambered up the incline, peered over the barbed wire at the Fort. "What are the chances, do you think, Mitchell?"

Mitchell took off her helmet, scratched her cropped sandy hair. "Some of them should hit, sir."

Benbow sighed. "Long as some do." He offered a battered old cigarette case. "Want one?"

"Thank you, sir." They lit up and smoked in silence, waiting for the command.

THE BATTLETRUCK

Jarrett turned and stood. "Sergeant Harper."

Harper and his team snapped to attention. "Reporting as ordered, ma'am."

"At ease."

The dark-haired sniper, Fox, had a half-smile on his face; Jarrett stared him down till it faded. The youngest, Greene, smiled too – but a twitchy, nervous thing. Practically a child – but an excellent shot. White and Carson stood stolid and straight, awaiting command. And Harper, as ever, was a rock; hard, unwavering, exactly the man she needed.

"We'll be launching an assault shortly," she said. "You'll use it to take up positions on the hillside. Take cover, hide, wait. Your mission will be to take out rebel command staff. Questions so far?"

None.

"I assume you've all been briefed on targets of particular interest, such as Helen Damnation and Roger Darrow?"

"Yes, ma'am," came back in a mumbled chorus.

"And of course, you shouldn't have much difficulty spotting who's giving the orders up there. *However.*" Jarret paused. "Having you in place will give us a vital tactical asset – but when you fire, you'll risk exposure. Therefore, if you identify a potential target, you'll contact me here before taking action, and fire *only* with my authorisation. Are we clear?"

"Yes, ma'am."

Jarrett pointed to the table; five sets of headphones with attached throat-mics lay there. "You'll use these to keep in contact. They're rare so try and bring them back in one piece." She half-smiled. "Along with yourselves. Questions?"

There were none.

"Then dismiss. And good luck."

BOWKITT LIBRARY
1220 HOURS

"Here they come," said Mackie.

Cov squinted through his binoculars. "Crow's Nest to Rook Actual."

"Rook Actual here."

"Range now about three miles. Approx thirty vehicles. I make twenty heavy 'cruisers, with five pursuit 'cruisers front and rear as escorts."

"Copy that, Crow's Nest."

BOWKITT

"Lock and load, everyone. Anti-armour teams in position, stand ready." Flaps tossed the mic to Newt. "Same order to Rook Two."

Newt relayed the command; on the embankment opposite, Flaps saw the fighters huddle down; ready, waiting.

REAPER CAMP

Walters stumbled from the landcruiser, through the camp. Reapers ran back and forth, pitching tents, stringing barbed wire along the top of the ridge that sheltered them.

He looked down at himself; his uniform still glistened, red and black. Blood coated his hands, sticky and drying. He still clutched the Browning; on the fourth or fifth fumbling attempt, he forced it back in its holster. He was shaking. He was gonna start crying any second, shricking like a kid –

"You!"

Walters stared at his hands, tried to rub the blood off them on his uniform, only dirtied them all the worse.

"You! Soldier!" A woman strode up – brown-haired, hard-faced. A corporal's stripes on her sleeve. The corporal from before, in the landcruiser; Walters remembered the man slumping back without a head and flinched.

"Stand up straight! Attention! What's wrong with you? You hit?"

"N-no. No."

"No what? No, *what?*"

"No corporal."

"Then what the hell are you doing? Where's your unit? What
—"

"Pete!" Someone wove towards him. "He was in the vanguard, corp."

The corporal's jaw tightened. "Name and unit?"

"Patel, corp. Second Battalion, Third Company, First Platoon. Same as him." Patel shrugged. "One of us got the short straw – I was in the battletruck coming here."

"All right – well, get him to your platoon commander for assignment. Next attack's about to start."

"Another one?" Walters was shaking, opened his mouth to scream it was madness, they'd all be killed, but Patel grabbed his arm.

"I'll sort it, corp. Come on, Pete."

Stumbling, Walters let himself be led away.

THE BATTLETRUCK

On the chart table, rows of counters. Pieces in the game. Jarrett focused on them. A chess board, nothing more; all anxiety, all excitement, all doubt must be pushed aside. All hatred too: even Helen must be put from her mind for now. There was only the game.

She pushed an intercom button. "All units report readiness."

"Rocket section standing by, ma'am."

"Medium landcruisers standing by."

"Support landcruisers standing by."

"Infantry standing by."

"Snipers standing by," said Harper.

Nothing from Wong; the sappers' work had already begun.

Jarrett took a sip of water to dislodge the lump in her throat. It tasted of blood. "You have your orders." A deep breath. "Attack!"

Silence; then the whooshing shriek of rockets, the crump of distant explosions, and the roar of engines.

"Rockets!" Helen shouted.

Wakefield stared; points of red and orange fire shot up from the Reaper lines, trailing white smoke, hurtling towards the Fort.

Shouts, shrieks, from the defenders on the walls. "Hold fast!" yelled Wakefield.

Some of the red dots flew off left or right; some fell short, exploded on the hillside. But others smashed into the wall. It shook, jerked – Wakefield lost her footing, fell. Then one screamed down and hit the parapet in a white flash. A trebuchet crashed on its side; a GPMG flew over the wall and three fighters fell screaming to the courtyard below.

"Up!" Wakefield stood. Helen crouched beside her, passed her a helmet. She staggered to the parapet. "Landcruisers!"

Ten medium ones surged forward, then swung about and stopped, side on. Muzzle flashes flickered, danced, then the dull thump of mortars, the whistle of shells.

"Incoming!" Helen shouted.

Shells exploded on the wall. Another detonated on the parapet; another still fell into the courtyard. The thudding blast of them shook the wall.

Wakefield made it to the parapet again; below, screaming, Reapers charged up the slopes, twenty small landcruisers riding with them, guns firing as they went.

APPROACH TO FORT

Patel was screaming as he ran, rifle fisted tight in his hands. Beside him Walters screamed too, face white under clotted blood, all the terror and rage and the things he'd seen howled out of him in a blast of fury at the rebels.

A mine thudded behind them; screams. Still a few of those left. The fire-ditches burning up ahead, snarls of barbed wire around them. Bullets buzzed and cracked past; a Reaper running on Patel's other side dropped, his face blown apart. Patel hunched forward over his rifle, screamed as he leapt a burning ditch, hit the ground, rolled, came up, scrambled on – keep moving, keep moving, weave, never be a sitting target.

Walters, where was Walters? But then he heard the screaming again, saw Walters running alongside him. Still going, still in the fight – both of them still alive, through all the fields of hail and fire.

Wall One
1235 hours

"Fire back!" shouted Wakefield. "Down there – hit the Reapers."

Filly pulled a spent magazine from her Bren gun. "Out of ammo!"

Wakefield ran along the parapet; a crate of it lay open. She scrabbled out a half-dozen clips, spilled them on the floor as another mortar round thudded into the side. Picked them up, ran. "Ballista, trebuchet – hit the medium 'cruisers. Rest of you, kill Reapers!"

The whistle and thump of the mortars stopped as she skidded to her knees by Filly. Helen – where was Helen? Then Wakefield saw – behind a GPMG whose gunner had fallen, firing down at the Reapers.

Wakefield's ears hummed. "Here!" She thrust the magazines at Filly. Throat was dry, burning – smoke and dust. Filly shoved a fresh clip into her Bren. As she aimed, Wakefield saw why the mortars had stopped. The Reaper infantry were nearly at the walls.

The mines left the hillside dotted with craters; Carson scrambled forward, then rolled in, flinging off the camouflage cape she'd worn; the black Reaper uniform blended better with the dark earth.

She crawled, keeping low, to the edge of it nearest the Fort, and unslung her rifle, reached up to mould the earth at the edge of the hole, forming a small gap for the rifle's barrel. She fitted the stock to her shoulder, adjusted the sights.

A grunt, and someone flopped into the crater with her. Carson twisted round, fumbling for her Browning.

Fox grinned.

"Fuck are you doing here?" she spat. "Orders were to spread out."

He looked down at her lower body. "I'm up for that if you are."

"Fuck off."

He moved closer. "I could smell how wet you were for me –"

She kicked out at him and he recoiled – rearing up, just a little bit too high. His helmet gave a dull clang as the bullet hit it. Fox fell forward, blood pouring down his face.

"Oh fuck." She scrambled for him: cunt or not, he was one of her own. The helmet came off as Carson rolled him over; the top of his head came with it.

"Fuck. No. Fuck."

In that moment she realised she was kneeling up and, like Fox before her, would be visible above the lip of the crater. She started turning to throw herself down, but as she did what felt like a booted kick smashed into her chest, drove the wind out of her. Couldn't breathe. She fell forward over Fox, and her mouth was full of blood and earth.

Bowkitt Library
1242 hours

"There," said Mackie.

Cov looked. "Rook One, this is Crow's Nest. We have visual on support column. ETA ten, maybe fifteen minutes."

"Copy that," came the reply, and the line went dead.

Outer Gate
1245 hours

Patel stumbled, nearly fell; Walters grabbed his arm and pulled him on, last few feet to the walls and gate. The ground ahead of them ripped as though a blade had raked it, three Reapers going down as it swept over them, too. Walters' rifle fired upwards, four rounds rapid; then he heaved Patel at the wall and flung himself after them.

Patel pressed flat against the stone as more bursts from above slashed down. Three Reapers knelt before the gate, trying to mould plastique into place, but an explosion flung them sideways like dolls. Another grenade exploded seconds later.

"Fuck!" Walters screamed.

Other Reapers had ropes and grapples; they swung them, flung them upwards, then started to climb.

"Give 'em covering fire!" a sergeant screamed.

Act. Fight. Do your job. Patel shouldered his rifle, aimed up at the battlements above, and fired.

7.

BOWKITT
20TH MARCH, ATTACK PLUS TWENTY-ONE YEARS
1250 HOURS

"Wait for it," said Flaps. "Wait. Wait."

The support column rolled forward, over the mines planted to the rear. Flaps flexed sweaty fingers on her Sterling, flicked the safety on and off. Glancing right, she saw the machine guns aimed down, the anti-armour crews wriggling into position to bring their M20 rocket launchers to bear on the heavy landcruisers. There were a couple of Carl Gustaf 84mm recoilless rifles too. Nearer to Flaps, Jazz had her hand on the detonator's plunger.

The column rolled past; Flaps turned her head, watching the lead vehicles closing in on the mines ahead. The earth looked smooth to her; you couldn't see where it had been disturbed. Not from up here, anyway – might be a different story from the cab of landcruiser. The sun was hot on her back.

She turned, looked at Jazz; the other girl's eyes met hers. Flaps looked back to the front of the column and –

A dull thud, and the earth shook; then three landcruisers flew up and crashed down. Smoke, flame, screams.

"Now!" Flaps yelled, nodding at Jazz. Another thud, and the mines to the rear took out the rearguard. Flaps scrambled to the bank and opened fire with the Sterling. Bren guns and GPMGs burst into life up and down the embankments on either side.

The .50 cals on the landcruisers opened fire, blasting showers of dirt from the banks. Screams, and half a dozen fighters went tumbling down. But a moment later the first salvo of 3½ inch rockets and 84mm rounds smashed into the convoy from either side. Explosions erupting up and down the column as they hit; smoke boiled out to fill the Devil's Highway.

Sud screamed over the battle as he fired the Sten in long, ragged bursts. He didn't even realise when it was empty, just kept pulling the trigger till Beak stopped shooting and punched his shoulder, shouted at him to reload. He ducked down – didn't need her to tell him this time – and fumbled a new clip into place as Beak shook her head and fired three rounds through the thickening smoke, knocking a machine gunner back out of his landcruiser.

Flaps emptied the Sterling's magazine in a burst at one of the surviving vanguard 'cruisers: the machine gun crew collapsed. She changed the clip, flung one of the ropes over the side.

The remaining 'cruiser from the vanguard roared forward, shunting one of its wrecked fellows out of the way, and shot forward. Another blast of smoke and soil exploded upward as Flaps swung down the rope – another band of mines, laid further up.

"Come on!" she shouted. Hit the ground, fired. More rebels jumped down with her. She ran for one of the heavy cruisers, tearing a door open and throwing a grenade inside.

The Battletruck
1315 hours

"And you've heard nothing else?"

"After the initial distress call, ma'am, no. We've tried to regain contact, but nothing. Should we keep trying?"

Jarrett shook her head. "They're gone." She took a deep breath. "We have the convoy's last known position?"

"We do, ma'am, yes."

"Then inform REAP Command – the loss of the column, and approximate location. That'll be where the rebel force in the Wastelands is based. Check ETA on the next support column, request a heavier escort, and recommend a strike on that position. That's all."

Jarrett looked down at the chart when the radio operator had gone. From outside came the rattle of far-off gunfire.

The Devil's Highway

The Walker strode along the top of the high embankment now, relishing the view of moors and ruins alike.

From behind came the clatter of gunfire, the dull thump of grenades. It turned, looked back, saw smoke rising in the distance.

Battle, pain, death. All irrelevant.

It turned away, walked on.

Bowkitt
1320 HOURS

Flaps stumbled along the road, weaving like she was pissed. Smoke boiled up, made her cough and choke. Bodies on the ground – open eyes, bloody mouths. She tugged the empty mag out of her Sterling. Her legs shook.

"Fucking yes!" Beak yelled. "Cop that you Reaper cunts!" She rocked with laughter, hugged Sud around the shoulders; he grinned and cried at the same time, shaking from the after-effects of the adrenaline. If anyone noticed the wet stain at his crotch, no-one said. He wouldn't be the first to do that in battle, or worse.

Whoops, cheers; the sound grated in her skull. "Fucking shut it!" shouted Flaps. "We're not done here. Find the artillery and fuck it up. Owt we can't shift, we cripple. No fucker's gonna use it on the Fort. Now crack on!"

A moment's stunned silence. Sud and Newt blinked at her; Beak sighed. Jazz pinched the bridge of her nose and nodded. "She's right," she said. "Let's get to it."

Ashwood Village
1322 HOURS

Gevaudan ran past the war memorial towards the wall. Stone chips flew from the parapet; a defender fell screaming, hit the ground with a dull crunch. He forced himself to look: no, it wasn't Helen. He scanned the parapet for her.

Gevaudan glanced behind him: a platoon of fighters were charging after him, but they were behind. He was almost there, but alone. Perhaps that would be enough.

Gevaudan bounded up the steps, head down, as bullets cracked past, drawing the Brownings as he reached the battlements. Bodies lay crumpled before him, blood soaking into the planks; all the defenders at this end of the wall were down. Movement to his left; a Reaper climbing over the parapet, a knife between her teeth. Gevaudan shot her in the forehead; she slumped forward.

"To me!" he shouted.

More Reapers further down the parapet. Gevaudan fired again, both guns; two men fell. A bullet plucked his coat-sleeve; he fell to one knee, firing the pistols empty; by then, the remaining defenders were overbearing the Reapers.

Gevaudan drew his revolvers, fired over the parapet at the Reapers climbing up, ducking back a moment later as a hail of fire spewed up at him from ground level. But now Wakefield and her defenders were firing down too with Brens and SMGs, and further reinforcements were charging up the steps.

Rocks went over the side, pots of boiling oil, and the Reapers fell or jumped. Some lay in broken heaps on the ground; the rest ran or were dragged back towards their lines.

Gevaudan ignored the cheering, reloading his pistols. A helmet clattered on the floor. It had fallen from the Reaper he'd shot; her dark hair was wet with blood. Gevaudan turned her over; the face staring back up at him seemed ridiculously young. *And still the young ones march.*

Helen was beside him. She swayed; he reached out, steadied her. "Thanks," she said, then ran towards one of the wounded.

"*What passing-bells for those who die as cattle?*" murmured Gevaudan. He scratched up a handful of bloody grit and laid it over the dead Reaper's eyes.

THE BATTLETRUCK
1335 HOURS

"Why are they falling back, Majid? I didn't order a retreat."

"They've taken eighty percent casualties already, Colonel. Even if they could get up the damned wall, they'd never hold it."

Jarrett punched the chart table, till the pain in her knuckles made her stop. She could arrest Majid, execute him – but no, that was a stupid idea. He was loyal, and an excellent second. History was full of leaders who'd turned on their own when their fortunes fell. She wouldn't be among them.

"Your orders, ma'am?" said Majid. "Ma'am?"

"I can't go back," she muttered to herself. What would wait for her if she did, in defeat? Demotion, disgrace; most likely, Winterborn would have her in front of a firing squad. Helen. Helen was taking everything away from her, again.

She looked up, and they stood across the table from her: Tom and Mandy, Mum and Dad. But not Helen, of course, because Helen wasn't dead. If they had Helen with them, maybe they'd go.

"Yes," said Tom. "But you knew that, didn't you, Nicola? It's her, or it's you."

Jarrett closed her eyes; when she opened them again, no-one was there. She took a deep breath and reached for the intercom. "Dr Kellett?" she said.

CATCH CENTRAL

"Dr Kellett?" When there was no answer, Jarrett's voice grew louder, sharper. "*Dr Kellett.*"

Kellett rocked in his swivel chair, hugged himself and giggled.

"Dr Kellett!"

He sighed; you could only make Jarrett's kind sweat for so long before they kicked down your door holding a gun. He reached for the intercom. "Yes, Colonel?"

Jarrett could hear the laughter in his voice. Loathsome little bastard. But that didn't matter, for now at least. "Get your toy soldiers out of their box," she said.

8.

"Whew," said Cov. "That was fucking noisy."

"Yeah." Mackie laughed.

There were two explosions on the road below; grenades, disabling a Reaper trebuchet. Three rebels took saws and axes to a ballista; two others pounded spikes into an artillery piece's barrel. They looted the landcruisers of their ammunition and explosives, then drove them away or spiked their boilers.

A woman was shouting, Cov could hear her even in the library dome. Her small lean figure clung to a rope halfway up an embankment; reddish hair gleamed in the light. "Flaps can kick arse, can't she?"

"Kick mine any time," Mackie sniggered. "Or owt else she wants to do with it."

Cov grimaced. "Don't even want to fucking *think* about that, mate."

He looked back down to the road. The last of the fighters were climbing back onto the embankments. Guns were reloaded, bolts pulled back. The wait began again.

THE WAR ROOM, ASHWOOD FORT
1340 HOURS

"Alannah?" Hei called. "Rook Actual for you, Scramble Two."

Alannah picked up the mic. "Osprey Actual."

"Yo," said Flaps. "We blocked the fuckers."

"'Blocked the fuckers'?"

"Fucking posho," she heard Flaps mutter. "First support column – we got them."

"Casualties?"

"All of them."

"*Your* casualties."

"Eight dead," said Flaps. "Ten wounded. Four serious. Rest can still fight."

"Okay," said Alannah. "Good work." She cut Flaps off. "Phoenix, this is Osprey, come in. Helen!"

WALL ONE

Helen leant on the parapet, slipped off her helmet, stumbled over to one of the wounded. She helped load the moaning boy onto a stretcher, met Gevaudan's eyes as he looked at her, then out across the wall towards the Reaper lines.

"Here." A young girl, no more than twelve, lugging a basket; she took out a bread roll and a hunk of smoked meat, held it out to Helen.

Helen realised she was starving; all she'd eaten that day had been part of a tin of pemmican on the drive to Listening Post 23. "Thanks," she said. She took the food and bit into it. Someone offered a water canteen; she gulped at it to wash the bread and meat down.

Below, the Reaper dead were everywhere, scattered below and before the walls; wrecked landcruisers smouldered and further down the slope about half the medium 'cruisers lay wrecked or overturned by artillery hits. The rest were gone, pulled back in the retreat.

Wakefield shouted orders, getting the dead and wounded cleared away, damaged weapons righted, calling for replacements to use them. She clutched a bread roll in one hand, split open and the meat pushed inside. Helen smiled; the tribes had finally rediscovered the sandwich.

As the whining in her ears from the explosions and gunfire faded, she heard her name called.

"Phoenix? Phoenix! Will you come in, Helen, for fuck's sake?"

Alannah. Helen picked up the communicator. "I'm here, Osprey," she said. "They've fallen back."

"I *know*," Alannah said. "Now will you please, *please* get your fucking arse back to the War Room where you can direct the bloody battle *properly?*"

Helen breathed out. Under the ground while the battle raged, and if the walls fell – she shook her head, opened her mouth, but a hand fell on her arm. She looked up: Gevaudan. "She's right," he said. "You're needed there."

That was all he said, but his eyes never left hers and she couldn't look away. Or deny what he'd said. Besides, she could feel the rush of the speed ebbing; she'd need a couple more of Alannah's pills. "Okay." She bowed her head. "Let's go." *Take me to my grave.*

She followed the Grendelwolf to the steps, heading back down to the courtyard and the village.

Wall Two

"Osprey for you," said the radio operator.

Danny leant against the parapet, watching the defenders on Wall One clear the bodies and wreckage away. Nearby, on the church tower, Scopes and Trex lay with their rifles. "Harrier," he said.

"Danny? You okay?"

"I'm fine," he said. "Been stuck back here doin' fuck-all, haven't I?"

"They hit the first Reaper support column on the Devil's Highway," Alannah said. "Some casualties, but they're okay. I thought you'd want to know…"

Oh shit. "What?"

"Flaps is okay. She's fine."

Danny breathed out. "Thanks," he said.

"Just doing my job."

Neither spoke; seconds past. "Well," he said. "Thanks again."

"Yeah," she said. "Osprey out."

"All good?" said Harp.

"Yeah." Danny knew he should be thinking of Flaps, but he was thinking of another face instead, framed by silver hair.

Wall One
1345 HOURS

The smoke on the hillside was thinning, and in it shadows moved. Wakefield moved close to the parapet, fumbled for the binocs.

As she did, the first of them walked out of the smoke, grey and helmed and masked; even without the binocs she knew what they were, but she looked anyway.

"Catchmen!" she shouted.

Bolts pulled back on the machine guns; Wakefield cocked her Thompson, but her gut was tight. Special weapons, Helen had said – they needed something special, to stop these. But what did they have here?

"Open fire!" she shouted, and the guns thundered. They didn't miss: the bullets hit and made the Catchmen jerk and dance. But only briefly: now, on they walked. A couple of mines blew, flinging Catchmen upward. But seconds after they hit the ground they got back up – even one Wakefield had seen lose its legs rose, its legs restored – and on they came.

They reached the fire-ditches as the bullets thudded into them without effect, stepped over the edge, fell into the flames. Then climbed straight out again, not even beating out the flames that flickered on them.

Someone on the battlements screamed.

"They won't go down," Filly shouted, sighting with the Bren gun and triggering a long burst into one Catchman, with no effect other than to slow it briefly down. "Why won't they fucking *die?*"

And Wakefield had no answer, nothing she could say. Cold dread froze her, held her throat so she couldn't speak, at the sight of them as they reached the wall and climbed, talons sinking in, heads tilting so they grinned up with their wide mouths full of teeth.

She remembered the Styr of Hobsdyke, the tunnels under Graspen Hill, and that was bad enough, but these were somehow worse. "Keep firing!" she shouted.

The first Catchman came over the walls, flung a Bren gunner from the battlements and slashed another's throat with its claws. The others followed. One came towards Filly; Wakefield thrust the girl behind her, blasted it in the chest with her Thompson. It staggered back, then grinned and screeched. She fired again into that red, open mouth; it choked and gagged – a moment's hope – then spat the bullets out to rattle on the floor.

A Fox tribe fighter didn't run – but these things couldn't die, so what else to do? Shame at her fear, but Filly was warm behind her, would stand and die if Wakefield didn't make the call. "Fall back!" she shouted, turning from the thing to run, seizing Filly's wrist to drag her after her. "Retreat!"

9.

"Thought you were supposed to be back in the War Room," Danny said, as Helen climbed onto the battlements.

"So did Alannah," said Gevaudan, before Helen could even speak.

"Yo, Creeping Death," said Danny.

Helen bit the inside of her cheek so as not to laugh – but then she heard the screams. She spun, looked towards Wall One – saw the defenders charging down the steps to get away from the grey figures stalking along the walls.

"Oh Christ," she said. She turned, grabbed Danny's sleeve. "Get someone to the armoury – get the bullets off Zaq. The special ones – the iron ones. And give me twenty of your men."

Danny nodded. "Harp, you're with Helen. Take A and E Sections with you. Lish, grab a couple of big 'uns and leg it to the armoury."

"Shouldn't you be in the War Room?" said Gevaudan.

"We've got to try and hold them here," said Helen. If they didn't, it was death anyway: better beneath an open sky than in a sterile tomb.

"Then you'll need help," he told her.

The yellow wolf's eyes were calm. She breathed out. "All right. Let's go."

They ran down the stone steps, past the church and down into the village. Wakefield and her team were well ahead; the Catchmen were only just starting down the steps on Wall One. After all, when you couldn't be killed, what was the rush?

"Wakefield!"

The Fox woman stared at her, wild-eyed. "They won't die," she said. "They won't –"

"I know." The Catchmen marched in a straight line, like an arrow aimed at the Fort, as they came down off the wall. "You and Gevaudan – circle back back through the village. Go round. Take up positions. They'll be sending Jennywrens over the wall after these things. They *will* die."

Wakefield bared her teeth. "And you?"

"Try and hold these off. If the right bullets come in time –"

"And if they don't?" said Gevaudan.

"We're short on options either way. Now fucking move, the pair of you!"

WALL TWO

1408 HOURS

Danny gripped the Lanchester, so hard his fingers hurt. Below, Helen and her people made for the village square as Wakefield, Gevaudan and their fighters peeled away. Some knelt, some stood, some lay down as the Catchmen trudged on.

All of them were fucked. No doll in his pocket this time; hadn't even had a chance to light a candle. Then again, he'd forgotten that before and lived. Once or twice.

"Boss?" Lish, along with four men carrying two crates. Danny pulled the lid off one. Arrowheads and magazines – the bullets were hard grey iron with something carved on each. He knew what it'd be, of course.

Danny pulled out two SLR magazines. "Get the rest to the village square," he said. "Now. Not you, Lish." The medic stopped, blinked at him. "We're gonna need you here if they don't hold."

Clutching the mags, Danny ran for the steps.

The Battletruck
1409 hours

The phone on the edge of the chart table rang. One of Jarrett's aides snatched it up. "Lieutenant Wong, ma'am."

Jarrett held out a hand. "Lieutenant."

"Good news, Colonel. We've reached the wall."

"What? Already?"

"We broke through into the cave system very quickly. There was just one tunnel, leading up the hill. Forks off in multiple directions from here on in, otherwise we could get further under the complex, but –"

"But you're definitely under the outer wall now?"

"We are. The sound's a lot more muffled, so there's something big and heavy overhead."

Jarrett was smiling; the expression felt so unfamiliar it almost hurt. "Excellent work, Wong. Excellent. Simply stellar. How quickly can you mine it?"

"We can set enough shaped charges for the job within an hour at the most, maybe sooner. The hardest part is done."

"Get on it immediately. Inform me if there's anything you need."

"Yes, Colonel."

Village Square, Ashwood
1411 hours

Helen shouldered the Sterling as the Catchman advanced. Slow, steady, relentless.

She pulled back the bolt. Clicks rang out as the rest of her group did the same. Her eyes felt gritty; she didn't feel as fast or nimble as she had minutes before. The Catchmen were grinning, their dim eyes glowing dully as they flexed their claws.

Helen's vision cleared; her heart quickened. Good old-fashioned adrenaline, coming back into play. "Fire at will!" she shouted, triggering a burst that hit one in the face. It reeled, but came on. The air thundered with gunfire and Catchmen twitched and jerked, but on they came.

Harp knelt beside her, fired a two-round burst from his Thompson, then another, and another. Helen fired, aimed, fired again. Acquire the next target. Fire a burst. Acquire another target. Don't think of the long game, of whether the bullets will come in time, of what happens when they reach you. Just think of the next shot.

Aim and fire. Aim and fire.

And on the Catchmen came.

St Martin de Porres Church
1413 hours

Danny legged it up the church tower steps, legs aching, lungs burning, kicked the door at the top wide. Two rifles swung towards him. "Whoah!" He dropped to his knees, gasping. "Here." He ran to them, held out a mag apiece.

"What's this?" said Scopes, taking one. "Magic bullets?"

"Bullets that'll stop those," Danny said, nodding down towards the village square. "Load up and do what you can."

Scopes wrinkled her nose, then shrugged. "Furry muff." She pulled the magazine out of her rifle, jacked the bolt to eject the chambered round, and slotted the new one in.

Trex took the other one. "You okay, mate?" Danny said.

A small smile. "Not bad." Trex changed magazines, cocked his rifle.

"We're on it," said Scopes. They turned away from him, both aiming over the church parapet. Conversation over; like Danny wasn't there any more. He was used to it by now – Scopes' way, and Trex had picked it up off her – but it still pissed him off.

He'd done all he could though; he ran back down the tower stairs.

VILLAGE SQUARE, ASHWOOD
1419 HOURS

"Coming through!"

Two fighters ran up – big men, heavy – carrying a crate. One pulled off the lid. "Load up."

There were magazines ready-loaded – for rifles, Sterlings, Thompsons, Stens. Helen grabbed two, pulled the one in the Sterling free and shoved one of the replacements in. A Crow warrior plucked the flint arrowhead from one of her shafts, pushed an iron one into place. Harp cocked his Thompson, sticking a spare clip through his belt, lips moving. Helen caught part of the Fox Tribe's battle prayer: *"...bring us victory, slay our enemies; if we die, carry our souls."*

"Look out!" someone screamed. Helen whirled, pulling back the bolt, as the Catchman swarmed into the square.

10.

Scopes sighted on the war memorial, tracked sideways to where Helen and the others were loading their weapons with the new bullets. Howling, the Catchmen closed in.

Scopes centred the 3LR's cross-hairs on the lead Catchman's helmeted head, and squeezed the trigger.

A neat hole appeared in the helmet. The Catchman screeched; pink slurry boiled from its mouth, from its eyes too as the lenses over them shattered, and it pitched forward. Scopes aimed again. Maybe it took a headshot, maybe not. She shot another Catchman in the chest; it howled, blood frothing through its fangs, then fell to its knees and toppled sideways.

She aimed and fired again, then again. She heard Trex fire too; more Catchmen fell, but there were over a hundred of them, and they kept coming.

Helen flicked the Sterling's fire selector to semi automatic. "Single shots only!"

She fired; a Catchman doubled over, clutching its stomach. Something hissed through the air and another fell, an arrow in its throat. Then a ragged volley rang out – rifles, submachine guns – and a dozen of them went down. Harp fired three shots, not even seeming to aim; each time, a Catchman fell.

The Sterling wasn't a long-range weapon, but at this distance it didn't have to be, especially with the Catchmen so closely packed. Helen sighted, fired again, and started forward.

WALL ONE
1425 HOURS

Gevaudan slipped from the outskirts of the village, ran for the wall and leapt. The wall's surface was jagged and uneven, chunks of stone and concrete jutting from the mortar; handholds and toeholds were easy to find.

Movement above: Gevaudan pressed against the wall, looked up to see the .50 cals swivel to point inwards.

Above him, the guns fired. Windows burst in the abandoned houses across the village. A body fell out from one; one of Wakefield's fighters. Submachine guns fired back from inside one house. The .50 cals thundered again: A haze of dust and chipped stone swallowed the house.

Gevaudan took a deep breath, fixed his eyes on the parapet above, and summoned the Fury.

Everything was too slow for him. He had to be at the top *now*. His palms were cut and bleeding, but that didn't matter: they'd heal soon enough. He went up like a lizard over rock.

Carson tried to breathe, tasted blood and dirt. She coughed, retched, rolled onto her side, hacked up spittle and blood.

Fuck. The wound in her chest throbbed. She was weak as a kitten. There was blood inside her uniform; when she moved it gushed out of the bullet hole.

Fox. She twisted round, stared at him. The mocking smile was gone from his slack and hanging mouth. The mess of pink brain and darkening, clotting blood inside his shattered crown looked sticky now rather than wet, the blood drying. Flies crawled over it, and his open eyes.

Carson twisted away. *Bastards.* Yes, Fox had been a cunt, she'd hated him, always taunting her – but he'd been one of hers.

Her rifle – it was where she'd left it, propped ready, the barrel hidden by the dirt. She dragged herself to it, tucked the stock into her shoulder, sighted on the battlements.

WALL ONE

Gevaudan swung over the parapet, landing cat-like on all fours beside a .50 cal's crew. The Reaper feeding the ammunition belt stared, mouth opening. Gevaudan backhanded him across the face, felt his neck snap. The machine gunner reached for a pistol; Gevaudan grabbed him, threw him over the wall. A thin scream, then a thud.

Something hit his shoulder; he spun, snatching up a fallen Sten. Along the parapet, a Reaper aimed a rifle at him; another tried to bring the .50 cal to bear. Gevaudan swept a short burst across them both; as they fell, he whirled to fire the other way along the parapet.

Figures came into a focus. A looming shape filled the scope: long black hair, a black coat. Something strange about him, something wrong, even before she saw the yellow eyes.

Grendelwolf. That would be something, to end him. But with one shot, even to the head? They could sustain appalling damage and still live. No; this would be her last shot. She'd make it count.

WALL ONE
1430 HOURS

Running feet on the steps below – Wakefield's fighters, coming in.

Four Reapers remained at the far end of the wall; three fell to a long burst that emptied Gevaudan's Sten. He ran at the last of them, as the Reaper tried to reload his gun –

The Reaper screamed once; then Gevaudan's claws slashed his throat. Hot blood sprinkled Gevaudan's face; he ran to one of the GPMGs mounted on the parapet, aiming down at the advancing Reapers, sick and shaking as the Fury ebbed. He checked his shoulder with his fingers; they came away bloody. He fingered the wound; it was shallow, a slash, and already closing. His palms were already healed. His body, endlessly erasing the damage it sustained, the better to wreak it on those of others.

"Trebuchet, ballista, cannon!" Wakefield shouted; her surviving defenders ran to the artillery.

Approach to Ashwood Fort

A tiny, bird-faced woman – some sort of tribal – ran back and forth shouting orders. Command of some kind; Carson stroked the trigger, tracked along.

The ground juddered. Shouts. Boots thundering. The whistle of projectiles through the air; as Carson reached the lip of the trench, she saw a trebuchet load of rock and metal smash into a group of Jennywrens and wipe them away in a flurry of corpses and body parts. A ballista bolt sang down, smashed into an oncoming landcruiser.

Carson coughed blood again. *Fucked.* She was dying. But she wasn't done.

Wall One

"Machine guns!" called a voice; as he slumped against the parapet, shaking from the Fury's after-effects, Gevaudan saw Helen run onto the battlements; the men and women with her grabbed at the machine guns, bringing them back around to aim towards the attackers. Standing up straight, she pointed to one of the GPMGs. "That one too." Harp ran to it, swung it around and pulled back the bolt.

No helmet, standing upright on the walls – was she mad? Gevaudan started towards her; he'd drag her to the War Room bodily this time, if he must.

Approach to Ashwood Fort

More movement on the walls. Carson tracked back again. A flash of red hair. She brought the gun back to bear, focused.

The face that filled her sights: a pale oval, grey-eyed, red-haired. She'd never met this woman, but knew her – who and what she was. An enemy. *The* enemy. They'd remember her, for a final kill like this.

The headset. She pushed the transmit button. "Mower, this is Scythe Four. Have visual on Target Alpha." Blood in her throat again; she gagged, coughed. "Mower, do you read?"

THE BATTLETRUCK
1432 HOURS

Jarrett took the mic. Everything was suddenly still; nothing else seemed to matter.

"Lieutenant Wong for you, ma'am," called another radio op.

Jarrett raised a hand for silence, brought the mic to her lips. "Say again, Scythe Four."

The voice was raw, in pain, but focused, taut. "Repeating: visual on Target Alpha. Permission to fire."

Helen. It wouldn't be doing the job herself, but it would be the next best thing. "You're cleared, Scythe Four. Take her."

APPROACH TO ASHWOOD FORT
1433 HOURS

Carson centred the cross-hairs on Helen Damnation's forehead, took up first pressure on the trigger. Then the face went out of focus, blurring. No. No. *Not this, not now. Let me have this at least.*

The face unblurred, then blurred again. Now, quickly, before she lost consciousness.

Carson fired.

WALL ONE

The crack was loud in Helen's ear; she flinched, stumbled sideways, blinking. What? She looked around? Then the saw Gevaudan charging towards her, mouth opening wide to shout, and she realised: a bullet.

Had to get down, had to hide – but everything was suddenly so sluggish and slow. The speed wearing off, burned out of her system, perhaps, or all the exhaustion and strain of the fight with the Catchman crashing in on her – catching up, ha-ha. And she moved to throw herself down, but everything was so slow, took so impossibly long, and –

APPROACH TO ASHWOOD FORT

Carson refocused through the sight. Still there. The bitch was still there. And realisation was dawning on her face. She'd duck, and she'd be lost.

Pull back the bolt. Eject the round. Chamber a new one. Sight.

Quickly. No time.

Helen was starting to sink down. Carson sighted again, cross-hairs on her temple, and fired.

WALL ONE

Helen heard nothing this time. What felt like a booted foot crashed into the side of her head, so hard she felt things break.

No pain, only weakness – weakness and fear, because the force of the blow, the sensation of things broken and shattered, told her the damage was serious, devastating. Mortal.

Her legs collapsed. She hit the ground. Blood on her face. Fluid trickling from her ears. The world around her flickered and greyed. Was gone.

APPROACH TO ASHWOOD FORT

Carson saw the red-haired woman drop, glimpsed the Grendelwolf fly across her sights, bellowing, to dive upon her. Too late.

Everything dimming now, but at least she'd seen that. She reached up to her headset, pushed transmit. "Mower One. Scythe Four. Target Alpha. Kill. Confirmed."

Carson's voice rattled in her throat. Her hands slipped from her gun and her limbs went limp; she slid down into the welcoming earth.

THE BATTLETRUCK
1434 HOURS

"Scythe Four? Scythe Four, come in." But there was only silence.

Jarrett lowered the mic. Kill. Confirmed. Helen. Dead. "Yes!" she shouted it. Everyone in the chart room jumped, staring at her.

Jarrett stared back. "Carry on," she said.

"Ma'am?"

"What?"

"Lieutenant Wong."

"Oh yes." Jarrett held out her hand for the telephone. "This is Jarrett."

"Colonel? Charges are in position. We can bring down the wall."

Jarrett was grinning, so hard her face hurt; first Helen, now this. No need for pills now: high on life. She'd always known it: kill Helen and it would all fall apart, the whole damned rebellion. "Then do it, Lieutenant. Blow the wall. Now."

"Yes ma'am."

Jarrett handed back the phone, picked up a personal communicator, strode outside, up through the camp to the barbed wire. There was the hill, and there was the wall. She raised the communicator to her lips and watched.

Thump. The earth shivered underfoot. The walls trembled. And then a great section of the outer wall cracked and shuddered and sank down into a rising billow of smoke and dust.

The rumble of the blast rolled over the camp. In its wake, as tiny and meaningless as the ant-like shapes that scurried on the wall or fell from it, came their thin piping screams.

And it was the sweetest of music to hear.

Jarrett pushed the transmit button. "This is Mower Actual. All units – attack. Repeat, all units. Attack."

PART THREE
FOR THOSE WHO FALL
IN DARKNESS

1.

Knee-deep standing water; swirling mist that sank through clothes and skin to the bone. Mosquitoes and midges swarmed in the air, but they left the Walker untroubled; the twisting clouds they hung in even parted as it passed.

Its robes were sodden; they and the ooze beneath the water clogged and slowed its steps. But on it came, straight-backed, undeterred.

Over to its left was the distant trickle of water; the river. And to its right...

The Walker half-turned, peered through the mist. The hiss and clank of landcruiser engines echoed through it, from the road. Another convoy, on its way. The Reapers and the rebels: games for children. Its game was a larger one by far.

There was solid ground ahead: the Walker climbed onto it and continued on its way.

"Clear the way!"

They scattered from Gevaudan's path gratifyingly enough. One advantage of being a Grendelwolf, at least. He bulled down the corridor, Helen in his arms, shoved in through the doors.

The sight brought him up short. The sick bay occupied half of the upper floor; normally only a few of its hundred beds were occupied, but now every one was in use, and most of the floorspace too. Nurses herded any walking wounded to the doors, guiding them out to make room. Another nurse ran up. "What do we have?"

"Gunshot wound to the head." Gevaudan's voice came out level, calm, as if unconnected to the rest of him. "It's – it's Helen."

"Jesus," said the nurse. "Nestor. *Nestor!*"

"Not now!"

"It's urgent."

"Fuck. One minute."

"We don't have a minute," said Gevaudan. Helen's eyes were open and blinking; blood ran from her nose, and her head – through the blood he saw white bone and –

"Okay, what?" Nestor swerved around the bodies; tall, athletic and black, hands and smock bloody, surgical mask hanging around his neck, bald head a-gleam with sweat. Gevaudan held Helen up to him. "Oh Lord Jesus," he said. "Okay – there."

A body was being lifted from a trestle table, laid on a heap with others – the porters couldn't drag them away as fast as they mounted up. Gevaudan laid Helen out; Nestor pulled up his mask and leant in.

"Okay." He pointed to the straw-coloured liquid seeping from her ears. "CSF."

"What?"

"Cerebro-spinal fluid. That's not good."

"She's been in shot in the head."

"I guessed. What was it? Pistol, rifle?"

"Rifle, I think. A sniper."

"Okay. I need water, here!" Nestor took a narrow-spouted jug from a nurse, rinsed the wound. Gevaudan hissed at the sight of the damage; the rent in Helen's scalp, the cracked white bone. But only bone. For a second he'd thought her brains were hanging out, but it had only been a ragged flap of scalp.

"She must have moved as the sniper fired," Nestor said. "It didn't hit her full-on, just a glancing blow. Otherwise she'd be dead."

"You mean she'll be all right?"

"I mean she has a chance, Gevaudan." Nestor's eyes met his. He was a good man; a barely-qualified GP when the War came, he'd lived by his skills ever since. It had kept him in demand, and as well-provided for as a non-Reaper could be: not many men in their forties were as fit as him. Gevaudan had to remain calm; Helen could be in no better hands. "CSF's never a good sign. We're talking a skull fracture at least, possibly an extradural haematoma."

Helen's eyes closed. "Is she —"

"Still breathing. Gevaudan, you need to step back so we can deal with this."

"Yes. Yes, of course." Gevaudan backed away till he was up against the wall, leaning against it. His legs shivered under him, then gave way; he crashed to the ground.

"Whoah!" Nestor started towards him. "What the hell?"

"I'll be all right." Gevaudan clenched his still-trembling hands. "Just the Fury. Burns up a lot of energy. Need food."

"Well, I can't let you eat the patients," said Nestor. "Or any of my staff. Even the lazy ones. We've got some cans of pemmican, though, if that would –?"

Gevaudan nodded.

"Okay, then." Nestor motioned to a nurse. "Sort that out, yeah? Now if you don't mind, I've got work to do."

Gevaudan nodded, eyes on the pale figure on the table as Nestor and his team crowded in.

231

To walk the Road again, Helen found, was almost a relief; she was free here of the lives that depended on her, the dangers. Funny: on this long, dark path, separated only from the dark beyond by the white bone cobbles that edged it, she felt almost safe.

"Safe?"

She looked up. In the distance she saw what she always did: the ruined City, its broken towers. But in front of her was Frank, his pale, bird-claw hand tangled in Belinda's matted hair. He smiled, showing the thin sharp needles of his teeth. "That's new, if nothing else."

"Frank." Helen folded her arms. "Belinda."

"Hello, Mummy." She giggled. "Tick-tock, tick-tock, and... stop."

"That's right," said Frank. "It's the end of the lullaby. Here comes a candle to light you to bed..."

Belinda giggled again. "...and here comes a chopper to chop off your head."

"I'm not going with you."

Frank laughed. "What makes you think you have any say in it, Helen? You're in the sick bay with a bullet in your head and your heart's just stopped."

"For good?" said Helen. Frank might taunt, might slant the facts, but she was somehow certain he couldn't outright lie. The smile on his face soured, as if he'd tasted something foul.

"Most likely," he said at last. "You've a chance – but only the slimmest. Far easier to come with us, now. But for now, you have a choice." His mouth turned down. "You've fought a long time, Helen, all because of this idea that it's Winterborn's soul, not yours, that we should have. And you've caused yourself further suffering with this continual stubborn insistence that you have some sort of right to live. So," he smiled, "before taking another step, you must remember, Helen. Go through it all again. *Live* it all again. And then, if you can – try to claim you have a right to live."

Helen's legs felt weak. Jennywrens, Catchmen, Styr, Tindalos – she'd face them all together rather than that. Indeed, that was half the reason she fought.

"Or," Frank said, "you could just come with us, and have done." The two of them smiled: hungry, gloating.

"Fuck off," said Helen.

"Such language." Frank covered Belinda's ears. "Have it your own way, then. Belinda?" He clicked his fingers. They stepped sideways in opposite directions, over the cobbles at the edge of the road, and were gone.

The Black Road stretched on. You couldn't go back, Helen knew, only forward. She took a deep breath, and then the first step. There didn't seem to be anything in her way. Maybe it had all been a bluff. She took another step –

And the Road was gone, and there was only the dark.

WULFDEN, LANCASHIRE

MAY 17TH, THE YEAR OF THE WAR

ATTACK MINUS FIVE MINUTES

Warm sun; birds singing. A gentle buzz of bees. She stretches on the lawn, reading. A wide-brimmed hat shields the back of her neck and a light blouse her back and arms. being a redhead, she burns easily.

Sheep bleat somewhere, grazing on the hills.

The book is about World War Two. It belongs to her Dad; he's always reading them. Helen wants to be grown-up, so she reads them.

Something's changed. She doesn't know where the thought comes from, but she looks up. She gets up and walks, in sandals on the heat-brittle grass, across the garden to the flowerbeds and weeping willow, then down the short path through them to the drystone wall and back gate.

The hillside falls away in a slow drop to the valley below. Beyond, moor and valley and other, further hills, lush and green in the late spring sun. In the distance, the town where Dad works.

Nothing's different. But something, yes; *something's* changed. After a moment she realises it's not a sight but a sound. The birdsong's stopped.

And that's not all. A hush has fallen over the whole valley. She can see the fluffy white dots of the sheep on neighbouring hills, but they're silent. Even the buzzing of bees has stopped. There's a car engine somewhere, and a TV on in a neighbouring house, but that's all. Nothing that isn't man-made – *human*-made, Mum would say. All of nature, bird or beast, is still.

And then the new sound comes.

A clattering, hard, like metal on metal, growing to a thunder as a shadow darkens the sun. She can't see where they're all coming from, but they rise and fill the sky: birds, taking flight, hurtling away. Black clouds boil up from the eaves of houses, the size of hills, flying lower and weaving. One whizzes by her head: a bat.

The sheep mill and bound across the hills. The sky clears, warm and bright again. For a moment, all's still.

She stands there, blinking, thin and red-haired and pale, the quiet awkward girl with grey eyes that look long and hard into things. Boys tease her; Mum says it's because she's pretty and they'll all want to marry her one day, but she knows it's not just that. She scares them, a little, or something in her does; something they see in the grey of her eyes.

Her name is Helen Winter, and she is ten years old.

And now there is a new sound; faint and far-off, but with nothing in it of nature. Makes her tummy clench, like a fist. A sound she's heard before, but only in films – the ones Dad likes, about the war. A low, metallic wail that rises high, lingers and falls back down, only to rise again.

Wailing.

Sirens.

Air-raid sirens. But the war's over, isn't it? The Nazis are long gone and now the Germans are our friends. Why would –

"Helen!"

Mum's standing on the patio at the back of the house, the glass doors flung out wide. She's dark-haired, olive-skinned – always said Helen had her Dad's looks – but now she looks white. "Get inside!" she screams it. "Now, Helen! Now!"

Helen runs; she's scared now, doesn't know why. Mum's terror, maybe, infecting her. She runs in through the kitchen, where Mum's pulling open cupboards, flinging tins and dried noodles into carrier bags. "Under the stairs!" shouts Mum. She runs to the cupboard under the stairs, pulls open the door and throws out the hoover and a box of old books from the charity shop. "In there now, darling, please!"

Helen does as Mum says. Mum's crying. The sirens wail; from outside she hears shouts, then screams, a baby wailing. Terror in the air.

Mum runs to the door, shoves the already-splitting bags of food in, then scrambles inside and pulls the door shut. There isn't much room – this is where all the odds and sods go, the camping gear they don't use and the bottles of spring water Mum likes.

Helen's crying too; she can't help it. In a few minutes everything's gone strange, gone wrong. She doesn't understand the world around her any more, only knows there's threat and danger and her lovely Mum is scared and crying too. "What is it?" she says. "Mum? Mum, what is it?"

And Mum's opening her mouth to tell her, but then the edges of the shut door go white.

Light. It's brilliant, terrible light and Helen screams to see it. "Don't look!" Mum screams too, and grabs her, buries Helen's face in her chest. Warm; a soft, light sweater despite the heat. A smell of fabric conditioner and the faint, unique smell of Mum.

But even with her eyes shut she can see the glow, burning red then orange. Mum screaming in her ear. It fades, slowly, and Mum's grip slackens, but when Helen sits up and opens her eyes, blood-red floaters are printed on her sight.

"What's happening?" she sobs again. "Mum, what's happening?"

Mum hugs her close, tight. "Sh. Sh –"

And then the rumbling drowns her soft voice out, like thunder but it doesn't stop, it goes on and on and on, getting louder, louder, louder. The floor starts shaking under them; the paint-pots and jam-jars on the shelves above them rattle and clatter and one falls off, scattering old screws over them. Dust falls from the ceiling in a hissing stream, and with a splintering sound – barely audible over the rumbleroar – it cracks open. Helen's screaming into Mum's jumper, but she only knows that because it's her doing it. Mum grips her tight, but she could scream or sing or shout a poem for all Helen can hear.

The whole house shakes and rattles. Then a BANG and a splintering crash, a hiss like the tide on the shore and the howl of the outside wind, and Helen realises the patio doors have burst inwards, showering glass across the kitchen floor.

And the howling wind – where's that from? Only seconds before it was so still a day.

Mum grips Helen tight, and Helen grips her Mum. More things crash and break – dishes, glasses, mugs, shaken loose from their place. Still not understanding, not knowing if it'll ever end.

But at last, it does; the rumbleroar fades away, and there's only the house's creak and groan as it settles after the fight and makes up its mind whether or not to fall down. Only that, and the terrible wind. And the screams and sobbing from outside.

Mum sinks back from her, prayered hands rising to her mouth as she sobs, and Helen makes her move. Mum won't tell her, so she'll see. And she flings the cupboard door open, hears Mum scream her name but doesn't listen, heaves herself out and across the kitchen floor, glass crunching under her sandals, towards the shattered glassless doors and the wind that whips the garden, the black and red sky beyond.

She reaches the doors, stumbles out onto the grass. Far off, a cloud is rising, wide and thick, drawing up a column of smoke and flame beneath it. Like a mushroom on its stalk. A mushroom cloud.

The sky above is turning black as night, a stain that spreads across the sky. And on the ground below, there's fire – a fire that stretches miles and miles.

"Helen!" Mum grabs her, slaps her face – she's never done that – and drags her back inside. "*In!*" She slams the cupboard door behind them, grabs Helen's shoulders as she sobs, her own face streaked with tears. "I'm so sorry, sweetheart. I'm so sorry. But you mustn't go out. You mustn't. Not till Mummy says."

Helen's still trying to understand what she just saw, what it all means. It's too big. This – how much is gone, how much is changed? And she keeps thinking that the answer's *everything*, but her brain won't accept that, and yet it's true. This is war and it will have happened everywhere. She hugs Mum tight and Mum hugs her back, and they both sob. Then Helen realises it's not just sobs coming from Mum, but a name; she's saying a name over and over again. *Carl*, she's sobbing: *Carl*. That's Dad's name. But Dad isn't here, Dad's at work, at work in –

And then Helen realises where the mushroom cloud was rising from, and one small piece of the catastrophe, at least, becomes real for her.

WULFDEN, LANCASHIRE
31ST MAY, THE YEAR OF THE WAR
ATTACK PLUS FOURTEEN DAYS

"Stay here," says Mum, and pushes open the cupboard door.

Helen moves her face close to it, catches a whiff of air. The cupboard's hot and stinks. Even with the bin-bags tied and double-bagged, the stench of them escapes.

Mum's feet crunch in brick-dust and broken glass. Helen hugs herself and shivers; she's still in the shorts and long-sleeved t-shirt she wore in the garden two weeks ago. It feels like another time now – like one of those glossy never-neverlands they show in holiday adverts on the telly.

Showed. Not *show*. *Showed*. Because it *is* another time now; it *is* a neverland. Times like that will never come again, never can. The history of the world divides, as it did at Christ's birth. Then it was into BC and AD (or BCE and CE, but she still uses – *used* – the old term); now it's Before and After The Bomb.

Two weeks ATB.

Mum's footsteps fade. Silence. No. Helen decides she can't wait. She stands, fishes an old coat down from a hook. She sways; her legs tremble; she hasn't properly stood since the Bomb.

She pushes open the cupboard door and crunches her way over the kitchen to the patio.

The sky is black. She's never seen it so dark in the day, not even in the worst thunderstorm. The garden is dead, the grass wilted, the flowers lifeless, the willow bare.

She crosses the garden and looks out over the hills. Great black stains of sooty ash cover the land, and the air reeks of burning. Where the town was, where Dad worked, there's only a great black scar. She can't even see anything that might be ruins.

She should cry at the sight, at this new confirmation of her father's death, but doesn't. All her tears were shed in the past fortnight, all feeling wept out of her.

The wind blows moaning across the hills. A sheep bleats forlornly. And no bird sings.

Helen turns and goes back into the house, goes through the kitchen and living room to the open front door. From the street she hears someone sobbing hysterically

Mum stands at the front gate, leaning on the wall. The street is grey, sodden, the gutters clogged with grey-black ash washed down by the rain. Windows are shattered, and car windscreens. People stand outside like stone, staring at houses, cars, one another, the hills. All look grimy and tattered, dazed and dirty and grey in the dull light. All frozen. None able to understand.

Everything's dim – in the grey, overcast day, there are no lights. Helen flicks the light switch by the front door, on and off. Nothing. Of course there's nothing.

Mum turns and looks at her. "I told you to –"

"Internet's down," says a voice. Helen and Mum both turn and look. It's Mark, a boy from a few doors down the road. He's older than Helen – fourteen, fifteen? Might as well be a decade. Long hair, wears black; skulls and devils on his shirt.

"Did you think it wouldn't be?" says Mum.

Mark shrugs. "Laptop's been going on battery power. Most of them don't – they're all f – I mean, none of them are working."

"EMP," says Mum. "Electro-magnetic pulse. Wrecks anything electronic."

"Hoped I could maybe get a signal," says Mark. "Find out something. Anything." He shakes his head. "Telly's the same. Couple of radios are still working."

"Anything on those?" says Mum.

Mark shakes his head. "Not really. Picked up a couple of things, sound like voices, but it's all too faint."

"Pauline." Mrs Radcliffe shuffles along the street to Mark's side, takes her boy's arm. She's older than Mum but dresses like girls Mark's age. Hair dyed blonde. *Mutton dressed as lamb*, Mum said once, then made Helen promise not to repeat it. The hair looks wilted now, and grey. No make-up today. She looks old, even older than she is. "Helen."

"Jean," says Mum.

"What are we going to *do?*" A whining note in Jean's voice; Helen sees Mark wince.

"We work together," says Mum. She says it loud; her clear strong voice, her teacher's voice. Heads turn; the dazed, bedraggled people in the High Street turn and look at her. "We're lucky to be here," she says. "We're far enough away that we didn't get the worst of it. There's a stream for fresh water, clean water. There are sheep, wild game. There's land to grow food. We can cut wood and turf for heating."

People start drifting towards their house. Helen hugs herself against the cold, comes down from the top to see Mum better. Her little Mum, standing up and telling them. Because Mum knows things.

"We can make the best of it," Mum says. "Keep ourselves alive. Take care of each other – keep going till some help comes."

"What if it doesn't?" says Mark. "What if no-one comes? If there's no-one left?"

Everyone looks at Mum. Mum stands up straight, looks back at them all, and Helen swells with love and pride.

"We keep going," says Mum. "No matter what."

WULFDEN, LANCASHIRE

12TH APRIL, ATTACK PLUS FIVE YEARS

"Mrs Winter? Helen, is your Mum around?"

Helen sighs. "Yeah. Hang on." She shouts through the open front door. "Mum, it's Mrs Green!"

"Don't shout, Helen." Mum comes out. "Hello, Alice. Are you okay?"

Mrs Green shakes her head. "Bloody rats," she says. She's close to tears. "Got into the pantry and…" She's shaking.

"Go and see Mrs Thomas, then," says Mum. "Tell her I sent you and she'll sort you out with any spares. We've got rabbits, haven't we, Helen?"

Helen huffs.

"Helen?"

"Yeah. Two. Hanging up out back."

"Well, get one for Mrs Green, please."

"I caught those for us –"

"Helen."

She snorts and stomps through the house. Brief laughter from Mum and Mrs Green; she hears Mum say "Even nuclear war won't stop teenage tantrums" and she slams the wooden door put up where the patio was. Tantrum. She hates that word, hates having her anger dismissed like that.

There are no flowers in the garden any more. They all died in the long winter after the War. Helen doesn't like to remember that time; how close they all came to dying, how many they lost. Besides, it's a kitchen garden now: no room in it for anything they won't eat.

At the end of the garden are a pair of lean-tos. One houses the toilet – a plank seat with a bucket under it, which gets emptied out every other day and no doubt helps the vegetables grow. The other's for hanging game – rabbits, pheasants, ducks, geese – till it's ready to eat. In the house, it'd stink the place out; in the open, flies and scavengers would be all over it.

She's good at catching food. Snares and traps for rabbits and rats, and sometimes Mr Farnham lets her go hunting with one of his guns. He's got a .410 shotgun and a .22 rifle. Long as she brings him back something for the pot. She doesn't mind that. It's payment for the gun: pays for itself. But giving it away –

But that's wrong. Mum's always saying that. Me me me and self self self, that's why they had the War. Work together, look after each other, share what there is – that's the way. That's why they're still alive after five years of this, why there's food and shelter still, even though no fucker's shown up and –

Helen glimpses movement from the corner of her eye as she reaches for the lean-to door. When she turns round someone's standing at the garden wall, looking out over it. She tenses up, fists clenching, but then she sees the jeans and trainers, the blue sports jacket and the bald patch, and she relaxes: it's only Dad.

It's happened a dozen times over the last few years; Helen thought she was turning into a space-casualty till Mum told her it was happening to a lot of people. Everyone had lost someone they loved – lost the whole world they'd thought they'd known while they were at it. And there was no getting away from it, because everywhere you looked something reminded you. So people saw the dead. Ghosts. Ghostlighting, they called it Mum said she saw Dad too, from time to time.

Dad turns and smiles at her. "All right, our kid," he says. "Hey, you seen this? Might wanna have a look."

He points over the wall. By the time Helen's reached it, some time between one eyeblink and another, he's gone.

Helen looks over the back wall, and goes still.

Down below's the hills and the moors. Across the moors, a road, leading from the long-burned town where Dad's ashes lie to who knows where, branching off in two different directions as it nears Wulfden: one towards the hill, the other way off into the hills.

And along the hill road, towards Wulfden, a procession of cars are coming. Helen sees a dozen or so of them; they look like pick-up trucks. That's all she can see from here. For a second she thinks they'll turn off, head towards the burned town, but they don't – and why should they, after all, when it's plain to see there's nothing there and smoke's coming from Wulfden's chimneys?

Help's coming. After all these years, help's come.

Helen runs back across the garden, into the house with its smell of burning turves and peat. "Mum! Mum!"

"Helen! Where's that rabbit?"

"Mum, there are people coming!"

"What do you mean, people?"

"Cars!"

Mum and Mrs Green both stare at her. Cars? The last drop of petrol in the village ran out years ago.

"You can see them from the garden!" Helen says, pointing. "Go and look!"

She expects Mum to be happy, but Mum's frowning as she pulls her woollen shawl about herself and goes into the house.

*

The trucks roll into the village twenty minutes later.

Everyone's turned out to meet them, and at first there are cheers. But Helen feels hers die in her throat, and the second wave of cheers is much, much fainter than the first.

The trucks themselves are a bit weird. They hiss and clank. There's a big humpy thing behind the cabin and a chimney leaking smoke. Steam, Helen realises. The hump is a boiler. But that isn't it.

It's partly that each truck has a machine gun mounted on the flatbed at the back. But it's more the people who crew them.

They all wear uniforms of black leather, and black helmets with visors. They all have guns – rifles or submachine guns, and pistols on their hips. Soldiers would be one thing, but these don't look like any soldiers Helen's seen before. The trucks all have a symbol on them – looks like a wheatsheaf, or a bundle of sticks. A wheatsheaf, she realises, because under them are four letters: R.E.A.P. As the first of the soldiers, or whatever they are, jumps down, Helen sees he's got the same symbol on each shoulder, and something else below that: a flash of white material. Under that, six small letters: GENREN.

The guns are aimed – not at the villagers, but not away from them. Over their heads, where they can be swept down at a moment's notice.

A man climbs up on a truck's flatbed. Black hair, an eyepatch.

"Good afternoon," he shouts. His accent's pure South London; whoever he is, he's a long way from home. "My name is Major David Roth, Genetic Renewal Division, Reclamation and Protection Command, Regional Command Zone Seven."

"What?" someone says – Mark, still in his battered old leather jacket – and the soldiers glance his way. Roth eyes him for a moment, then turns back.

"There've been a lot of changes," he says. "The REAP Command incorporates all branches of government, the military, the security services, the lot. The country's divided into fifteen Regional Commands. You're in Number Seven."

Roth puts his hands on his hips. "Big chunks of the country are still radioactive. Contamination belts have settled everywhere. It's taken us – is still taking us – time to find where's safe and where isn't, and plot a way through. To reclaim what was lost. And then to protect it. It's taken us a long time to get to you, but we're here now. You're under the protection of the REAP Command. That means you're part of the country again. In exchange for a percentage of your produce."

"What percentage?" Helen nearly jumps when she realises it's Mum who's spoken. Hasn't she seen anything, the cold eyes of the soldiers? But of course she has. Her back's straight, chin up, arms folded. Defiant and proud. And Helen's proud, too, proud of her – but also scared. "How much of our produce?"

The black-uniformed men and women, hard-faced, unsmiling, are watching her. Roth looks down, with his one cold eye. "It'll be fair," he says. "The Reapers –"

"Reapers?"

"Yes, love, Reapers." Roth's voice is harder now, and Helen sees redness rising in his neck. "Reapers. Reclamation and Protection, see? The Reapers are putting this country back together. You contribute and we help you. See? Team effort. We're all in this together." He looks away from Mum. "Tell you what. Who's in charge here?"

"No-one's in charge," says Mum.

Roth looks back down at her. "I very much doubt that," he says.

"We work together," says Mum.

"I'm sure there's someone," says Roth. "Or several someones. A Steering Committee or whatever you bloody call yourselves. I'd like to discuss it with them, if I can. Brief out exactly what's gonna happen, work out exactly what the quotas and the deal are gonna be." He smiles. "This evening, say? Twenty hundred hours?"

His eyes meets Mum's.

No, thinks Helen.

After a moment, Mum nods.

*

"Mum, I don't think you should go."

"Of course I have to, love." Mum pulls the shawl around herself.

"*Mum*."

Outside, it's dark.

"We need to negotiate with him," Mum says. "Major Roth will have done this before. He's not a bad man, I'm sure. Just a little rough."

Mum's used to talking, to sweet reason. Let's all work together. Be reasonable. We can work it out. She's the best Mum in the world, and the best person Helen's ever known, but she's got one flaw. You'd think she wouldn't have it now, that no-one would, but she does. At heart, she believes, everybody, deep down, is good.

And even Helen knows – how could she not, in this fallen world? – that just isn't true. And those black uniforms, those helms and visors, those guns and cold dead eyes – when she looked at them she thought she knew how a rabbit felt when it stared down the barrel of her gun.

She opens her mouth to speak again, but Mum shushes her. "It'll be all right," she says. "Don't wait up. This might be a while."

She smiles once, goes out. The door clicks shut.

But Helen decides she *will* wait up. She won't sleep till she's seen Mum safely home. She sits by the kitchen table, a candle burning in an old jar for light, and reads. One of Dad's old books. Read it a dozen times now, till it's falling apart. Even World War Two seems comforting somehow; that other world, long lost.

Shots ring out: the *rat-tat-tat* of automatic weapons, then a succession of single shots. Helen cries out, jumps in her chair.
Mum.

She runs through the house, pulls open the door – and a helmed Reaper strides up the path, thrusting a gun at her.

"Back inside!" Helen opens her mouth and there's a click – the gun being cocked. "Back inside now!"

Helen slams the door in the Reaper's face, then flings herself down, in case the violence of the gesture brings a hail of shots in response. But it doesn't. Outside, there are shouts and screams, another burst of gunfire, then slamming doors and silence, but for a barking dog.

Helen crawls back against the wall and sits there, hugs herself. Hugs herself and waits for dawn.

WULFDEN, LANCASHIRE
13TH APRIL, ATTACK PLUS FIVE YEARS

She doesn't sleep that night, can't. When the light coming in through the plastic sheeting at the windows turns silver-grey,

245

the High Street starts coming to life; she can hear voices, sounds of movement.

She gets up slowly, goes to the door. Tries the handle and it opens.

In the street outside there's a Reaper. Might even be the one from last night. She motions to Helen. "Go on," she says. "Take a look."

The villagers are shuffling up the street, towards the village square. The first ones have already got there: Helen hears them wail, and she knows what she'll find. But in truth she always has, ever since those shots rang out. That knowledge has been her one companion, all through that long night.

The bodies lie in the village square, chests and stomachs torn across by burst-fire, foreheads and faces punctured by single rounds. Helen knows them all: there's Mrs Thomas, the greengrocer. Mr Farnham who lent her his guns. And there, in front of her, flies crawl into Mum's mouth, and across her open eyes.

*

"For the time being," Roth says, standing on his landcruiser's flatbed again, hands once more on hips, "this village will be under my direct control, as the senior serving officer of REAP Command. Any questions, concerns, issues or disputes should be brought to my attention."

Around Roth's 'cruiser are his Reapers, rifles held ready. No-one answers, much less comes forward. The village square is hushed; the bodies are gone, but the blood's still drying on the pavement. No-one knows where the bodies of the dead went: people asked, but were ignored.

"In due course," he added, "a permanent area commander will be appointed. Now, a word about that. REAP Command effectively combines the functions of the government, civil service, security services, the judiciary, the military, the police, under one umbrella. More efficient that way. Actually gets things done. So whoever takes charge will be a Reaper.

"However, it's easy to apply to join. And obviously there would be real advantages to having a local resident, with the associated skills and knowledge, in command here. So: REAP Command is recruiting, ladies and gentlemen. Those who serve in it get better conditions and rations than the rest, because they're doing the vital task of putting our country back together." Roth's eyes linger briefly on Helen. "It's open to all able-bodied citizens," he says. "If they impress me."

It's all she can do not to recoil; the meaning behind the words is bad enough, but the insult there is worse: that she'd let him fuck her – in her head, she uses the word, blunt and crude and brutal, because it's the truth – after he had Mum killed. But she gives nothing away; she's not stupid. She knows what will happen if Roth ever guesses how deep – and lethal – her hatred of him is.

But others? She can already see them glancing at one another. *Work together. Help each other.* All gone now. Instead: become a Reaper and get more than the rest. Creep to Roth and be rewarded with more power.

Me me me and self self self; that's what got us into this mess. Mum had never seemed so right: the villagers would stab each other in the back to curry favour with Roth. Not enough that he murdered Mum. He has to destroy everything she built.

No-one comes near Helen's house as the day wears on, as though she's tainted. They all remember how Mum spoke up, the voice of resistance. They act as if it's catching.

The house; she can't stay in it. The silence, the space and emptiness of it will drive her mad. She goes for a walk, passes the pub, listens by the wall of the old beer garden where the locals huddle, gulping the strong foul beer Wendy the landlady brews out back.

"Heard a couple of 'em talking," she hears one voice say. She knows it: it's Mark.

"Yeah," says another one. It's high-pitched, with a snuffly quality to it: Mark's mate Joe. "So what?"

"They're not getting it all their own way," says Mark. "Said there's a resistance."

"Resistance?"

"Yeah."

"Where?"

"Out in the Wastelands."

"The fuck's that?"

"West, that's all they said."

"Well, that's not fucking much."

"Better than stopping here. What do you reck, maybe twock one of those 'cruisers?"

"Never manage that, and they'd come after us. Reckon we just slip away."

"What, tonight?"

"Nah. They'll be keyed up after what happened. Tomorrow."

Joe thinks about it. "Kay," he says after a moment.

Helen walks on. She'll catch up with Mark when he comes out, speak to him alone. See if she can go too.

A hand touches hers. She spins. Mum stands next to her. Dad's beside her, holding Mum's hand.

"No," says Mum, "you bloody won't. You're going to go home, shut the door, and wait till morning."

Helen opens her mouth to protest.

"Do it," Mum says.

"Listen to your Mum, our kid," says Dad.

Helen blinks away a spittle of rain. When her sight clears, they've gone. She glances up and down the street; a Reaper stands outside the pub, rifle at port-arms, watching her.

She turns and hurries home.

WULFDEN, LANCASHIRE

14TH APRIL, ATTACK PLUS FIVE YEARS

The screaming wakes Helen. She rolls onto her back in the double bed that was Mum and Dad's, then Mum's, now hers. What's the song Mum liked? *Tears On Your Pillow*. She's left a lot of those, crying for the loss she's had, howling them into the pillow, using it to muffle the screams because Roth mustn't know her hate for him.

Can he really not suspect, though? Or what kinds of people has he met in the last five years? How like animals that they'll shrug off the deaths of those they love in exchange for a dangled promise of power? *Life goes on; that's how it is now; you accept it and do as you must to live.* But then she's seen it happening here in Wulfden; it shouldn't be a surprise.

Let Roth think that of her, then. Let him not suspect. And then –

The screaming. She registers it properly. She recognises it; it's the same sound she muffles in her pillow.

Helen gets out of bed, fully clothed: it's still so cold all the time. She pulls her boots on, goes down the stairs.

Outside the front door, the High Street's damp from a mizzling rain; the sky's grey and a hazy mist swallows the hill. And that desolate screaming echoes through it.

It seems to ring from all around, but she guesses where it's coming from; she walks up along the High Street to the village square.

The old lampposts are still in place, never been taken down. Usually they hang candle-lanterns from them. Today, two of them have something else.

Jean Radcliffe's on her knees in front of them. Helen doesn't recognise her at first, her face is so twisted out of true by the scream that pours from it. She clutches at the lamppost, unable to reach Mark's feet as he swings to and fro in the damp air, the long hair only half-screening the face. Joe, hanging beside, has cropped hair, so the damage done is more visible, his face purple and bloated.

Around each one's neck, a sign's been hung. On them, in big red letters: SUBVERSIVE.

Jean howls and keens. Footsteps sound on the damp pavement, and a crowd gathers to watch, to digest the lesson the Reapers have taught.

*

Helen waits until dark, sits in the kitchen a long time, with a backpack beside her filled with dried and smoked and pickled foods, a compass and a couple of blankets and anything else she could find that could be of use. Like the knife in its sheath that she straps to her arm.

"Helen."

She looks up. Mum and Dad sit across the kitchen table from her, holding hands.

"We're worried about you, our kid," Dad says.

"Please, love," says Mum. "Just go. Get over the wall and run away. Don't do anything else. Please."

Helen pulls the backpack on and slips out into the back garden, keeping low and quiet, climbs over the wall, crouches in the lank tall grass in the fitful moonlight.

The Reapers patrol the hill, but it's nothing she couldn't slip through. It would be easy enough to do that; head west, look for the resistance Mark had mentioned. It also wouldn't be enough.

Helen grits her teeth and nods, then slips along the back of the back gardens till she's behind the old Post Office. A Reaper patrols the yard. After a while, he moves to a corner, unfastens his trousers and starts to piss. Helen climbs the low wall, cat-foots across the yard and presses herself against the Post Office's back wall. Then she reaches for the drain pipe and starts climbing.

Halfway up, she dares to look down. The Reaper is patrolling again, back and forth and back and forth. He doesn't even look up.

Too many villages like this, perhaps. Too many easy conquests. Too many people shrinking before their guns, jumping to their tune.

She gets a window open and climbs inside; a little box room. Manages not to knock anything over; she eases the window shut behind her.

Quiet. She's done well. But then she's had practice; more than once she'd slipped out at night and shinned a drainpipe to meet with Mark. A kiss and a feel, never going all the way. It had been something, anyway.

She tiptoes onto the landing, hears snoring from one room. Eases the door open, teeth gritted lest it creak. It doesn't. She pads inside.

It's Roth, all right. His uniform is on a chair beside the bed. A pistol on the bedside table. A black Browning automatic. Helen thinks of the single shots she heard ring out the night Mum died. Was that him? Did he fire a round into her little Mum's head?

Control. Calm. She tiptoes the last few steps to the bed. Picks up the pistol, pushes in through her belt. And then she draws the knife.

Roth stirs, mumbles. Helen freezes, but he doesn't wake.

And so all that remains is what to do next. Sneak out again, with or without the gun? Or finish what she started, do what must be done?

She doesn't stop to think about it; even then, she knows that it would be the death of action. Instead she leans forward, lays the knife to Roth's throat.

"Helen," says Mum's voice. She knows they're there, her mum and dad, across the bedroom from her. But she doesn't look up.

Roth's eye opens, and Helen's draws the blade across.

She steps back quickly, but some of his blood splashes her. It makes a hissing sound as it sprays from his slit throat. He chokes, gags, but can make no sound.

Helen gets in close, her face to his, then whispers in his ear so he'll carry her voice with him to Hell. "Pauline," she says. "Her name was Pauline Winter, and she was my Mum."

And then she steps back to watch him die.

It seems to take a long time.

When he's dead, she goes through his belongings. He has a submachine gun too, so she takes that, plus ammunition. A first-aid kit. And there's a lighter, and even a bottle of fluid.

She squirts the fluid over Roth and the bed, then flicks the lighter, sees the sheets flare into flame. At the bedroom door she looks back and sees Mum reaching towards her, eyes full of tears, and Dad gently but firmly drawing her back.

Quick now, she darts across the landing and into the box room. Flames crackle; the air grows hot and thick with smoke. Helen peers down into the yard; that fucking Reaper's still patrolling back and forth.

Shouts, running feet from the landing. Helen aims the SMG at the door, but it doesn't open. She looks back down at the yard, sees the sentry run inside. Then she flings open the window and climbs down fast, runs across the yard, jumps over the wall.

Scrambles into bramble bushes nearby as the Reapers on guard further down run up to investigate; looking back, she sees the fires have taken hold, that the Post Office is a beacon in the night. It'll be some time tomorrow before they work out she killed Roth, if ever, and by then she'll be far away.

She doesn't know it yet, but she's seen her parents' ghosts for the last time. They'll never appear to her again.

Helen gets up. She has a clockwork torch, she winds it up, and keeping the beam low, runs off into the night. Into the west; into the Wastelands.

2.

"And the heavy weapons?"

"No joy, ma'am, sorry. The ones that survived the wall breach were put out of action by the rebels before they pulled back."

Jarrett fought back a yawn. "Surprisingly well-trained for half-ferals. Anything else?"

"Yes, ma'am. Lieutenant Wong reports that the explosion caused a roof collapse in the cave, but her team's at work digging through. Once they've done that, they'll try and find their way under the second wall."

"Good. What else?"

"Just one thing, ma'am. CATCH Central's on the line. Requesting clearance to pull the Catchmen out."

"Really?" Jarrett smiled. "Now that's entertainment. Put him through."

"Colonel?" Kellett said. There was a sharp edge to his voice, querulous. "Are you there?"

God, his *voice*; it grated on her ears. Jarrett rubbed her eyes. "Yes, Doctor. I understand you want your toy soldiers to leave the party."

"The rebels have a weapon that's effective against them."

"Join the club, Doctor."

"They're being killed, Colonel." Kellett's voice rose.

"And this is a bad thing because…"

"They have been useful to you, Colonel."

"They were forced back."

"After advancing further than your Jennywrens had succeeded in doing at any p –"

Kellett broke off. *Knows he's gone too far.* Jarrett's hand clenched white on the mic; she breathed hard. So easy to tell him to fuck himself, let his abominations be wiped out. But he was right. They'd been of use, and might be again. Besides, the battle would now belong to the Jennywrens – and so, therefore, would the victory. "Very well," she said. "You may recall them."

"Thank you, Colonel."

"And if you ever speak to me like that again, I'll have a bayonet pushed so far up your arse you'll taste your own shit on the end of it."

Silence, then Kellett trying to speak, or splutter. Jarrett handed the mic back to the comms tech, then shook two more white pills out of the jar.

WALL TWO
1508 HOURS

"They're pulling out!"

"What?" Danny turned, ran to the radio op pointing over the battlements. The GPMGs and .50 cals stuttered. Bullets whined and cracked in the air. Below, Wakefield, Harp and the last of the Wall One defenders were falling back towards Wall Two.

"The Catchmen. See?"

Fucking had and all. The grey-suited monsters had turned about and were marching off back through the village; the advancing Reapers dodged around them as they went. "Fucking great. Just leaves an army of those cunts to deal with. Keep that covering fire goin'!" He yelled at the other defenders. "And stand ready at the gate!"

The gate swung open. The machine guns blasted and hammered down at the Jennywrens. Danny knelt, aimed, fired a wild burst from the Lanchester, saw a Reaper fall.

"Coming through!" someone shouted below. The defenders poured in, the Reapers a hundred yards behind.

Harp staggered up the steps. "Right behind us," he said. He grinned at Lish, ruffled her hair. "Gerroff," she said.

"Gates shut!" Danny shouted. "Hit the fuckers with all you've got. Shove 'em back."

"Boss!"

"What?"

Lish caught his arm. "Trex and Scopes!"

"Fuck." Danny stared at the tower of St Martin de Porres; the two snipers were still prone there, rifles cracking, dropping the Jennywrens as they fell back through the village. Bursts of gunfire cracked off the battlement stone.

"Gotta get 'em out," said Harp.

"Can't." Danny ducked as another burst of gunfire blew a shower of dust from the parapet. "They're digging in, got a clear field of fire. No way they'd make it from the church to the gate. Cut down before they'd gone ten steps. Fuck." He breathed out. "They're safer there for now."

From the church, more shots. A distant cry echoed from the village in answer to one.

"More than the Reapers are," said Harp, and grinned.

SICK BAY, ASHWOOD FORT

Darrow halted in the doorway; the reek of blood and excrement, of opened bodies and incipient decay, was so thick and strong he felt as though he'd walked into a wall. He breathed in through his mouth, went forward.

Nestor glanced up at him from the table, didn't speak. On it was Helen. Darrow had forgotten how small she was, and how pale. She looked fragile beyond words, almost childlike. And that wound in her head.

Darrow looked away, back up at Nestor. "Doing everything I can, before you ask," the medic said. "And no, I don't know if she'll make it or not. Still trying to evacuate the haematoma. If I can do that she'll have a chance, barring infection and so forth. Beyond that, can't say. And now I need to get on with this."

"Of course." Darrow looked around, saw what he'd come for. "Carry on. And thank you."

The Grendelwolf was cleaning blood off the floor with rags. "Gevaudan?" said Darrow, approaching.

"Darrow."

"Are you – "

"All right? Of course not." He nodded towards the table. "They don't have room for people to stand around. So I said I'd help out."

"Gevaudan, there's a battle on."

"Surely you jest."

"We're holding at Wall Two, but only just. There'll be a further attack at some point. I need anything and anyone available to throw the Reapers back. You're no good to me scrubbing floors."

Gevaudan looked up; Darrow managed not to flinch back from the yellow glare of his eyes. "You can't do anything for Helen here," he said. "But she will certainly die, along with everyone else here, if the Reapers break through. Please?"

Gevaudan glared at him, then looked over to Helen on the operating table. Finally he nodded and rose, cleaning his hands, then tossed the rag in a bucket and followed Darrow out.

"Fuck me." Walters ducked as a chunk of stonework burst above his head, then ducked into a doorway, sweeping his rifle about the inside of the house to make sure no-one was there.

"No thanks," Patel shouted back from the house opposite, hunkering down behind a garden wall. He aimed up, fired.

Walters peered out around the doorframe, shouldering his rifle. Smoke and dust in the air, gun-thunder, explosions, screams. Up ahead, the second wall, with guns firing all along it, the bullets smashing down into the village. Little stick figures moving on the parapet. He sighted best he could, flinching from the spray of chips and dust and the bullets that flew about; fired, fired and fired again.

WALL TWO

"Fuck." Danny ducked as his helmet clanged from a bullet impact. "Fuck." His head throbbed. He took off the helmet, checked it. A big dent, but no break. Touched his head; sore but no blood. Put the helmet back on, glared down at the village.

More Reapers pouring in through the breach, into the village. Lish ran along the battlements, head down, lugging a crate of .50 cal ammo half as big as she was. "Keep firing!" Danny yelled. "Pin 'em down. Harp?"

"Yo?"

"Gimme the control."

Harp swallowed, then nodded.

The firing control was pulled over, the wires. Danny pulled the plunger up, spat on his hands and took a deep breath.

Harper dived in through the doorway, hit the floor, then rose, the Browning aimed in both hands. Kept low as bullets thudded into the house, smashed through the windows.

Work to do. But first, check all's clear. He swept the lower storeys of the emptied house, then went up the stairs. Checked again, room by room. Nothing. Nada.

Good. Harper reached up, touched his headset. "Scythe One to all Scythe Units. Come in."

"Scythe Two." White.

"Scythe Three." Greene.

"Scythe Four? Scythe Five? Acknowledge." Nothing. Just the static hiss. Harper's lips tightened as he moved, crouching, towards the front bedroom, watching the window. He could see the inner wall, the guns on it flashing, and the church tower. "You'll pay for that, you bastards," he muttered, then hit transmit again. "Scythes Two and Five, I'm taking up position in the village. Both of yous, move in."

"Acknowledge, Scythe One," said White. "Wilco."

Harper lay on the floor, crawled to the window. He put the Browning on the floor beside him and unslung his rifle, resting the barrel on the window sill and propping it on the windowframe, then drew back the bolt.

He adjusted the sights; the wall sprang into focus. He scanned along the battlements – then tracked away, towards the church tower. He glimpsed the barrel of a rifle; he settled the cross-hairs, waiting to catch a glimpse of the sniper. Just let the wee glipe show his turnip for a fraction of a second and Harper would chop him.

Harper sniffed.

To live this long, you had to be aware of things – the things that would give you away to the enemy, and those that gave your enemy away to you. Especially if you were a sniper. Sound, Silhouette, Shape – and another S: Smell.

Through the reek of smoke and dust, he detected something else, something out of place. A sweet smell. Familiar, but it didn't belong here.

Harper frowned. Then he recognised it: something he hadn't tasted in over twenty years. Marzipan.

And then he remembered them telling him in army training, all those years ago, how something else that smelt like marzipan was –

Plastique, he opened his mouth to yell, but then the world ended in a blinding flash.

WALL TWO
1521 HOURS

For a second after Danny pushed the plunger down, nowt seemed to happen. Then dust and smoke puffed out from inside the village houses and from under them, and they burst apart, their wreckage tumbling and dissolving into the black and grey haze that boiled up.

The wall shook and the deafening bang of the explosion slammed out. Danny ducked, wincing. Bits of dust and stone rained down.

And as the explosion faded, he heard the screaming from the smoke and flame where Ashwood Village had been.

ASHWOOD VILLAGE

Walters was underwater. All the sound was swimmy and vague, slow and echoey. The street – rubble, smoke, flames, scattered body pieces – swelled and blurred in his vision as if through a distorting lens.

Nothing is real. Nothing is real. Piece of a song he'd heard once, an old song. *Nothing is real. Nothing is real.* It felt right.

He looked down at himself. His uniform was ripped apart. He was bleeding. How bad? Couldn't tell. Didn't feel too bad. Warm wetness trickling down his neck on either side, coming from his ears. He touched them. Blood on his fingers.

Dead bodies. Men and women screaming: bloody mouths, missing limbs, guts hanging out. Others swaying as if pissed, glassy-eyed, dazed. *Do I look like that?*

...ete?

Walters blinked.

Pete?

Turned.

Patel there, shouting his name. Walters heard it, a blurred echo; took a weak, swaying step towards him.

Then something smashed into him and the ground was gone. He hit it again a moment later, and pain shocked through him. He screamed, or tried to; could barely hear a thing, so no knowing if he did or not. He twisted on the ground, felt shattered bones grate together; tried to breathe and found blood instead of air.

Hands grabbed him, dragging him to the shelter of a broken wall. A blow smashed into his shin; he screamed again without sound, looked down and saw his foreleg hanging by shreds of gristle and meat. Screamed again, vomited, choked on both it and his blood when he tried to breath. The road surface danced as if in heavy rain, only the sprays and founts were of tarmac, stone and dust. The guns on the second wall, raking the ruins for any who'd survived the blast.

Hands pulled him to shelter, sat him up. Patel, looking down at him. *Saeed. Mate.* Saeed was crying. Trying to say something, too, but Walters couldn't make it out, was still trying to when the dark came in and took everything away.

"I don't care how many casualties they've taken," Jarrett shouted. "Send more in, Majid. They can't blow up the village twice. If we don't reinforce, they counterattack, and we lose the ground we've won. Hold the breach and the village, no matter what. That's an order."

She tossed the mic aside. She'd never been a spendthrift of her Reapers' lives. But sometimes such sacrifices needed to be made. The Reaper Creed; that was Britain now, what anchored it together. And the Jennywrens most of all: *My soul for my country; if I never see Heaven it is a price I gladly pay.*

Just words till now, but she had to wonder. This battle was all or nought; at the end, how would she stand? Would it all have been worth it?

She dismissed the thought. *I am in blood, stepped in so far...* what was that, Shakespeare? Yes, that was it: *Macbeth.* Was it worth it? After all she'd done, the blood she'd shed – little of it hers, to be sure – there couldn't be any other answer than yes. Nothing else would redeem her career, or her.

"Is that what you tell yourself?" She looked up to see Tom lounging against the table; behind him, little more than shadows, were Mum and Dad and Mandy. "Too scared to admit you might have been wrong? And look where it's got you, Nicky. Just look."

"Ma'am?" The comms tech ran up. "Commander Winterborn on the line for you."

"Right." Jarrett straightened, saw the tech's face. "What?" But she knew, of course, felt the fear's cold stirring in her bowels. "*What?*"

"We're picking up some snatches of their comms traffic," the Reaper said. "And there was something..."

"Tell me?"

"It's Target Alpha, ma'am. She's still alive."

Tom threw his head back and laughed. Jarrett gripped the edge of the table.

"She's in a bad way, ma'am," the tech said quickly. "Critical condition, touch and go. Gunshot wound to the head. She's probably had it, but…" she faltered. "Just thought you should know, ma'am."

You fucking idiotic bitch, Jarrett thought but didn't say. *Then comes my fit again*. Another line from *Macbeth*. "Thank you," she said, and steadied herself. She closed her eyes; when she opened them again, the ghosts were gone.

The bitch was still alive; just when Jarrett had been sure it was done, all bar the mopping-up. But now the task was still undone. She drew herself up: no matter. Helen was out of action, at least. And when they took the Fort, Jarrett would find and kill her personally. She smiled, returning her attention to the comms tech. "Put the Commander through," she said.

Ops Room, the Tower

"So she's still alive?" said Winterborn.

"So far, sir, but we don't know in what condition. Unlikely to play any part in the fighting from here on in, certainly."

Winterborn swayed a moment. Helen. Dying, maybe dead: that was good, surely? And yet – and yet, again, there was a memory of warmth, one he sought to banish and silence at once before it could take root and bloom.

"Commander?"

"Yes." Winterborn straightened, glanced to each side, making sure he drew no mocking or critical glances. Beware; show no weakness, do nothing to shake their faith in you. "Yes, Colonel, continue."

"We've breached the Fort's outer wall. They mined the whole area – the old village. Took heavy casualties. I've reinforced, of course, and we're holding, but we're encountering strong, well-organised resistance."

"You expected anything else?"

"No sir, of course not. But we need support here – reinforcements, and most of all, heavy weapons."

"All of which are on their way," said Winterborn. "You'll have all you need, Jarrett, to deliver the results you've promised." He paused a moment, let the veiled threat sink in. "Now get on with it."

He handed the headset back to the comms tech; drew himself up, held himself straight. *Pull yourself together, boy.* Whatever Helen was in the past, it was in the past. She was the enemy now. He must have order. Stability. And it would come.

ASHWOOD VILLAGE

Patel crouched behind the wall, shaking, not daring move in case it exposed him to the gunfire hailing down from the battlements. The next wave of Jennywrens poured through the breach, bellowing, scattering out among the ruins in search of cover. But there was little or none.

Still, after a time, the guns on the battlements fell silent.

Silence. Just the hum in Patel's ears, the belltone. He looked down at Walters, stretched beside him. Hand shaking, he scooped up dust to pour over Pete's staring eyes. "Sorry mate." His voice hitched. Crying. *Tighten up, boy. That's not the GenRen way.*

A shot rang out. Patel ducked, grunted. Shouts in the distance. Another shot rang out, then another. He looked towards the church tower.

Sniper.

THE BATTLETRUCK
1540 HOURS

"All Scythe units," said Jarrett. "Acknowledge."

"Scythe Two acknowledging."

"Scythe Three acknowledging."

Otherwise, silence. "Scythe One?" she said. "Sergeant Harper?"

"Sergeant Harper went first through the breach to scout ahead, ma'am." Scythe Two was talking – the Lance-Corporal, White. "He'd taken up a position in the village and ordered us to follow him in, but then…"

Harper. How long had she served with him? Back in the Civil Emergency, he'd served in her Predator unit, hunting down and killing the rebels' stay-behind units during Operation Clean Sweep. But he'd been with her even before that. Perhaps the closest thing she'd had to a friend… no, she dismissed that notion. He'd been a subordinate, and a capable, obedient one. Nothing more.

"What about the other two?" she said. "Carson and Fox?"

"Lost contact with them before the breach, ma'am," said White. "We were advancing under heavy fire. There was always the risk."

"Damn." Jarrett sighed. "All right. The two of you, here are your orders. There are two rebel snipers in the church tower. They're slowing the advance by picking off officers and NCOs. You're to infiltrate the village, and take them out."

"Wilco."

"Wilco," said Greene, the younger one, but there was a nervous tremor in his voice.

"Get on with it." Jarrett changed frequencies. "Captain Majid?"

"Ma'am?"

"I want you to designate some units – three or four – no, make that five. They're to get over the outer wall anywhere they can to attack the inner wall. Let's see if we can't distract them a little. And once that's underway, have Lieutenant Benbow and his rocket section move in."

"The breach was clearly created by some kind of mine," Darrow said. "And reports of the explosion all confirm the same thing – it came from beneath the wall."

"Sappers?" said Gevaudan. "But surely they couldn't have dug their way as quickly as that from the Reaper camp?"

"Normally, they couldn't," Darrow said. "But it appears they didn't need to."

"Ah," said Gevaudan. "The cave system."

Alannah spread a map out on the table. "The caves have never been fully charted, but a couple were explored before the War. One runs down the hill from under the Fort and gets most of the way to the Reaper camp before veering off to the west. It emerges a couple of miles away, so they couldn't get in there directly from where they are, but they wouldn't have to dig very far before breaking through into it."

"Whereupon," said Gevaudan, "they just need to walk up and find themselves under Wall One."

"Right," said Darrow. "But as you can also see from the map, the cave branches after that. About four or five different tunnels, all leading no-one knows where. Added to that, the explosion probably brought the tunnel roof down, so they'll have had to dig their way through, but…"

"Wall Two would be their logical next target," Gevaudan said.

"Yes. Our best bet would be to send a team down through the tunnels to intercept the sappers, ideally collapse the tunnel with charges."

"But the tunnels are uncharted."

"Yes."

"So your best chance is someone who can see in the dark and has acute hearing," said Gevaudan. "Someone like me."

"Quite simply," said Darrow, "yes."

Wall Two was the next target; Danny was on Wall Two.

If Wall Two fell, Danny died. And the Reapers would pour through. And Ashwood would fall.

And Helen, no matter Nestor's skill, would have no chance then.

Gevaudan nodded. "Very well. I'll go now."

Alannah held out a large, heavy backpack; an old army bergen, stuffed full. "You'll need this stuff," she said.

Gevaudan nodded. He took off the coat, laid it over the back of the chair. "Take care of that for me, if you would."

He pulled on the backpack and went out of the War Room, headed for the door at the end.

"Gevaudan." Darrow followed him. "Do you – don't you want a weapon?"

"I have these." He indicated the pistols in their shoulder and hip holsters, then held up his hands and extended the claws, saw Darrow grimace and flinch. "And these."

He spun the locking wheel, opened the door, and stepped through into the caverns' cold blackness. The door swung shut behind him, shutting out the last of the light.

"*The bright day is done,*" he murmured, "*and we are for the dark.*"

WALL TWO
1548 HOURS

"Wakefield," called Danny, keeping below parapet level. For now the Fort was silent. Harp knelt behind a crenellation, gun shouldered; beside him was Lish, with an SLR she'd snatched from somewhere. As she scuttled towards him, he heard a rifle crack from the church and answering bursts of gunfire from the village, hammering the tower. Then silence, stretching out.

"What?" said Wakefield. Her eyes were red. Dust: it caked their skin and clothes, along with smudges of soot.

Danny took a gulp from his water canteen, then handed it to her. "I want you to sort some patrols out. All round the wall." He gestured around them. "Reapers could try and come at us from any of those."

Wakefield nodded. "Done," she said. "Filly, with me."

Filly drank the last of the water, tossed the canteen to Danny and crawled after Wakefield, who hissed out other names as she went.

THE CAVES

Gevaudan had a torch with him, but did his best not to use it, though even his Grendelwolf eyes were next to useless here. His hearing was good, though, and the trickle of water was easy enough to follow. And the caves were tall enough that he moved through them without having to stoop too far.

There'd been plenty of water in the caves, a small lake from which multiple streams flowed, disappearing into cave mouths as they went. He'd chosen the widest stream, hoping this would lead all the way down. If he was lucky, it would converge with the others to form the tunnel the Reapers had used; if not, it would peter out in a dead end, or veer off in a completely different direction.

Gevaudan hadn't come close to true unease in some time – well, not until he'd fought the Catchman and found himself apparently battling an enemy he couldn't kill. This was different, and in a way worse; even a Grendelwolf could get hopelessly lost and starve to death. Or worse. There was one true, deep fear all Grendelwolves knew; one peculiar to them, one whose effects they had seen at close quarters.

How long till he was next due to take the Goliath serum? How long ago had the last dose been, without which his body would begin to break down and devour itself? To be trapped down here, perhaps with the battle ended and the Fort fallen – how long might he last? And not only that death – the most terrible death of all – but to suffer it here, in the darkness and alone.

He mustn't think about that, could only press on. And so down into the dark he went.

"Yo yo yo!" said Mackie.

Cov looked up, wiping sweat from his neck and forehead. "What?"

Mackie pointed, the telescope to his eye. "There."

Cov looked too; in the distance was a new convoy of heavy landcruisers, barrelling down the Devil's Highway, rolling towards the tangled wreckage that blocked their path. He reached for the radio mic.

THE CAVES
1555 HOURS

Gevaudan stopped; listened. Water dripped and echoed – but he heard something else. He crouched, cupped his hands to his ears.

The scuff of boots on wet stone. The mutter of voices.

He moved along the tunnel, feeling ahead of him. And then a beam of light flashed out ahead of him, as if to bar his path.

The voices, getting louder. He inched forward, saw that the cave opened out into another tunnel that ran across its path. He hunched low, beside the entrance, and peered round. A dozen or so head-torches shone, light gleaming off the walls. Black-uniformed figures wore them; they carried rifles. Gevaudan ducked back.

"Wait," someone called.

"What?"

Gevaudan eased his arms out of the straps of the bergen, lowered it to the floor.

"Thought I saw movement."

The click of bolts drawn back. Gevaudan drew the Brownings, eased the hammers back with his thumbs. No element of surprise, then; a simple test of speed and skill. His against theirs.

"*Ah, well*," he murmured, "*'tis very well.*"

He drew breath, leapt out into the tunnel and fired. Rifles crashed and bullets flew. He flung himself to the ground and fired again, as bullets whined and ricocheted about him.

BOWKITT LIBRARY
1556 HOURS

"What sort of numbers?" said Flaps.

"Looks about the same as the last one."

"Right." Flaps hissed through her teeth. "No more mines, but we're okay for rockets and the wreckage should stop 'em. Ought to be able to –"

"Cov," said Mackie.

"In a minute, mate."

"Cov!"

The big lad was pointing – not at the Devil's Highway, but at the land beside it. Level with the convoy but now pulling ahead were small black dots, expanding as they travelled, a thin dust haze rising behind them. Cov squinnied through his binocs, and they sprang into focus: fast-pursuit 'cruisers, each with a half-dozen fully-armed Reapers in the flatbed. Cov swept left, across the Highway to their side, and saw another group of landcruisers nearing the town there too.

"Fuck me," he said, grabbing for the mic. "Crow's Nest to Rook One and Rook Two – hostiles approaching overland. Twenty FPCs apiece, fully armed. they're coming right at you."

"Us," said Mackie, as Cov lowered the mic. "Coming at *us*."

Gevaudan stood, holstering the revolvers, then picked the empty Brownings up from the wet cave floor.

They were easily found; light spilled from the Reapers' surviving head-torches to bathe the floor.

He reloaded as the gun-thunder's echoes faded, to be replaced by the drip of water; when he shifted position, gravel and cartridge cases crunched underfoot. He couldn't avoid looking at the men and women he'd killed. In particular, his gaze was drawn to the officer; a small Chinese woman, little more than a teenager.

Her shoulder-flashes were grey. CivEng – the Civil Engineering Division. Building roads and bridges. Chances were, her parents had pushed her forward for the Reapers, hoping she'd have a chance of a better life.

Another young one, marching to the abattoir like a lamb. He scooped muck from the cave floor to cover her eyes. "I'm sorry," he whispered.

He dragged the bodies up the tunnel, laid them out in rows. Then he did what had to be done; he took the explosives they'd been carrying and rigged them to bring down the ceiling, inserting pencil fuses to set them off, then retreated back along the way he'd come.

When the charges blew, the whole hill seemed to shudder, dust and pieces of stone falling around him. A moment's fear that the collapse would bury him too, leaving him trapped and helpless – there were things even a Grendelwolf's strength couldn't overcome. *Till famine cling thee*, he thought. Or lack of Goliath serum.

Clouds of dust billowed down the tunnel; Gevaudan coughed and choked, then walked into them as they began to clear.

The tunnel ended in a wall of rubble.

Gevaudan stepped over the bodies to fetch the bergen. Inside were more explosives, and motion sensors; he planted them in and around the rubble, then started back the way he'd come.

Bowkitt Library

"Oh, fuck me," Mackie said. "Fucking fucking fuck me."

Cov couldn't argue with him.

In the ruined town below, either side of the library, the Reaper landcruisers were pushing their way relentlessly through the remains of the streets. The chatter of the .50 cals and crump of grenades sounded, plumes of smoke and dust rising. Flaps and Goll were holding them off for now, but that left no-one to watch the Devil's Highway.

Below, the second convoy had reached the town. With no fire coming down from above, men ran out of the heavy 'cruisers towards the wreckage that blocked the road.

3.

Cold morning. Helen shivers in a woodland bivouac, crawls out to piss.

The embers of last night's fire smoulder. She has some twigs and kindling left, and uses them to build it up again. Boils water over it for dandelion coffee, gnaws on a piece of smoked rabbit.

A twig cracks; she reaches for the Sterling beside her. Neither it, the pistol, nor the knife are ever far from her now. She sits and listens and waits, but there's nothing more. Just an animal.

The first three nights, she slept without fire, afraid the Reapers were searching. If so, they'd failed to find her. Perhaps they never linked her vanishing with their CO's death, assumed he died in an accidental fire and decided one runaway teenage girl wasn't worth the effort to find. Probably thought she'd die out here in the Wastelands alone, save them the chase and the bullet.

Helen's starting to fear they're right.

Maybe they know it was her, but now they have the whole village up in arms. Maybe the Reapers have all been chased out of Wulfden, or hang from the village square lampposts like Mark and Joe, or litter the stones with bullets in them like M –

The grief blindsides Helen from nowhere; she almost drops her coffee with the shock of it. She grips it close, nursing the warmth as she sobs.

When the crying fit passes, she blinks and sits up straight. How long was she out of it, lost in crying? Anyone could have come up and shot her.

You're a woman now. Not a child. Fifteen years old. That's old enough. So no more crying. Harden up. You want to fight. So fight.

Helen stands, packs her gear, and travels west.

*

She's slept under hedges and broken walls, shivered in the cold, risked water from unfamiliar streams. Could be dying slow already, a creeping dose. The Wastelands are as the name implies: empty woodlands, desolate hills, abandoned farms, burned-out villages. The closest thing she's seen to life are the rabbits she's killed for food. The taste of them cloys in her throat now.

Today, as she walks, she sees crows circle over her, and tries to tell herself it's not an omen.

In almost a week since killing Roth and leaving Wulfden, she hasn't seen one human soul.

And now it's growing dark, and she follows an old, long-unused B-road with slow, plodded steps. She knows it's riskier and more exposed than the harder route of travelling the moor the road cuts across, but she's starting to stumble. She's bone-tired, struggling to keep her eyes open, but she needs a place to sleep and can't see one; the moor is flat, not even a wall or stand of trees in sight for a bivouac. Or if there is, she's missed it in her exhaustion.

The Wastelands are empty. Resistance? A myth. Must be. Maybe that was the Reapers' plan: have all the troublemakers run off into the west, seeking allies but finding only loneliness and death. That's why they haven't followed her. She's done their job for them.

Helen's laughter is weak but wild as she goes, reaching a hump in the road – something to break the monotony of the moor. The stupidity of it all, believing she'd find anybody here –

But then she sees a light up ahead.

She blinks and stands there, looking. Off the road, maybe half a mile across the moor, is some sort of structure. And in or near or by it, the light of a fire.

Helen checks the Browning's secure in Roth's old holster at her hip. (The knife that slit Roth's throat pierced extra holes in the belt so she could pull it tight enough.) Makes sure the Sterling's uncocked, the chamber empty, but the safety catch is off. The knife that killed Roth is in her boot. She leaves the road and sets off across the moor.

It's slow, hard going without her torch – it's in her bag, but the light would warn whoever owns the fire that she's coming. For all she knows – with her bloody luck – they'll turn out to be Reapers.

The building takes shape as she approaches. It's in ruins, but not from the War – she's seen a place like this before. Old pillars, high, ornate arches, thick with ivy. An old monastery or abbey.

Below one high wall, the fire burns. Some men and women sit around it. She sees tents. She quickens her step – and in the dark, something snaps underfoot.

Sudden movement, the snapping back of rifle bolts. "Who goes there?" A woman calls.

The moment stretches out; for a second she thinks she can't speak, that she's forgotten how over the silent days, or that the fear of the moment's paralysed her. Then she thinks the only sound she'll make is laughter, because she could end up being shot by the people she's been looking for because she's too panicked to speak. But then her throat unlocks, and she says "Don't shoot. Please."

"Show yourselves," says someone; a lean, greying man crouching by the fire with an old tommy-gun in his hands. "Keep your hands where we can see them."

"It's just me," she says, raising her hands. "I'm on my own." She comes forward. So fucking tired. Every step is an effort, as if she's wearing boots of lead. Movement above her; she looks up and sees a gaunt woman in her twenties with cropped black hair perched in a niche on one of the broken walls, covering Helen with a Bren gun. A lookout, probably the one who called out. Helen never had a chance of sneaking up on them unawares; she tells herself she'd already be dead if that's what they wanted.

They stare at her as she comes into the firelight. The lean, greying man stands, lowering the gun. She sees no black Reaper uniforms, just a mix of old clothes from before the War and stuff that looks home-made – rough woollen sweaters, trousers of animal skin.

"Well?" she says at last. "Are you the Resistance?"

But before she can answer, she's falling.

*

When she opens her eyes, she sees stars. Not a metaphor or anything – real stars, up in the sky. Millions of tiny points of light. Glittering dust. She stares at them for a long time before someone speaks.

"Beautiful, aren't they?"

Helen starts. Realises she's under a blanket, another folded under her head. She's dressed, but her guns are gone. She twists round on her side; sitting nearby, his back to the dying fire, is the greying man. Beside him is her backpack, the Sterling and the Browning.

He smiles slightly and looks up at the sky. "You couldn't see them at all for the first couple of years. Do you remember? So much dust in the atmosphere, blotting out the sun."

"Yeah." Helen remembers the – literally – dark days that followed right after the War, the long bitter winters.

"Started clearing after that, but it's only really been the last year or so that you could see them again. My name's Darrow, by the way."

"Helen."

Darrow nods. "Oh, and the answer to your question is yes."

"My...?"

"You asked us, before you collapsed, if we were the Resistance. We are." He glances around the camp. A couple of people, one of them the gaunt woman, sit talking by the fire; two other adults and a young boy sleep beside it, and Helen sees someone standing near a pillar with a rifle, keeping watch. Otherwise, it's just her and Darrow; the tents are zipped up tight. "A small part of it, anyway," he adds.

"I've been looking for you," Helen says.

"I assumed as much."

They study each other in silence for a few seconds, while the firelight flickers and shadows stretch across the ground. "It isn't an easy ride, you know," he says.

"I didn't think it —"

"Everyone has to work," he says. "To play a part."

"I know that," says Helen. "That's why I was looking for you. I don't want to hide. I want to fight."

"To fight?" Darrow looks at the guns beside him. "Do you actually know what you're asking when you say that, Helen?"

"I killed my first Reaper seven days ago," she says. "I cut his throat, and I took his guns."

Darrow's expression is hard to read. Pity? Sadness?

Helen tells him what happened. He sighs. "I wish I could tell you I haven't heard the same story before. The Reapers have started expanding in earnest, trying to take back control of areas that have been left uninhabited or to fend for themselves. Did you notice a white shoulder-flash on the ones you encountered?"

"Yes," says Helen. "There was a word on it. GENREN."

"Genetic Renewal," says Darrow. "They call them the Jennywrens. Of all the different divisions the Reapers have, that one's the worst."

"What's so bad about them?"

"They were set up after the War. There were a lot of children born after the attack with birth defects – deformed, mutated. Many died, some lived. The Reapers decided to eliminate them. So they set up extermination squads. The men and women in them – some were violent criminals, offered a pardon in exchange. Or Reapers would be assigned to them as a punishment. Later the job expanded to deal with anyone they wanted to dispose of. Tea?"

Darrow wraps a rag around the handle of a jug at the edge of the fire, fills two tin cups, holds one out. "Thank you," Helen says.

"It became a badge of pride to the Jennywrens," Darrow goes on. "That they were strong enough, ruthless enough, to do anything, no matter how terrible, for the good of their country. The Reapers use them to get rid of those they don't want. It's often dangerous work, especially in the Wastelands – there are bands of feral children living out here, grown up wild after the War. They're tough, dangerous. So the Jennywrens were trained up in wilderness survival, counter-insurgency, special forces techniques – and now they're the Reapers' shock troops. They kill anyone who stands in their way, even for a second."

"I know."

"Of course. I'm sorry."

"I want to fight the Reapers, Darrow. That's all. That's why I'm here. Will you show me how to do that? If not, I'll go in the morning."

Darrow smiles – a little sadly, she thinks. "All right," he says. "I'll teach you. Now drink your tea and sleep."

Abbey Ruins

21st April, attack plus five years

Darrow's people have two landcruisers parked behind the ruins, a curtain of ivy draped over them; by the time Helen wakes in the morning the boilers are stoked and ready.

"I hear you want to fight," a voice says. Helen looks up from the pottage they've given her for a breakfast, sees the gaunt woman looking down. She smells sour and looks hard and wild: a little frightening, but at the same time someone you'd want at your side.

Helen isn't sure if she's being mocked or not, so she just meets the hard dark eyes and nods. "Yes."

"Good. Girls should learn to fight." The woman nods at Darrow, grins. "Can't leave it all to the men." She offers a hand. "Mary Tolland. Scary Mary, they call me."

Can't think why, Helen thinks but doesn't say. She shakes the offered hand. "Helen." She doesn't give a second name. Helen Winter is gone.

Mary lets go of her hand, steps back. "Perhaps I'll be seeing you, then." She nods in farewell and strides off towards one of the landcruisers.

"We're moving out," says Darrow. He motions Helen into the flatbed of one of them, climbs in after her. The small boy sits across from her. He twists his head away when she looks towards him, but not quite fast enough to stop Helen seeing the burn scars down the side of his face.

"This is Noakes," says Darrow. "Noakes, Helen."

Noakes looks at her and nods. The side of his face is buckled and shiny, and looks as though it half-melted, then set. But both eyes are intact, bright and alert.

"Too young to fight," says Darrow, "but he wants to learn. Kept stowing away on the landcruisers when we went out on patrols, didn't you, Noakes?"

The boy hides a half-smile, the unburnt side of his face going red. When Darrow looks away from him to Helen, she sees Noakes look up at the older man with something close to worship.

"It was easier to let him come along," says Darrow, "to watch, and learn. Anyway." He holds out a length of rag. "If you don't mind."

"What's this?" she says. She can't help noticing he's holding her bag in one hand, the Sterling and holster-belt in the other. She reaches for her boot, but the knife's gone too.

"You'll get those back later," he says. "In due course."

"What's that?" Helen asks again, pointing at the rag.

"It's a blindfold, Helen." He sees the look on her face and sighs. "Where we're going is a secret place. We can only afford to let people we can trust absolutely know where it is."

"So you don't trust me?"

"I trust you enough to give you the chance to prove yourself. The rest has to be earned."

He tosses another blindfold to Noakes, who dons it without a word. Finally Helen nods, and puts hers on.

THE REFUGE

21ST APRIL, ATTACK PLUS FIVE YEARS

She isn't sure how long they drive. An hour? Two? She feels wind on her face, a smatter of rain, a hint of sun. She can sense the light outside the blindfold. And then voices call out; there's a grinding of metal and stone, and a moment later that's all gone. The air is chill and slightly dank, and there's only darkness as the stone and metal grinds again.

Then she can sense light once more, and the air's warmer. Fingers touch the back of her head; she jumps. "Take it easy," says Darrow, and the blindfold comes away.

The two landcruisers are rolling down an underground tunnel; walls of earth and stone shored up by wooden beams and rafters, lit by electric light. Across the flatbed, Noakes sits up, rubbing his eyes. Helen looks back; as the grinding sound fades, she sees a shrinking rectangle of pale light narrow and vanish as doors swing shut.

"Where are we?" she says.

"Old drift mines," Darrow tells her. "Take care not to wander. There's miles of these tunnels and we only use some at present."

"This is where you live?"

"Where we live," says Darrow, "and where we plan. This is where the Resistance to the Reapers is coordinated from." He glances at her. "And where we train people to fight."

Helen nods. "Good."

Darrow smiles. "Welcome to the Refuge."

OLDHAM, LANCASHIRE

7TH OCTOBER, ATTACK PLUS SIX YEARS
OPERATION CHICKENHAWK

The street is rubble. The terraced houses were flattened by the blast, to bricks and wall-stumps. Reapers or looters carted most of it away, but a low ridge of broken masonry, like a tide-mark, lies at the edge of the roadway's buckled tarmac strip.

Helen crouches behind it as the hiss and clank of a landcruiser sounds, glancing each way along the line of young fighters either side of her. Most are her age, a couple younger; two or three older. All look to her.

Ashton raises his eyebrows. A stocky man in his early twenties with long, brown, shaggy hair. Another of Darrow's protégés, here to watch and take charge if Helen freezes or fucks up. She understands that; hates it, but understands.

The engine sound grows louder, directly opposite them, then trails off into a sigh of steam. Booted feet clomp on the pavement. "Everybody off!" yells a voice.

Helen nods to the rest, climbs up the bank and peers over. It's a heavy landcruiser; she head-counts some twenty Reapers and best part of a hundred children. Still surprises her there are so many of these, but Darrow's told her the birthrate spiked up from a couple of years after the attack. One of the few ways left to get some pleasure in life, and for too many girls and women it's all they have to barter for food, shelter or any other need.

The oldest children look about twelve. A lot of the younger ones have birth defects – malformed limbs, microcephalous heads, vestigial hands. There's a boy with a port-wine mark, a girl with a hand lacking all but a finger and a thumb who can't have been less than nine. Born before the bombs; her defect's nothing to do with the War, but they've rounded her up anyway.

Other kids have no external disfigurements; their damage is within. Helen sees the blank, thousand-yard eyes of the space-casualties, and the grimy, spitting, snarling ferals, most of them naked. Others wear rags and tatters of clothes and their eyes are half-clear, half-wild – tribals from the Wastelands nearby. The unwanted and the damaged, the useless eaters, the lives unworthy of life. Operation Monitor, the Reapers call it. An obscenity that's provoked the rebels to test their strength at last with their own campaign: Operation Chickenhawk.

Movement in the landcruiser's cabin. Three Reapers inside; far as she can tell, the rest are all on the road, shepherding the kids across.

She slides back down the slope. "Twenty Reapers, plus three in the cabin," she says. "Mike, take two of yours and deal with them. Don't let them get a call off."

Ashton nods.

"Rest of you are on me. Spread out, aim high. We want to rescue these kids, not do the Reapers' job for them." She holds up the whistle round her neck. "On my signal."

Nods all round. Helen puts the whistle in her mouth and climbs the rubble; the others follow.

The Reapers have herded the last of the children out of the 'cruiser to the other side of the street, where three of the broken walls of an old mill still stand. The wall facing Helen's collapsed, and so have all the floors, right down into the basement, leaving it a hollow shell. A ready-made burial pit.

Helen pulls back the bolt on her Thompson gun. Wishes she had the Sterling, but no – there aren't enough of those to go round. The newer, up to date weapons have already worn out and broken – these older ones are sturdier, but the ones from caches mothballed in the '80s and '90s are highest in demand. In the meantime, she gets Second World War army surplus. Still, Dad always liked stories from that time. Maybe he'd be proud to see her now. Or not.

The Reapers cock their guns and Helen shoulders the Thompson. "Belay that," shouts a voice. The officer in charge, hand on the pistol on his hip. His other hand holds a long, heavy canvas bag; he throws it on the ground. "Use those. Don't waste bullets."

The Reapers gather round the bag and take out iron bars. *Bastards.* Helen glances left and right along the line. Ashton's looking at her. She looks back to the road, gets the officer in her sights as the bars rise in the air, then blows the whistle and fires.

The Reapers spin at the whistle, and the officer ducks sideways as she pulls the trigger; the burst meant for his chest smashes his shoulder instead. He bounces off the front of the truck with a scream, pistol skittering away. As he does a salvo crashes out. The children scream and dive – except for the space-casualties, who just stand and stare – but more than half the Jennywrens are scythed down on the spot.

The cabin windows explode in spraying glass as Ashton and his two rake it. Helen ducks as a shot cracks overhead, fires back. A Jennywren's visor shatters; she slumps forward, blood pouring down her face.

The guns crack and chatter for no more than a minute, then all's still again, except for a thin shrill whine in her ears and someone screaming. It's coming from the road. Helen looks back and forth along the line, sees no casualties among her fighters.

She gestures to Ashton. "You three cover us."

He loads a new magazine into his Sten. "Will do."

"Rest of you, with me." Helen gets up. "Everyone to my left, make sure they're all dead. Everyone else, get the kids back on board the truck."

The kids wail and sob, their world, already precarious, blasted to insanity by the day's events. Dragged from holding camps and homes, bundled aboard a truck to be killed, now this. Another of the older fighters, Alannah, enfolds three or four of the little ones in an embrace, speaking softly, then shepherds them back towards the 'cruiser. Shots ring out as Helen's team finish the job; the wounded Reaper's screaming stops. No-one even thinks of mercy. The Reapers show none, and these are GenRen – everyone's seen the white shoulder-flashes.

Movement ahead, glimpsed through some of the children still on the road. A black leather uniform. "Out of the way!" Helen shouts, raising the gun; the kids scatter.

It's the officer, fumbling for his pistol with his good hand, the other hanging limp and useless at his side. He's weeping – perhaps with terror, perhaps with pain. When he sees Helen, he screams, dropping the pistol and raising his good arm. "Don't shoot," he says. "I give up."

Helen keeps coming towards him. He crawls away, till he's up against the mill's broken wall; behind him, she can see the pit.

The basement is littered with masonry and flooded with grey-white, stagnant water. In the water there are corpses. Two, three hundred; maybe more. Heaps of them; some form little hills. Rats crawl over them; a couple of crows flap down to peck. Some bear bullet wounds, but most have crushed skulls and broken limbs. And all of them are children.

"Don't," begs the officer. "Please. Don't. Please don't shoot me."

Helen looks down. A Reaper lies on his back, staring upwards, an iron bar near one outstretched hand. "Don't worry," she says, "I won't." She reaches down. "I don't waste bullets."

The iron bar whistles through the air. The officer screams He stops after the third blow, but only because she's shattered his jaw. Helen heaves him over the broken wall; he hits the slope, bouncing, and lands among a pile of the dead. She thinks he's still moving as the rats close in. Hopes so, at least. She throws the bar after him and turns away.

"Good work," says Ashton. "Let's go."

The last of the kids are almost on board, but as Helen watches, one runs away from the landcruiser. Alannah comes after him, but he keeps backing off.

"Easy." Helen holds up a hand for Alannah to stay put. "What's this then?" she asks, approaching the boy.

"I want to know what you're going to do with me," he says. His voice is light and high, but very clear. He's pale, with blond hair and light blue eyes, and almost angelically beautiful.

"Do?" Helen crouches. "We're going to take you somewhere safe. We're going to give you a home."

"No-one will try to hurt me?"

"No," she says. "No-one."

The boy's isolation and aloneness is so familiar; despite all their differences, Helen might be looking in a mirror. She holds out a hand. "Come on," she says. "Please?"

"Helen!" shouts Ashton. "We need to go."

Helen ignores him, keeps her hand extended. "Helen?" says the boy. "That's your name?"

"That's right. What's yours?"

"I don't have one," he says. "I am – I."

"Would you like a name?" she asks. After a moment, he nods. "Then come with us, and we'll find you one."

He looks at her, then at her hand. Then he takes it, and she leads him to the truck.

NURSERY, THE REFUGE

10TH OCTOBER, ATTACK PLUS SIX YEARS

Helen goes down the tunnel, knocks on the door. Kate opens it, smiles.

Helen smiles back. It's always hard not to with Kate. "Here I am," she said. "What do you need?"

Kate's smile dims a fraction. "Just a few minutes. In here, if that's okay?"

"Sure."

The nursery's a large chamber, partitioned with wood planking: two or three 'quiet rooms', the dormitory, the playroom, and a small office for Kate. It's this Helen steps into now.

Kate motions Helen to an old, soft armchair. Helen sits, fidgeting; she's never comfortable around Kate. Not out of dislike; the opposite, in fact. You feel warmth in Kate's presence; safety. A round-faced, pretty woman in her fifties, with curly blonde hair – used to be a therapist or counsellor, something like that, before the War. Worked a lot with children, someone said. Explains a lot.

And that's just it. Everything about Kate says *you can talk to me; you can tell me how you feel.* And Helen's not doing that, not with anyone. The things she's seen and done and felt are old shrapnel: lodged deep, imperfectly healed around, locked where they can't cause pain except when the wind blows cold.

"So?" says Helen.

Kate sighs, sits facing her. "It's about the little boy."

"Which one?" But Helen knows, of course.

"The little one you rescued the other day. About ten years old. Blonde hair, blue eyes. No name."

The blue eyes; Helen hasn't been able to get them out of her head, the need in them. "What about him?"

"He's been having panic attacks," says Kate. "Very bad ones. Hyperventilating, nearly passing out yesterday."

"Poor little sod. But that's – I mean, isn't that what you deal with?"

"Normally, Helen, yes. But he doesn't seem to want to talk to me." Kate looks at her steadily. "He just keeps asking for you."

"Me?" The fear of any kind of intimacy, of opening herself to hurt; the sudden warmth of being needed. "Why?"

Kate spreads her hands. "I don't know. He obviously sees something in you. Without knowing about his childhood, what stages in his development he's missed… but he's definitely bonded with you, I think. You might be the first person that's happened with."

"Bonded? Wait, wait." Helen raises her hands. "I'm a fighter, Kate. I'm not a nurse."

"All I'm asking is that you see him. Go talk to him, see if you can bring him out."

"Out? What's happened – he turned into a casualty?"

"No, nothing like that. In fact, I don't think I've seen anything quite like this. Whatever he's been through, it's affected him deeply, but in a pretty unusual way. He's polite – very, very polite."

"And that's wrong?"

"Not wrong, just… strange. Not many of us still have anything in the way of social grace, and certainly not children his age. Too many of them orphaned, fighting for survival. It's a defence, I think. He uses manners and etiquette to hide how he feels."

"Manners and etiquette?"

"No child his age, in all of this, should be as well-mannered and self-contained as he is most of the time. I'd guess most of it's from books. He reads a lot, voraciously. Spends most of his time in one of the quiet rooms with a stack of books and he's happy as a clam."

"Then what's the problem?"

"It can't last. It's a way of not feeling, I suppose, a coping mechanism. A shield, but a very brittle one. Sooner or later it'll break, and I don't know what'll happen to him then. You're the one person he has any apparent emotional attachment towards. I mean, look."

Kate picks some drawings up from the table by the chair and holds them out. Helen takes them. They're of a female figure – she thinks – with a gun. In a dull blue suit or coverall, like she wears – like many rebels do. But the giveaway's the hair; bright red. "Why me? Why not someone else? Why not Alannah? She was the first to see him, and she loves mothering the little ones."

"Your guess is as good as mine right now," says Kate. "It might just be that you're a fighter."

"So's Alannah."

"But also a nurturer, a mother-figure. You're a warrior – you're not helpless, not vulnerable. Maybe that's it. Maybe he thinks he can rely on you not to die on him."

Helen hands back the picture. "Okay," she says. "I'll talk to him."

*

She taps on the quiet room door. Behind her, the other kids play – the other orphans, the ones who haven't been found adoptive parents or are still too damaged or disturbed.

"Please go away," says a voice from inside. Calm, quiet, but ragged with tears.

"It's Helen," she says. Silence. She bites her lip and pushes open the door; the Reapers would be easier to handle than this.

The nameless boy curls in a corner, surrounded by his books. His little body shakes with sobs. Helen goes to him and kneels. She doesn't know what to do. Like the first time she had to field-strip a gun; she knew what the object was but hadn't a clue what to do with it.

After a moment, she reaches out, hesitant, and touches his shoulder. The boy reacts as if stung, head whipping round to glare at her – and then recognition dawns. A moment of stillness, and then he moves, flinging his arms around her, a grip so tight he'll never let go, she thinks, and the sheer gentle need of him makes the grip unbreakable.

She's rigid in his embrace at first, but as he sobs and clings, tries to bury himself in her, his anguish is like a fine oil, the kind that trickles deep into machinery, loosening, cleaning, making parts stiff from lack of use capable of movement again. And she can't help it; her arms fold around him, pulling him as tight to her as she's pulled to him, stroking his back. She kisses his hair, and she sings to him, an old song her mother taught her.

And as she does, she feels the boy quieten and relax, resting against her, warm and quiet and still, his head in the hollow of her shoulder, so neatly it's as though they were carved for one another. She realises her face is wet, and her throat hurts. She's been crying too. Did Mum feel like this about her? Perhaps. Or perhaps it's more how she'd have felt towards a little brother, if she'd ever had one.

*

They sit in the corner, the boy curled against her; she strokes his hair with one hand and reads to him from one of the books that litter the floor. Greek myths. He loves those: Oedipus and the Sphinx, the Labours of Hercules – and, most of all, Perseus and the Gorgon, how the young hero killed Medusa, whose gaze turned men to stone, and rescued the Princess Andromeda.

It won't be till years later that Helen wonders whether Kate brought them together as much for Helen's sake as for the boy's.

"Perseus was brave, wasn't he?" says the boy.

"Yes."

"Like you."

Helen has no answer to that.

"And he saved Andromeda from the monster," says the boy.

"He did."

"I'd save you," the boy says. Helen looks at him; he's looking up at her with that earnest, solemn look. "The way you saved me. If you were in danger, I mean. If there was a monster. I'd be like him."

She touches his cheek. "I know you would, love." She feels warm, tender – capable of things she thought she'd lost the skill to do.

"Can I be Perseus?" the boy asks shyly.

"How do you mean?"

"You said you'd find me a name," he says. "Can that be mine?"

"Okay, then," says Helen. "Perseus." She thinks of the teasing, of how cruel kids can be, even now. "Percy for short?"

He grins. "Percy for short."

And she draws him to her, and he nestles in her embrace, and they gently rock in silence.

In just nine years, he'll be dead.

4.

BOWKITT

20TH MARCH, ATTACK PLUS TWENTY-ONE YEARS
1615 HOURS

The house was roofless but the walls still stood; it gave Flaps and the others some protection from the bullets hammering their position. She poked the Sterling out through a window and snapped off a burst, though she doubted she hit anything in the swirling smoke and dust.

Beak's rifle banged out a rapid tattoo as she fired through a gap in the brickwork; beside her Sud huddled, sobbing. Flaps crawled past them to Newt. "Rook Two, now," she said, then took the mic. "Rook Two, what's your status? Rook Two." Silence. "Goll, fucking well talk to me."

A voice she didn't recognise came on the line. "Goll dead, Rook One."

"Fuck. Okay, what's your status?"

"Fucked. Goll trying to get us in line – then they hit. Everyone giving orders at once, so nothing done. Overran us. Pushed us back. Now we're – oh fuck!"

Shouts. Screams. Gunfire – and then the transmission cut. "Rook Two?" said Flaps, knowing even then there'd be no answer. "Come in, Rook Two."

It was still sinking in when a dull thud came from her left, then another. The Highway. Flaps spat out dust. Fucking hell, she was thirsty. "Shit. Crow's Nest, Rook One here. What's happening down there?"

"Fucking carnage, Rook One. Rook Two's nearly wiped out – last few of them are falling back towards here."

"What about the Highway?"

"Reapers are setting charges to blow the wrecks, clear a way through."

"Shit."

"Rook One, we're armed up here, we got rifles. We could –"

"*No*," said Flaps. "We need eyes and ears there. Don't give away your position, just watch. Keep us briefed." She tossed the mic back to Newt. "Jazz!"

The other woman raised a hand, crawled over.

"Take a squad and get to the Highway. Don't let the fuckers clear it."

Seconds after Jazz had gone, something seemed to crash into the house, and the inside filled with smoke and dust. Flaps coughed, spluttered; someone grabbed her arm and dragged her to the floor. Bullets flew in through the window and smashed into the walls. Two fighters, male and female, who didn't get down fast enough were hit; the man's head exploded and the woman was almost cut in half.

Flaps wriggled to the window. Over the sill, she saw the landcruisers rolling in. They spread through the streets, or over the parts of the town flat enough to roll over. They spread out wide, a single advancing front, no one spot to concentrate the rebels' fire, travelling at a near crawl. Their .50 cals swept back and forth across the ruins, firing continuously; their spread meant they could hammer everything with heavy weapons fire, and the speed meant their pace was slow and steady.

The Jennywrens followed on foot, mopping up. There were screams, bursts of gunfire, then silence. The Reapers were a killing wall that moved, pushing relentlessly in.

An orange flash; an explosion, and bodies flew from a landcruiser. Then another was hit, and another. The rocket teams. But then other explosions erupted in the rebel lines; Flaps saw a pair of Reapers aiming a Carl Gustaf of their own over the top of a landcruiser cabin. A chunk of brickwork by the window exploded in her face as a bullet smashed it; she fell back coughing and choking, clutching at her blinded eyes.

"Flaps!"

"Fuck!"

Hands grabbed her, dragged her to a sitting position. She coughed and spat; her hands were to her eyes. They were streaming tears and stinging, but as she wiped at them her vision cleared. "I'm okay," she said. "I'm okay." Then she saw who was kneeling in front of her. "Jazz? The fuck are you doing here?"

Jazz's forehead was bleeding, and she was as dust-caked as Flaps. "The demolition crews on the Highway are guarded. Blasted the hell out of us. We couldn't get near."

From the Devil's Highway came two more explosions; another fusillade smashed into the house's tottering walls.

BOWKITT LIBRARY
1620 HOURS

Like slow black poisonous beetles, the landcruisers crawled through the burned town across the way; below the library, the remains of Rook Two hid behind burned-out rusted cars and heaps of rubble to make their final stand.

"Fuck this," said Cov, and reached for his SLR.

"The fuck are you doing?" Mackie yelped.

"They're gonna be wiped out down there," said Cov.

"Flaps told us not to!"

291

"If they go, so does the Fort," said Cov, "and then we're all fucked anyway."

"But they'll see us."

"Then they see us."

Who first? Rook Two or Rook One? Rook Two needed all the help they could get, but even if a few survived, there weren't enough left to do any damage to the fucking convoy. And if Rook One didn't get help and fast, there wouldn't be enough of them left either. Cov crawled to the window and sighted across the Highway towards the line of 'cruisers. He got one of the machine gunners in his sights, then fired. The man pitched over the flatbed from the impact. He sighted on another and fired, again, and again.

"Twat!" Mackie scrambled across the floor, with his own rifle. "If we get killed 'cos of this, I'll fucking do you, you fucking knobhead."

Cov grinned and fired again.

BOWKITT

The hammering fire from outside faltered, became lighter, more sporadic. Flaps looked out; nearly a third of the .50 cals were already unoccupied, and another gunner fell as she watched. A Reaper taking aim with a Carl Gustaf tumbled from his landcruiser. Thin and faint, she heard a voice shouting. "Get on that .50 cal!"

"Now!" she screamed. "Get on them, Newt – tell everyone, hit the cunts now! Beak, Sud, cover us."

"Come on!" Beak shouted at Sud, firing over the wall. Flaps saw the boy's shoulders hitching, faster and faster, with his breathing; then he screamed and opened up with his Sten. Almost automatically, Beak reached across and pushed his head down.

Flaps shoved a new mag into the Sterling and charged out, weaving through the wreckage and keeping low. Single shots and bursts rang out behind her. A 3½ inch rocket blew out another 'cruiser. She ducked behind a 'cruiser-sized chunk of concrete, aimed over, sprayed a burst that hit one of the remaining gunners as she tried to bring her weapon about.

With a hiss and clank, the landcruisers reversed; a Reaper who didn't get clear in time screamed as the wheels snapped his bones. The other Reapers ran, keeping the landcruisers between them and the enemy in their retreat. Others were left exposed; Flaps aimed and fired, burst after burst, knocking one after another down, while other guns cracked and volleyed. As the landcruisers rolled back, they left a scattering of beetleblack bodies in their wake. Flaps came out from behind the concrete and went after them.

BOWKITT LIBRARY

Gunfire raked across the library windows and smashed the tiled ceiling, showering Cov with broken ceramic and glass. Dust billowed out and filled the air.

A rocket shrieked towards them. "Fuck!" screamed Mackie – but the projectile shot past, clipping the side of the dome. Pieces of tile fell past a window; Cov scrambled to another one, ducking as a .50 cal fired again. He snapped off a shot in reply, but couldn't tell if he hit anything or not.

"You fucking bellend," said Mackie.

"Shurrup," said Cov. "Tool up and take the stairs. Cunts'll be trying to come on up."

BOWKITT

Flaps reloaded as the landcruisers pulled back to regroup. Jazz scuttled to her, tugged her sleeve.

"What?"

Jazz pointed across the road; Flaps saw bullets kicking dust from the library dome, a muzzle flash at the windows. "Shit."

"What do we do?"

"Can't do fuck-all, with Rook Two gone." Flaps took a deep breath. "Grab some launchers, get another squad together and hit that fucking convoy. Newt! Get me Osprey."

THE WAR ROOM, ASHWOOD FORT

"Field-Bases Three and Twenty are holding off Reaper attacks too," said Darrow. "There isn't anyone."

Alannah picked up the mic. "Rook One, this is Osprey Actual. Negative on back-up. Other bases are also in combat."

"We can't hold with what we've got," said Flaps. "We need support here, or that convoy's getting through."

Alannah turned to Darrow. "There are other forces further up the Highway, right?"

"Yes, in case anything gets past them."

"That's a big fucking convoy, Darrow, and by the sound of it Flaps' people haven't made a dent. The others aren't equipped to hit them as hard."

Darrow nodded. "Good point. All right. It's your call."

"Thanks." Alannah pushed transmit. "Osprey Actual to Rook One. Hold on. Help's coming. But they can't get through. Whatever happens, you've got to hold them."

"Roger that, Osprey. We won't let you down."

ASHWOOD VILLAGE
1625 HOURS

Long beats of silence stretched across the village's smoking ruins, broken by the rattle of loose rock as someone moved, bursts of fire from the second wall and answering salvos from the ruins.

What there *hadn't* been, Lance-Corporal Sara White was grimly aware as she inched through the rubble towards St Martin de Porres, was a rifle shot from the church tower. The other snipers knew they were coming, and they were on alert.

Two rifles poked over the church tower parapet. Slowly, White eased a hand up to touch the earpiece in her headset. "Scythe Three."

"Yes, Scythe Two." Greene's voice was cracked and trembly. This was too new to him; never been under heavy fire before, and more than half their team was already gone. Harper, even. Christ. Harper couldn't be dead. But he was. White pushed how that felt to one side. Kill now. Mourn later. "Two rifles. See them?"

"Yes, I have them."

"Target the one on the right," said White. "I'll take the left."

She kept the intersection of the cross-hairs above the barrel. Just show me something. Just for a second. All they had to do was try to take a shot, and that was it.

Get an officer or NCO to move, catch their attention? Unlikely. These two were both bloody good at what they did. If they'd worked out there were counter-snipers after them, they knew this was a duel. They could let nothing else distract them, any more than White let the click and rattle of movement over stone behind her register in any real sense.

Tie the snipers up, and she and Greene bought time for a strike team to get into position to hit the inner wall; it took a sniper's eye and scope to spot the subtle signs of movement as Jennywrens in camo gear crept in. When that happened, the two in the church tower were fucked anyway. But that was too easy. Less than they deserved. White wanted to be the one who brought their deaths. One sniper to another. But the time was ticking down for that.

She wondered if she'd ever know their names.

Movement; the rifle barrel to the left dipping, a helmet rising behind it. That one mistake; for whatever reason, that one mistake.

White fired, and the bullet hit; the helmet clanged like a dinner gong. But no blood or brains, and it didn't fall.

That one mistake.

She just had time to register that before something smashed into her skull and the world turned white, then black. She didn't hear the bullet; travelling faster than its own sound, it left no time for that.

BELFRY, ST MARTIN DE PORRES CHURCH

Scopes ducked down, hitting the floor – strewn with bat-shit – as a rifle bullet punched through one of the louvres in the side of the belfry. Then another. Then a shot rang out from above. After that, silence.

Scopes peeped out of the slit again. Below, she made out the female sniper, slumped over her rifle, blood thickening and darkening the dust around her head. A second sniper had fallen half into the road, his rifle beside him. Blood spread round him too, but he was still moving feebly. Looked like a throat wound. As she watched, he shuddered once and then lay still, open eyes staring up.

Scopes nodded once to herself, worked the Lee-Enfield's bolt to eject the cartridge and load a new one, then climbed back up to the roof.

ASHWOOD VILLAGE

Benbow crouched behind the broken wall as the latest volley of shots settled, then glanced over at Mitchell. "How are we doing?"

"All set up here, sir." The sergeant nodded at the five rockets set up on their stands behind the wall. "The other groups are nearly ready too."

"Right, then." Benbow blinked, pulled off his glasses and rubbed his eyes. "Better let Jarrett know, then. Tell them all to prepare to fire."

"Yes, sir."

St Martin de Porres Church

Trex grinned as Scopes crept over. Her L1A1 was still propped against the parapet, the helmet and the stick he'd lifted it on lying on the floor. She put the helmet back on.

"Good job," he said.

She grinned back. "Yes, that wasn't bad, was it?"

Then she heard something whistle through the air.

Scopes turned, saw the rockets streaking from the edge of the village ruins. Two, targeted on the church. One overshot and exploded behind; the other hurtled towards the roof. No time.

She dived down, pulling Trex with her, knowing as she did that it wouldn't do any good.

The rocket hit a second later.

Wall Two
1630 hours

Rockets smashed into the battlements, explosions erupting, flinging bodies skyward. Some screamed as they fell. Danny was flung sideways. *Fuck*, he thought. And, *Alannah*.

He saw the parapet pass under him; below were the other defenders on the ground, staring up. Oh fuck, oh fuck. Not even a quick death. Die slow and broke, live a cripple –

And then it was as if he could fly. He stopped, hung in the air for a second, then flew back, down, lighted safe on the parapet.

Gevaudan let him go. "Are you all right?"

"Fuck me." Danny nodded. "Yeah. Yeah. Cheers, Creeping Death."

"Yes, you're clearly fine, and still have a death-wish."

"Eh?"

"Never mind."

"Good to see you."

"Just came back from a little errand for Darrow. I assumed I'd be of most use here."

The rockets had stopped; from below were screams and shots and bellows from the Reapers. Danny looked over the parapet; hundreds of the fuckers, charging.

"Open fire," Danny yelled, but when he looked he saw the battlements near-empty but for the dead. Harp and Lish were still there, Lish pumping shots from her rifle rapid-fire, but the rocket salvo had been a sight more accurate than the one that'd hit Wall One. Huge chunks of parapet had been blasted away, and what remained of Wall Two's defenders were streaming back down the steps to the inner courtyard. "Get back!" he yelled after them. "Get fucking back here."

"No use," said Gevaudan, as the first grappling irons clanked into place and fists hammered at the gate below. "We can't hold here. Fall back and regroup." He picked up a GPMG. "I'll follow."

"Fuck." But he was right.

Harp dragged Lish away from the wall; Danny ran with them back down the steps. Behind him, the machine gun chattered. It was only as he ran across the courtyard that he remembered: *Scopes*.

St Martin de Porres Church

"Scopes? Scopes?"

She opened one eye. Trex was prone beside her.

"Are we dead?" She said.

"Don't think so."

"How did we manage that?"

Outside, gunshots and bellowing. "Fuck." Trex rolled onto his back, staring. "They're storming the fucking wall."

The communicator crackled. "Scopes? Trex? This is Harrier."

Danny pushed a finger in his free ear, pressed the handset to the other to hear Scopes over the gunfire. "Yeah, we're okay. It was a dud. But we're stuck."

"Not gonna forget about you," said Danny. "Just hang on in there."

"Do what we can. Fuck. They've clocked we're still here. Got to go, Danny. We'll hold them off as long as we can."

"War Room for you," the comms tech shouted.

Danny grabbed the mic. "Harrier."

"This is Falcon," said Darrow's voice. "They've broken through?"

"Yeah," said Danny.

"All right. You're in charge of all remaining defences, Harrier. Sending you everyone we've got left."

"Roger that. Won't let you down."

"I know that, Danny."

ST MARTIN DE PORRES CHURCH
1635 HOURS

Scopes aimed over the tower parapet, snapped off three fast shots; two Reapers went down. One kept screaming; others dragged him back. Submachine gun fire spattered across the edge of the parapet. She ducked and rolled, came up and fired back, then ducked again.

Sweat ran into her eyes. She hacked a strip from her shirt, bound it round her forehead. Out on the roof in the sun and working hard. Her mouth was parched, throat dry; she needed water. Scopes took a gulp from her canteen; it was almost empty.

Across the rooftop, Trex's rifle cracked rapid-fire, half a dozen rounds in quick succession. "Watch your ammo," Scopes said.

"Three down. Another wounded," he said.

Not good enough. Should be one shot, one kill. Even then they were up against it. The Jennywrens had the church surrounded. Every few seconds, another group moved in.

Scopes did the maths. One of them up here or both – either way, sooner or later, the Reapers would get in. But she was fast – fast enough that on her own she could keep circling the top of the tower, do some damage. "Trex!"

"Yo."

"Need to hold the stairs, in case they get in. That's you. On it, now."

"'Bout you?"

"I'll be fine. On it!"

Trex nodded once. Hesitated. Looked at her; she looked back.

"On it," Scopes said, softly, again.

Another nod. Trex grabbed rifle, Thompson gun, a satchel full of mags; headed down the stairs.

Scopes opened her mouth to call him back: best to stay up top, cut them down as they came single-file up the narrow stairs. But he was gone, and then shots came bouncing off the parapet again. She rolled, came up to the side, fired down. A dozen Reapers moving in towards the main entrance. Bunched together, the silly cunts; she sighted and fired, fired, fired. Just a split-second's work to twitch the barrel left or right or up or down a hair – and with each shot, down a Reaper went.

She ducked and rolled again to avoid another burst of fire, but whooped as she did, grinning. One shot, one kill, every single time. Eight shots, eight down, and half of them were headers. She ran back to the parapet to go again.

Inner Courtyard
1640 hours

Danny felt the shelter judder under bullet impacts. He crawled through the sandbag tunnel, peered out through a gun slit. The Reapers were on the battlements, but heavy fire from the fighters were hitting them. Some of the defenders were in the upper storeys of the Fort, firing down.

One of the defenders grunted and fell back, jerking. "Lish!" Danny shouted. The medic barrelled through the shelter, dropped to her knees by the wounded man, but even as she did, he coughed and was still, eyes fixed and unblinking. "Get him out," Lish shouted. "And take his ammo."

Danny crawled to Gevaudan, who knelt nearby, firing short, killing bursts up from a Bren gun. "How's it look?"

The Grendelwolf bared his teeth; soot and grime smudged his white face, and his yellow eyes shone. "Holding. Just about. They have the wall, but they can't get further."

"Not till they get those fucking mortars up there, they can't," Danny said.

"Ah, yes. I really should have remembered those." Gevaudan sighed. "We'll need to do something about that, won't we?"

"One of us will." And there was Scopes and Trex. "All right, mate. You'd better gear up for some covering fire. Counter-attack time."

St Martin de Porres Church
1650 hours

Scopes was dripping sweat now as she bolted back and forth across the tower roof. Like a dance; spin, dive, roll, come up and fire. Two more Jennywrens spun about and fell as the heavy rounds from the SLR hit them, another fell writhing and

301

screaming with a shattered leg. Three shots, two kills. Slipping, Scopes. So thirsty.

A light foam filled her mouth; she spat, and the SLR's barrel hissed and smoked. Sounds of movement: Scopes rolled again as a grapple landed on the roof, hooked over the parapet. She came up, fired five rounds rapid down. Screams. She threw herself back as a wave of shots crashed and sprayed against the church tower. Unhooked the grapple, threw it down. Came up again, aimed on two Reapers, fired; the gun was empty.

"Fuck." She searched the ammo satchel; one mag left for the SLR. The iron bullets from Danny. The rest were the chargers for the Lee-Enfield.

"Last mag!" Scopes shouted down the stairs, and grinned to herself as she slapped it home and jacked back the bolt; she'd always preferred the Lee-Enfield anyway. It'd been hers since she was old enough to shoot; better by far to fight her last fight with it, if that was what this was.

*

The first squads of Reapers had swarmed into the church through the main entrance; Trex had downed nearly all of them with the rifle, rapid-fire, but now the SLR was empty, with even the iron bullets gone.

Now he was down to the Thompson gun. Good gun; didn't have the SLR's range, but he didn't need it in here. The heavy .45 rounds it spat hit hard, dropping his targets. Two round bursts: the stick mag held twenty rounds. Each burst meant one Jennywren; each clip, ten.

The Reapers flung themselves down behind pews, fired over them; bursts from the Thompson smashed straight through. The thin wood wasn't a shield for bullets; the stone of the doorway around him was.

The Thompson emptied. Trex loaded another clip. Last one. Fuck – thought he'd had more. A Reaper ran for the doorway, screaming, another dozen rising to rush after him; Trex fired one-handed from the hip. The man jerked sideways, sprawled forward. Sloppy – at least five rounds in that burst. Trex dropped to one knee, the Thompson shouldered, two hands now, and fired out the weapon in neat bursts, then dropped it and pulled the Browning at his hip instead. Two-hand grip, double taps. The last of the charging Reapers turned, tried to run back; Trex put the last round in the back of his head. Better doing that now than him facing you with a gun.

Another one rushed him, now his gun was empty. Trex's hand dropped to his hip, plucked the throwing-stick he carried. Drop a rabbit with that, he'd told Danny once; Reaper, too. This one had a helmet on; Trex aimed for the throat, threw. The stick whipped through the air and hit. He heard the Reaper's voicebox crunch and she went down, choking.

Nasty way to go, but they'd come here for a fight, so it was all on them. The Reaper who'd charged him lay at his feet, a Sterling in his hands. Trex reached to pick it up.

Someone punched him in the stomach. That was his thought; near enough the last coherent one before the pain burst in him. Worst he'd ever known, knocking his legs from under him and – oh fuck. His bowels had gone. Shat himself. Hot warmth pooling in his trousers, blood and shit.

The Reaper with the crushed throat; smoke coiled from her rifle. Then it clattered on the floor and she slumped over it. The other Reapers came out from behind their pews.

Cunts. Coming out for the kill. Trex grabbed the Sterling and fired, raking it across them. Three down. He hauled himself to the stairs. Grabbed the handrail. Managed to stand, doubled over with pain. Shit running from his kecks. Hold onto the gun. One hand. A black helmet appeared round the doorway. Trex fired at it, kept backing up. Another burst as another Reaper appeared.

He was almost at the top when someone's hand stuck a pistol round the corner and fired up the stairs, working left to right and back. Another in the stomach, two more in the chest. Another smashed his left shoulder; he hung onto the Sterling with his right, fired another burst, but the recoil jarred it from his hands. He dragged himself up the last couple of steps, pulled himself to his feet with the doorframe. "Scopes," he got out, and then the floor was gone and he fell forward.

Scopes dragged him back from the doorway, kicking it shut. Her eyes stung, throat threatened to close. Fuckers. Pulled Trex into the middle of the roof, knelt over him. Rifle, Thompson, pistol. That was what she had, and she'd use them all to keep them back from him.

A Reaper ran up into the doorway; Scopes shot him through the chest and he fell back. Pulled back the bolt for another round as more feet ran up the stairs. Then a clank behind her – another grapple going over the parapet. Fuck. She threw aside the Lee-Enfield; it wouldn't fire fast enough, love it though she did. She snatched up the Thompson, cut down two more Reapers in the doorway to the roof, spun and raked the parapet as one climbed over.

Clank and *clank* and *clank* rang out. More grapples, going over the wall – left and right, in front, behind. Scopes palmed a spare clip, held it ready as she fired burst after burst, spinning this way then that way then right the way round.

They kept coming and coming and somewhere at the back of her head she knew they'd win, that there was no stopping them, but she ignored that voice, along with the one that offered the hope Danny would be in time. They weren't relevant anyway, didn't matter. All that mattered was the next move, making it the right move. Now left, now behind, now right, now the door. Turn and be there in time to shoot, and hit your mark. Not that she had to worry about that. Best shot in Darrow's crew, she was; had always been. The day she missed was a cold one in Hell. It was all a game, a game of chance and skill. And she was as good as anyone got at it. She was a machine, clean and smooth and coldly efficient, that swivelled and aimed and shot.

Dimly, she registered that Trex lay still. Her eyesight blurred with tears, but only for a second. The Thompson emptied. She slammed a fresh magazine in, pulled back the bolt, raked the doorway as a group of Jennywrens tried rushing it, then spun and fired at the parapet.

Another magazine emptied. Then another. One left. Her shoulder ached from the recoil, her eyes from smoke and tears.

She was slowing; two Jennywrens burst through the doorway as she shot another one off the parapet, guns rising. The Thompson swept across them and they fell.

And then the Thompson was empty.

She threw it down, reached for the Enfield revolver on her hip. Trex had liked his Browning, but Scopes never had; she didn't trust an automatic, had only used the SLR under protest and as long as they'd let her keep her old rifle. Revolvers didn't jam and if they misfired you just pulled the trigger again. But she could have used the Browning's thirteen shots instead of the Enfield's six.

She fired two-handed, pivoting left, then right. Bullets spanged off the roof and then she was hit – in the leg, in the side. Scopes swung left and fired, hitting the Reaper who'd poked her Sterling over the parapet in the face. The woman fell from the tower, screaming.

Something hit Scopes in the back. With a broomstick crack, her spine shattered and her legs were gone. Scopes fell forward, over Trex. Booted feet ran in: over the walls, from the doorway. She tried to lift the Enfield, but they kicked it away. Then kicked her, over onto her broken back. Kicked and kicked. And then they fired – pistols, rifles, SMGs. Kept on firing, long after she was gone.

INNER COURTYARD
1700 HOURS

"Oh no," said Gevaudan.

Danny stared at the Grendelwolf. He'd never heard him sound like that before. He was staring up through the gun-slit, towards the wall. "What?" said Danny, moving towards another slit.

Gevaudan put a hand on his shoulder. "I wouldn't," he said. "You don't want to see."

Danny pulled away and looked though the slit.

Normally you couldn't see the church tower for the wall, but a couple of rockets had hit together and blown a chunk of battlement away, so now you could.

It took him a couple of seconds to work out what he was seeing. Something pale and splashed with red, hanging from the parapet. Two limp pale stalks hung down. Arms. And there was a dangling mop of hair, wet and matted with blood. And just as he understood what he was looking at, they slung Trex's body over too, naked and broken and hanging upside down.

"Bastards!" He punched the sandbags. "Fucking cunts!" He grabbed the Lanchester. "Right. We're fucking having the twats now."

"Wait." Another hand, on his wrist. He looked: Wakefield, Filly behind her. "They want that," she said, voice unsteady. Her eyes glistened. Her and Scopes had got on, Danny remembered, and Trex had been one of her tribe. "Want you angry. Not thinking. Then you fuck up. And they kill you."

Danny breathed out. Yeah. Made sense. *Deep breaths. Control.* What Darrow always said. "Right," he said. "But we've got to hit 'em anyway."

Wakefield grinned. "I know."

"Harp?" shouted Danny.

"Here."

Harp scuttled over; Lish was beside him, still tightening a wound dressing on his arm. "Keep still, will you, for the love of Mary?"

Harp snorted and waved her away, then yelped as Lish pulled the dressing tight.

"When you've finished dicking around," said Danny. "You and Wakefield, get whatever's left of your lot together. We're taking the wall. Me and Wakefield're on those steps —" He pointed to the flight to the gate's left. "You lot're on the other set. Clear?"

"Clear," said Harp.

Danny turned to Wakefield. "And after that, you sort those rockets and mortars out. Rest of us'll cover you."

Wakefield licked her lips, but nodded. "Will do."

"Gevaudan?"

"I'm here, Danny."

"Yeah. *Stay* here. This doesn't work, we're gonna need you to keep 'em back."

"Even I can't hold them off on my own."

"You won't be on your own. Come on, Wakers."

1710 HOURS

Hunched at the entrance to the shelter, the Lanchester in his hands. Felt weird. So used to barking orders for others to run and shoot he'd nearly forgotten how it was. Half-scared. Half-glad. At least in that kind of fighting it was simpler; just his life lost if he fucked up.

A deep breath; heart hammering. Fear. The dark grey afternoon and the guns flashing on the battlements. Shouts and cries.

Bullets punching into the sandbags; sand running out. Bullets punching divots out of the ground. And he wanted to run into that?

Danny's eyes found the gap in the wall; the church tower and the two torn and broken forked things hung from it. Let himself remember them both. Trex at Hobsdyke; Trex beating out a rhythm on his guitarback and chanting some tale of his tribe. And Scopes. Scopes at Station Five, dropping Reaper after Reaper with her rifle, and – and how many more? They'd grown up together. Scopes was family; Scopes was blood.

Danny cocked the Lanchester, glanced behind him at the other fighters ready to charge. "All right, then. Wakefield, on me. You ready, Creeping Death?"

"I believe so," said Gevaudan, shouldering the Bren.

"Right." The fear rose high now; for a moment it threatened to close off his throat and deny him all speech, but then it cleared. "Go!" he shouted, and threw himself out through the door.

The guns opened fire from the shelters, and the ones on the wall hammered down. The ground burst and shattered; men and women dropped and spun; fell and lay still, fell screaming. Danny almost went down as the woman running alongside him pitched sideways. He caught her, staggered, then let her drop; half her head was gone.

A Reaper leant over the battlements; Danny fired a burst from the Lanchester and the man pitched over the rail screaming. Danny ducked again, ran on and reached the bottom of the steps, pressing flat against the wall.

Reapers above, firing down; he threw himself flat and the bullets flew over. Cries and thumps of falling bodies from behind. He fired up, heard another SMG fire behind him. Fired the Lanchester up the steps, zig-zagging the barrel. Two Reapers rolled down them. "Come on!"

Danny up and charging, firing bursts as he went. Muzzles flashed above. A cry; someone just behind him fell backwards down the steps, shot in the throat. Danny advanced and fired, advanced and fired. Slow progress, step by step, bullets cracking by and chipping the wall. The Lanchester emptied; as he changed sticks he saw a Reaper appear at the top, aiming his rifle.

Someone slammed into Danny, sending him sprawling; a submachine gun chattered and the Reaper fell. Wakefield helped him up.

More Reapers up above, taking up positions; Danny pressed flat against the steps, trying to make himself as small a target as he could. By then, Harp and Lish's group had reached the top of the steps and opened fire. A grenade went off. Two Reapers were flung over, fell shrieking to the courtyard. Guns fired.

"Up!" yelled Danny; rose and charged. The Reapers at the top spun back towards him, but he was already firing from the shoulder as he went. So were Wakefield and the rest. The Reapers fell; Danny gained the top of the steps and charged along the battlements. The Lanchester emptied again and he swung it like a club, the butt smashing into a Jennywren's unhelmeted head and crushing bone. He dropped to one knee to change magazines; Wakefield charged past, clubbing a Jennywren with her Thompson gun, taking another in the throat with her knife.

By the time Danny had reloaded, the last Jennywrens on the battlements were dead and the machine guns were firing down into the advancing Reapers again. The rocket crews were almost at the wall, were setting their weapons up. Fired at an upward angle, the rockets would come down in the inner courtyard, maybe on the Fort itself.

The grapples still hung from the battlements; Wakefield grabbed the rope and swung over the side. "With me!" She rappelled quickly down, the others following.

"Give them covering fire," Danny yelled. Machine gun fire swept across the rocket crews. The survivors turned to run, but Wakefield and her team dropped from their ropes and ran at them.

*

"Mitchell!" Benbow dragged himself out from under a body, screaming as his shattered leg pulled free. He twisted sideways, vomited at the pain. He didn't even dare look. "Mitchell!"

The sergeant knelt in front of him, staring his way, but she didn't see. The top of her head was gone. As Benbow watched, she pitched sideways and lay still.

Screaming: Benbow turned, saw the tribesfolk rushing in. A tiny bird-faced woman ran at him, a Thompson gun in one hand, a short spear in the other, howling as she charged.

Benbow screamed too. He fumbled for the pistol at his belt; he'd never used it, but it was all he had. He was still screaming when she drove the spear into his throat.

*

Someone thundered up the steps; Danny swung round, but it was only Gevaudan, the Bren in his hands.

"Oi, Creeping Death," Danny said. "I thought I told you to stay back."

"Just thought I'd see if you needed a hand."

"If I had, I'd have told you."

Gevaudan sighed. *"How sharper than a serpent's tooth…"*

"Eh? Never mind. Cheers, anyway."

THE BATTLETRUCK
1723 HOURS

"I'm sorry, Colonel. They didn't just collapse the cave, they rigged it with enough explosives to bring it down all over again. Vibration sensors everywhere."

"You're telling me you can't get through, Lieutenant Castle?"

"We could, eventually. But it'll take hours."

Soft laughter; if Jarrett looked up, she knew she'd see Tom. She refused to. "How many hours?"

"Ten, twelve. If we're lucky."

"We don't have ten hours," Jarrett said at last. "All right, Castle. Pull back." She breathed out, closing her eyes. "We'll have to find another way."

CATCH CENTRAL
1725 HOURS

"CATCH Central."

"Dr Kellett." Jarrett's distaste was sweet as honey to him. "Prepare to deploy your Catchmen again."

"Things not going well, Colonel?"

"Do *not* push your luck with me, Doctor." A pause. "The rebels have retaken the inner wall and seized the mortars. The outcome of this siege will matter to us both."

"I live to serve, Colonel," said Kellett.

He managed not to giggle till the intercom went dead. Then he reached for the controls and sent the Catchmen marching.

5.

MAIN CANTEEN, THE REFUGE

CHRISTMAS DAY, ATTACK PLUS TEN YEARS

The big canteen's all decked out: boughs of holly, bright shards of glass and plastic hanging from a Christmas tree. At one end are ranks of trestle tables stacked with vats of stew and beer; at the other end a group of musicians with a drum, guitars and comb and paper play 'In Dulci Jubilo'. Against the other walls, rows of chairs and tables, a clear space in the middle to dance.

What little they have, pooled to celebrate. There's not much of faith in it; there are Jews and Muslims here, Hindus and Sikhs, and they're as welcome as the rest. And there's the new faith whose shrines are dotted about the Refuge – pictures and models of the lost, for the grieving to light candles. Superstition, the lot; Helen has no time for any of it, but something in her aches at the Christmas wreaths and songs, the Yule tree. They wake a faint echo, of another, better time.

Percy holds her sleeve as they walk in; her hand rests on his back. She doesn't let her fingers touch his smooth neck;

he's fourteen now, more or less a man by today's standards. Physically, at least.

They find a table; Helen slips something from a pocket in her coverall. "Percy? Happy Christmas."

He blinks at her, stricken. "I... I didn't get you anything."

"It's okay," says Helen, kissing his cheek. "That's not the point. Happy Christmas."

The gift is wrapped in a pre-War plastic bag. Percy unravels it, draws out what's inside. A small metal box. Once it might have shone like silver; it's scratched and tarnished now. "What is it?"

"Open it," she says.

He fumbles with the lid, and it clicks back. A tune plays. She sees his eyes fill; it's the song she sang to him that first time, the one he still most loves to hear.

He just sits there, blinking tears, staring down at it. Does he like it? Hate it? She can't tell; at times like this, his face is a mask. "I thought it might help," she says. "You know, if I'm ever not there. If I'm away, and you have an attack. You can listen to the song, and it'd be like me singing. Next best thing."

Percy looks up; still teary, but smiling. Helen breathes out: relief. "Thank you," he says; gets up and comes around the table, hugs her tight.

The music plays. There's laughter, song; she hugs him back. Helen glimpses Noakes in the background, disgust on his face: Noakes hates the weak, says there's no room for them, and that's all he sees when he looks at Percy. Helen glares back at him till Noakes looks away.

But what *is* going to happen to Percy? He's almost a man – hopefully, at least – but she can't see him ever standing on his own. Too much damage; he's been left too frail. So many like him; the Reapers let them die or have the Jennywrens do Nature's work for her. The rebels don't; do they weaken themselves, or find uses for kids like Percy? She hopes they can.

Helen gets up.

"Are you getting food?" says Percy.

"Not yet. A beer, maybe."

"Can I have some?" he says. That earnest, solemn look; the child so desperate to be a grown-up.

"Okay," she says. "You don't have to finish it if you don't like it. All right?"

"Thanks."

Helen goes up to the tables with the vats, gets a couple of beers in earthenware mugs. As she steps back, someone bumps into her from behind. She loses her balance, drops one mug and sends the contents of the other spilling over the floor.

Laughter and applause. "Sack the juggler!" someone shouts. Helen feels her face flame red, and she rounds on whoever she collided with – but he's already kneeling, picking up the pieces of the broken mug.

"Sorry," he says. "Gimme a second." He's about her age, stockily-built without fat, with cropped blonde hair. He holds out his hand for the other mug and after a second Helen hands it over; he goes to the serving-table, comes back with two fresh drinks. "Here you go," he says, offering one.

"Thanks." That should be the end of it, but Helen doesn't turn away and neither does he. When he moves to get clear of the growing queues she goes with him. "Haven't seen you before."

"From Yorkshire way. Sheffield. Only been here a few days." He holds out a hand. "Frank McCall."

"Helen Damnation."

He laughs. "Seriously?"

Her face burns red again. She took the name soon after joining Darrow. Hide her connection to Wulfden, lest the Reapers take reprisals on the locals. Bury Helen Winter and her grief at her mother's death. But most of all, a statement of intent: a promise of what she'd bring the Reapers. It had seemed clever then; foolish now, but the name had stuck. "Yeah," she says, and the twinkle in his eye sets her laughing too. She glimpses Percy – watching, frowning.

"Listen," says Frank, and she looks back at him. "You want to dance, Helen Damnation?"

And she's about to say no, but then stops. He's a good-looking boy, this Frank McCall, and it's been a long time since there was kissing and hands caressing her, a naked body twined with hers. And it's Christmas and it's cold outside, and the next time she goes out there she could die, and when she's not out there she's got Percy to look after and she's a lucky girl, really – she has shelter and food, more safety than most folk outside the REAP Command can dream of, and shouldn't she live, just a little, while she can?

So she says, "Okay," and Frank reaches out to take her arm. "Just a sec," she says, takes the beers and goes to their table. "Here you go," she tells Percy, then steps back.

"Helen?"

Calling after her like this, he sounds querulous now; nagging, whining. "It's okay," she says, hoping she doesn't sound too sharp. "Just having a dance. I'll see you in a bit."

And she lets Frank take her hand and lead her to the dancefloor, where the band strike up something fast and glad, and she's almost able to lose herself in the music and the dance entirely. Almost; she feels Percy's eyes on her back, hungry and needing, the whole time.

HELEN'S QUARTERS, THE REFUGE
21ST APRIL, ATTACK PLUS ELEVEN YEARS

It's warm in the room, hotter in the bed. The last hour's passed like honey, falling slow and golden from a spoon. When did she last taste honey? She's sure she has since the attack, but the only memory that comes back is Mum's kitchen at Wulfden, Mum drizzling it slowly into Greek yoghurt.

Helen flicks her head to toss the memory away. Mum has no place here – sorry Mum, but you don't. There are some things a parent doesn't like to see their child do. And besides, she doesn't want the past flooding back to haunt her every day. Surely she can build new memories, good ones? Find some joy, even in the ruin of the world?

She kisses Frank deep as they roll from side to side; now him on top, now her. He's deeply tanned, his skin gold-brown against the white of hers. Honey on cream. Or Greek yoghurt.

She grunts and pushes him over on his back, hands on his chest, pressing down: *stay*. His skin's slick with sweat, as if he's dipped in oil; when he runs his fingers down her arms she knows it's the same for him. Her skin tingles at his touch. It's all pure sensation, and it takes everything away, stops her thinking, so being stroked and pleased and loved is all that's left.

She slides her leg across to squat astride him. Slips a hand down to aim and steady his cock, rubbing the head of it against her. He groans and so does she. Feels good, but it's teasing too, both of them knowing there's far more and wanting it badly.

It's easily done; all she needs do is relax a little and sink down. He pushes inside her, until the back of her thighs touch his. Filled. For a while at least. She kneels and circles her hips, moves slowly up and down.

Frank reaches up to hold her breasts, rolling the nipples between finger and thumb. Unwelcome little thoughts come in to niggle at her, nibbling at the edges of awareness like tiny fish at a piece of meat. He's beautiful, so beautiful, and she doesn't want to think of what a bullet might do to him. But he has the same fear for her, and she knows he wants her to stop fighting; everyone works at the Refuge, everyone does their part, but that doesn't mean everyone takes a gun and goes out against the Reapers. She could do something different, but doesn't want to.

And so it goes unsaid. It's not the only thing that does, of course; there's one thing in particular that she hasn't said to Frank, but she's going to have to; it won't stay quiet much longer.

Later, later; all that for later. For now it's just the two of them; their hands on one another, him inside her, her surrounding him. She moves faster, feeling the tingling heat gather as she approaches orgasm; his breathing is ragged and she knows he isn't far behind. An explosion, a beautiful explosion, a white flash that doesn't kill anything but thoughts and fears. At least for a time. She's close; she's almost there.

Bang, bang, bang. Someone's knocking on the door.

"What the fuck?" says Frank.

"Shit." Helen's back in the present, the now – it all crashes in on her, the spell broken. She climbs off Frank, feels him slip out of her, pulls the sheet around her and strides to the door. The sheet clings damply; a smell of musk and sweat.

Helen pulls the door open. "What?"

Percy stares up at her, dazed – by her anger, or by the sight of her, near-naked and her hair all wild, face flushed red. "What do you want?" she demands.

He blinks. "I just –" His voice fades to a whisper as he looks away. "Just wanted to see you."

"It's not a good time, Percy."

"But –"

"Percy, I'll see you later."

She slams the door. Huffs out a long windy breath as she turns away. But it takes her anger with it, because as soon as she's done it she feels ashamed. She starts to turn back, hesitates. No, fuck it. She has her own life. She's looked after him this long. Surely she deserves to have *something* for herself.

So, back to the bed, where Frank wakes, curled and shivering without the sheet, the sweat on him suddenly chill. And she folds the sheet around them both, but there's no heat to that either, and she can feel the damp of their sweat. They huddle close for warmth, now, and only that; the interruption's killed the mood. Even snuggled to his chest, Helen feels alone. And now she remembers what she hasn't told him yet, and must.

"You okay?" he says.

"Yes," she says. But he can hear it in his voice.

"What's wrong?"

She could say *nothing*, she could lie, but what would that achieve? Only a delay. Helen lifts her head and props her chin upon his chest, looks up into his brown, gentle eyes. "I'm pregnant."

Winterborn looked round. He'd felt as though someone had whispered a name in his ear. *Helen.*

Winterborn stood up straight, gritted his teeth, clenched his fists behind his back. He would show no weakness. He would *not.* But even so, the floor beneath him felt ready to give way.

INFIRMARY, THE REFUGE

15TH NOVEMBER, ATTACK PLUS ELEVEN YEARS

Percy's footsteps echo down the corridor as he reaches the infirmary door. In one hand he grips a cake from the canteen, wrapped in cloth. He straightens, coughs and clears his throat. Composes himself, and pushes through the doors.

The infirmary's quiet today; only half a dozen beds are occupied right now. Helen's is at the far end. The cot's beside it, but she's holding the baby to her breast.

Percy doesn't know where to look. Helen's been as good as blood to him, but the only time he ever saw her less than fully clothed was a few months ago, when she flung the door wide, wrapped only in a wet sheet. When she'd snapped at him and slammed the door in his face. As if he wasn't anything to her any more.

She found him later, hugged him and apologised, and they've both tried to pretend it never happened and that everything's as it was before. But it's not, not really; it's still there. Can't trust her like he used to, to catch him when he falls.

Nothing's really been the same since Frank came. And now this – a chain to link Frank and Helen for life. Ever since last Christmas, deep down Percy's hoped that it will end and it'll be just Helen and him again. But that'll never happen now. He's been like blood to Helen, but that's not the same as *being* blood. And where does that leave him? "Hello," he says.

"Percy." Helen smiles; glad to see him, at least. But how long for? "You okay, sweetheart?"

Percy takes the word like a starving child snatching food from a floor. "Y-yes." A stammer. He offers her the cake. "Thought you'd like."

She unwraps it. "Oh, babe. Thank you. C'mere." A one-armed hug, a kiss on the cheek. The baby squalls, as if to get rid of him. "Sh, sweetie. It's okay. Percy, this is Belinda. And Belinda, this is Percy. Percy's your big brother. Aren't you, Percy?"

Blood. Percy forces a smile, looks at the tiny red-faced thing in Helen's arms. Brother. Sister. And he tries so very hard, to feel something, *anything,* for the child that isn't jealousy or resentment. But he can't. "Yes," he says. "I am."

In six and a half months, Percy will be dead.

HELEN'S QUARTERS

2ND FEBRUARY, ATTACK PLUS TWELVE YEARS

Nights like this, Helen wishes she was out in the field fighting Reapers, where Frank is. She will be again, when Belinda's a little older, but she wishes it could be now. Out there, you get too tired to do the job and a bullet ends it all. But this? Doesn't matter how tired she is, the baby's drilling cry, designed so perfectly to be like a knife thrust into the ear, still rings out to rouse her.

But not now; now, after two unending hours of walking up and down the room, Belinda is asleep. Slowly, slowly, Helen leans forward and puts her in the cradle, straightens up, not even daring to breathe unless –

Someone taps at the door.

Helen spins, a hand to her mouth. Fright, then rage: if whoever it is has woken Belinda she'll fucking kill them. But when she turns back, Belinda's snoozing on.

Helen pads to the door – quick, before they knock again – and opens it, a finger to her lips.

"Hi," whispers Kate.

"What is it?" Helen whispers back.

"I thought you'd better know. It's Percy."

"Percy?" She wants to cry; Belinda's demands are draining enough, but does she have to attend to his too? He's a man now, or he should be. His need of her is corrosive, vampiric. Then guilt chases the thought away – what if something's happened to him?

"He's having a panic attack," says Kate. "Very bad one. Worst I've seen him with in years. He could really use you."

So it is that, after all. Helen leans against the wall and shakes her head. "I can't."

"I can stay and mind the b –"

"No. No. I can't do it, Kate. I just can't. I'm fucking falling down here."

"He really needs –"

"I don't care, Kate." That sounds horrible. "Not right now," she amends. "Please. I've been on my feet for – I need to sleep."

She's braced to fight, braced for Kate to trot out sweet reason and persuasion to make her go. Kate, endlessly giving – another's need is her obligation. Yes, a fucking saint. But she expects Helen to follow her example, and Helen can't, not tonight.

Kate doesn't argue, though; maybe she sees it'll be hopeless. "All right," she says, "I'll do what I can."

Disappointment on her face. Fine; let her think less of Helen, then. Helen just nods and closes the door on her, stumbles to her bed.

OPS ROOM, THE TOWER

20TH MARCH, ATTACK PLUS TWENTY-ONE YEARS

Winterborn swayed, suddenly unsteady. From nowhere, he was afraid; his palms were damp with sweat.

Why? No cause. Jarrett was at the Fort's gates; the second convoy was about to break through and then the job would be finished. Helen, Helen was dying with a bullet in her head; surely that was a good thing? No cause, no cause, for him to feel afraid.

And yet he knew these symptoms, knew what was coming. Not here. Not in front of them all. Quickly now, before it was too late.

"I'll be in my office," he told Thorpe. "Inform me of any further developments."

He felt all their eyes on him as he walked from the room.

PERCY'S QUARTERS, THE REFUGE
2ND FEBRUARY, ATTACK PLUS TWELVE YEARS

Can't breathe.

He *is* breathing, of course – but with fast, in and out breaths, too short and shallow to help. Dizzy, falling. Dying. Going to suffocate.

The music box on the floor. Reaching for it, fingers fumbling.

"This?" says Kate. "You want this?" She puts it in his hand.

Percy flips open the lid, and the song begins to play. *If I'm away, and you have an attack*, she said. *You can listen to the song, and it'd be like me singing.* And it's worked before.

But it doesn't now. Today it's just a reminder that Helen isn't here, not because she couldn't come, but because she wouldn't. She doesn't care; he doesn't matter enough to her any more. And the music box is just a reminder that she doesn't; a mockery of the comfort that she gave. Kate's soothing words are just words – no, not even that, they're just noise.

Percy will very soon be dead.

And to sing him on his way, there's only the mocking tinkle of the music box, the tune, the mocking echo of the words that Helen sang him:

I dreamt I dwelt in marble halls, with vassals and serfs at my side,
And of all that dwelt within those walls, that I was their hope and their
pride...

COMMANDER'S OFFICE, THE TOWER
20TH MARCH, ATTACK PLUS TWENTY-ONE YEARS

...I had riches all too great to count, and a high ancestral name,
But I also dreamt, which charmed me most, that you loved me still the
same.

Winterborn breathed in and out of the leather bag as the
tune played. The music seeped into his blood like a drug; the
bag steadied his breathing, calmed him.

At last it was done; he flung the bag down, leant over the
desk and snapped the box's lid shut.

PERCY'S QUARTERS, THE REFUGE
2ND FEBRUARY, ATTACK PLUS TWELVE YEARS

Percy lies there, sobbing, face burning, heart thundering, spent.
He shakes.

"Are you all right?" asks Kate.

"I'm fine." His voice trembles. He doesn't look at her; won't.
"You can go."

"Perhaps I should stay until –"

"Get out!" He screams it; her endless, boundless calm and
warmth swallow the look of hurt and anger on her face, but it's
there, however briefly. He almost feels bad, because it's Helen
he's angry with, Helen he h –

No, he doesn't hate Helen. He doesn't, does he? The
opposite; he loves her. That's why it hurts so much; that's why
he wants to lash out in return.

But "All right," Kate says, rising. "You know where to find me, love." And she closes the door behind her and she's gone. And he could go after her – but he won't, can't. He's humiliated himself, been humiliated enough for one day.

The music box. The fucking music box. Percy snatches it up and flings it, all his anger behind it, at the wall.

He hears things break on impact, and at once horror and regret come to wash the rage away. But it's too late.

He cradles the box, opens and closes the lid, but there's no sound. No music plays.

Percy begins to sob.

In three months' time, he will be dead.

CANTEEN, THE REFUGE
1ST MAY, ATTACK PLUS TWELVE YEARS

"Today," says Darrow, "is the day the lost are found."

The dining hall's hushed; he turns from the lectern to a table holding a stack of old telephone books. "These six lost everything in the War, even their names. So today, to mark their passage into adulthood, they choose new ones. They may choose one from here, or elsewhere. This is their first true choice."

One by one, the other boys and girls go first to the table, then to Darrow, who announces their new names. A Blacksmith, a Taylor, a Gebregergis – Percy has no idea where *that* name originated, but doubts any ancestor of the pale red-haired girl who's claimed it came from there. Probably she just likes the sound. What's in a name, after all? Nothing, Percy knows. And everything.

Lanterns light the hall; Percy looks out over it, seeking the one face that isn't there.

At last it's his turn. He walks straight to the lectern. Darrow gestures to the table, but Percy shakes his head.

"You've already chosen?" Darrow says.

322

Percy looks out one last time, hoping he's wrong, but Helen isn't there. He sees Mary, yes, but Mary has little use for boys at the best of times, and none at all if they can't fight. Noakes' half-seared face jumps of out of the crowd at him, and he looks away. The only halfway friendly face there is Ashton, and he isn't Helen, and Helen isn't there.

There's something in Percy now, a feeling of loneliness and cold: it comes from a time before Helen, when he'd scavenged like an animal in the ruins and the winds of the long winter that followed the War. The aftermath, the waste: he hadn't been born in that winter, yet he had. "Yes," he says, and whispers the name.

Darrow turns to announce it, but Percy touches his hand, flinching as Darrow looks sharply down. "There's something else," he says.

Darrow frowns. "Yes?"

"I want to change my first name too."

"That's your right," says Darrow. "What name do you now take?"

Perseus, slayer of the Gorgon, rescuer of maidens; glorified, loved and set among the stars. That's not him any more. Never really was, any more than Helen will ever be his Andromeda — or, it seems, anything else to him again. No; Perseus dies today.

But if he isn't Perseus, then who is he now, this boy, this *man*, without a name? There was another Greek king. A different one; what he desired, he took by force, without regard for laws of gods or men. Yes. Him.

He whispers it in Darrow's ear; Darrow raises an eyebrow, but nods. "Very well," he says, and speaks the new name: "Tereus Winterborn."

6.

St Martin de Porres Church
20th march, attack plus twenty-one years
1730 hours

"Engineers." Danny pointed to the shattered Wall Two gate. "Fix that, then the battlements. And sort some new sandbags out for the shelters. Wakefield?"

"Here." The Fox led the remains of her force back from the ruins of Ashwood, dragging mortars and bombs.

Danny forced himself to look up. Flies were already circling and settling on Trex and Scopes. "Get them down, now."

Wakefield nodded. "Want new look-outs up there?"

Danny shook his head. "Got some on the Fort roof. Safer." He looked at Scopes again. "Should've thought."

Wakefield didn't say anything else, just led her people into the church. The bodies were pulled up, then carried down on blankets. Danny didn't want to look – that many other corpses lying about, so what did these two matter? But they did, like it or not.

Wakefield came down after the rest, something in her hands: Scopes' rifle. Not the SLR, but the Lee-Enfield she'd had long as Danny remembered. It was broken in two, and the stock shattered. Wakefield knelt beside Scopes, the smashed weapon in her hands. Danny remembered her presenting her spear to Scopes like that, before Hobsdyke. *Can see you real fighter. You love your weapon. Part of you. Same for me.*

She laid the gun on Scopes; folded the broken, bloody hands over it, then nodded and watched them carry the dead away.

Danny swallowed, blinked, looked down across the village's smoking ruins. His communicator crackled. "Harrier."

"Lookout One here. Reapers regrouping. Looks like a counter-attack."

"Everybody in position!" Danny shouted. "Thanks, Lookout."

"Something else, Harrier. Vanguard of the attack –"

"What about it?"

"Catchmen. Hundred, hundred and fifty of them."

"Shit." Danny ran for the gate.

WALL TWO
1745 HOURS

"You, you, you, you –" Wakefield ran along the shattered battlement, tapping rifle-holders and Crow archers as she went. "Get the iron bullets, iron arrows. You kill Catchmen. Rest of you – kill Jennywrens."

Someone behind her. She turned: Danny. He grinned. "What she said," he shouted. Magazines were handed out; arrows too. "How many we got?" he muttered to her.

Wakefield pulled a face. "Not enough."

"Here they come," someone shouted.

The Catchmen spread out into a line and marched over the rubble. A rifle cracked; one jerked and fell.

And the Catchmen broke ranks and charged.

Bad enough when they'd marched like machines. Now they wove and darted, hit the ground and scuttled. Shots fired, arrows flew, but too many of them missed.

"Try these." Gevaudan appeared on the battlements, two crates heaved on his back. One was full of rifle rounds and arrows, the other –

"Blades?" said Wakefield.

The Grendelwolf picked out a pair. "These should help."

Wakefield grimaced, but took two knives. She unbound the flint head from the short spear she carried on her back and lashed one of the blades there in its place. The other she thrust into her boot.

Machine guns chattered; bursts punched into the Jennywrens as they charged. Rifles barked and arrows flew, hunting Catchmen.

"Gevaudan." Danny, communicator in hand. "Get your arse to the War Room."

"But the Catchmen –"

Danny swallowed, face even whiter than normal. "We got to hold by ourselves." Wakefield saw him clip the communicator to his belt on the second attempt, heft the Lanchester. "Darrow wants you, now."

For a second Wakefield thought Gevaudan would say no, but he nodded. "Good luck," he said. Looked at Wakefield. "All of you."

Wakefield nodded; the Grendelwolf nodded back. He clapped Danny on the shoulder and headed down.

"There!" yelled someone. Wakefield looked; four Catchmen, shinning up the wall.

Harp shouted orders. Rifles cracked; a Catchman fell. Another dropped, an arrow in its throat, but the other two were fast, zig-zagging. Knew they could be killed now. Wakefield pulled spear and knife; no magic bullets in her guns.

The Catchmen reached the battlements; one near her, the other further down. Screams, a body flying, shots. Danny staggered back from the one nearest Wakefield, fired the Lanchester into it; she leapt forward, rammed the knife into its back. She felt it falling and spun, spear cocked for throwing as the second charged along the battlements.

The grinning, screeching, toothed horror of a mouth; the dull, blank glow of its eyes; the black Styr claws. Wakefield spat a curse and threw; missed. The Catchman bayed as it closed; then its face exploded and it fell. Behind it, Lish lowered her rifle, nodded to her. Wakefield nodded back.

"Archers, watch that fucking wall!" yelled Danny. "Pick off any climbers. Rifles, try and do your jobs so they don't get that bastard close. And cheers, Wakers. And Lish."

Lish smiled and aimed back over the battlements. Wakefield grinned, pulled the knife from the first Catchman's remains, and went to get her spear. Blood on the battlements. Bodies dragged away. Shots.

She and Danny reloaded their submachine guns with the magic bullets. Wakefield got back in position, spear in one hand and Thompson in the other, barrel propped ready on the battlements. Beside her, Danny shouldered the Lanchester. And so they waited, for the next wave to crash against the failing wall.

THE WAR ROOM
1755 HOURS

"Gevaudan." Darrow looked up from the chart table. "Thank you for coming."

"Why am I here?"

"Because you're needed."

"Yes – on Wall Two. The Catchmen are attacking –"

"Danny and the others are armed with anti-Catchman ammunition," said Darrow. "That should be enough."

"It had better be." Alannah spoke up from the other side of the table. She met Gevaudan's eyes; nodded.

"The next two hours will decide the face of everyone here," said Darrow. "And that of the rebellion against the Reapers. The support convoy's escorts are fighting it out with Flaps and her team, and it isn't going well. Reinforcements are en route, but even they won't necessarily be enough."

"And if the column gets through?" said Gevaudan.

"Then all Jarrett has to do is wait for her artillery to arrive. Wall Two will be lucky to hold for five minutes after that. And if Wall Two goes…"

Darrow's face was grey, the lines in it cut deep. "If Flaps is able to stop the column, do we have a chance?" said Gevaudan.

"We may have a chance in any case. It depends on you."

Gevaudan had to smile. Darrow had a certain knack for gaining one's attention. "I'm listening."

"The tunnel you blocked."

"Yes?"

"Alannah intercepted a transmission. Jarrett's abandoned any attempt to get through the rubble and pulled her people back from there. There's a guard post at their end, but it's small. Easily dealt with using trained fighters."

"And the small matter of the blocked tunnel?"

"The booby traps are activated by vibration sensors. Practically impossible to disable if you're coming in from their side, but very easily done from ours. The rest is just time and elbow grease."

"And what do I do at the other end?"

"Look." Darrow pointed to the chart. "We've managed to get a general idea of the camp's layout. Our lookouts on the roof and some recon scouts – they managed to get in close, at great personal risk. You have their vehicles, tents… and these structures here."

"I'm assuming the larger one is Jarrett's battletruck?"

"Yes. But that's not your primary target." Darrow pointed at the smaller structure. "Here. Reports indicate most of the Catchmen were gathered outside it. Not now, of course; they've marched to attack the Fort. There's some sort of aerial…"

"It's where they're controlled from," said Gevaudan. Where Kellett controlled them from. He saw Alannah watching him, biting her lip.

"Yes. You fought a Catchman, Gevaudan. You know what they're capable of."

"I do. Even with anti-Catchman weapons, they'll win sooner or later in those numbers, especially with the Jennywrens behind them. But if we can shut them off at source, we might hold."

"I'll put together a team to go with you, if you like."

"I'll handle this better by myself."

"I didn't doubt that. But once you shut the Catchmen down, you'll be in the middle of the Reaper camp. With a little support…"

"I'm with you. And then you'd attempt a counter-attack to repulse the main Reaper force?"

"Exactly."

"One question," Gevaudan said. "What's to stop the Reapers sending a force of their own up through the tunnels once they realise they're clear again?"

"They won't be," said Darrow. "As soon as you and the others are through, the sappers will reseal the tunnel and reactivate the booby traps."

"Of course. So, a one-way trip if things don't work out at the other end."

"I'm afraid so."

Gevaudan sighed. "When do we start?"

"The sappers are already at work."

"Good thinking." Gevaudan rose. "Then I'll go and join them."

"Gevaudan?" a voice called as he strode down the corridor outside.

He turned. "Alannah."

She came close. "Will you be all right?"

He raised an eyebrow. "I'm touched by your concern."

"I meant that I know who Martyn Kellett is."

"Ah." Anger, and a giddy hint of something like fear.

"You'll be okay? You can cope?"

"I'll cope," he assured her. "Now, if you'll excuse me."

He spun the wheel, pulled the door wide, stepped into the dark of the caves.

Flaps tried to dig herself into the ground as the sill above her head disintegrated. Fuck-all cover left. They'd been pushed back; all the Reapers had to do now was keep firing. She tried to breathe, coughed and choked on acrid smoke and dry stinging brick-dust.

Beak and Sud sat huddled against a stub of wall, Beak's arm around his shoulders as she reloaded one-handed. Flaps wriggled sideways, towards a bit of cover that'd at least let her kneel up. Two Reapers ran in. Flaps dropped one; the second swung his gun towards her. Beak fired her rifle from the hip, nailed him through the head. Sud scrambled up into a crouch, clutching his Sten.

"Flaps!" The communicator on her hip screamed.

"Flaps! Flaps!"

"Yo!" she shouted.

"It's Jazz. They've cleared the highway. Not enough of us left. We need more fighters—"

"I've no-one," said Flaps. "Barely holding here as it is."

She peered across the highway, saw the landcruisers around the library. Muzzle flashes from the top floor. Reapers fell. Cov and Mackie were putting up a good fight, but this could only end one way for all Flaps' folk.

"More landcruisers!" Sud shouted. "Oh fuck, *more*!"

"What?" Flaps scrambled over; Sud was squinnying over the wall. "There!" he said. "See? Right there —"

"Sud," screamed Beak over the gunfire, "will you get your fucking head d —"

Bullets smashed into the stonework; Sud fell without a sound, hit the ground, was still. Even from where she was, Flaps saw the fist-sized hole in his forehead. His eyes blinked, then stayed open, glazing, as blood widened around his head.

"Cunts!" Beak sprang to him, fired back. "You *cunts*!" Then she was just screaming, no words in it, only blind fury and pain as she opened up with the rifle, rapid-fire. A Reaper fell; guns crashed in reply. Two exit holes bloomed in Beak's back, and she collapsed across Sud.

"Fucking hell." Flaps helped drag Sud and Beak behind the chimney breast. She looked, saw two dozen new landcruisers tearing into the town behind the Reapers.

Beak cradled Sud, coughing blood and weeping. Flaps pulled the spent clip from her Sterling. The others were all looking at her. What for? For a second she hated them. She'd no ideas left – and there'd be no quarter, no prisoners –

The .50 cals on the newly-arrived 'cruisers muzzle-flashed and Flaps ducked, but no rounds hit their position. The Reapers closing in on the house fell, a couple dancing briefly as the bullets stopped them falling.

"They're ours!" Newt said. He stared out at them, shaking, crying.

A couple of the Reaper cruisers brought their .50 cals to bear on the new arrivals, but fresh volleys smashed into them, sweeping the Reapers off the flatbeds like dolls.

Flaps wanted to laugh, but might never stop if she did. "Everyone but G Squad, go help Jazz," she shouted over the guns. "The rest of you, with me."

She ran, head down, through the dust that blizzarded in the wind. A Reaper stumbled out of it; she cut him down with a short burst, ran to one of the abandoned 'cruisers. "Get on those .50 cals," she shouted. "Finish the job." Then ran towards the new landcruisers, arms raised, hands empty. "Friendly!" she shouted.

"Hold fire," yelled a voice. A small, wiry girl jumped down and ran to her. Nut-brown with quick black eyes and a snaggled grin, black hair tied back. A Fox-triber, like Wakefield. "Flaps!" she called.

The name came back to her just in time. "Pin!" They punched each others' shoulders. "Thanks."

"Glad to."

Shots from across the way; through the dust, across the road, bursts of gunfire from the Reaper 'cruisers around the library sent dust spewing from its walls. Flaps squinnied through her binocs: Reapers clustered round the entrance. Now and then a couple darted in, and there was shooting. Cov and Mackie; still holding on.

"Borrow a couple?" she said, pointing to the 'cruisers.

Pin sniffed, looked around. The Reaper 'cruisers were either still, or crewed by Flaps' team, directing fire into the ruins after the scattered Jennywrens. "Reckon."

"Thanks." Flaps jumped aboard one, pointed across to the library. "Let's go!"

BOWKITT LIBRARY

Crouched on the staircase above the ground floor, Cov aimed at the hole in the library wall. Two Reapers darted through, running for the stairs; he fired five rounds rapid and they fell.

Fresh movement at the entrance; he aimed and fired again, but this time the rifle fired two shots, then jammed. "Fuck!" He ducked, bullets smashing into the staircase wall above his head. He clawed at the hot breech, but the bolt wouldn't move.

Mackie scrambled down. "I'm empty, mate."

Cov pawed out a spare clip, but the Reapers were already pouring in, raking walls and stairwell. Mackie screamed, ducking down, hands over his ears.

Cov reached for his pistol – but it wouldn't be enough, they were coming, guns at the ready. But then Mackie was shouting, standing, arms raised. "Family Man! Family Man!"

The Reapers hesitated; their weapons dipped. And then the edges of the hole in the wall, the broken wooden door-frames, exploded in a hail of splinters and dust; the walls juddered and shook from .50 cal bullets, and the floor broke and splintered. And in the middle of it all, the Reapers spun and staggered, danced and fell.

More bursts hit the library; Cov heard landcruiser engines approaching. Flaps to the rescue. He laughed, turned towards Mackie.

Mackie.

Family Man. Family Man.

Mackie saw it in Cov's face, and stared back at him, wet-eyed, bottom lip trembling.

"Family Man?" said Cov. "Mackie?"

Mackie was crying.

"Oh come on, mate," Cov said. "No."

"They had me," Mackie blubbered. "When we were trying to get out of the city, back round Christmas."

There'd been a couple of days they'd been split up – their crew half-killed and scattered, hiding out, trying to find the right moment to regroup and make a run. No-one knew where Mackie'd been. He'd turned up with a story about hiding in a cellar. But instead the Reapers must have had him. And instead of kill or torture him, they'd turned him instead. Sent him out to find the rest of the runners, lead the Reapers to their base.

"Oh fuck, mate," said Cov. Mackie was sobbing his heart out, and Cov felt like he was about to do the same.

"I had to," said Mackie. "Had to."

Cov could only shake his head.

More gunfire; the library shuddered, fresh dust exploding in through the entrance as .50 cals raked the walls again. Flaps' unit, finishing off the Reapers now pinned up against the library, the way the last of Rook Two had been. The air boomed and sang with it.

Cov turned back towards Mackie, and went still.

Should have seen it coming, of course. Mackie had a gun on him. The barrel waggled to and fro; poor fucker's hand shook.

"Mackie," he heard his voice say, thin and faint, lost in the racket coming from outside. "Mate. Don't."

Still crying, Mackie pulled back the hammer with his thumb. "I'm sorry," he said. "I'm sorry. I'm sorry."

The lone pistol shot was lost in the machine guns' thunder, like a tear in the sea.

Stone scraping stone; now and then a curse. Otherwise the sappers worked in silence.

Gevaudan stood, his back to the tunnel wall. He'd offered to assist but had been politely but firmly refused. So now he only waited.

A hand brushed his arm; he looked up, then released a long, slow breath through his teeth. He glanced behind him to ensure no-one was too close, then turned back and whispered: "I thought I wasn't going to see you again."

"Never's a long time," said Jo; she leant against the wall, smiling. "Your past's a very hard thing to get rid of."

"I know." He sighed. "I've missed you."

"I know."

"Twenty years, and I still miss you."

"I know you do." She put a finger to his lips. "But I'm not here for that. You need to be very careful, Gevaudan."

"Danger." He shrugged. "I've been there before."

"Many times," she agreed, nodding. "But this is a different kind of danger, isn't it?"

He looked away. "Perhaps."

"There's no perhaps about it, Gev. You've just had a lot of old wounds opened up again, haven't you? And they hurt. Right?"

"I'll be careful."

"You want to be cruel, don't you?" she said, very softly.

"It's how they built me," he whispered back. "How *he* built me."

"Don't lie to yourself. You can't afford to do that now. It isn't the Grendelwolf who wants blood this time, it's you."

"Yes," he said at last.

Jo reached up and touched his face. "Don't let him change you that way. You're better than that, Gevaudan. You really are."

"We're through," called one of the sappers. Gevaudan blinked and stepped away from the wall. He glanced to his side; Jo, of course, was gone.

Footsteps sounded; Wakefield grinned from a side-tunnel. "Grendelwolf!"A slim black girl followed her – Filly, that was her name – and a dozen, twenty more, all creaking with grenades and extra magazines. A couple wore backpacks; plastique, he guessed.

"Shouldn't you be on the wall?" he said.

Wakefield shrugged. "Darrow called. Wants me to go with you. Kill Reapers. Proper fight. Beats the Wall."

"Danny?"

"Still fighting. He's good." Wakefield stepped close, gently knuckled his arm. "Danny be fine. This way we save him."

"Hello?" The sapper called. "Whenever you're ready."

Gevaudan hushed him with his yellow stare, then turned to Wakefield's crew. "All right, then," he said. "With me."

As they followed him, he murmured to himself:

"It seemed that out of battle I escaped
Down some profound dull tunnel, long since scooped
Through granites which titanic wars had groined..."

BOWKITT LIBRARY
1815 HOURS

Flaps jumped from the landcruiser, ran fast across the rubble. She jumped bodies – Reapers, rebels, didn't matter – reached the hole in the side of the building. Held up a hand as two of her team ran up behind her. Last thing she wanted was getting shot by her own fucking crew in a panic. "Friendlies," she shouted. "It's Flaps. Mackie? Cov?"

At first she couldn't hear anything; just the whine in her ears, still fading. From the Devil's Highway, screams and dull explosions, the rattle of gunfire, the rebels raining bullets and anti-armour rounds down onto the convoy. Smoke billowed up, the fighters leaping down onto the road to finish the job. Faint cheers rang out over the guns.

In the distance, the sun was a red and orange ball of dull fire, like molten metal, pouring away behind the hills; a cold night wind blew through Bowkitt's ruins, raising whirls of dust like ghosts. As it settled, Flaps saw a thin woman with cropped hair, arms folded, watching her. Behind her were the others, the rest of the crew – Lelly, Telo and the rest – in a line, with a gap there for an extra body. For whenever it was Flaps' time. Mary said nothing; she just nodded. And then the dust billowed up again, and she was gone.

A sound came from inside the library; a low, desolate sobbing, muted and muffled. "Cov?" called Flaps. She peeped round the side of the hole, then took a deep breath and stepped through.

The floor crunched underfoot: pigeon bones, cartridges and powdered brick. Blood soddened the dust in spreading patches, from the bodies scattered inside: Reapers in their black uniforms.

Mackie sat at the bottom of the stairs, his rifle on one side of him, pistol on the other, face in hands. He sobbed. Cov lay at his feet, eyes open; what was left of his face looked more surprised than anything else.

Flaps walked slowly to him, waving back the others; Mackie's weeping grew till it abolished all other sounds, till there was no other in the world. She stopped and squatted before him; after a moment, she reached out, touched his shoulder. "Hey."

The blood around Cov was fresh, hadn't quite stopped spreading even though his heart had clearly ceased to beat. Must have been in the last minutes of the fight, with Flaps and the others just outside. Awkwardly she reached out, hugged Mackie tight.

"It's okay, mate," she said. The big lad stirred, clumsily folded his arms around her. "It's done," she told him. "You did well." She squinched her eyes shut tight; sealed in the tears. "You did well."

7.

THE REFUGE

4TH OCTOBER, ATTACK PLUS FIFTEEN YEARS

Late one night, Belinda asleep. A rare night; quiet, and they're both here. Command hardly ever sends both parents out in the field at the same time; they try to find families for orphans here, not make new ones.

Neither talking much; they don't, any more. Better that way. Helen slumps on the bed, close to sleep. Frank doesn't. Fidgets. Something he wants to say. She waits; it comes.

"Heard they need somebody new to run the catering section," he says.

The hell? "Good idea."

"Yeah?"

"Yeah – you should apply."

"What?"

Helen nods towards Belinda in her cot. "Got to be better for her if one of us isn't out in the field all the time. What?"

"I meant you."

"Do I look like a cook?"

"Do *I*?"

"Back in the kitchen where I belong? That's the plan, is it?"

"That's bollocks."

"No, it's not." And she's on her feet, like a cat with its spine arched and fur on end. "It's exactly what you want from me."

"No, Helen." His voice rises a fraction. "What I *want* is the woman I went dancing with at the Christmas party, that's what I bloody want."

"Hello?" Helen waves her arms in the air. "She's here."

"No, she's bloody not," he says. "She's gone and there's this cold bitch instead."

"Bitch? *Bitch*?"

"Forget it."

"No, I won't forget it, Frank. Bitch, am I?"

"I might as well sleep with a bloody corpse at night."

"Well, if that's all you want, don't let me stop you. Go on out and fuck away till your dick drops off, pal."

"That's not what I —"

"Mummy!" Belinda squalls it from the crib, face already red, crying. Helen turns away from Frank, grateful because he really doesn't understand. It isn't the fighting, it's the fear. Not for herself, but him. She'd felt that loss once, that pain — never again. She picks Belinda up. "Sh, sweetheart. It's okay."

"Oh," Frank says, "*now* you give a damn about her, when it suits you."

"Stop it," Helen mouths. She holds Belinda tighter, twists round to keep her back to him. Too sharp, that one; too close to the bone. She acts the loving mother, but every time it feels fake. A performance. She keeps doing it, though; do it often enough and maybe it'll work; maybe she'll love the child.

"Why are you and Daddy shouting?"

What can she say? "It's all right, Belly. We were just playing." She hears Frank snort, tightens her grip on Belinda, makes it relax. There's so little harshness you can hide a child from in this world now; she'll hide this much, if Frank will only let her. "It's okay. Playing, that's all." She sounds fake even to herself;

how can she ever keep the performance up long enough not to wound Belinda?

Someone knocks at the door. Frank's across the room before Helen can say a word; his anger's like embers hit by rushing air; flaring up from nothing into fury. And that anger needs somewhere to go.

He yanks the door wide. "What do *you* want?" he shouts, and Helen, moving after him, sees Tez's white stricken face beyond him in the doorway. "Fuck off!"

He slams the door in Tez's face. Belinda's the only thing that stops Helen flying straight at him then – Tez, Percy, whoever he calls himself, he's always been the closest thing to blood she has. Of course he isn't any more – that's Belinda – but then that's the secret Helen tries to hide and knows she fails to, at least from Frank: she feels more for Tez. And it shames her.

But with Belinda there are requirements, obligations, things she has to do before she can think of any others' needs, even her own.

Like now. Because she has to cross back to the cradle and put the child down, then stride across the room. Frank moves to intercept, reaching for her, but steps back when he sees her face, the killing wrath in it; if he doesn't move she'll knock him down. He's done it now; shattered the pretence Helen tried to maintain. Fuck him, then. Let him deal with the bloody mess here. She has to find Percy.

She slams the door behind her. Percy's already halfway down the corridor, going at a clip, head down, fists at his sides. "Percy!" She breaks into a run. "Percy!"

"It's Tereus," he spits back at her, not turning. "Tez, if you can't manage that."

He's rigid; if Frank's anger is fire, Percy's – Tez's – is water, flooding him till he threatens to burst. But when she catches up with him, turns him to her, he's nearly in tears.

"Sweetheart," Helen says. Hugs him close. He's crying, and so's she. She's dead; feels nothing for her husband now, nothing beyond a faint flicker of occasional warmth for her daughter. Who else is there? Darrow, maybe, but he's distant; she can't come to him like this. Tez, Tereus, Perseus, Percy – whatever the name, he's the one constant she has. Even though he's grown more distant from her – a cruel, seemingly inexorable process, ever since Frank, even more so since Belinda.

She's struggled to bridge the gap. The land in ruins, the war against the Reapers, but even here, the human heart wreaks its havoc; she's fought to fit the time in, between the fighting, between marriage and motherhood, to tend this one fraying human connection.

Which of them is crying more? She can't tell for certain, but now he's the one comforting her. He strokes her hair. Gentle. Tender.

His fingers touch her face. Slender; delicate. Helen looks up at him, and sees how beautiful he is. That blonde hair to his shoulders; the blue eyes, the alabaster skin, the soft red Cupid's bow of a mouth. Not a little boy any more. Nineteen years old; a grown man.

But he's her brother too, her little brother. *Don't do this. It's wrong. Wrong.* A small voice tells her that, but seems now so far away.

"Tez," she says.

"Percy," he replies.

And then they kiss.

Tez's Quarters, the Refuge
5th October, Attack plus fifteen years

As soon as Tez wakes in his narrow bed, he knows something's different. He can feel the wall against his back. That's not normal; usually he curls up small and tight, the covers wrapped around him, but in the middle of the bed. Habit, ritual; ever since the rebels brought him here, he's ensured that as few details of his day to day life have changed as possible.

Something else is different too. The bed is warmer than usual. No, that's not it. There's warmth in the bed, a source of it other than himself. He can feel it on his skin. His bare skin.

340

And he feels skin, bare skin, against his own as well. Smooth, soft, like a caress. A warm breath brushes his face.

Memories stir; slowly Tez opens his eyes.

Beside him, head resting on the pillow, is Helen. Eyes closed, red hair spilling across that long white face.

Tez blinks, then slowly lifts his head and looks around the room. Yes, it's his familiar little room – the narrow bed, a chair and desk – scavenged by Helen on some mission or another – in one corner, two old plastic bins in another (one full of neatly-folded clean clothes, the other with those for washing.) Neat, precise, ordered. A place for everything and everything in a place. And now, here: Helen. Order disrupted, a threat of chaos; and yet it's glorious.

And he's just staring in amazement, in disbelief; one shaking hand reaches out to stroke her face, gentle as a brush of cobweb, afraid to wake her. And Tez is actually happier than he can ever remember being.

Everything has changed, now. She turned from Frank and came to him, took him to her bed. Well, to his bed, if he's being accurate, but that's semantics.

But they've been like brother and sister. Isn't there a taint of wrongness to this?

No. He rejects that. How could there be? The two of them did this, together; they both chose freely, embraced it. There's no real blood between them. A difference in age, yes, but that means far less now than when they met, less still each with passing year.

So some might call their love abnormal; what of it? What's normal, now? Normal burned to ashes fifteen years ago. This is a new world with new rules. Morality? Guilt? This world's a Hell; people find whatever joy is to be found. Neither of them forced the other, so where's the harm?

This – and now memories of the previous night come back to him, and Tez wanders among them, this gallery of images. He and Helen, naked together. The kisses; the sex. Yes, sex. His first time; there's never been anyone else. And it was beautiful, lovely. And with the one person he truly loves.

There's only ever been one soul Tez has known any real intimacy with, and he thought he'd lost her – but no, if anything he's gained her more fully than he ever dared hope. Helen's his again; Frank's gone. Tez has her back.

If this can be okay, his life will be perfect.

"Mm." Helen stirs; her lips twitch, trying to shift the strands of hair sticking to them. Tez reaches out and brushes them away.

The grey eyes flicker open. A blurred moment where she isn't sure where she is, who with. Then focusing on him. He sees the recognition in her eyes. And then she goes very very still.

The moment hangs, suspended. Her face, her eyes – what he sees there isn't what he wanted, or hoped for. Not joy, not acceptance; instead, revulsion and withdrawal.

No; it may be a prayer, perhaps the only one that Percy, Perseus, Tez, Tereus has ever made. *No. Please.* But like all prayers, it goes unanswered.

He reaches out again to touch her face, but this time she's awake, and pulls away from him.

"Helen?" he says.

"Tez," she whispers, staring. "Oh God."

"Helen?" he says again, and hears a slight crack in his voice.

"It's okay," she says, but now won't look at him as she dresses, pulling her clothes on under the covers – she doesn't even want him to see her now. "It's okay. I'd better go."

Words; there have to be words, haven't there? To make her stop, to make her stay – make her see that this isn't wrong, it's right. But if there are, Tez can't find them; he's still trying when she goes, almost running, her boots' unfastened laces flapping as she does. She'll trip, she'll fall. But she doesn't, and then she's gone.

And Tez is alone.

HELEN'S QUARTERS
5TH OCTOBER, ATTACK PLUS FIFTEEN YEARS

Frank's gone; Belinda too. Helen's not worried about that. Frank's unit was due to go out this morning; he'll have gone with it, and taken Belinda to the creche. Helen isn't ready to go there yet, to face the questions and the looks.

She's glad they're gone. She's a bad liar; she might twist the facts to her ends, but outright deceit, at least to those she loves – no, that's no strength of hers. Or even to those she once loved, or is supposed to; she isn't sure which category her husband and her child fit into. Either way, she can't lie.

And Tez – oh God, Tez. She can't think of him now. And she has no right to feel disgust for him, even though she does. But she feels much more for herself. His face, everything about him – the whole relationship's blighted, poisoned, soured. She can't picture his face without wanting to vomit. She's destroyed everything with her weakness.

Stripped, she crouches over the waterbowl. She washes herself out, then scrubs her skin. Hard, over and over. It hurts, but she doesn't care; her traitor skin deserves it, for having taken pleasure from his touch. When she looks at the water in the bowl, it's pink with blood.

A knock at the door; Helen closes her eyes. She knew this was coming. Every second when it didn't was a joy because it delayed what's about to happen, and a torment because it meant the worst was still to come.

And now it's here.

He knocks again.

Her eyes are still closed. If time could just stop, here. Or if she could just wait until he gives up and goes. But time won't stop, and sooner or later she'll have to face him.

Helen stands and pulls her coverall on. She's a lot of things, she knows. She's weak and she's selfish. A terrible mother; a terrible wife. So damaged and afraid of further hurt that she's incapable of love. So weak and so selfish and so damaged and so afraid that she destroys the little love she's had.

But there is one thing she isn't, and refuses to be: a coward. Not this kind, at least.

She strides to the door barefoot as he knocks again, pulls open the door. He stands there, outside, his blonde hair mussed, blinking at her with those blue eyes. Those huge, beautiful eyes.

"What?" she says. He blinks at her, silent. "What?"

"I…" The hurt in his face. She wants to melt; reach out, hold him. But she mustn't. She has to end this now. "I just came to see you," he says, in a near-whisper. "Make sure you're all right."

"Yeah," she says. Keep it short, formal, cold. "I'm fine."

"I thought you might want some help," he says, "moving your things."

"My things?" Oh no. Inevitable, of course, but she'd prayed it wouldn't be.

"Well, out from…" He gestures limply through the door. "Out from… here." He trails off, looking at her.

Cruel to be kind. Cruel to be kind.

"Percy," she says, "I'm not going anywhere."

"But last night – "

"Was a mistake." It hurts to say this, so much. "It was wrong. We shouldn't have."

"No," he says. "Helen, no, it wasn't, it was beautiful – " He reaches out to her.

"No!" She recoils. The look on his face, as though she struck him. "Percy, I can't do this. I can't. Just – just go. Please, just go."

She shuts the door, but of course he doesn't leave, not at first. She hears his voice outside: "Helen?" Then again, cracking. "Helen?"

Then he screams it – *Helen! Helen!* – and starts bashing on the door. If someone came to intervene, would that be better or worse? Probably worse. Thankfully, no-one does, and so Helen just slumps down with her back against the door, sobbing silently, biting at her wrist, till his cries turn to weeping and at last she hears him stumble away.

The canteen's silent today. A young couple sit a few tables away, thin and pale, munching bowls of stew. An older man with his leg in splints cradles a mug in two unsteady hands. A few littl'uns at a table at the far end, their giggling like splintered glass scraped over metal. Other than that, Tez is alone there.

Most of the men and women, the ones who fight, are away. He knows enough of what's going on: the Reaper Commanders were massing a combined force at Sheffield to sweep south and east through the larger Command Zones, rolling over the rebel-held territories, seeking out and destroying the bases.

Not just another battle, this one; let the Reaper army move out and they'll be unstoppable. What's the word? Yes: *Juggernaut*. And if the rebels can stop them there – hit them with a pre-emptive strike, take out the bigger weapons they still have, blow up the barracks where the soldiers sleep – the Reaper Commands will never be able to act in concert again. They'll only have enough to hold their own territories, and the tide will be turning; from the Refuge, the rebel commanders will be able to conduct a campaign to break each Command, one by one.

No, this battle will be decisive, so they're all gone. All that's left is a skeleton staff, the children – and those, like him, that no-one knows what to do with.

And so Tez sits alone at his table, staring at the wall.

No, not Tez. He isn't Tez any more, no more than he's Perseus or Percy. Tez is a soft name, a nickname – it's the name that Helen gave him, not the one he took for himself. His name is *Tereus*.

It'd been the same at the start. He'd taken a name for himself, but she'd tried to replace it with one of her own. Perseus: Percy.

In a way, he supposes he should be grateful to her. She showed him what love means, what it's really worth. So much better now he's let it curdle into hate. Curdle? No: better to say that it's fermented, it's matured. This state is the better one, the lasting one. Love depends on how the other feels. *Reciprocity*; he mouths the word to himself, enjoys its feel. He takes pride in the words he's learned: more than most here will ever manage. Half of them grunt like animals.

Hate, though: hate is hard, adamantine, and if it's strong enough it doesn't matter how the other feels. They'll never soften it; their wants, their needs, don't influence it at all. Hate wants what it wants, and does all it can to get it.

It was the lesson he'd needed to learn; the only way to truly become Tereus, to kill weak, clinging Perseus once and for all. Even after the naming, he hadn't lost the dream of resurrecting Perseus; there'd been some nagging, stupid hope of rescuing his Andromeda from the sea serpent of her marriage. But Helen had never been Andromeda; Cassiopeia, perhaps, vain and selfish. She'd used and discarded him.

Tereus glances around the canteen. A few others sit at tables. None of them mean anything to him. He looks and sees the grubby and the weak, the old, the stupid, the broken. The worthless.

Was there ever anyone else he cared for, other than Helen? His mother, perhaps, though he can't remember her face – or any other detail, really. For a time Helen meant comfort; stability, security. But people can't be relied upon; only power will keep him safe.

"We did it!"

Someone runs into the hall: Noakes. He's got a bandage round his head, from a concussion he took in a recent scrap; that's why he's stuck here instead of at Sheffield. Heads turn and people stare. Noakes looks around; his eyes linger on Tez for a moment and a half-smirk twitches his mouth: contempt at the sight of the weakling, the milksop, the one who can't fight. Only for a second, before Tez looks down, but it lasts an age. Then Noakes shouts: "We won! Sheffield! They smashed the Reapers! It's over!"

For a second, silence; then the whoops and cheers begin. People slap each other on the back. The man with the splinted leg lumbers over, tears in his eyes, gives Tez a hug. Stale sweat;

stale beer. Tez pats the man's back, stiff with loathing, knowing his face is screwed up in disgust.

Now they have their victory, and want to celebrate. So now they see him. Now he matters. Otherwise, he doesn't. He can't bear the hypocrisy of it any more; he gets up and goes out.

"Tez," calls a voice. He grits his teeth, clenches his fists, swallows the urge to shout *It's Tereus, you fucking idiot.* Instead, he turns and smiles.

Darrow's pushing a wheelchair down the tunnel. A woman sits in it, head lolling forward, silver hair screening her face. Still, but for the occasional twitch. Tereus sees no wounds, so the damage is within. The worst weakness of all; he wants to run, but stands his ground.

"Do you remember Alannah?" says Darrow, nodding to the woman in the chair.

"Alannah?" Wait – yes. From the raid on the mill, where Helen rescued him. Her hair had been darker then. Tall, warm, folding the rescued children in her arms. But he hadn't wanted her; no, instead it had been the redhead with the gun, the one who beat Reapers to death with an iron bar. If he'd gone to Alannah instead, would he be here now? Or would he still have seen through all the lies and illusions in the end?

He studies Alannah, grey and stooped in the chair. Perhaps Darrow's waiting for him to ask what happened to her. He should, of course; he knows the things he's expected to say and do. But he no longer cares enough to make the effort. Instead, he looks up at Darrow and asks: "Is it really over?"

"Not quite," says Darrow. "Not yet. The Reapers will struggle to put a major army in the field again, but it'll still be a long hard battle. We could still lose." A faint shadow of a smile. "But things are on a more equal footing now, and the tide's turning our way. Excuse me." He pats Tez on the shoulder, walks on.

The chair's wheels squeak as Darrow pushes it away. The cheers from the canteen echo down the corridor.

Tez remembers Alannah as she was; straight-backed and fearless, the children in her arms. Now she's this broken grey thing. Given the choice, she might rather have died that day.

Perhaps he should have too. At the time it seemed like a new world, a better life.

But in the end Helen used and discarded him, threw him away without regard – and worst of all *she's* made *him* feel dirty, as if *he's* the one who was wrong. The new life has led nowhere. If this is the world the rebel victory builds, better if the Reapers had killed him that day.

There's no softness in the Reapers; none of the deadly falseness of romance or emotion. Being Perseus to Andromeda has led only to anguish; it's left him alone, nothing and nobody.

The Reapers take what they want. They have what matters: power, stability, control. And that offers a safety that doesn't exist here, amid all the soft, impossible nonsense about compassion, love, sharing, making the world a better place. The Reapers are about holding on to what you have, then gaining more. About surviving.

The rebels are Perseus, but the Reapers are Tereus: they take what they want, as Tereus did.

He leans against the wall, breathes deep. Revelation. Epiphany. Two other words he knows that half those in the Refuge wouldn't understand. And in that moment, the last trace of Percy is finally gone, and Tereus Winterborn is truly born. And he knows where he belongs. He sees Noakes looking at him, and Tereus Winterborn smiles and holds his gaze, unblinking. And this time it's Noakes who looks away.

THE CHARR

21ST OCTOBER, ATTACK PLUS FIFTEEN YEARS

Tereus walks shin-deep in soft grey ash, so fine it swirls and billows up around him with every step and fills the air with the stench of the fire that burned this forest fifteen years ago. He has a cloth across his face so he doesn't choke on it.

The trees are blackened but petrified; their dead branches form a canopy and the ashes they stand in have never fully hardened or blown away. The War turned these woods into a wound, and it's never really healed.

He'll stink of smoke after this, but he knew that before he entered the woods; he left a change of clothes behind on the outskirts, and bottled water to wash with. The old clothes he'll burn before returning to the Refuge.

At last, he reaches a clearing. The black shapes in its centre aren't trees: there's a landcruiser and a squad of Reapers around it, all bringing their guns to aim at him.

"I come in peace," Tereus says, raising his hands. "I believe the password is *Philomel*."

The guns are lowered. Tereus pulls the cloth down from his face. The landcruiser's cabin door opens and an officer steps out. A big man in his forties, tall and bull-shouldered, with iron-grey hair; half his face is a shiny, buckled ruin of keloidal scars. His eyes are dark and hard.

"Major Richard Dowson, CorSec," he says. "Who the fuck are you?"

"My name is Tereus Winterborn."

"Congratulations. Why should I care?"

Winterborn says nothing. Dowson sighs. "All right," he says. "What do you want?"

"I want to make a deal."

"Deal?" Dowson says. "Well, that's funny. What do you *want*?"

"I want to be a Reaper."

"Then go to the nearest city and find a recruitment office."

"Not just any Reaper," Tereus says. "I want a commission."

"Well," says Dowson, "I wants don't get." He half-turns – to leave, or to give his men the order to fire? The danger of the game gives Tereus a small, half-scared thrill.

"Not even," Tereus says, "I wants who can offer something that *you* want very, very much?"

Dowson turns back. "And what's that then?"

"Oh, nothing much. Just the location of the Refuge." Tereus looks in his eyes and smiles. "The location, and how to get inside."

Dowson goes still. A breeze blows; ash billows up into the air. Dowson coughs and spits.

"Okay," he says at last. "That could be… of interest."

"I'd have thought it would be very interesting," says Tereus. "But first of all, an officer's commission."

"I'll consider it," says Dowson.

"No, Major. You'll give me what *I* want, or you won't get what *you* want."

"Oh, really?" Dowson smirks. "What's to stop me *making* you tell?"

"This." Tereus puts something in his mouth; he holds it between his front teeth, lets them see, then shifts it to his back molars so he can talk. "Poison capsule," he says. "I bite down, and you have nothing."

"Bollocks," says Dowson.

"Not at all." Tereus shrugs. "You see before you a man with nothing to lose, Major. With the rebels, I have nothing. If I have a future, it's with the Reapers. They're the way I need to go – that we all need to go."

Dowson purses his lips.

"Think about it, Major. Quite apart from everything else, wouldn't that be a coup for you? Here's one who lived among the rebels, was raised among them, but who of his own free will came to see that the only way this country will have a future is through the Reaper Creed."

"I'll say one thing for you," Dowson says, "you could charm the bloody birds off the trees when you want to." He glances about him. "If there fucking were any around here, anyway. And you're not short of balls. Could use that, definitely. Second Lieutenant?"

"*Full* lieutenant," says Tereus.

"All right," sighs Dowson. "*Full* lieutenant. Word of honour."

"You're a man of your word, then, Major?"

"Well, if you didn't bloody think so, you wouldn't be here, would you?" Dowson says.

He grins, and Tereus finds he can't help but smile back. "I suppose not," he says.

And they shake hands.

The Refuge

Helen dries her hair, watches Belinda sleep. She sniffs a strand of hair, sighs her relief; at last she's washed the reek of smoke out of it. She dries off and starts to dress; as she laces up her boots, the door opens, then clicks shut again.

She doesn't turn. Who? She hasn't spoken to Tez since that horrible morning after; glimpsed him a couple of times in passing, in corridors or the canteen, only for him to turn and vanish before she could call out. No more than she deserves, of course, but she wants at least to talk to him, make sure he's okay. Maybe that's part of the price she pays, never knowing what damage she's done.

But mixed in with the concern, there's the fear. Tez was broken enough before; he's still more broken now. And broken things have sharp, cruel edges; broken things can become weapons, and wound. She doesn't want to believe Tez could hurt her, but she's fought too long, seen too much, not to.

But then she hears the heaviness of the footsteps, and breathes out. "Hi, Frank. Heard you were okay."

"Yeah. Sorry about that."

Helen half-smiles, turns to face him. His clothes are dirty, face grimed with soot. "Just got back?" she says.

He nods. "Mopping up in Sheff."

"Nice to be home?"

He shrugs.

"There's water," she says. "If you want to wash."

He nods, then crosses to her side. For a precious minute or so there's no bitterness between them; they just stand together watching Belinda sleep, this thing they made. Small and pink and perfect. Nearly three now, and she might actually grow up in a land without the Reapers. Helen can't help but envy her, and on the heels of that there comes a wash of the love she so often tries and fails to feel.

"Are you done now?" says Frank.

"What do you mean?"

"Now it's over."

"But it isn't over, Frank. The Reapers aren't finished yet."

"It'll never be over, will it?" Frank says. "Not for you."

Helen closes her eyes. Too much to hope the peace could last for long. And she's so weary, so bone-fucking-tired of it all. "If you mean I'll never be what you want me to be," she says, "then no."

"You were, once," Frank says.

"Was I?"

"Yes."

Helen sighs. "If you say so," she says, and goes out.

*

Helen walks the corridors, the Browning bouncing against her thigh. She should really have stowed it; you're not supposed to carry weapons on base, but she forgot. People clap her on the shoulder as they pass, pat her on the back. Someone cheers. And she smiles. But it's all hollow. Nothing's there.

She sees faces she recognises, but never the one she wants. She goes to Tez's quarters, knocks on the door; no answer. Calls his name through the door. "Just talk to me, Tez. Please. You don't even have to open the door." But there's only silence.

She tells herself he's not there; she'd rather think she's made a fool of herself than imagine him sitting there, silent, ignoring her.

She goes to the canteen. It's the likeliest place she can think of. It's crowded; there are tables set up with vats of beer. Let them celebrate the victory at Sheffield. Groups sway side to side, arms round one another's shoulders, singing. She sees Mike Ashton with a girl on his arm, sees Scary Mary with two. She even sees Noakes, when he comes up for air out of a clinch with another fighter – boy or girl, she can't tell, and does it really matter anyway? Fair play to him as long as both partners are willing.

But she can't see Tez. Then again, he wouldn't be here. He'd hate everything about this: crowds, drunkenness, all of it. So where is he?

And then a klaxon blares, its loud harsh bray echoing in the tunnels. Laughter, then the conversation fades. But it can't be real, can it? The Reapers are beaten. They're on the run. The combined force was broken at Sheffield, and the alarms are only supposed to sound if –

But as the laughter and talk stops, Helen hears the other sounds, further off, under the klaxons' bray. Screams. The dull faint stutter of guns. Then a dull crump, and the canteen's walls shiver, dust falling from the ceiling.

Impossible. Unthinkable. But it's here.

Frank, Belinda –

Helen pulls the Browning and jacks the slide. A two-handed grip, aiming down at the floor. And then she's running through the tunnels. More screams, more gunfire. And a smell of smoke. Something's burning. Screams ring out, some of the worst things she's ever heard.

Helen cuts through the crowd, weaving fast. She's going against the flow, she realises; everyone else is going the other way. But all that counts now is the mission, the job: find Belinda. Find Frank. After that, she'll find Tez if she can.

The shooting gets louder as she nears her quarters. And the smoke. And there's heat, too: the burning.

She turns the corner into the corridor and coming the other way down it are half a dozen Reapers. Most carry SMGs, but the lead one has a flame-thrower; she stops and blasts a jet of fire into each room as she reaches it, then moves on as the screams sound. A burning figure, tiny, reels out of a doorway; one of the other Reapers cuts it down with his Sterling.

The next doorway down from them is Helen's.

One of the Reapers sees her; shouts, points. The flame-thrower swings towards her. Helen drops to one knee, firing. The Reaper falls, torching the ground; a second later the fuel tank explodes.

Helen dives and rolls as the fire surges across the ceiling. Screams. Burning Reapers stagger back and forth, bouncing off the walls. One bursts out of the smoke, blackened but unburnt. Helen fires, three rounds rapid, and the Reaper falls back into the fire. "Frank? Frank!"

"Helen?" He's in the doorway, Belinda sobbing and screaming in his arms.

"Come on," she says. "Move."

She runs along the tunnels, him behind her, and tries not to laugh. For now, at least, they're a family again.

There are a dozen exits from the Refuge, but the Reapers will be waiting outside most of them. There are a few others, though – emergency ones, further off and known only to a handful of rebels. She's one of them. If they're lucky, whoever's betrayed them to the Reapers – and it could only be an informer – won't have known about them all.

Explosions shake the tunnel walls. Dust, smoke, billowing everywhere.

Belinda's crying. Frank says nothing; doesn't ask where she's headed. He trusts her in this, at least.

"Helen!"

She spins, gun raised, but points it down. It's only Darrow, with Ashton beside him. Behind them are Scary Mary and Noakes, holding up Alannah. Helen can barely look at her friend; gaunt and hollow-eyed, hair matted and grey, she's barely recognisable as who she was.

"Which way are you going?" says Darrow. He's grey-faced and there's blood on his clothes – not his, though, that she can see. Smoke drifts from his Thompson gun.

"North-west exit. You?"

"We were heading for the south one. Which do you think –"

The tunnel shakes again from another explosion; the ceiling cracks, spilling clouds of dust. "God knows," Helen shouts. "You keep going your way, we'll go ours. Better chance of one of us making it. Regroup later."

Darrow shakes his head. "How did this happen?"

"Someone sold us," Helen said. "We were lucky. Looks like it ran out." She goes to Alannah, touches her hair. Alannah grunts and recoils, flailing blind at her. Helen steps back; the sight of her friend like this burns. "Take care of her," she says.

"I promise," says Darrow. "Good luck, anyway."

"Roger!" He turns back. "Have you seen Tez?"

He shakes his head again. "I'm sorry."

"Good luck," she says.

Darrow turns and leads his party into a side-tunnel; veils of smoke engulf them and they're gone. Belinda sniffles; Frank stares at Helen. "Which way now?"

She swallows, points. "This way."

MOORLAND

23RD OCTOBER , ATTACK PLUS FIFTEEN YEARS

It takes Helen, Belinda and Frank nearly an hour to reach the north-west exit, and along the way they run into other survivors who've got lost in the warren of tunnels fleeing the Reapers. "With me," she tells each group. "I know a way out." And they follow.

No-one says much else. What else is there to say? Everyone's reeling from it; this, so soon after victory. The only home most of them have had since the War, breached and ruined, in flames. Friends, loved ones, dead or just missing, fates unknown. Tez. So on they march, each silent in their own private grief.

A thundering boom – bigger, this one, and louder than anything else they've heard, and the mines shake. Dust rains, rocks fall from the ceiling. Two people are crushed and killed, and the earth keeps shaking long afterwards. They're setting off charges inside the mines, to collapse the tunnels, crush anyone who's escaped them or trap them to suffocate.

"Bastards," Helen whispers. She spits out dust. "Come on."

Finally the tunnel they're in slopes up. The air clears – cool and fresh, a light breeze – and through a mesh of gorse and bramble, she sees stars.

Helen ventures to the entrance. All seems clear. She motions to the rest, and they move.

The north-west entrance is hidden by thick bushes. They tear their way out, scratched and bleeding. The ground underfoot shudders again, as the Reapers continue their work.

"Where to now?" asks Frank.

"I don't know." Helen shakes her head as the other survivors stumble out after them; she's had no thought till now other than getting clear of the Refuge. All around is the empty moor, grass and heather. "If we head west, maybe we'll – "

Light explodes in front of them; then to their left and right, and from behind. Helen reaches for the Browning, but her stomach falls hollowly away and she knows it's hopeless, that the betrayal is complete. Gun bolts snap back. Light glints off helmets, visors, black leather uniforms. Reapers.

Who sold us? But she knows; even before a shadow moves into the light, its fresh black Reaper uniform gleaming, she knows who it'll be, and wants to laugh at the vile, perfect symmetry of it.

"Helen," he says. "I thought it would be you."

"Percy," she almost whispers. What's she going to beg for? Her life? Frank's, Belinda's, those of the others? Doesn't matter. She never gets that far.

"No." He pulls back the bolt on his Sten.

"Tereus Winterborn. Open fire!"

Helen dives for a nearby hollow; a submachine gun chatters and something punches her in the thigh. She yelps, rolls for cover. Submachine guns are firing – a dozen, twenty. People scream. One of the voices is Belinda's.

Helen twists around. Most of the group are down already; the others fall as she watches. A couple jerk and dance backwards as they're hit. It takes her a second to find Frank. He's kneeling, coughing blood – it hangs from his lips in strands. He still has Belinda in his arms, but she's limp and still, arms like rags, head dangling; unblinking eyes.

Frank's eyes meet hers. There's nothing in them but a dull reproach. He opens his mouth as if to talk, but two or three bursts hit him at the same time and he falls backwards, still holding Belinda.

"Cease fire," calls Winterborn. Not Percy any more, not Tez. Tereus Winterborn. This is who he is, is it? All right then. Let him take the consequences.

Helen draws the Browning, cocks it. She's dead. Fair enough. But she'll kill him first. She has to smile. It's quite apt, really. His story will end with hers. Bound together, even at the end.

"Drag them away," he says. "There may be more to come."

The Reapers start forward. She hears a couple laugh, now it's over. Hears their boots scuff the heather, then squelch in blood-wet earth. She'd kill them all if she could, but she has thirteen shots in the pistol and only seconds left before she's seen and they finish the job.

Helen aims, gets him in her sights; he's silhouetted against the headlights, a perfect target. A headshot. Perfect. They'll see her any second, but she'll make her one shot count. She crooks her finger round the trigger and squeezes.

Click.

Misfire.

Winterborn starts at the sound, turns – she sees his face, his blue eyes. And he sees her.

"There!" shouts someone.

She pulls back the slide, ejects the dud round, tries to aim again. But there's a stutter of gunfire and the hummock she's behind explodes. She's punched again and again, and there's a blow to her head. She falls back. Lies there, feeling her blood run into the turf; staring at the sky, unable to breathe. The stars die one by one. Then nothing.

MOORLAND

24TH OCTOBER, ATTACK PLUS FIFTEEN YEARS

A cold grey dawn, and mist swirls through the dead brown heather and bare bramble snarls. A couple of fires burn, streaming smoke into the dull sky – lit for warmth, no other reason.

Wider columns of black smoke lift skyward in the distance: from the main entrances, from ventilation shafts, from places where the ground's collapsed. Fires still burn underground; perhaps some of the coal seams have caught alight. Winterborn remembers reading of a place where that happened, before the War. The town above it was evacuated. The ground would crack open or fall away.

The thought of that happening here has a certain appeal. The rebels' dream of Heaven, turned into the pit of Hell. He smiles to himself. The whole moor a blighted, burning ruin; the vengeance of Tereus Winterborn.

"Drop, sir?" one of the Reapers, offering a hip-flask.

Winterborn's about to refuse – the man's coarse-looking and grimy, and the flask's been in his grubby mouth and who knows how many others – but he forces a smile. "Thank you," he says, and wipes the flask's neck as surreptitiously as he can before taking a sip. He grimaces at the burn of it in his throat, but smiles and hands the flask back to the man with a nod. The Reapers are his family now; he must win their acceptance and respect in order to rise. Not for warmth or companionship; he neither wants nor needs them any more. Simply for power. Control. Stability, order, *safety* – they're all that matter now.

There's a crunch and scrape of shovels. He wanders over to inspect the hole. Wide and deep. "That should do it," he says. "Throw them in."

By the pit lie the rebel dead. Bare and naked, pathetic-looking now they've been stripped of clothes and weapons. The Reapers take the bodies and throw them in. He glimpses faces he recognises, and feels nothing. The last three bodies: Frank goes in first – nothing. Then Belinda, so smashed and torn by the bullets that her clothes are almost all that hold her together. Still nothing.

And then Helen.

Only then is there a flicker of feeling. He's seeing her naked, one last time, though her bare white skin's caked in blood. Then she falls among her dead family, and it's done.

"Fill it in."

As he walks back to the landcruisers, there's the hiss and clank of another approaching. Reapers snap to attention and salute; Winterborn follows suit.

Dowson steps out of the cab. "At ease." He nods. "Winterborn."

"Sir."

Dowson jerks his head. "Let's walk."

They step away from the Reapers, the fire, the mass grave being filled in behind them. "One word of advice," says Dowson. "That burial shit. Knock it off in future."

"Yes, sir."

"In the cities, they've got pits where they dump the dead – along with all the shit and the household waste. Gets used for fertiliser. Out here – well, sometimes the Jennywrens burn 'em, but most of the time they're just left for the crows. Makes a nice little public warning, see?"

"Yes, of course." He's irritated with himself. "I should have seen that."

"You're young. We all were, once." Winterborn glances at Dowson and the Major snorts. "I wasn't fucking *made*, you know."

He's expecting a smile in response, Winterborn realises, so he obliges. "Was the operation successful, sir?"

"I'd say." Dowson bares his teeth in a grin. "All the patients died. There's a few of them got out, but we're mopping up. Any we don't get –" He shrugs. "Doesn't matter. We've cut off the head. They've no central command now, can't co-ordinate."

"Can we, after Sheffield?"

"It's just troops and materiel we're short of, not comms. We keep in touch, share info, make sure we're ready for any rebels trying to leg it from one RCZ to another. We'll do it. They're done for now." He looks at Winterborn. "Largely thanks to you."

Winterborn smiles.

"You did good work here," says Dowson. "I wasn't sure about you at first, but now – now I think you've got steel. I think you'll go places. I'll be keeping an eye on you, Winterborn."

At the time Winterborn isn't sure if that's a promise or threat. Later he'll wonder just when Dowson looked at him and saw a future Commander. Surely not then. But he'll learn that the current Reaper Commander for RCZ7 is weak and incompetent, that the rebels came close to victory partly because of the stupid mistakes he's made. Dowson, and others, are looking for a new one; to everyone's surprise, they'll eventually realise that they've found what they're looking for in one young officer, a former rebel who's risen fast through the ranks, whose ideas are bold but practical and whose methods are ruthlessly effective.

But that is the future.

"That's enough," he calls to the Reapers filling in the grave; the bodies are more or less just covered in earth. "I don't think any of us mind if the foxes dig them up, do we?"

Laughter. Some trapped part of him mewls and squirms at the thought, but he ignores it. It's the worthless part of him, and it'll soon be dead. "Let's head back," he says.

Sitting in the landcruiser, he feels something dig into his thigh; it's in one of the pouches on his uniform. He takes it out: it's the music box. For a second he's tempted to toss it over the flatbed's side, but he doesn't. For now, at least, he'll keep it. He can't explain why.

Winterborn looks back once as they drive towards the city; at the black smoke smudged against the sky, and the raw patch of earth that marks Helen's burial spot. And he feels nothing. He tells himself that, over and over. He feels nothing.

COMMANDER'S OFFICE, THE TOWER
20TH MARCH, ATTACK PLUS TWENTY-ONE YEARS

Winterborn breathed slowly in and out, then reached up and wiped his eyes. His fingers shook. No. Not possible. This wasn't right.

"I feel nothing," he whispered. That seemed to help, so he did it again. "I feel nothing. I feel nothing. I feel nothing. I feel nothing. Nothing." There was a silence; his fingers stroked the music box. After a moment, he whispered again. "Helen."

THE GRAVE

24TH OCTOBER, ATTACK PLUS FIFTEEN YEARS

Pain. Hot foul air. Stale. Struggling to breathe. When she does, she sucks in dirt and grit. Coughs. Retches.

She can't move. She's pinned.

Dark. Can't see.

Tries to breathe steadily. God, the air's foul. Okay, then; breathe through your mouth. She does. It helps, although she tastes blood.

She's alive. Somehow. She doesn't understand how or why, as the memories come back. That last sight of Frank, of Belinda a shattered, ragged doll in his arms – her mind keeps skating around and away from it, unable to touch the wound.

Speaking of wounds – there's the one in her leg, and the rest. The meat of her upper arm, one in her side. She feels the pain of them. And the throbbing pain in her head.

The hummock must have shielded her. Maybe there was hard rock under the covering of earth. That might explain it. But there's the long blurred period after.

Not all black, though. She vaguely remembers lying on the ground. Remembers hands dragging her, remembers her clothes being torn off and a twinge of fear that she'd be raped – vague and distant, as though she were a character in a story she was reading. Hands taking her, throwing her. It's all fragmented, disconnected. A blow to the head; concussion, maybe. She's probably bled a lot from her wounds – she feels weak, shaky – and when she winces she feels a crust of dried blood on her face crack. She wouldn't have been moving; she'd have looked dead enough in the dark.

In the dark, where she is now, lying on –

Helen realises two things. First, she is naked. The second is that the surface she lies face down on is cold and smooth, but lumpy. Feels rubbery. And cold wet things are touching her. Her hands feel shapes – a hand, a face.

Oh Christ. Oh Christ, she's lying on the dead, and on top of her –

The third thing Helen realises is that what's pressing down on top of her is earth.

She starts screaming, screaming into the dead beneath her. Things shift and stir in the earth. They're waking. Frank and Belinda, the others, all the ones killed, they're coming for revenge. Because this is her fault, of course it is. How can it not be? Who betrayed them? Percy. Why did he betray them? Because of her. She used him, fucked him, threw him away. He was fragile and she shattered him, and the broken pieces reconstituted themselves as a monster called Tereus Winterborn. Her screams become howls of anguish – not only grief, but torment. There was a saying she'd heard somewhere – from Mum? From Darrow?

Hell is truth seen too late.

And now she's in Hell. The dead are waking and coming for her, to tear her apart.

Something squeaks. Rats. They must be burrowing, to get to the food. Oh Christ. They can always tell when you're helpless, rats. Is that the next level of her Hell, to feel them stripping meat from her face, biting out her eyes?

She's nothing but a scream now, thrashing madly in her prison, her tomb.

And then she feels the earth give.

As she recoils from the corpses she lies on, the ceiling of solid dirt pressed down against her back shifts.

Helen is still for a moment, blinking in the dark. No. She can't have felt that. Not possible. She's finished. They've buried her in a mass grave. The only question now is how she dies – suffocation, infected wounds, hunger or thirst, the rats or the hungry dead. She can't, doesn't dare let herself hope.

If she tries to move again, nothing will happen. She only imagined it. It'll be solid as rock.

Helen takes a deep breath of the thinning air, and pushes slowly down with her hands and knees, pressing her back up against the earth above and trying to lift herself.

Softness, give, and then resistance. Of course; the earth around her might be looser, but above it'll be solid-packed. But then it gives again; above her, she feels something crack and break. And there's a hint of cooler, cleaner air.

How deep is the earth? A foot? Less? The Reapers don't usually go in for mass graves; they just leave the dead to rot. Perhaps – perhaps, just possibly, there's a chance.

"No," says Frank's voice: she hears it, clear as day. "You've no right."

Voices whisper in the dark, echoing him. "No right. No right. No right. None." She hears stealthy movement; they're stirring, ready to come for her.

Deep breath. She pushes down again. For a second the weight on her back's intolerable, and then the crust of earth breaks open and light floods in – weak and grey, but dazzling after the total blackness here, and she cries out. The cry becomes a scream of effort as she rears up, forces herself to her knees, tearing free of the ground.

Brilliant light; cold air. She gulps the air, shields her eyes from the light.

Scrabbling at the ground, she pulls herself free; curls up, bare and cold and shivering.

Reapers. Where are the Reapers?

She opens her eyes and looks. The moor is empty, except for plumes of smoke. She's alone on the surface of the grave.

Helen gets shaking to her feet, looks down into the hole she's come from. Dead faces stare back up at her. Among them are Frank's and Belinda's. *You did this. This is on you.*

Sobbing, she kneels and claws the dirt back over them.

Where now? Anywhere and nowhere. Just run.

She scrambles away, on all fours at first.

Like the beast you are.

Naked, filthy, blooded, hair matted with dirt, death and madness in her eyes. Then she stands and runs.

The run becomes a walk becomes a slow, dull shamble. Helen's feet hurt; she's pretty sure they're bleeding. She doesn't know how long she's been going for. Can't have been long, surely? The cold is eating into her and her wounds ache. How much blood must she have lost?

She's lain in the dirt, with corpses, with open wounds. A matter of time before infection sets in. One or the other will kill her; she laughs, and it echoes over the moor. Survived all that, only to die later on. But that's human life in a nutshell. She laughs again.

Then, at the top of a rise above her, she sees a landcruiser silhouetted against the sky.

She stands there watching it, but there's no movement. In fact, she realises, there's a body hanging over the side.

She starts walking again, till she reaches the 'cruiser.

There are more bodies; some Reaper, some rebel. Some of the rebel dead are children. Mown down. But they fired back, and they took their killers with them.

A dead woman in a coverall; killed with a headshot, so her clothes aren't damaged. She's about Helen's size. Mumbling an apology, Helen strips her, dresses, searches for a pair of boots.

In the landcruiser's cabin is a tin box with a red cross on the lid. First aid. She grabs it.

The 'cruiser won't be going anywhere; the fire's burned out, and there's no fuel left. But the boiler's still hot, so it's warm in the cab. There are rations – pemmican mostly, dried meat and berries. She devours two cans of it, then undresses again. The medical kit has bottled water, bandages, antiseptic. She scrubs her body with both, paying particular attention to her wounds. Clean them. Disinfect them. She yelps from the pain of the anitseptic, but it'll do its job.

The pain in her head is from a lump that feels as big as a tennis ball. A chunk of rock, maybe. Hit her, concussed her.

Saved her life. The wound in her side is a through-and-through – the bullet passed through the soft skin below her ribs. The entry and exit holes are only inches apart, and there doesn't appear to be any serious injury. The shoulder and thigh wounds are also minor.

There are iron tablets, even antibiotics in the kit. She takes the iron tablets, keeps the rest for later.

Dressed again and cleaned again. Her hair's still clogged with dirt – there wasn't enough water for that. She'll find a stream, wash it properly. She loads up with food, then searches the dead for weapons.

She takes a Sterling from a dead Reaper, and as many bullets for it as she can carry. Now for a pistol. She finds two, weighs them in her hands; a Browning, like Roth's, and a .38 calibre revolver with SMITH & WESSON carved on the barrel.

Six bullets in one; thirteen in the other. But she remembers Winterborn, and how she would have had him, back there, if not for that misfire. She looks at the Smith & Wesson; if she'd had this, she could have just pulled the trigger again for a second shot, and that would have been enough.

She tosses the Browning away, finds as many bullets for the revolver as she can. And then she walks again.

THE WASTELANDS

31ST OCTOBER, ATTACK PLUS FIFTEEN YEARS

Helen wakes with a cry, grabbing for the Sterling. The night around her is silent; an owl hoots, a fox barks, then nothing.

She huddles back against the wall of the ruined cottage, hugging the blanket round herself, as the nightmare fades. She's covered in sweat, but cold; she shifts closer to the remains of the fire she set before. There's still some heat. It occurs to her she's come full circle: sleeping rough in the Wastelands with weapons taken from a Reaper's corpse, her loved ones dead behind her.

"Helen," says a voice from the dark.

"Who – " She aims the Sterling at it. And then they walk out of it, hand in clawed hand. Dead-straw hair and needle teeth. Cracked white clay for skin; clotting blood for eyes.

Frank picks Belinda up and sits down, dandling her on his knee. He doesn't speak, just looks at her, smiling. Helen lowers the Sterling; she has the sense to know there's no killing these.

"What did you dream of, Mummy?" Belinda says.

"Dream?" Helen licks her lips. She can't look away from her daughter's needle grin and blood-clot eyes.

"Before we came," says Belinda. "You were having a nightmare, weren't you, Mummy? What about?"

Helen doesn't answer. Can't.

"She dreamt of a road," says Frank. "Didn't she, chicken? She dreamt of a long black road."

He grins, and then he laughs. So does Belinda. Helen can't stand it; she grabs her things, her blanket, weapons and backpack, and stumbles away. God knows what's out there, but it's better than this.

"You can't outrun us, Helen," Frank shouts after her. "You can't get away from your dead. And the Black Road will be there whenever you sleep."

And Helen runs on, into the night.

The Black Road

20TH MARCH, ATTACK PLUS TWENTY-ONE YEARS

Pebbles of white appear out of the dark as she runs; cobbles of bone, marking the edges of the Black Road. Then they stop, and there's only a black void ahead. Helen stumbles to a halt.

"Road's End, Helen," says a voice behind her. She turns; behind her, gouged into the road, is an open mass grave. Standing on the naked, bloodied corpses in it are Belinda and Frank. "You've nowhere to go," he says, and holds out a hand. "Come here; join us."

"No," she says.

"You've no choice," says Frank. "What's back there for you anyway? Him?"

He points, and Helen turns. Something strides from the void up ahead, black coat flapping round him.

"Gevaudan," she says, but stops. There's nothing she recognises in his face, only hatred. There's a jagged, Y-shaped scar on his left cheek, which shouldn't even be possible; Grendelwolves always heal without a mark. Yet here he is, and there it is.

He stops before her, snarling. The yellow wolf's eyes look at her, see only prey.

"Gevaudan?" she says again, but even as she does she sees his claws slide from his fingertips. She flings herself backwards from the lunge; Gevaudan vanishes just as the blow reaches her, so she's never sure if it connected with her or not. The ground crumbles underfoot and she flails for balance, teetering on the edge of the grave. She twists round to see the bodies in it stir, moaning, fumbling blindly up at her. There are faces she know. Ashton. Noakes. Mary. So many, many more.

"He will destroy you," says Frank. "Why not stay here, Helen? With us?"

The dead reach out their hands, rising to their feet.

"You know you deserve it, Mummy," Belinda says, and grins, baring her teeth. So does Frank, and so do all the dead: dead hair, cracked-clay skin, needle teeth and blood-clot eyes.

And she backs away, but it would be so easy. Just stand and wait and let them take her. It would all be over. She can go on battling to keep ahead of the ghosts, out of some need for revenge on Winterborn, out of some vague nostalgia for an older, better time, or – release. Just stop, and rest with dignity.

After all, even if the ghosts do leave her alone afterward, what's left? It's all dust, anyway. *Please, tell me your vision*, Gevaudan said once. She'd had no answer, has none now. She might tear down what exists, but offers nothing to replace it. Yes. Perhaps it would be better.

"Yes," says Frank. He steps out of the grave and inches along the road towards her, extending a hand. Black talons like a Catchman's, crusted with blood. Helen starts reaching out; Belinda and the others grin behind Frank, avid.

Helen turns, looks back into the dark.

"No!" Is that fear on Frank's face? She looks at him, then the others. Yes; fear. She takes a step back. "Helen," he says, and lunges forward, reaching for her hand. She snatches it away.

"Helen!"

Helen turns and runs, then jumps, flinging herself into the void ahead.

Frank, Belinda and all the dead scream.

The world explodes in white fire.

Tell me your vision, Gevaudan's voice whispers.

If you live, tell me.

8.

The searchlight behind Danny exploded, and he dived. He wriggled along the battlements, glass fragments falling from his jacket and hair. "More flares!" he shouted. "Lish!"

A few feet away, two more flares erupted into dazzling life; the medic flung them both out over the wall.

Danny rose to a crouch. One hand gripped the Lanchester with its iron bullets, the other a fallen Thompson gun with normal ammo. He peered over the parapet, saw a Reaper climbing up, fired a short burst from the Thompson; the man dropped without a sound, dead before he'd begun to fall.

Twilight in the ruins, and everything seemed to move and crawl. The last of the searchlights they'd brought up was gone; now the only light came from their dwindling stock of flares.

Further along the battlements, Danny saw Harp, sitting back against the wall and tightening the dressing on his arm again.

369

Their eyes met; the tribesman winked and grinned, but it was fake, a thin mask ready to peel off.

Lish shouted a warning; Danny turned to see a Catchman's grinning face appear over the parapet. It heaved itself towards him, gaping mouth coming at his face. Danny brought up the Thompson, shoved it under the thing's chin, then jammed the Lanchester into its chest and fired.

He scrambled away from the thing as it collapsed, dissolving, and got to his feet again. Swaying, tired, ready to go down. Unless Darrow pulled something off soon, there'd only be one end to this. But till then, he was doing his fucking job.

Sapper's Tunnel
1850 hours

The Reapers guarding the tunnel mouth were just inside the entrance, behind a wall of sandbags with a GPMG and a searchlight they hadn't used. Grendelwolves had been designed for stealth as well as all-out battle; Gevaudan was on them before they realised.

The Fury wasn't required, and they died quickly. A slash from his talons felled one; a heel-handed punch to the chest, smashing ribs into heart and lungs, another. The third turned to run, mouth opening to cry out; Gevaudan caught her head in his hands, snapped her neck with a twist, lowered her to the floor and slipped to the entrance.

"Clear," he whispered into the dark behind him. Wakefield and Filly emerged seconds later, the rest of their squad with them.

They peered out of the tunnel entrance. The sun was down and the grey haze of twilight had fallen. Lights shone inside tents and above the tunnel along the perimeter fences; some of it spilled backwards across the camp. Lamps were mounted at intervals, but deepening shadows thickened like silt between the pools of light.

"All right," said Gevaudan. "I'll do my job, you do yours."

"Luck," said Wakefield. As Gevaudan moved ahead, he heard her mutter *"Fox's Spirit, run with us..."*

He slipped through the camp; silent, fast, ghosting from shadow to shadow. He soon saw Jarrett's battletruck; the portacabin with the mast wasn't far away. No Catchmen stood outside it now; Kellett would have despatched all his creations to the wall. There was his target, and the distance to be covered wasn't great. The only question was crossing it without being spotted and raising the alarm. Men and women sat and ate; a squad marched past. Even he couldn't take on the entire Reaper force single-handed.

He studied the potential routes between the tunnel entrance and Kellett, calculating the danger points along each one where he risked being observed. It didn't take long; what the Reapers' engineering hadn't achieved, rigorous training had.

That done, Gevaudan crouched in the shadows and waited. He could hear the chatter of guns and the thump of explosions. Everything now was a question of time: how long Danny could hold Wall Two against the Catchmen and Jennywrens, how long it would be before someone checked up on the guard post and how long it took before one of the routes to Kellett's portacabin cleared. He pushed aside all but the last consideration, waiting for his moment.

And at last, it came.

CATCH CENTRAL
1855 HOURS

Kellett pressed another button, and the view on the monitors changed, from the foot of the wall to its parapet. A machine gun tipped backwards as the Catchman got over the wall; a rebel fell choking to her knees, her jawbone torn away. The other gunner's face filled the monitors, screaming.

Kellett smiled, one hand slipping down to caress his groin. This aroused him too; not as much as the other, but enough. Perhaps there were children in the compound, and he could see them through the Catchmen's eyes before they died. Or perhaps Jarrett would let him have one to play with; a reward for faithful service.

The cabin door opened. Kellett snatched his hand away, furious, face burning red. "You're supposed to knock bef –"

The black-clad man closed the door. Man? No, there was something about him not quite human; the smooth perfection of his face, the fluidity of his movements. And then Kellett saw the yellow eyes.

Grendelwolf.

Kellett's hand moved towards the intercom button.

"Don't." The Grendelwolf was armed, but made no move for his guns; too much noise, and at close quarters, he didn't need them anyway. "I'd reach you long before, Doctor."

Not just any Grendelwolf – but of course, there was only one left now. "Shoal," he said, and smirked. "Well, you seem to have overcome your aversion to violence. But then we knew that already."

"I should have killed you at Sheffield," said Gevaudan. "I thought I had."

"Can't keep a good man down." Kellett licked his lips. He wasn't dead yet. If he could keep Shoal talking, a way to alert the others without him knowing, or to summon the Catchmen, would present itself.

"So they tell me," Gevaudan said, "but that still doesn't explain your survival."

He advanced, his shadow falling on Kellett. No time left, none – Kellett shrank back in his swivel chair. It skidded less than a foot across the floor before colliding with a bank of equipment. "What do you want?" he demanded. The Grendelwolf couldn't just want him dead, or that would have been done by now.

Gevaudan was looking at the screens. "I see your appetites haven't changed," he said. "What do I want? Your pets, Doctor. Shut them down."

"No." Kellett shook his head. "I won't."

"Then we've nothing to discuss, and now you're going to die." Gevaudan raised his hands; Kellett watched the sharp claws extend from his fingertips. "And be assured, Doctor, it will hurt."

Shoal had always been intelligent. It had been rare that he was anything other than in full control. But Kellett saw little in the yellow eyes now that wasn't wholly feral. He could already feel the pain of the claws slicing, rending, tearing, "All right!" his voice was higher and sharper than he'd meant. "All right. I'll do it."

He fumbled at the control panel. His hands shook. He prised up a section of smooth metal. "Had to keep this hidden," he said. He realised he was crying. These were, after all, the closest thing he had to children of his own. Underneath was a raised red button.

"Do it," said Gevaudan. "Or…"

"All right. All right." You fucking mutant cunt, he wanted to say, to spit in that white face, but didn't dare. He gripped the button and twisted it through a hundred and eighty degrees. A click, and it lit up.

On the screens, a screaming face. The shrieks came tinnily through the speakers, interspersed with chatters of gunfire. Shoal's breath rasped in his ear, blowing hot through a grid of teeth. Weeping, Kellett pushed the button down.

WALL TWO
1900 HOURS

The Lanchester spat two last iron rounds and was empty. The Catchman fell, but another leapt over the wall at Danny; he got out of its way just in time, but he was stumbling. Tired, running low. One mistake and he'd be fucked. He locked eyes with the Catchman. Stare it down, don't look away, else it'll attack. Wakefield'd told him that, or had it been Trex? What you did with wild dogs out here if they came at you. Might not work on this fucking thing, but it was worth a shot.

He fumbled for one of the magazines clipped to his belt, trying to ease it out. Pull out the old clip, slide in the new. Don't look at the gun, don't break contact.

No point looking for help; it was every cunt for himself up here. The Catchmen were on the wall with the Jennywrens charging in behind. Wall Two was gonna fall – minutes, seconds, it was going down. But he wasn't falling back.

The Catchman took another step towards Danny, reaching for him, then stopped, hand hovering in the air. Clotting blood and skin-shreds on talons inches from his face.

And then it screamed. All the Catchmen did, on the wall and off it. Its fanged red mouth went wide; its back arched, and it juddered. And then a thick pink slurry boiled out of its mouth. Its lenses shattered and the same matter spewed from them. Danny jumped back as it splashed on him. The Catchman crumpled to its knees, and crumpled was the word: Danny wasn't sure if it was falling or deflating as the liquid poured out. Its arms and legs shrivelled and its torso crumpled; the bottom part of its face collapsed and it fell forward.

The pink slurry stank; Danny gagged, switched to breathing from his mouth as it lapped round his feet. And it was all over the battlements, because every Catchman, every fucking one of the twats, was down.

Someone cheered. "Fuck that," Danny yelled, jabbing the Lanchester over the battlements at the Jennywrens. "Hit those fuckers." He fired down at the Reapers climbing up; two fell. "MGs – someone get fucking on them!"

Danny and Harp managed to right one of the GPMGs and unkink the ammo belt. Danny pulled the bolt back, aimed, squeezed the handles, sweeping it across the Reapers below. But then a Bren began sputtering, fitfully, and then another. Further down the battlements, one of the .50 cals kicked into life. Jennywrens fell from the wall; the lines of advancing troops began to fall, then to break and scatter.

The monitor screens were blank, a sea of white noise. All the lights on one panel flickered off.

Kellett slumped over the panel, weeping. "There," he spat. "You've got what you wanted. Happy now?"

"Ecstatic," said Gevaudan. He took a step back from Kellett. He didn't want to be any nearer the man than he had to. "Just one small detail," he said, and drew one of his Browning pistols.

Kellett heard the hammer click back and stared up at him. "No!"

"Yes."

"You promised –"

"I promised nothing," Gevaudan said. "All I'm giving you is a quick death. And that's for me, not y –"

He ducked as Kellett wheeled, heaving the control panel at him. Stupid. You didn't stand and make speeches at a time like this. Not even with Kellett, with whom there was so much unfinished business. He straightened; Kellett was charging towards the end of the portacabin, between the rows of equipment. Was there another door there? Almost certainly. Gevaudan fired, hitting him in the back; more rounds smashed into the equipment. Loud bangs, sparks, smoke; then fire as Kellett crashed to the ground, crying out. Instrument panels exploded; the smoke thickened, catching at Gevaudan's throat. Flames darted out, clung to the ceiling and spread. In the smoke, Kellett screamed in fresh agony as they found him.

Shouts from outside. Gevaudan drew the second Browning, flung wide the door.

He dived, rolled, came up firing. Jennywrens fell; he dropped the empty guns, snatched an SMG from a corpse, and summoned the Fury.

Wakefield grabbed Filly, dived, as the first charges blew. There were shrieks, a roar of flames; the Reaper tents were burning. A dull thud sounded; flame and smoke billowed up and a medium 'cruiser crashed on its side.

Guns firing, shouts, screams. She looked up, soon saw it in the firelight; the Grendelwolf, a GPMG in his arms, firing into the Reapers.

"There!"

A Reaper shouted, pointed at them. Wakefield snapped up the Thompson, fired; the Reaper fell. She grabbed Filly's arm; their eyes met. Wakefield smiled, touched her hand. "Not forget," she whispered. "Stay –"

"– with you," said Filly. "Yes."

Wakefield nodded, raised her voice. "Go!"

Then ran through the burning camp towards Gevaudan.

THE WAR ROOM, ASHWOOD FORT
1905 HOURS

"Rooftop lookouts are reporting explosions in the Reaper camp," Alannah said.

"Can you get hold of any of the scouts?" said Darrow.

"It's obvious what's happening. I mean, the Catchmen are all –"

"You're right." Darrow would have rather known if Gevaudan and the others were still fighting or if their attack was already over, but it didn't matter. Even the Grendelwolf could only hold so long, and there wouldn't be another opportunity. No Catchmen, no support convoy, the distraction of an attack in their camp: it was now or never. If he had the strength to order it. "Full assault," he said. "Everything we have. I want every Reaper pushed out past Wall One."

Alannah nodded, white-faced.

"Alannah?"

"Yes?"

"Tell Danny I want a small force maintained on Wall Two – in case of a Reaper counter-attack. Under his personal command."

Alannah smiled. "Thanks."

Darrow nodded. "Let's end this."

THE BATTLETRUCK
1915 HOURS

Another explosion; the truck shook with it. "Majid," shouted Jarrett. "Majid, report!"

"They used incendiaries," he said. "Torched the tents where the reserves were sleeping. Still estimating casualties. They must have infiltrated the camp, set charges everywhere. They're still going off."

"Where are they now, these saboteurs?"

"Fell back and regrouped to one of our sentry posts."

"Waiting for relief to come, no doubt." Jarrett breathed deep. "They must have cleared Wong's tunnel. Send two platoons down there in case of further attacks. Then surround that sentry position and blow it to Hell."

"We're still fire-fighting in the camp, ma'am – " Another explosion thudded, shaking the battletruck.

"Majid, I gave you an order – yes, what now?"

The Reaper holding out the signal flimsy flinched back from Jarrett's glare. "The rebels, ma'am. They've launched a counter-attack. Our forces can't hold. They're being pushed back out of the Fort."

"The reinforce them! Majid, sent reinforcements!"

"We can't!" he shouted back. "It's chaos here. We're still trying to get it under control."

"I will not let this happen. Not when we're so close. Find men. Send them."

"Half of them are dead or wounded!"

"Then send the other half. And where the *hell* are my heavy weapons?"

Another explosion, and the battletruck lurched, heaved sideways. Jarrett went sprawling, then clutched at the chart table, pulling herself to her feet. Under the truck itself – the scum had actually dared to plant a charge under her. But she was still alive. They hadn't killed her. They wouldn't. She wouldn't, couldn't die, not till Helen was dead.

"It's over," said Tom, standing over her. "Just accept it, Nicky."

"Fuck off," she spat, and lashed out at him. He vanished before the blow could land. The radio mic – where the hell was the radio mic? She found it, snatched it up. "Majid? Majid?"

But there was no answer.

1920 HOURS

Majid dragged himself clear of the landcruiser, knocked over by the latest blast. Black smoke boiled skywards, from all over. How the hell had they done it? They were everywhere. Must have been tribesfolk – those scum were like rats, could get in everywhere.

On the wind, another sound; a roaring that wasn't fire. He stumbled about the white flames rushing up from the remains of the reserve tents, stared up at the hill. Something black was flooding down it; it took him a moment to realise it was the Reaper force in full retreat. And the rebels were charging after them; a line of landcruisers, firing into the Reapers as they fell back, with the infantry bringing up the rear.

The battletruck – he ran towards it. It was listing badly on one side, the wheels gone, but otherwise undamaged. The battletruck's door hung open. Majid pulled himself inside, staggered across the tilted floor, shoving Reapers aside as they bailed out. They at least had seen the writing on the wall. Jarrett clung to the edge of the chart table, as if she'd fall without it.

"Ma'am. Ma'am!"

She blinked, stared at him.

"The rebels will be here in minutes, ma'am."

"Then prepare a counter-attack. I thought I gave the order."

"We can't, ma'am." Majid kept his voice level. He had to make her see. "We can't hold, not with this damage and these casualties, not with both support columns destroyed. Even if Command sends a third column, even if it gets through, there'll be no-one here *to* support."

Jarrett turned to him. Her eyes were muddy glass. "That is defeatist rhetoric, Captain Majid. That is conduct unworthy of a Reaper officer, let alone a GenRen one."

"Ma'am, it's the simple truth. You have to order a retreat — quickly, now, while some of us are still left."

"And face a firing squad when we get home."

"Even if that's the case, at least some of our men will survive."

The screams and howling from the hillside was louder, rolling closer. Gunfire sounded. Another explosion outside; the battletruck shivered like a dying beast.

Majid looked at Jarrett: he'd admired her, followed her without question. Until today, the idea he'd ever question her leadership, much less defy her, would have seemed insane. But he couldn't let this happen. "You have to order the retreat, ma'am," he said, and reached for the radio mic. "If you won't, I will."

Jarrett stared at him, put a hand to the Browning on her hip. Majid breathed deep, brought the mic to his lips. "This is Mower to all units."

She drew the Browning, pointed it at his face. "Don't."

He turned away from her. "Abort operation. Repeat, abort. Return to base —"

The Browning's hammer clicked back. Majid closed his eyes. "Repeat, return to to Central Command. E Company, you're the rearguard. Cover the retreat, make sure everyone gets away. This order can't be countermanded."

From outside, shouts, engines, running feet. Majid felt a sweat-bead trickle over his temple and held his breath, waiting for the bullet. But it didn't come; slowly he opened his eyes and turned, found himself alone inside the crippled battletruck.

REAPER CAMP
1925 HOURS

"Go!" shouted Wakefield, and jumped over the sandbags round the sentry-post, charging after the Reapers as they ran. Filly landed beside her, ran with her, shooting too. Gevaudan ran past, firing from the hip.

And the Reapers fled.

Weapons clattered on the ground; black-clad men and women flung themselves aboard teetering landcruisers as they rolled away. The Jennywrens fleeing down the hill poured into the camp, sweeping through their own defences; with a roar, the main rebel force flooded after them.

Bullets cracked past. There were cries. Gevaudan pivoted right towards an oncoming group of Reapers, and Wakefield saw there were only four of her people standing to her right. Everyone else – gone.

"Filly," she said, and turned left. But there was nobody. Wakefield turned, looked back; where the firelight hit the ground in the near-dark, she saw only bodies.

A scream escaped her. She rammed a fresh magazine into the Thompson. "Come on!" she shouted, and charged, firing.

APPROACH TO ASHWOOD FORT
1927 HOURS

The last wave of rebels passed; the hillside was quiet again as the stars came out in the night sky.

Gunfire and explosions echoed up from the Reaper camp below, but the Fort's broken walls were silent, the rubble and corpse-strewn slopes still. Smoke drifted from the black gouged craters in the grass and the burned-out fire-trenches. Here and there, one of the dying moaned.

In the grass, Jarrett stirred under a camouflage hat and poncho, and started crawling up the slope. She didn't look behind her. It was dark now, all fires and headlights, and even if the sun had still been up, what was there to see? She knew the story already.

Her forces were smashed and falling back. Majid had been right; even with her gun at his head, he'd calmly given the retreat order. That wasn't a coward's act. Majid had never been one of those, and he hadn't begun today.

In that moment, the wild rage – near hysteria, she admitted – had passed and she'd accepted the truth. Operation Harvest had failed. An utter rout. Majid would get who he could back to Manchester and with luck he'd be spared Winterborn's wrath. After all, he'd have Jarrett to blame for the failure. Even if she wasn't there.

Jarrett crawled to the edge of a crater. A faint moan; a dull gleam of black leather, a white face with a bloody mouth. One of hers. Not that Jarrett considered stopping to help, even for a second; that would have been as pointless as going back. The rebels didn't take prisoners. Especially not if they were Jennywrens.

Jarrett couldn't tell if the wounded Reaper saw her or not. It didn't matter, anyway. She crept on. She wanted to get up and charge, but she'd be dead before she'd gone ten steps. No: slow, steady, methodical – that was the way.

She snorted to herself. She should have found Wong's tunnel, tried to get in using that. Then again, they might have resealed it. No, this would have to do.

She felt light as she crawled; she smiled, even hummed softly to herself till she remembered her training and fell silent. The rebels weren't the only ones trained in stealth and infiltration.

Shadows fell across her; four figures standing above her, looking down. They were only silhouettes, but she knew them, of course. She looked down and crawled on, her dead family's gaze on her back. She could feel it: it burned. But at last it was gone, and when she looked back down the hillside, so were they.

No more responsibility; no more command. Everything was delightfully simple again, as it hadn't been in years. She was done, beyond question; Winterborn would execute her for this failure. But that didn't matter any more. She'd realised that in the second she accepted Operation Harvest had failed. Fine, then; let it fail. It had only ever been a means to an end.

In a way, in fact, it hadn't failed at all. It had brought her where Helen was.

That was enough.

Jarrett fixed her eyes on the shattered outer wall, and continued to climb.

Road to Ashwood
1932 hours

Patel was close to falling; didn't feel as though he could run another step. He let his rifle drop, clattering on the road. A little less weight to carry. He staggered a bit further, reaching out, almost touching the rear of the landcruiser ahead.

Hands caught and raised him, pushed him forward; other hands reached from the landcruiser and grabbed his arms. He was pulled aboard; he collapsed on the flatbed, sobbing. Someone patted his back. "It's all right," a voice said. He looked up, saw a woman looking down at him. Brown hair, hard face. Familiar. He remembered her from the camp, barking orders at Pete – Pete, who was lying back there in the rubble of Ashwood Fort, torn open and unburied. "It's all right," she said again, and he saw that she was crying.

Patel sat up, stared over the end of the flatbed. He could just about make out the hill and the shattered Fort in silhouette against the clear night sky. Men and women still ran on the road, trying to keep up with the column. The landcruisers would stop and let them on – but not yet, not till they were clear. He could see bodies on the road – the wounded and the exhausted, left behind to whatever mercy the rebels would offer. There wouldn't be any, of course. Not as if the Jennywrens would have done any different.

And they still had to make it back along the Devil's Highway, past whatever was waiting for them there.

Saeed Patel realised that he was crying too. The road and Ashwood Fort blurred behind his tears. The corporal patted his arm.

WALL ONE
1940 HOURS

When Jarrett reached the outer wall, she huddled behind a wrecked landcruiser, peeled off the poncho and hat and turned them inside out. The other side was the dull grey of rubble and dust. She put the gear back on.

She lifted the poncho's hem, then pulled up the cuff of her trousers. Underneath was an ankle holster holding a 7.65mm Walther automatic and a compact silencer. She took out both, screwed the silencer to the barrel, then crawled though the wall breach and into the ruins of Ashwood Village, eyes fixed now on the inner wall.

ST MARTIN DE PORRES CHURCH
1955 HOURS

Danny stood among the rubble and the dead. Burning and dust, blood and – already – the smell of things starting to rot. Harp sat on a chunk of rubble nearby, eyes red and glazed.

"Falcon, this is Harrier. Got anyone you can spare? Lot of corpses to clear here."

Darrow's voice came back at him. "Still mopping up below just now, but it's all over. The Reapers are in retreat. No sign of Jarrett, though. Strange. I always thought she was the type to go down with her ship."

"Ship?"

"Doesn't matter." Darrow sounded ready to drop, and the old git hadn't even been in the fighting. "We'll get some people to you as soon as we can, Harrier."

"Right."

Fires burned in braziers on Wall Two, and at intervals between the church and the village ruins. Rippling pools of low warm light, with belts of shadow between them. Danny looked up at the church tower; the walls were riddled and pocked with bullet holes, streaked with dried blood where Trex and Scopes had hung. Suddenly he was close to skriking, like a sprog. He choked it back. Not in front of anyone. He was in charge. Had to look it.

He leant against the wall, shaking.

"Danny!"

He turned. On the battlements, Lish was waving. "Up here, boss, fast!"

He ran to the gate, then, when it opened, up the steps to the battlements. Lish stood over two bodies. "Look at this."

Danny looked. Each had been killed with a single shot to the forehead; one had been stripped of his coveralls and had no submachine gun. A grapnel was hooked over the parapet – probably left over from one of the attacks. But the wounds were fresh, the blood still wet. Something lay crumpled beside them. Danny picked it up; a camouflage poncho.

"Shit," said Danny, and ran back to the steps.

REAPER CAMP

1957 HOURS

Cheers rose skyward with the smoke. But not from Wakefield.

She found a landcruiser, shoved the dead driver from his seat and sat. Tired. The deep after-battle weariness. Normally you were happy first, at least, that you'd lived. But not her. Not today. *Filly*. Wakefield's eyes prickled. She wiped them.

She looked around. The living and the dead. Gevaudan sat against the tilting battletruck, shivering in the firelight, shoving hunks of pemmican into his mouth from a can. She looked away.

"Wakefield?"

The voice. She turned. Dirt and smoke-smudged, bloody from cuts on her hands and face, but standing, smiling, weaving towards her: Filly.

And the joy she should have felt with battle's end came at last. Wakefield laughed, jumped down from the 'cruiser, threw her arms around the girl, felt warm arms hug her in return.

Ashwood Fort

1959 hours

One of the men Jarrett had killed had worn a cap; her hair was tucked under it, the brim pulled over her eyes. His coveralls were several sizes too big, but they'd be easier to ditch when the time came. Under them she was still in full Reaper uniform, the Browning holstered on her hip. The silenced Walther was in a pouch on the coveralls.

She had enough of a disguise to pass inspection, but the moment she was challenged she'd be fucked. And she didn't know the Fort's layout well enough to get where she was going. She'd need to find someone to ask, and quickly.

Footsteps. Laughter. Jarrett ducked into an alcove. Voices:

"Christ, it's a mess up there."

"Least it's bloody over now."

"Good job. Nearly out of bandages."

A weak laugh.

Medics. Helen had been shot; she'd be in sick bay. Perfect. Jarrett slipped the Walther from its pouch, eased back the hammer with her thumb.

Two women drew abreast, both clad in bloodstained smocks. Jarrett would only need to question one of them; the other was surplus to requirements. When they'd gone past, she stepped out and shot the first one in the back of the head. The other turned, mouth opening, and Jarrett shot her in the stomach.

The woman went down, mouth opening to scream. Jarrett jumped on her, a hand over her mouth, and wedged the silencer in her throat before dragging her into the alcove. "Listen to me. *Listen*." She leant in close, staring into the pain-dilated eyes. "Tell me what I want to know and live. Otherwise you die. We clear?" She took her hand from the woman's mouth. "Helen Damnation. Where?"

The woman pressed her lips together. Defiant. No time: Jarrett jabbed her wounded belly with the Walther, muffled her scream with her free hand. "Where?" she said again, removing the hand.

"Sick bay," the woman moaned, eyes screwed shut.

"And where's that?"

The woman's eyes opened, focusing again. "Fuck off."

Jarrett shot her in the stomach again, muffled the screams once more. "This is getting monotonous, darling," she said. "*Where?*"

"Top floor," the woman said at last. She coughed blood. "Oh fuck."

"So Helen's on the top floor?" After a moment's hesitation, the woman started to nod. Jarrett pushed the gun into her belly again, hard. "*Are you sure?*"

"No!" The woman was crying with pain. Gut wounds did that. She'd held out better than many would, Jarrett gave her that. At least she'd tried. "Roof," she said at last. "Wasn't room for everyone, so they moved some of them. I saw. Her, I mean. Can't miss her. Everyone knows her."

"Yes," said Jarrett. "I know."

She stood, aimed, fired: a neat hole in the forehead, a spray of blood and brains up the wall. As she straightened, another rebel came round the corner. His mouth opened when he saw the bodies; he reached for a gun.

Jarrett fired once; the man fell to his knees, then pitched forward, coughing and moaning as blood pooled around him. The Walther was empty; she threw it away and ran down the corridor, unslinging the Thompson. No point finishing him off; why waste time? When they found him, living or dead, they'd know what was happening, and who the target was. All that mattered now was that Jarrett got there first. And that Helen died.

9.

A cool breeze touched Helen's face. She smelt smoke on it. Urine. Excrement. Blood.

Bright light, through her closed eyes. She opened them, blinked.

Above was the black night sky; lantern-light glowed around her. She blinked again. She lay on a hard surface. Stone? There were voices. Low murmurs.

She turned her head. When she shifted position, metal dug into her thigh. Her .38, she realised; she was still fully clothed.

Other bodies were lying on the hard flat surface. Ventilator hoods jutted up at intervals, and a cupola with louvred sides. The edge of the surface ended abruptly, and beyond, in the fitful glare of flares and searchlights, she could see the inner and outer walls of Ashwood Fort – one breached and shattered, the other still standing but with sections of battlement blown raggedly away.

The roof. Her head hurt when she turned it and she felt sick.

She heard screams, but they were distant, muffled. From below. Of course. Nestor would have moved casualties who were out of immediate danger up here.

It was coming back now. The battle. The blow to her head. She propped herself up on one elbow – waves of pain and sickness swept through her and she closed her eyes till they passed – and looked out to see flames dancing in the woods where Jarrett had been. What she could see of the village was smoking rubble, strewn with corpses, but rebels in their coveralls were dragging them away, heaving them onto landcruiser flatbeds.

Over, then, and they'd won. Must have, as the battle was clearly done and if they'd lost, the Jennywrens would be at work wiping out the survivors. She wasn't sure how she felt. It was finished and they were still alive, but she'd missed it. It had been her fight and she'd been flung out of it. Others had completed the work that should have been hers.

Perhaps she'd fought a different battle, though. That had been won too. And the victory was hers alone.

"Take it easy." Nestor knelt by her, a hand on her shoulder. "Lie back down."

"It's over?"

"The battle is. As usual, the long part's going to be fixing the damage." He pressed her back down. "You took a bullet to the head, Helen. It took a lot of work to keep you alive, so I'd appreciate it if you waited a bit before trying to kill yourself again."

She managed a smile. "I'll try."

ASHWOOD FORT
2011 HOURS

Danny ran into the Fort, looked both ways. The corridor to the left of the entrance was narrower, quieter; that was the way he'd have gone, keep out of people's way till he'd found out where Helen was.

He rounded a corner and there the bodies were. One in the middle of the corridor, one propped up against the wall, another collapsed at the far end.

He ran to the first two. Both dead; headshots. The one sitting up had two gut wounds. When Danny looked up at the third body, it moved, groaning.

He legged it over, propped the man up. He'd been hit in the chest; lung blood frothed from his mouth.

"What happened?"

The man tried to speak; a whisper came out. "Jarrett. Saw her fucking face. Colonel fucking Jarrett."

Danny pulled the communicator out. "Falcon, this is Harrier. Falcon, come in. *Urgent.*"

"This is Falcon," Darrow said.

"Jarrett's inside the Fort," said Danny. "Sound an alert." He ran for the stairs. "She'll be heading for the sick bay."

THE WAR ROOM

"Full alert," said Darrow, then turned towards Alannah. "Alannah –"

He reached for her, but she pulled back. Jarrett was here. The room wavered, threatened to fade and fall away. The bare concrete walls, the cold face and that hard nasal voice. *All you have to say is* yes.

"No," she muttered. She waved Darrow off, backing up till she was against the wall. It was solid. Hard. The floor felt ready to melt. Her legs wouldn't hold her up. She pulled up a chair, slumped into it. Jarrett and the torture cell faded; she was in the War Room again.

"The Fort's on alert." Darrow was crouching beside her, trying to take her hand. She wouldn't let him. "Helen's safe."

"Sod Helen," she said. "That bitch is here."

"We'll find her. Alannah, we'll find her. She will not come near. Do you hear me, Alannah? She will not come near you."

Outside the War Room, klaxons began to sound.

Outside Sick Bay, ashwood fort
2015 hours

Jarrett stopped on the stairwell, glancing up as the klaxons blared. So, they knew. She smiled. Didn't matter, really. Didn't matter at all. Nothing mattered, as long as Helen died.

She was almost at the doors at the top of the stairs. Beyond them she saw sky. The roof. Where Helen was waiting for her.

Jarrett took out the Browning, checked the magazine was full and the chamber loaded, then holstered it. Checked the Thompson's magazine next. Then she unfastened the coveralls; they slid down and she stepped out of them, kicking them aside. She brushed specks of dirt from the black leather.

She was a Reaper again. An officer. A Jennywren. She slipped the pill jar from her pocket, tossed two more pills into her mouth. There were still two left, but she flung the jar aside. She didn't need it any more; one way or the other, those sleepless, haunted nights ended today.

Jarrett breathed deep, rolled her head to flex the tense neck muscles, and smiled. It was time.

Ready or not, Helen, here I come.

Ashwood Fort Roof

Helen opened her eyes to see Nestor coming back; wincing, he knelt beside her. "All right," he said, "now let's—"

A thud and crash. Someone shouted; then the *rat-tat-tat* of a submachine gun. More screams. A body fell. The submachine gun fired again.

"Nobody move," said a familiar voice. "Where's Helen?"

*

Nearing the top of the stairs, Danny crouched low. He was sure he'd heard gunshots, but it was hard to tell over the blaring klaxons. He shouldered the Lanchester, wedging the communicator between his jaw and shoulder as he moved towards the doors.

*

Helen lifted her head; Jarrett stood at the doors opening onto the roof, a Thompson gun in her hands. Two bodies lay at her feet.

No-one spoke.

The submachine gun swung to aim at one of the patients, a sandy-haired woman in her forties. "Let me explain something," said Jarrett, and fired. The woman's face shattered, and she flopped backwards. More screams. "Tell me where Helen Damnation is," said Jarrett. "Or I'll kill every one of you."

"Quickly," she heard Nestor say. "With me, now."

He moved behind her; his hands got her under the shoulders, lifted. A nurse – a thin dark-haired girl, no more than sixteen – crouched and took Helen's legs. She struggled feebly – let her get free, walk – but she was too weak to escape.

They carried her behind the cupola. The nurse held her upright as Nestor fumbled with the edge of the louvre. There was a click and it swung open; inside the cupola hung a metal cage.

"Service elevator," said Nestor. He pulled the cage door open, got Helen under the arms; she waved the nurse away, managed to stand. "In here, q –"

A chatter of submachine gun fire, and the nurse collapsed, her white smock turning red. "Helen!" shouted Jarrett, and her boots thundered along the roof towards them.

Danny saw it as he reached the doors; the woman in Reaper uniform firing, a white-clad body falling, then the Reaper charging across the roof towards the cupola. Even through the doors he heard her screaming Helen's name.

He flicked the communicator to transmit and crashed through the doors.

"Alannah, Darrow, it's Danny – the roof! Jarrett's on the r –"

He should have radio'd first, then gone in; Jarrett spun towards him and he was trying to aim, but it was clumsy, slow. He flexed his shoulders, let the communicator drop as he fell to one knee. The Thompson's muzzle flashed. *Rat-tat-tat*, and the bullets flew over his head. A buzz, like wasps. Danny pulled the trigger, and the Lanchester kicked back against his shoulder, spitting brass cases from the ejection port. But Jarrett was already diving, hitting the floor, prone, the Thompson gun at her shoulder.

Move, aim, fire. Danny tried to throw himself sideways, sweeping the Lanchester's muzzle down towards her, but he knew already he wasn't going to make it. Not fast enough, not nimble. The Thompson flashed again, *rat-tat-tat*, and something kicked him in the chest. Felt like it anyway. And he flew backwards and hit the surface of the roof, and he couldn't move – too weak – and he couldn't breathe.

Should have lit that candle, he thought as the stars wheeled above and dimmed. *Should have made that doll.*

The War Room

"Danny!" Alannah shouted into the mic. "Danny!"

"Alannah –" Darrow tried to take the mic, but she struck out at him. He turned away, cursing. "Hei – get a squad up on the roof, now."

He turned back to her. She let the mic fall; her hands had gone to her mouth. She said nothing, and nor did Darrow. There was nothing to say.

Ashwood Fort Roof

"In," gasped Nestor, "quickly." He bundled Helen over the threshold into the service lift, pulled the cage shut behind them, fumbled with the controls.

"This thing work?" said Helen.

"Think so."

"You *think?*" Helen fumbled for the pouch on her coveralls that held her revolver.

"No other way down – oh shit."

Jarrett rounded the side of the cupola and saw them in the exact moment that, with a grinding of gears, the cage began descending. Helen tried to tug out the .38, but her fingers were thick, weren't working. The Thompson swung up.

"Down," Nestor shouted, grabbing her and pulling her to the floor. The Thompson fired; bullets spanged off the cage door, ricocheted off the walls. But then Jarrett was gone, and the lift going down; from above Helen heard a scream of rage. Then, a second later, the Thompson was firing again, and a series of clangs, cracks and thuds sounded from above as bullets hammered into the cage roof. Something cracked loudly, and the lift fell, plunging faster and faster down.

*

Jarrett fired another burst from the Thompson, and then the gun was empty. She lowered it; below her, the lift cage dropped out of sight into the dark. Perhaps she'd smashed something and the cage would just fall now, plunge all the way to the bottom of the shaft and smash Helen and her doctor to a pulp. Perhaps. Probably, even. Almost certainly. But Helen had died before, or seemed to, and then come back.

No. Jarrett had to be sure. No doubts this time. Had to look into her eyes, see the light go out, put a round through her head to make sure or even cut it off.

Shouts from across the roof; more rebels had arrived. Well, that had been inevitable. Jarrett wouldn't be leaving here; she'd known that when she'd left the battletruck. Even if she lived, where would she go?

Where Helen was, of course. To see her die.

Jarrett tossed the submachine gun aside, pulled a pair of gloves from a pouch on her uniform and tugged them on. Then she reached into the cupola, grabbed the lift cables, swung her legs inside and started sliding down.

10.

"All right," Alannah heard Darrow say. "Thank you. Now organise a level by level search. Find them before she does."

He crossed over to Alannah, knelt. "Alannah."

"Danny?" her voice sounded tiny, cracked. All she could think of was Christmas; Danny asking her to dance, the hurt on his face when she rebuffed him. Hadn't wanted to be weak, dependant. Much less take a lover so young. It wouldn't have been right. Or had it really been simpler – *no, I'll look pathetic, an old woman with a boy?* After everything – the War, the Civil Emergency, the torture – after *everything*, could she really have been as shallow as that? And now it was too late to put right. All she could see was Stephen's face, after he'd died. So pale and so still. Stephen, Danny; Danny, Stephen.

"Listen to me." Darrow took her hands. "Danny's been shot."

"By Jarrett." It wasn't a question.

"By Jarrett. Listen to me, Alannah –"

"Where's Jarrett now?" She said it through her teeth.

"We're looking. There's an old service elevator on the roof, still in working order. Looks as though Nestor got Helen into it and escaped, but we don't know which floor."

"Jarrett?"

"Far as we can tell, she climbed down the shaft after them. Alannah, *listen* to me. First, I have people searching every level. We *will* find Jarrett and we *will* find Helen. But Alannah, listen to me – Danny's alive, all right? She shot him, but she didn't kill him."

Alannah looked at him. "How bad?" Darrow didn't answer straight away. "How bad, Roger?"

"It's bad," he said.

Alannah nodded. "I thought so."

She got up, walked out.

"Alannah!"

Alannah went across the corridor into the Intelligence Centre to her desk. There was one personal communicator left in her drawer; she took it out. "Keep me posted," she told him. On her way out, she motioned to the two fighters standing guard outside the door. "You two, with me."

SERVICE ELEVATOR

The lift plummeted; Helen saw the floors flash by the cage. Then her legs buckled; if not for Nestor's supporting arm she'd have fallen as the pressure rose. The floors slid by more slowly; the cage was decelerating. The lift jerked hard, and they staggered. For a moment she thought it had stopped, but it continued descending, this time at a constant, steady pace.

Floors went past. Which level now? "What..." Her voice was a dry croak. She swallowed. "What floor did you push?"

"Second," he said. "But I think we've gone past it."

A final set of doors went past, and then the shaft's brick walls were replaced with wet, dripping rock.

"What the hell?" said Nestor.

Helen huffed a weak laugh. "Think the lift goes further down than you thought." The blast shelter's unknown architect's doing, she guessed.

With a whirr, groan and clank, the cage halted before a metal door. Nestor pulled the cage door open. Outside was blackness and the drip of water. The only light was the dim glow glimmering down the shaft. Nestor glanced up at the ceiling. "Don't know if we should stay put or –"

There was a bang from above, and something hit the roof of the lift cage. Hit it and smashed through, punching into the floor. "Christ!"

A tiny point of light showed where the bullet hole was, from the light at the top. Another shot rang out, and Helen threw herself backwards just in time; she felt the bullet skim past her face. Jarrett must be using steel-tipped bullets. "Out, now," she gasped, stumbling for the threshold.

Nestor went after her, arm around her waist as more shots rang out. He pulled her to one side as Jarrett kept firing; two or three bullets ricocheted off the floor and cracked into the tunnel walls. Helen's hand touched something; fabric, she thought, but damp, slimy. She fumbled up it; a coverall, hanging by the lift.

Helen groped higher, found something cold, hard, smooth: plastic. Dome-shaped, with a peak. A helmet. And on the front of the helmet, something round and hard and drum shaped. A headlamp.

Two more bullets crashed through the cage roof. Helen's fingers probed the circumference of the headlamp, finally found what they were after: a raised piece of plastic that gave slightly.

Perhaps; just perhaps.

She pushed at the switch; it clicked, and light flashed into the tunnel. "Jesus," said Nestor, flinching from the beam. It was watery, wavering, but it was light.

Three shots in quick succession punched through the cage; one whined down the tunnel. Helen put the helmet on.

"Careful," said Nestor. Helen felt the gauze pad under the bandage press against the head wound and swayed for a second. She turned, shone the beam along the row of hooks beside the lift door; on them hung half a dozen coveralls, most of them now rotten, and five more helmets. She took one and gave it to Nestor. "Let's move," she said; above, she could hear muffled grunts and scraping metal as Jarrett climbed down.

Nestor switched his headlamp on. The beams lit up the cave ahead; it bent round after a dozen yards.

Hide in the earth, Frank had said. Where was he now? The cold dark weight of the ground pressed in around her; she swallowed with difficulty.

They started along the cave, ducking as more shots rang out behind.

LIFT SHAFT

Clinging to the lift cable, Jarrett ejected the empty magazine, heard it clatter on the cage roof, then took another from a pouch on her belt and clicked it into place. She tugged the slide and it snapped forward. She started climbing down again.

She'd shinned down quicker at first, using both hands, but when the cage had slowed and stopped she'd had to chance a shot. She gauged the distance to the lift below – ten, maybe fifteen feet. Close enough.

Jarrett let go of the cable and dropped in the dark. She crashed into the cage roof, slipped and fell sideways, arms raised to protect her head. Her shoulder hit the shaft wall. "Fuck."

Helen. Jarrett fired five rounds rapid through the cage roof. No sound. She might have hit them both, but she'd heard a mumble of voices from below; chances were, she knew, Helen and the doctor had got out. She tugged at the roof hatch, aiming down at it.

Noise above; grating metal, grunts of effort. Light spilled into the shaft. Jarrett looked up; the doors on the level above were being forced open. They slid wide; three figures were silhouetted against the light. Rebels, looking for her. She aimed up and fired, four rounds left to right and four rounds right to left. The doors vanished in a haze of smoke and jumping brass; when it cleared, they were gone.

Quickly now. The rest of her life was likely minutes long; all that mattered now was Helen. She yanked the hatch open, jumped down into the empty cage, ejected the empty magazine and reloaded once more.

Down the cave outside the door there was light, and there shouldn't have been. Light, and two dim silhouettes. One turned, and the light flashed into Jarrett's eyes. She raised the gun, fired; shouts and running footsteps, and the cave was dark again.

The light. The light had been at head level. A headlamp. She'd only glimpsed Helen and the doctor in the lift before it descended, but she was sure neither of them had had one, and there'd been none in the lift itself. That meant – Jarrett ran her hands along the wall each side of the door at head-height, heart thumping, snarling in frustration as fingers grubbed over wet rock, till at last they found smooth plastic. She donned a helmet, found the lamp and switched it on.

She bit back a cry as faces jumped out of the shadows in the torchlight. Mum, Dad, Tom.

"There's no way back from this, love," Mum said gently. "Even now, you could stop."

"Not any more," said Dad. "What's she going to do? Where'll she go? Think she'll have a chance to put things right now? Who'd trust her to?"

"You could try and get away," said Tom. "Find a way out of the caves. Go into the Wastelands. Choose something different. Change."

Jarrett snorted and strode forward; they fell aside. The torch beam fell on Mandy's tiny face, ahead of her. Her eyes were full of tears.

"Don't," she said. "Please, Nicola. Don't."

"Leave her, love," Dad's voice called out of the dark. "She's made her choice."

Mandy bowed her head, and stepped out of the light. The only sound was the drip of water, and the distant echo of footsteps.

Jarrett squared her shoulders, then started down the tunnel, Browning aimed ahead.

CAVE SYSTEM

The cave opened out. The headlamp beams shone upwards; stalactites shone like wet yellow fangs. Below them, stalagmites sprouted from the floor. The cavern stretched out about twenty feet to either side, and further still ahead; the weak beams from their helmets reached only into the dark

"Graspen fucking Hill all over again," said Helen.

"Huh?"

"Forget it. Come on, let's…" She blinked and swallowed; her head swam. "Let's keep going."

"Shit," said Nestor.

Helen opened her eyes. About fifteen feet ahead of them, the floor ended. The crevasse was at least thirty feet wide; no jumping over that. The headlamps picked out a jagged rock face, but couldn't find the bottom.

Helen's legs gave way. Nestor steadied her. "Okay," he said. "Here." He pulled her back towards the back wall of the cavern, found a niche in the rock, helped her sit. "You're in no state to be moving."

"Not much choice," said Helen. Was her voice slurred? Sounded like it.

Nestor reached over, turned off her headlamp. "I'm going to try and lead her off," he said.

"Lead her where? There's nowhere."

"I'll do what I can."

"Wait." Helen unbuttoned the pouch, pulled out the revolver. "Take this."

"I don't use them, Helen," he said. "Never have, never will. Besides —" he smiled. "If you get the chance, you'll do a better job with it than me."

He got up before she could protest, and his footsteps clicked away.

LOWER LEVEL, BLAST SHELTER, ASHWOOD FORT

Blinking, Alannah sat up. No pain. Didn't feel as though she'd been hit. She scooted back against the far wall, looking herself over. No visible wounds.

She got up. The two men with her hadn't been so lucky. She'd thrown herself backwards faster – perhaps because her first instinct on seeing Jarrett's face had been to recoil – so the bullets had missed. The other two had been hit in the head and chest; both were already dead.

She took out the communicator. "Roger? Jarrett's in the cave system." She didn't know she was going to say it until she did. "I'm going in after her."

"Alannah!"

She tossed the communicator aside. It clattered on the floor; she heard Darrow's tinny voice still calling her name, and smiled.

Alannah could see the roof of the car below. She leant into the shaft, reaching for the lift cables.

CAVERN

Helen huddled deeper into the niche, teeth clenched. She was shivering; sick, dizzy, weak. Wetness trickled down her neck. Water dripping, or was she bleeding from the ears again? She gripped onto the .38, so that the metal dug into her palms.

Keep me awake.

Looking out, she saw pale light splash across the cavern floor. It moved and shifted, but there was no sound. No clue as to what might be going on.

Helen pulled her knees closer to her chest as the light lapped closer to her hiding place, in case her feet were sticking out. The .38's milled hammer spur dug into the ball of her thumb. She should have cocked it before. Easier to pull the trigger that way, if she got Jarrett in her sights.

Water dripped, echoing in the dark.

"Helen?"

Not Nestor's voice. A woman's.

"*He*-len?" The voice crooned, gloating and triumphant. "You know who this is, don't you?"

Slowly, she eased back the revolver's hammer.

The light flickered back and forth across the floor.

"I've got your friend, Helen," Jarrett said. "You can save him if you want, you know. Then again, what's one more?"

Helen pushed herself to her feet, swaying as another wave of dizziness swept through her.

"Go on, Doctor," she heard Jarrett call. "Tell her. Let her know you're still with us for now." Silence. Then a cry of pain.

"Fuck you," she heard Nestor say.

"When I give an order, Doctor, it's obeyed," said Jarrett. "Well, Helen?"

Helen peered round the edge of the niche. Jarrett was ten feet away, her Browning at Nestor's head. "Kneel," she told him. Jaw clenched, Nestor obeyed. Jarrett pressed the Browning to the back of his skull and cocked it. "Show yourself, Helen."

Helen stepped out and aimed one-handed; the other reached out to switch on the headlamp. Click, and the light shone at Jarrett's face. She didn't look round. "This gun has a hair-trigger," she said. "If you shoot me, this man dies." She glanced round, smiled. "And you're not looking too steady just now anyway."

She was right; Helen's gun-hand shook. She used both hands to aim; the barrel still wobbled. Then again, Jarrett didn't look good either. Muscles jumped in her white face, her eyes were bloodshot, and while the gun stayed steady, the fingers of her free hand twitched non-stop. A thin thread of blood ran from her left nostril. She was burning up; all she cared about was who burned along with her.

"Simple choice," said Jarrett. "Put down the gun and let me finish what my sniper started. Otherwise, he's dead."

"You'll kill him anyway," said Helen. "You got me that way before."

"Ah," said Jarrett, "that. What was her name again?"

"Shell." A child. Twelve, maybe thirteen. She'd been in the wrong place at the wrong time, nothing more. Jarrett had put a gun to her head: *Surrender or she dies.* Helen had surrendered, and Jarrett had blown Shell's brains out anyway.

"Should have known," said Jarrett. "You remember all the names. But if you think back, Helen, I never *promised* to spare her, as such. I never gave my word."

"And that would have made a difference?"

"Of course it would. Thought you knew me better than that, Helen. My honour's all I have." The gun at Nestor's head, steady as a rock; the .38's barrel shook and wobbled, and Helen's vision blurred in and out of focus.

"If I put my gun down," she said, "do you give me your word you won't harm Nestor?"

"You have my word," said Jarrett. "I'm just here for you."

Helen glanced around the cavern, looking for Frank and Belinda. Surely they wouldn't want to miss this. But she'd turned from them on the Black Road, after everything; maybe she'd finally exorcised them, laid them to some kind of rest. Now they were about to get what they'd always wanted, and they weren't here to see it.

Helen started laughing. Couldn't stop herself. It went on and on, shaking her like weeping.

"What?" demanded Jarrett. "What's so funny? What?"

But Helen just laughed. It was one small victory, at least.

She uncocked the .38 and threw it down. Her laugh ebbed into silence.

Water dripped.

There was something like gratitude in Jarrett's face.

"Thank you, Helen," she said, and began to raise the gun.

And then a fresh beam of light shone into the cavern, and a voice called Jarrett's name.

*

Jarrett squinted towards the glow, keeping the gun at Nestor's head. "Stop there," she said. "Or he dies."

"No," said the woman. "Put your gun down, Colonel."

The woman stepped forward. Beneath the helmet, silver hair fell around her shoulders. She held a massive revolver, aimed at Jarrett.

"Do you remember me, Jarrett?" Her voice shook; her dark eyes glistened.

Jarrett glanced from her to Helen, saw Helen looking at the pistol on the ground. "Don't," she said, then looked back to the woman. "Who are you?"

"You don't remember," she said. "Do they just sort of blur together, then? The people you tortured?"

There *was* something familiar. It was the dark eyes; the pain in them, as if whatever Jarrett had done to her had only just ended. As if she had an eidetic memory, for instance, where nothing ever went away. "Vale," she said. "Alannah Vale."

"Drop the gun," the woman said.

"Unlikely." Jarrett smiled, but behind it she was torn between disbelief and rage. Alannah Vale was an irrelevance; Jarrett had broken and discarded her years ago. How dare she come between her and this? And yet the gun was real, and aimed at her. Jarrett looked at Helen again; Helen looked down at the fallen .38. She looked steadier on her feet than she had a minute ago, her eyes clearer.

The gun in Vale's hand shook. Frightened, damaged; weak. Worthless. Jarrett had no doubt she could spin and shoot fast enough to drop Vale before a shot came near her, but Helen might reach her gun. And she might just be fast enough, and accurate enough. Jarrett couldn't chance that.

No. It wasn't even a choice.

Jarrett looked back towards Helen.

Alannah cocked the Webley; a loud click echoed in the cave. "Jarrett," she said. "Look at me, you bitch."

But her voice wavered and cracked, broke into a sob. She was crying, she realised; she felt the tears on her cheeks and she felt her arm shake. Partly the gun's weight, yes, but not all. Just the sight of Jarrett weakened her.

The memory of her torture never really left; it was always there, like a permanent stain. The electrodes clamped to nipples and genitals; the needles inserted under fingernails, the lighted cigarettes. The beatings, in the glare of a third-degree light: the Reapers who'd kicked and punched her had been faceless, but Jarrett had sat watching it all from her chair. Sometimes not even watching; seeing it had bored her. She'd just wait for the latest round to finish, then wave her thugs back and ask her questions again.

All this and so much more, and Alannah could forget none of it.

Even with a gun, what could she do? Jarrett was her monster; for years now, the nightmare in the dark, the thing waiting in the shadows when the lights went out. Everything she'd built up in the years since, in the months since she crawled out of hiding to fight, all of it just crumbled away. Jarrett was the truth. The torture was the truth. Naked and battered and bleeding, bruised and burnt, muscles still twitching from the electrodes, on a filthy concrete floor, broken and waiting for the footsteps to come again, the door to open and light to shine through to illuminate another torture session, that was the truth.

I don't have the power in this room, Alannah. You do.

I do this because I don't have any choice.

Jarrett looked back at her, and smiled.

Do you know how much power you have, Alannah?

Weak, the smile said.

You have so much power you can stop all this with a word.

And then Jarrett looked away again, and swung the Browning towards Helen.

All you have to say is —

"No," said Alannah, and fired. The Webley's crash shook the cavern, rang off the walls and ceiling. A squealing and squeaking and flutter of wings as bats scattered, swarming in the light above.

Jarrett spun sideways; her left arm flapped and dangled like a strip of cloth, hung useless as she fell to one knee: shattered bone. The scream she let out wasn't pain, but rage. Through the flurrying black wings and bristle-furred bodies Alannah saw the Browning sweep towards her, but suddenly she was calm, the fear gone, and Jarrett seemed to move very slowly. She pulled the trigger again, and the hammer rose and fell. The revolver kicked and a second blast rolled out: Jarrett flew backwards, hit the ground, rolled to a halt two feet from the crevasse and was still.

Nestor had dived to the floor. He got up slowly, blinking, then ran to Helen as she fell to her knees. Alannah looked from them to Jarrett, then walked slowly towards the body, gun aimed down.

The air was full of the shots' echoes, the clatter and squeak of bats and the thin high belltone in Alannah's ears, but through it all she heard Helen ask: "She dead?"

Perhaps her voice did it, woke whatever strength Jarrett had left to remind her of her mission; the body moved, twisted, the pistol in its hand thrusting towards Helen. Alannah fired again; Jarrett jacknifed, screaming, but the gun stayed in her hands. Alannah kept firing as she walked, and Jarrett thrashed like a broken-backed snake. With a final heave of her body, she rolled away, to the edge of the crevasse, then over. She dropped into the dark and was gone; Alannah heard a scream, then a distant sound of impact.

Alannah realised she was still pulling the trigger; the Webley clicked and clicked. She knew she should stop, but couldn't. The pleasure it had given her, of seeing Jarrett break and fall and scream; it was already fading, and she wanted to hold onto it.

A hand rested on hers; Nestor's, his other arm supporting Helen. "She is now," he said. "Come on."

The last of the bats fluttered away, back to their roosts. Alannah shoved the Webley back into its holster – it took only three or four attempts – and helped him prop Helen up. They started back through the cave to the lift shaft; she could already hear voices calling out to them.

Afterwards, she'd send someone to get Jarrett's body. Not to gloat, not really. Just so that she could be sure.

*

Jarrett lay alone in the broken dark, shattered on the rocks and breathing blood.

So thus it ended. Failure. The Jennywrens smashed and broken, driven back home in full flight. And Helen still alive. Couldn't even finish that. Perhaps the bitch would still die. She'd been shot in the head, after all.

Pain. Suffocating. The copper taste and smell of blood, wiping out all else.

Earth fell on her: a light sprinkle at first, then a heavy fall of it. A shovel-load.

There was light – she could feel it on her closed eyes. She opened them and looked.

A rectangle of grey sky, with earth sides. Swirling mist, and around the edges of the grave, her family. Each with their shovels. Mum and Tom on one side, Dad and Mandy on the other. Mandy with her little plastic seaside spade.

One after the other, they began to shovel the dirt. It fell on her. And as it fell, they spoke: the same words, over and over.

"How could you, love?" said Mum. "How could you?"

"I *hate* you," shouted Mandy.

"You disgust me," said Tom. "I never want to see you again."

And Dad just shook his head. That was all they said, all he did, as they slowly, steadily, buried her deep. And she screamed and she begged, but all to no avail, thrashing in her grave as the earth closed over her.

But like Helen before her, she tore through the crust of earth, broke out gasping into air and light. Around her was a dilapidated cemetery; wild grass and weeds, tilted headstones, sunken graves. And mist. The four of them walked away from her, joining hands, and vanished into it, even as she screamed after them.

Jarrett stood and ran after them; with vague surprise, she noted that her smashed limbs and body were suddenly healed. The mist swallowed her and there was only whiteness and echoing mist, uneven ground underfoot. No sound but the echo of the pleas she screamed after the ones she'd lost, begging them to come back.

Nicola Jarrett blundered on into the mist, trying to find them. But she never did.

APPROACH TO ASHWOOD FORT
2100 HOURS

Filly's arm was round Wakefield's shoulders. Wakefield's held the black girl's waist. Wakefield wasn't sure how that had happened, but decided it was good as they trudged back up the hill.

The grass squelched underfoot. Blood, still wet. Bodies still scattered on the slopes. Crows flapping down to peck at their food.

"Glad you're okay," said Filly, squeezing Wakefield.

Wakefield squeezed back, grinned. "Same."

Filly stopped. "You hear that?"

Wakefield was about to say no, but then she heard it too: low moaning, over the to the right. Wounded. She scanned the bodies, saw none moving. The moan came again — a crater, nearby. She pointed and they waked to it, now hand in hand.

Two bodies in the hole, both in Reaper black. A dead man, the top of his head blown off, and a woman lying on her back, beside her sniper rifle, coughing blood. Wakefield's hands moved without asking her head: the Thompson gun was cocked and aimed, her finger on the trigger.

The Reaper looked up at her; her eyes were dull with pain. Didn't much care either way, guessed Wakefield. Too far gone. After a moment, she looked to Filly, then lowered the gun, looking over the hillside instead, to where nurses were loading bodies onto 'cruisers. "Over here," she shouted. "Prisoner."

She watched, Filly's hand warm in hers, as they lifted the Reaper from the hole. Her eyes looked even more dazed than before, not understanding this. "Your lucky day," said Wakefield; then she and Filly walked on.

Ops Room, the tower
2130 hours

Thorpe lowered the mic and licked his lips, then turned and started towards Winterborn.

The Commander had returned to the Ops Room a little under two hours ago, and had stood, silent and motionless, as the reports had rolled in: the loss of the second support convoy, the attack on the Reaper camp at Ashwood, the final humiliating retreat. It hadn't ended there, either; the Jennywren force had been hit again and again as it fell back along the Devil's Highway, with a final devastating enfilade from M20s, Carl Gustafs and light machine guns as it cut through a burned town in the Wastelands.

And through it all Winterborn had stood, that marble-angel face without expression, those blue eyes giving nothing away.

Thorpe swallowed and approached. "Commander?" Winterborn didn't answer. Thorpe cleared his throat to speak again.

"Yes, Colonel?" Winterborn didn't look at him. Normally, he was most dangerous when he was smiling and jokey, but on a day like this, there was no knowing when his rage would erupt, or at whom. There *hadn't* been a day like this before; neither the Civil Emergency nor the December Rising had marked so utter and abject a defeat.

"The PeriSec units have rendezvoused with what's l – with the column," said Thorpe. "They're being escorted back to REAP Thurley."

"And Doctor Kellett?"

"Missing presumed dead, sir."

"And Colonel Jarrett?"

"Still missing, sir." No 'presumed dead' there; Majid had made it clear what had happened. Not that Thorpe could blame her; even Jarrett wouldn't be psychotic enough to face Winterborn after this.

"*Quintili Vare, legiones redde*," murmured Winterborn.

Thorpe blinked. "Sir?"

Winterborn nodded. "Orders, Colonel."

"Yes, sir?"

"Place Captain Majid and all surviving officers under arrest, pending debriefing. All survivors to be confined to barracks until further notice."

"What about wounded, sir?"

"Arrange treatment, but they're to be segregated from other patients. I want a lid kept on this as far as possible."

No hope of that, and Winterborn must know it as well as Thorpe did; word of this disaster would be across RCZ7 in days, the other Commands within the week. But he had to try.

"Place PeriSec divisions on high alert in case of retaliation," said Winterborn. "Ditto CorSec divisions. Always the chance that word of this will lead to further unrest." A half-smile. "One would hope we cured the urban population of any rebellious urges back in December, but it's best to be prepared. Carry on, Colonel. Inform me of any further developments."

Without another word, he turned and left.

Commander's Office, the Tower
2147 hours

Winterborn's breathing slowed at last; he dropped the bag onto the surface of the desk, then slumped forward, eyes slowly focusing.

"*Quintili Vare, legiones redde*," he whispered again. "*Quintili Vare, legiones redde.*" It had almost become a mantra. *Quintilius Varus, give me back my legions.* Augustus Caesar had shouted that,

411

over and over again, after three of his legions had been wiped out in the Teutoberg Wald. Of course, the failure there had been Quintilius Varus', their commander's, alone, and Varus had paid with his life. But Jarrett's failure was a taint that would spread. Perhaps fatally, to him.

Winterborn breathed deeply, in and out, again. Perhaps, but not yet: not at all, if he could prevent it.

He slid the drawer open, took out the silver box. He should have thought of it before, but he'd barely shut the office door before the panic attack he'd been fighting off in the Ops Room finally overwhelmed him. He was calming again. At least for now, until the next time he found himself struggling with the full scope of the disaster.

He breathed in, deep, then out. He opened the lid of the music box and closed his eyes. It played a few notes, soft and soothing. Then slowed, and was silent again.

EPILOGUE

CHEETHAM HILL ROAD, CITY OF MANCHESTER
3RD APRIL, ATTACK PLUS TWENTY-ONE YEARS
1700 HOURS

The road was lined on either side with gutted, roofless brick buildings that had been shops. Some were missing, having collapsed or been pulled down after the war. The vacant lots where they'd been were filled with shelters built from rubble, old planks or plastic sheeting. Tarp or sheeting was stretched over the missing roofs of the surviving buildings.

Late afternoon and overcast; candlelight already burned in windows or in the crude shelters on the vacant lots. They were on high ground, so the Walker could see a long way, out to the hills rising in the distance and distant ponds of blue sky in the waste of rubble-grey cloud. Here and there the hills were dotted with points of fire. And ahead, rising like a polished silver spar, was the Tower.

The Walker had waited in Thurley Marsh for days, till it judged the time was right. And then it had begun walking again. It looked towards the Tower: now its journey was almost complete.

The exact moment, carefully chosen, was nearly here. But not quite. That didn't matter. The Walker was patient.

The road was busy; the lucky ones rode to the city in carts, the rest went on foot, all carrying produce, for which they'd be paid in food. A landcruiser rolled past, coming from the city centre. None of them spared the Walker so much as a glance, which was as things should be. It stepped out of their way, sat on a broken stub of wall, and waited.

COMMANDER'S OFFICE, THE TOWER
1705 HOURS

Winterborn tightened the last screw and took out the eyeglass, blinking as he refocused. He put the tools back in his drawer and opened the music box lid.

The tune played, and he settled back in his chair, eyes closed. Occupying himself with further repairs had helped distract him from everything around him; now the music washed it away instead.

The music slowed and stopped. Winterborn reached for the box again, found the key and started winding. But his fingers felt thick and shaky; the box slipped back onto the table.

He rocked in his chair for a moment then stood, striding to the window. Below was his city; beyond were his hills. As far as he could see was his domain.

But for how long?

Any Reaper or civilian saying that in Winterborn's hearing would have been branded a traitor, and fortunate if they only faced a firing squad. Had Jarrett been here, he might have consulted her on suitably painful methods. Or not. Winterborn's own imagination was fertile enough when it came to imposing torment. As well he knew: that was where the traitor was. You couldn't kill a voice in your head, except by killing yourself.

Besides, it was a useful question. They were still trying to gather intelligence from their few sources, but it seemed there'd been talk of a plan to spread the rebels' command out across multiple bases. Unconfirmed, but hardly a surprise. As Jarrett had said, the Fort had replicated the mistake made by the Refuge, and the rebellion almost ended as a result.

But words like *almost* and *nearly* meant nothing. The rebellion continued. It was only a matter of time before they struck back. And in the meantime, Winterborn knew the murmurs would have begun. In the other REAP Commands, and within his own. He'd been successful, achieved much, but that was the past. Now he was the Commander who'd tried and dismally failed to end the rebellion, and lost half his Jennywren forces in the process.

One defeat, if bad enough, set everyone to questioning you. And then came the whispers, and the secret plots, and at last the knife in the dark.

Many years ago, Winterborn had read the Qu'ran; a line from it came back to him now.

Wherever you are, death will overtake you, though you are in lofty towers.

Winterborn pressed his palms flat against the window, watching the sun's slow sinking. The night was still far off, but it would come.

SICK BAY, ASHWOOD FORT

1715 HOURS

The sick bay was quieter now. Most of the wounded were well again – able to walk, anyroad. Or they'd died, like Beak, despite all Nestor could do. Flaps reckoned Sud dying had been what had done it; it had broken something in Beak that the bullet hadn't.

A few, though – a few were gonna need longer than that. There was Helen, still under observation after the head wound and what had come after; there was a short, sandy-haired girl called Stock – Flaps had written her off for dead after seeing the Catchman pull her guts out – who lay thin and pale and quiet in her bed, fed on a liquid diet. And there was Danny.

Flaps sat by his bed, arms folded, watching him. Her back ached and her eyes felt full of grit. But she stayed.

"Here." A mug of hot tea, steaming next to her face.

"Ta." Flaps took it, wincing as it burnt her palms.

Gevaudan nodded towards Danny. "He *will* live, you know."

"You dunno that."

"No, but Nestor seems fairly certain. And he's usually right. The danger point's come and gone. He's healing."

"Then why's he like this?" She pointed at Danny: the still body, the shut eyes, the white slack face.

"It was a very bad trauma," said Gevaudan. "A shock. Damaging. His body's working hard to repair itself. It takes a lot of energy, and so he sleeps."

"Whatever." Flaps took a sip of tea, then nodded to the far end of the ward. "How come you're not with the missus?"

"Helen is not my *missus*."

Flaps just looked at the Grendelwolf over the rim of her mug. Gevaudan stared back, till she had to look away. Couldn't handle those yellow eyes for long.

Someone else came in, stopped by the bed. Flaps eyed the newcomer. "Back again?"

Alannah sighed. "Here to see Helen, if you must know. Is that all right with you?"

Flaps shrugged. Alannah shook her head and strode on up the ward. As she did, the door opened again.

"It's like Grand Central Station today," said Gevaudan.

"Like where?"

"He'll tell you later," said Darrow.

"Will I?"

"I'm sorry, Gevaudan. I need a moment with Flaps, if you can spare it."

"Of course." Gevaudan stood; he glanced at Danny, nodded to Flaps. "Darrow," he said, and slipped outside, the door swinging shut behind him.

Darrow sat in the vacated chair. "I wanted to talk to you, before I left."

"What's up?"

"Well, as you know, I'll be leaving soon."

"I heard. Back to Manchester, right?"

Darrow nodded. "New crews to recruit. The same as before."

"Like you did with Mary and that?"

"Yes." He smiled. "I remember when I first went in, after the Refuge fell. Mike Ashton had gone ahead of us. I was with Noakes."

"Who?"

"Before your time. He didn't make it."

"Right."

"And we brought Alannah in with us."

"Must have been fun."

Darrow looked half-irritated, half-amused. "She was practically a vegetable then. Didn't talk, couldn't do a thing without help."

Pity she didn't stay that way, Flaps nearly said, but didn't. Darrow was softer with her than with some of the sprogs, but not *that* soft. He was still Darrow; there was still a line.

"Anyway, a few more drifted in. A handful of survivors from the Refuge. And we each recruited a crew. And now we have to start again."

"Think you can?"

"I'd say so. I just need a few people with me who know the city. Who I can trust." Darrow was looking at her, hard. Took Flaps a second to twig.

"What, me?"

"Yes, you. I think you'd be perfect for it, in fact."

Flaps looked from him to Danny in his bed. Posted to the Wastelands, she saw him little enough as it was. In the city, she might as well be dead.

Darrow nodded, sighed. "Think about it, anyway," he said at last, and stood. As he slipped out through the door she saw how thin he looked, how faded the grey of his hair.

"No way," said Helen. "So that was why?"

"Yup," said Alannah. "Meant to tell you before, but I sort of forgot in all the excitement."

"Join the club. I'd forgotten I even asked. Getting shot in the head'll do that, I suppose."

"It didn't seem that important. I didn't tell Darrow, even at the time."

"How come?"

"I thought about it, but… Roger might have started second-guessing himself and not sent him. And it *was* our best chance, by then. Anyway. There's news."

Helen looked at the water jug on the table beside her. Alannah grinned and poured her a glass. "Enjoy the slave labour while it lasts."

"I'm not supposed to move from the bed unaided."

"Yeah, yeah. Whatever." The smile made Alannah look younger; it stripped away the years and the silvering of her hair. "The council met earlier today, minus you, of course. Took another vote on that plan of yours."

Helen's hands tightened on the bedsheets. "And?"

"And they've decided you were right."

"Well done for spotting the bloody obvious."

"So our command structure will be spread out over a network of forts, instead of just this one," Alannah said. "Communicate by radio and messengers, come together only when strictly necessary." She smiled. "The intelligence centre stays here, though. So at least I don't have to move."

She glanced sideways, to the other end of the ward where Flaps sat by Danny's bed.

"What is it?" said Helen. "There's something else."

Alannah sighed. "They took another vote on Roger's proposal, too. About him taking charge of the city crews."

"You're joking."

Alannah shrugged. "Now the Reapers know where the Fort is, no-one thought it was a problem." She swallowed, feeling her eyes prickle. "So he's going."

She couldn't say anything else. After a moment, Helen squeezed her hand.

*

Flaps sipped her tea, started as she heard a moan from the bed. Danny was stirring. His head lolled from side to side. His lips moved; he mumbled something.

"Lover?" Flaps got up and went to him. Leant close. She was smiling; she could feel it, making her face ache. "Babe?"

His lips moved and he mumbled it again. One word: "Alannah."

Flaps straightened up. The smile had frozen on her face. She felt it shrivel and die. She stood looking down at him. Her throat tightened; her eyes prickled. She wiped them, turned and strode up the sick bay towards Helen's bed, fists clenched.

Alannah saw her coming and got out of her chair, taking a step back. The corners of Flaps' eyes throbbed with rage. "He's all yours," she said, jerking a thumb back towards the bed. "You're fucking welcome to him."

Then she wheeled and strode out, slamming the doors wide open with her hands. Outside, in the corridor, Gevaudan stared at her, took a step her way; Flaps shook her head and kept walking.

*

"I, um…" Alannah looked at the doors to the ward, still swinging back and forth, then to Danny. She wiped her eyes. "I think I should… I mean, in case he comes round."

Helen snorted, rolled her eyes, as Alannah hurried down the ward. "Fine," she called. "Leave me on my own."

She settled back against the pillows, closing her eyes. As the quiet rushed back in, she remembered that last thing she'd heard on the Black Road: *tell me your vision*. It came back at moments like this, and always brought with it the knowledge that she had none.

A shadow fell on her; someone by the bed. Helen opened her eyes. "Gevaudan. Hey." Then she saw what was in front of him.

A half-smile touched the Grendelwolf's lips, and he looked down at the wheelchair. "I thought you might like some fresh air," he said. "Nestor had no objection."

Alannah had Danny's hand in hers, stroking it gently. It felt very private, like something Helen had no right to see. She looked back to Gevaudan and smiled. "Okay," she said. "I could do with a change of scene."

St Martin de Porres Church Tower
1745 hours

The crenellations around the tower's parapet looked like chipped broken teeth, and the bloodstains on the sandstone flags hadn't come out and probably never would.

From below came the clang of tools, and Zaq's voice echoing inside the battletruck as she berated the crew she had trying to fix it. One concrete gain this latest blood sacrifice had won. Along with their lives, of course.

In a couple of corners of the tower roof, brass glinted in the afternoon sun; cartridge cases that hadn't been cleared away. Darrow crouched, wincing as hips and knees complained, and picked a couple up. The 7.62mm NATO cartridge could have been a Reaper's gun, or Trex's, but the other was .303 British. Darrow smiled. Only Scopes' Lee-Enfield would have used that.

He straightened and stood, head bowed. He wasn't an emotional man – didn't consider himself one, anyway. But nonetheless, the crews had been his children. So many had been lost last December, it was impossible to grieve them all. But this was a sharper, more particular loss; one of the last of his crew.

She'd always been a strange one, Scopes – quiet, introverted, hardly ever lighting up except when she had her precious rifle. He'd never quite understood what it was about that weapon, the connection with it and why it had affected her – never would, of course, now – but it had been there. He wasn't sure how things had been between her and Trex – friends, comrades, lovers? None of his business, really. But he found himself hoping they' had been lovers. He would have liked to think she'd known that much happiness.

Someone rapped lightly on the shattered wooden door. "Yo."

He turned. "Flaps."

"Thought about it," she said. "I wanna go with you. That still okay?"

"Well – yes. But what about –"

"Right, then," she said, then turned and went down the stairs.

"Glad to have you," he called after her. Would he ever know why? Probably not. He wasn't the kind of father children had long heart-to-hearts with.

He closed his fist around the cartridge, put it in his pocket, and followed Flaps down the stairs. There was one more goodbye to say.

SICK BAY, ASHWOOD FORT
1800 HOURS

Alannah didn't hear Darrow come in; the first she knew was when she heard him chuckle. She turned and glared at him, feeling her face burn red; he was looking at her and Danny, smiling.

"So that's it," he said. "I saw it from the beginning."

"Piss off." Alannah looked down.

"Don't be ashamed, Alannah." He crouched beside her. "The fact we can still make fools of ourselves even after all this is one of my few remaining sources of anything resembling optimism."

Alannah laughed. "Oh, sod off." She shook her head. "You're going, aren't you?"

"Yes."

"Are you ever coming back?"

Darrow shrugged. "With luck."

"You can't forgive yourself, can you?" She couldn't keep the anger out of her voice.

"It's not that."

"What, then?"

"I owe them something. All of them. Nadgers, Nikki, Hinge, Thursday, Telo, Lelly... Mary, too. And Mike. And all the ones whose names I can't remember."

"They're dead," said Alannah. "We don't owe the dead anything."

Darrow's smile was sad. "You know better than that."

"So what do we owe them?" she asked.

"A meaning for their deaths?" Darrow stood. "I should go."

Alannah took his hand. "Be well, Roger."

Darrow kissed her hand gently. "And you, my lady." The moment hung between them; *what might have been*, she thought. Then his hand slipped from hers, and he was gone.

She turned back to Danny and waited. She didn't see Stephen there any more: only a boy called Danny Morwyn who was a third of her age, big-hearted and plucky, that she wanted to be with. If she was lucky, he still wanted the same. His eyes moved to and fro under their lids; she ached to know those dreams. He sighed; his eyes opened. He blinked and licked his lips. "Alannah?"

She poured a cup of water with her free hand, brought it to his mouth. "I'm here," she said.

"What about Flaps?"

"She's gone with Darrow," Alannah said. "It's just you and me. Assuming you want me."

He said nothing, but she felt his hand squeeze hers.

OUTSIDE ASHWOOD FORT
1900 HOURS

The little stone bridge had been smashed; the stream now frothed white around the fragments that lay in the current.

Everything changed, and usually ended up broken; but there could be beauty, even there.

The sky above was blue, marred only by scattered shreds of cloud, the air fresh. The sun was warm but low in the sky; another half-hour and it would be down.

Gevaudan sat on the broken stonework and looked at her. "You seem different," he said.

"I'm in a fucking wheelchair, Gevaudan."

"Temporarily."

"Huh."

"Another week or two of bed-rest and you'll be your usual unbearable self again. Or perhaps not."

"What *are* you on about?"

"I don't know." He spread his long white hands. "If I had to try and define it, I'd say you no longer seem to have a devil on your back."

"No," she said. "Not for now, anyway." She wanted to believe Frank and Belinda were gone for good, but there was no certainty with them. She scowled at Gevaudan; the way he just sat there studying her, looking wise, suddenly annoyed her. "What about you?"

"What about me?" he said.

"Alannah told me," said Helen. "About Kellett."

"Ah," Gevaudan nodded and looked down at the water. "That."

Something had come into his voice, or gone out of it; Helen regretted saying anything. "I don't think we ever really talked about my past," he said. "Did we?"

"Not that I remember," she said. "Look, if you don't want to – "

"When the attack came," he said, "I wasn't with my family. That was why I survived. I was a pacifist, you see. A peace activist. Much to my parents' embarrassment."

Helen smiled. "Black sheep?"

"My father was a military officer. There was a long tradition of it in our family. My brother, Gideon – he carried it on, at least for a while."

"He died?"

"In the War. He was in prison. I went there, looking for him, but it had burned. All I found were ashes and bones."

"I'm sorry."

"Anyway. The authorities deemed me a subversive and I was arrested a few weeks before the War. After the attack, I was able to break out of the detention facility. My family had all been at home when the attack came. My wife, my daughter, my son-in-law, my grandchildren. Radiation sickness. By the time I got there, they were all gone. I survived after that – God knows I didn't want to, but some sort of instinct kept me going. I stayed free, for a few years. Until the Reapers caught up with me. They put me on a clearance crew."

She'd tried lecturing him about the clearance crews once, right at the beginning. *I am* very *familiar with the clearance crews*, he'd said at her through his teeth. No wonder.

"I lasted longer than expected. I was lucky, especially at my age. But it couldn't go on forever. One day a medic came and took blood samples from everyone on the crew; shortly afterwards they brought me to the Major's office. Kellett was there. I didn't know his name at the time, of course. They told me I'd been assigned to an experimental programme."

"The Grendelwolves?"

"Kellett had devised the Goliath serum before the War, but it had been considered unethical. Inhumane. The Reapers, of course, aren't concerned with such things. I later learned they'd injected hundreds of prisoners with it. Most died, so they looked for common denominators among the survivors. Interestingly, age and general health weren't factors, otherwise I wouldn't have had a chance."

"That's the second time you've mentioned your age," said Helen. "How old –"

"At the time of the War," said Gevaudan, "I was sixty-six years old."

She stared at the smooth, ageless face, the black hair. He shrugged. "The Goliath serum repairs and reverses damage. That includes any caused by the ageing process. Even helps repair the damage and trauma it causes when it recalibrates your entire body. The only question is whether it can do so

424

more quickly than it can damage you. Kellett had found that all the survivors had two things in common."

"And you had both."

"I was male, and my blood type was O-negative. Hence the blood samples. They didn't tell me all this at the time, you understand. Possible survival as a human guinea pig, versus a slow death from radiation. Even if I'd been given a choice, I'd probably have agreed."

Gevaudan released a long shuddering breath. "Another time, I'll tell you about the change. It's not a memory I wish to revisit today. I will say this, though – it was prolonged and extremely painful, and nearly killed me several times. Even using O-negative males, only one in nine subjects survived and became a Grendelwolf. One other thing – all throughout the process, Kellett was there. Partly it was to take notes. But mostly, it was because he liked watching the suffering he'd caused."

Helen could say nothing. Gevaudan stared into the stream. "Having survived the change, I couldn't continue to survive without the serum. I think I told you how they once made an example of an insubordinate Grendelwolf by showing us exactly how slow and agonising a death that would be."

"Yes."

"Kellett presided over our training, too. And he took particular satisfaction in overseeing mine."

"Because you'd been a pacifist?"

Gevaudan nodded. "They had to train us, of course – we were to be their shock troops, and they had to be able to control us. But Kellett saw it as a particular triumph to make me act against everything I believed in. I loathed him, Helen. Hated him as I've hated no-one before or since. I thought he'd been killed at Sheffield, when the Grendelwolves rebelled."

"And then he showed up here, alive."

The stream bubbled and chuckled. "The worst part was the things I wanted to do to him. I would have made his death last hours, *days*, if I could have."

"You didn't."

"Not the point. It was something I couldn't blame on what Kellett had done. It was entirely human, and entirely me."

"So's the rest of you. You're more than that."

"Kellett almost turned me into a monster. I came close to turning myself into one here."

"The memory – what he'd done – it hurt that much?"

"Not that."

"Then what?"

Gevaudan was silent, head bowed. "Loss." he said at last. "You can resign yourself to having lost what matters to you. Reconcile yourself to it. The hard part is reconciling yourself to having something like it again, when you know what it is to lose it. And if you think you *have* lost it… you can find yourself somewhere very dark." Still he wouldn't look up. "I don't fight for a cause. I fight for you."

Helen looked for a reply, found none.

"Yo."

She turned; Flaps. "Just came to say hi before I went."

"Heading back to the field-base?" said Helen.

"City. With Darrow."

Helen remembered Flaps' words to Alannah. "Flaps, are you sure –?"

"I'm going. Glad you're alright, anyway."

"I will be." Helen touched the bandage around her head. "And – thank you."

"For?"

"Couldn't have won without you."

"I know," said Flaps. "Our job, innit? Dying so you stay alive."

The worst of it was that there wasn't any bitterness in it; it was just a statement of fact. Helen couldn't answer, any more than she could meet Flaps' steady, cold blue eyes.

"You're sure this is what you want?" said Gevaudan.

"What I said. Wish folk'd believe me."

"My apologies."

Flaps coughed, tugged her nose. "Went your cottage. Just to pick me stones up."

"Of course."

"Find somewhere safe for them once we're there."

"All right." Gevaudan swallowed hard. "Be well, Flaps."

"You too, Creeping Death."

She hesitated for a second, swaying on the balls of her feet, then darted forward and threw her arms around his neck. Gevaudan blinked, then patted her back with his long white hands. She stepped back, bright red. Helen wasn't sure which of them was more surprised by what had just happened.

They stared at one another a moment longer; then Flaps turned and ran off. Gevaudan stared after her. Helen looked away.

"Can you stay out a little longer?" she heard him say after a few moments.

With his coat around her, she felt warm enough. "I think so."

"Good. There's something I think you'll like."

Gevaudan wheeled her back through the outer wall and the ruined village. The road had been swept of debris, rubble gathered into heaps. Crude shelters of tarp or animal hide had been rigged for those who could be housed here, for now: the rest were crammed into the Fort.

Golden evening light painted the village square, streaked by the war memorial's long shadow. The cenotaph was scarred and peppered with bullet holes, the stone cross at the top shot away. A crowd had gathered around the square's edges; some stood, while others sat on chunks of rubble. Helen saw faces she recognised among them: there was Wakefield, sitting with Filly. Hei, Nestor – even Zaq was there.

"Helen!" Alannah waved to them. In front of her sat Danny in another wheelchair, a blanket around his shoulders, another on his knees.

Gevaudan steered the wheelchair to park it beside Danny's. Helen saw him nod to Alannah; she nodded back.

Helen looked at Danny. He looked small in the chair, and paler than usual. That wasn't surprising, nor was the look in his eyes.

"How are you?" she asked quietly.

The blanket round his shoulders lifted and fell. "I'm alive, aren't I?" he said.

"Yes. We both are."

"How's the head?"

"I've still got one."

After a moment, he smiled back, then stopped. She sat looking at him, waiting.

"Got Alannah to light a candle," he said. "In the road-shrine."

Helen didn't answer.

"Always do it before a fight. Didn't, this time."

"That's not why you got shot," she said.

"No?"

"Just – luck. Good, bad – it's all there is."

He shrugged. "Don't wanna take chances, anyway." He was silent for a while, not looking at her, then spoke again. "It's Scopes. Trex, too. I keep seeing them."

"I heard what happened."

His eyes glistened. "I should have got them out. I was in charge."

She remembered her first sight of him, at the shantytown by the Irk – bright and eager, big puppy-dog eyes. The light in him was almost gone now. Helen wanted to believe it would shine again; if it was gone for good she was as guilty of that as Danny was for Trex and Scopes.

She reached out and squeezed his hand. Danny started, looked at her in surprise. From the corner of her eye, Helen saw Alannah looking sharply at her. She wondered if Gevaudan was doing the same. "You did what you had to," she said. "You were in charge of stopping the Reapers, and you did it."

"With a bit of help from old Creeping Death there."

"You're welcome, Danny," said Gevaudan. "Wakefield and company played a part, too."

"That doesn't change the fact you're one reason the rest of us are still alive," said Helen. "And still in the fight. That's all I can tell you."

"The performance is about to begin," someone called. The low babble of conversation faded to silence.

Someone squeezed past them: a big lad whose face Helen vaguely recognised. "Soz," he muttered.

"Hey Mackie," said Danny. The big lad glanced back at him, twitched a smile, then lumbered on to the other side of the square.

"He looks a bit haunted too," said Helen.

"Bit of a not-right," said Danny, tapping his forehead, "but he did all right out on the Devil's Highway. His best mate got killed there. Poor sod."

1938 HOURS

The sun bled and burned away along the line of hills; as the glow faded, the square was hushed in the twilight. Danny pulled the blanket tighter round his shoulders against the sudden wind.

He saw Flaps in the crowd, with Darrow. She looked at him once, then away. That hurt, but he thought he knew why. Knew who he'd dreamt of before he woke, whose name he'd called. There were a few others from the Wasteland outfits there, too: he recognised Pin, and Newt. And there were other faces, too: Nadgers and Ashton, Nikki and Hinge, Thursday. A flash of grey hair above a young face: Trex. And beside him, Scopes. The living and the dead.

Thirty men and women shuffled in. He saw tribesfolk: Fox, Crow, Fish, Hawk. There were crew-members from the cities. There were folk in garb from all different parts of the Wastelands – among them was Lish. Harp watched her from the crowd. She and two of the boys carried guitars; others had bone whistles or onion flutes. Two Hawk tribers rubbed fat of some kind into their lips. A Fox and a Crow stood on either side without instruments of any kind, their hands behind their backs.

A Fox knelt, put a drum between his knees.

Hei stepped into the square. He fidgeted, looking nervous. "Two weeks ago, the Reapers came to kill us all," he said. "But we're still here. Many men and women died in the fight. We're here to remember them."

He licked his lips, looked round at the others. "From the tribes and the crews, from all the different communities in the Wastelands who fight with us, we called together singers and rhymers, whistlers and bards, hummers and drummers." The rhyme got a laugh. "We fought together," said Hei. "We grieve together. We remember together. And so this – this is us, together, too. We have named this… piece, 'For Those Who Fall In Darkness.' Um…" Hei looked around, at the crowd. "That's all." He stepped out of the square.

"He organised it all," Danny heard Gevaudan murmur to Helen. "His idea. A bright lad."

"Interesting title, anyway," said Helen.

"It's quite good, actually."

"You've heard it?"

"Of course," he said. "They needed a little advice. Didn't I mention I once taught music?"

Old Creeping Death, trying to sound like he didn't give a shit. Danny heard Helen chuckle. "So they really did bring everyone together."

"Sh," said Alannah, as the drummer began to beat a steady rhythm. Two others joined in. The onion flutes set up a low, sad hum that rose and fell. Two notes, then three, then a fourth. Circling round and round; rising, falling, rising again.

Dirge, that was the word. Where'd Danny heard it? Darrow? Gevaudan? With the drums it was a slow, steady march, for carrying the dead to their grave.

One of the boys on guitar played next, joined by the other, a layer of low strumming rhythm between the drums and onion flutes. Then Lish began to play, picking out a slow, sad tune – bit like something Gevaudan might have played.

Now the bone-whistles came in, thin and high and sharp, swirling about over the low dark hum like wind. Danny thought of faces screwed in grief, crying it out to the sky. The Hawk-tribers pursed their lips and joined in, before their mouths opened and the sound became a wordless keening.

The drum's rhythm quickened to a march and the music became faster, more jagged. It spoke of battle now, of danger and threat. Then the Fox standing to the side began to speak, in rhythm to the drums. He was a Rhymer, Danny realised, like Trex had been. He named Wakefield and the others who'd fought beside her on Wall One. Other names, too, ones Danny didn't know. Other fights and skirmishes he hadn't even noticed in the thick of his own scrap.

The Crow took up the rhyme, speaking of how the Catchmen had struck the wall and those who'd died and fallen back. Then the Fox again, on Helen standing firm in the village, of Gevaudan and Wakefield retaking Wall One. The Crow: Helen's wounding and Wall One's collapse. And so on. Danny heard his own name spoken, and it felt mad. Not real.

And then at last, spoken by the Fox, came another rhyme:

> *"All about St Martin's Tower*
> *A hundred Reapers lie.*
> *They came across the Wastelands*
> *On backs of steel to die.*

> *To hold the Tower against them all*
> *Was Scopes the sniper true;*
> *Trex the Fox to guard her back;*
> *Against that horde, these two.*

> *And up St Martin's Tower's stairs,*
> *A hundred Reapers more*
> *Paid in blood for every step,*
> *To reach the topmost floor.*

> *Call for Scopes of Darrow's Crew,*
> *Call Trex the Fox again,*
> *Her rifle's broken on the floor,*
> *You'll call them both in vain."*

Danny realised his fist was pressed to his mouth and he was biting at it. He was shaking. He rocked forward, letting go, not caring who heard or saw, sobbing. Alannah leant forward, hugged him from behind and kissed his hair.

He opened his eyes, trying to blink the tears back, and saw he wasn't the only one to weep. A lot of them were. Across the square he saw Mackie rocking to and fro, hugging himself as the tears streamed down his face, mumbling Cov's name.

CHEETHAM HILL ROAD, CITY OF MANCHESTER
1950 HOURS

Where Cheetham Hill Road met the A6, at the edge of the river and beside the ruins of a huge glass and steel building, a wall rose. The gate in it was open, and a ragged line of figures stood before it. Reaper landcruisers drove up and down the road, .50 cals aimed over the crowd's heads. Hard-faced CorSec troopers eyed them, rifles and submachine guns ready for use.

The Walker passed the ragged line. It side-stepped a landcruiser; the Reapers' eyes passed over it without reaction.

The Walker went through the gate, and the Reaper guards didn't even look up. It walked on into the city, eyes still fixed on the Tower.

ASHWOOD VILLAGE
2000 HOURS

All the sorrow in the world was in the music now, as the drumming slowed again and the last rhyme came to its end. Now Hei returned, and unravelled a paper scroll. With each beat of the drum, as the music still rose and fell, he called out a name.

Helen wiped at her eyes. Danny sobbed helplessly in Alannah's arms. The song had reached him more deeply than her, but that was good. If there was something left in him to damage, there might be something left to save.

And it wasn't only him: wherever Helen looked, she saw bowed heads, eyes wiped at roughly with sleeves. The big lad, Mackie, rocked to and fro, face in his hands. Why not her? Was she so dead inside? Or perhaps, having lived through the Refuge anew, she was empty just for now. Nestor had told her that, while unconscious, she'd cried. Perhaps, just perhaps, she had something left to save as well.

Gevaudan's head was bowed, black hair hiding his face. Perhaps the music had reached him too; perhaps she was the only one it hadn't turned inside-out.

She sank back in her chair. She felt alone, but with that came a degree of clarity. And with that clarity came sight at last.

Gevaudan leant towards her. "Are you all right?"

"You said to me, once, *tell me your vision*," she said. "Do you remember?"

"I remember."

"It's bugged me ever since," she said. "What happens when, *if*, we win? I didn't have an answer. And now I know why. I've been asking the wrong questions. It's not about *my* vision, it's about *ours*. Everyone's. Don't you see? We have to create it together. Otherwise we're just another bunch of things giving orders."

She fought for the words; Gevaudan stayed silent, letting her speak.

"We've been doing it all wrong, Gevaudan. We need something bigger than all of us – something that can't be stopped, whoever the Reapers kill."

"Useful, if it could be managed," he said. "But how?"

"A book."

"A book?"

"A book," she said. "Setting out what we want, what we're about."

"Which is?"

"Everyone being able to live their lives, as they see fit. And the rest – the rest is how-to. How to fight, build weapons…"

"An instruction manual," said Gevaudan, "and a manifesto. So anyone with a copy can be part of the fight."

"Yes."

"Leaderless resistance," said the Grendelwolf. "Not a new idea. But an effective one."

"You knew about it?"

"I learned a thing or two, along the way."

"But you never thought of it?"

Gevaudan shrugged. "Nobody asked me."

"And there's our problem in a nutshell," Helen said. "That's what has to change."

Gevaudan chuckled. *"Rise like lions after slumber, in unvanquishable number…"*

"Gevaudan?"

"Yes, Helen?"

"Shut up."

"Yes, Helen."

"Just for now."

"As you wish."

MILLER STREET, CITY OF MANCHESTER
2020 HOURS

The Walker strode up Miller Street, past the patrolling landcruisers, and stopped at last before the Tower. Even now, its frontage still gleamed: it wasn't hard to find people to risk their lives cleaning it in exchange for a few days' food. And so it shone in the thickening dusk, a gleaming symbol of the Reapers' might, visible for miles.

In front of the Tower was a concrete plaza, reached by flights of steps from street level. At the top of the steps were machine gun nests; further back, a pair of concrete pillboxes and guards with rifles outside the doors.

The Walker climbed the steps, skirting the machine gun nests and the hulks of the pillboxes, its footsteps clicking on the concrete, towards the entrance to the Tower.

Ashwood Village
2030 HOURS

As the song's last echoes rolled away across the hills, the applause began. Cheering, too. And weeping. Hands were shaken, embraces offered. By then the ruins were deep in twilight; candles were handed out and lit, and the crowd began breaking up and drifting off – alone, in groups, or, arm in arm, hand in hand, in pairs. A procession of tiny lights, going up the hill towards the Fort.

Wakefield watched the Grendelwolf wheel the crazy ginger away. Alannah stayed seated by Danny's wheelchair, holding his hands in hers, then leant towards him. Danny leant towards her, and at long last, their lips met in a kiss.

"Finally," said Filly.

"Took them long enough."

"I know."

"Sweet," said Wakefield, so soft it was nearly a breath.

"Yes," said Filly. Her warm, soft hand squeezed Wakefield's. "It is."

She smiled at Wakefield; Wakefield smiled back.

"Come," said Filly, and led Wakefield from the square.

The Tower
2035 HOURS

The guards outside the Tower's main entrance neither blinked nor moved as the Walker passed. It stepped between them. It raised a hand, and the door opened.

Neither did the guards inside spare a glance as the Walker crossed the lobby to the elevators. It reached out and pushed a button; the doors slid open with a soft chime.

The elevator went only to one floor, could not be used without authorisation. The sound should have alerted every guard on the floor, yet no-one moved.

The Walker stepped into the elevator: the doors shut behind it.

*

On the Tower's highest floor, the Commander's personal guards stood at attention. Their job was to challenge anyone who reached this floor with guns aimed and ready to fire. Yet none of them heard the lift doors open; none of them moved.

The Walker passed between them to stand before the door they guarded. Then it raised a pale, grimy hand, and knocked.

*

Winterborn pulled open his desk drawer. No-one got as far as his door unless he'd been told, and authorised it. But Operation Harvest had failed, Jarrett was dead, the Jennywrens crushed and scattered. You only held power because others believed you did: failure turned it all to dust.

Might his guards have let an assassin through – or were they here to do the deed themselves? Winterborn took his pistol from the drawer. "Who's there?" he called, and pulled back the slide.

When the door opened he raised the gun, but there was nothing there. After a moment, the door swung shut again. Winterborn blinked – and was no longer alone.

It stood over him in a long, grey cloak, face hooded. Winterborn thrust the pistol towards it, but a white hand plucked it from his grip.

Winterborn recoiled. He could cry out, but if this thing had made it this far, he'd surely get no help from his men. His swivel chair thumped back against the wall: Winterborn jumped out of it and darted towards the window, tensed for a run towards the exit.

The hooded figure turned to watch him go. He assumed so, anyway: he couldn't see its face, just the shadows inside the cowl. It put the pistol on the desk and spread its pale hands.

"Don't be afraid, Commander." Its voice was grating and raw. "If I meant you harm, I'd have done so by now."

Winterborn stood still, studying the visitor. "What do you want?"

"To help."

"Who are you?"

It chuckled; Winterborn flinched from the sound. "I'm hurt, Commander. Given our association, I'd have thought you'd recognise me."

It raised its grimy hands to grip the edges of the hood and pushed it back. The salt-and-pepper hair beneath was tangled and matted, and the glasses that he'd always worn were gone, but the face was the same.

"Doctor Mordake?" said Winterborn.

Mordake grinned as the hood slid all the way back. The back of his head was hairless, swollen. His grin widened and he turned, showing Winterborn what was there: a smooth white oval face, female, starkly perfect, right down to its small neat chin, the eyes closed. A mask, Winterborn dared to hope, until the eyes opened: they were as smooth as the skin, and utterly black.

The face smiled; the teeth were white and perfect. When Mordake spoke again, its lips moved too; as he turned back to face Winterborn, the Commander saw both mouths moving in unison. "That's right," he said. "I'm back to offer my services."

"What services?"

"My expertise, Commander. I'm sure you can use it. In fact, you already have. Who do you think gave you the information to create the Catchmen?"

"Ah," said Winterborn. "Of course. Although since Helen remains alive and Ashwood Fort didn't fall, I can only be so grateful."

"A bad workman blames his tools, Commander," Mordake said. "It's hardly my fault Colonel Jarrett failed, is it? In any case, don't worry. I've come back to give you an even more

powerful weapon." The two mouths smiled. "And to destroy
your enemies, Commander. Once and for all."

THE END

THE BLACK ROAD CONTINUES IN

WOLF'S HILL

WOLF'S HILL

QUEENSWAY TUNNELA, LIVERPOOL/BIRKENHEAD

The smell was worse inside, and the dark was thick and cold from the river above. Gevaudan felt it press in around them as he led them on.

The stink of urine and excrement worsened. The tunnel curved first one way, then another, snake-like. It had curved, ribbed white walls, now streaked with green and black, and four lanes, two going each way. In them were more vehicles: cars, trucks, buses.

The ground crunched under Gevuadan's boots. He glanced down; it was littered with cockroach shells and animal bones – bats, rats, birds – all in a soup of animal waste that had dropped from the ceiling. The mire clicked and scuttled as still-living insects scattered from his path.

Up ahead, something long and white hung down. A sheet of some kind, ragged and tattered. The lantern-light caught more of them, further down the tunnel. Then Gevaudan drew closer, and saw it wasn't cloth at all.

A gasp – he turned and saw Pin frozen, staring. She'd almost walked into another web, and the spider in it hung in no more than a foot from her face. The light gleamed in eight black shiny eyes; its legs seemed as thick as Pin's fingers, and three or four times longer, its body bigger than Gevaudan's fist. Pin shifted sideways, and it moved.

Neap screamed; the spider hunched, crouching. It was going to jump.

"Quiet," hissed Gevaudan, stepping forward; the spider scuttled upwards, haring up the strands of the web. "Keep quiet," he said, "and still. They won't be dangerous unless you panic them." He smiled. "They're probably more frightened of you than you are of them."

Pin didn't look convinced, especially as they carried on through the tunnel, skirting the webs, and encountered the shrivelled remains of birds, bats, rats and what looked like a small dog hanging in them. Nonetheless, she kept going – determined to set an example, Gevaudan guessed. She was doing well.

He kept low, staying close to the vehicles, the Bren gun at his hip. He passed a car, a truck and then a double-decker bus, its windows unbroken, but streaked, like its two-tone green paint, with rust and moss and slime. Inside, the passengers were still in their seats. What he could see of them was little more than rag and bone, but they were barely visible, cocooned as they were in the ballooning clouds of spiderweb that filled the vehicle's interior.

One of the bodies raised a skeletal hand and pressed it to the window. Gevaudan froze, staring, then relaxed when he saw the hand had too many fingers. The spider stared at him through the dirty glass for a moment, then scuttled away into the depths of its lair. Gevaudan breathed out, and they all moved on.

A noise; movement. A snap and crunch. Gevaudan raised a hand, heard the movement of the others behind him stop, and dropped behind a car. He shouldered the Bren and inched forward, then stopped to listen again.

A soft drip of water; a faint rustle of things moving on webs and floor. Something larger moved on the ground nearby;

Gevaudan aimed towards it. A rat glared beadily back at him, then scuttled away under the bus. Gevaudan rose, turned to the others and motioned them on.

The darkness exploded into light.

Fiat lux, Gevaudan thought detachedly as his eyes tried to reattune themselves. The sheets of webbing glowed, the spiders black scrawls that zig-zagged up through them towards the ceiling and the shelter of the dark.

Running footsteps thundered. "Halt! Remain where you are!" an amplified voice boomed. "Lay down your weapons!"

"Go!" shouted Gevaudan; he spun back and opened fire.

Webs jerked, flapped, tore. A clattering sound from above and blackness spilled from the ceiling to flood the tunnel; bats, frightened from their roosts.

Gunfire thundered in response. Webs jumped and tore again, some falling asunder. Dirt-covered windscreens exploded, and the bodywork of cars juddered and clanged as bullets slammed into them.

"Move!" shouted Gevaudan at Pin and the others. He could glimpse the Reapers through the webs – vague silhouettes, advancing and firing. He emptied the Bren's magazine in a long burst, saw two of them jerk back and fall. "Move!" he shouted again, then charged after his team, changing magazines as he ran.

One of the boys blundered into a web that tore and flapped around him; the boy screamed, fell to his knees. One of the spiders was on his shoulder, biting at his neck. Gevaudan snatched it up, crushed it, but the boy fell forward and he saw three more of them clinging on.

"Keep going!" he yelled after Pin and the rest. "Stay low!" Cocking the Bren, he knelt to check the fallen boy, but the tribal's eyes were open and unblinking, and there was no pulse at his throat. Before he could turn to fire back at the Reapers, fresh light exploded in the tunnel, from the Liverpool end.

This time there was no warning. The Reapers' guns crashed again; Gevaudan's team got off a few bursts in reply, but one by one they dropped. Pin ran past him, shouting; then she spun, slammed against the side of the spider-filled bus and collapsed beside the door.

Gevaudan fired back, and then something smashed into him and he fell against a car. Pain in his stomach; he looked down and saw his black sweater was dark and stained. Another round hit him in the shoulder, but he kept hold of the machine gun, firing first one way down the tunnel, then the other.

Shadows ran towards him: he jerked the Bren their way, then pulled it up. It was Neap and two others; the last of his team.

The Bren gun emptied; Gevaudan threw it aside and straightened up. There was still the Fury. Injured as he was, he didn't know how long he could sustain it, but he could at least try, give the rest of his team a chance to –

A hissing screech echoed down the tunnel, and everything went still. The firing stopped; even the scuttling of rats and spiders was gone. The only other sound was the fading flap and squeaking of the bats as they fled away.

"What?" said Neap. "What's that?"

Gevaudan looked towards the Liverpool entrance, saw the hunched shapes advancing, silhouetted against the webs before they tore them down with their clawed hands. Steel-helmeted heads; round, palely-glowing lenses for eyes.

"Catchmen," he said.

"But they're dead," said Neap. "They all died."

"Not all, it seems." Gevaudan didn't reach for the pistols he carried; they'd be worse than useless here. Instead he crouched and drew the knives sheathed in his boots. They whispered free; the light glinted on steel blades, and the symbol carved on either side of each one.

At first glance it resembled a crucifix, but a closer inspection would have shown the proportions weren't quite right, that parts of it weren't quite straight or at the right angle. Only one church he knew of depicted such a cross: the one that still stood in the village of Hobsdyke. Only it, carved on iron or steel, could kill the Night Wolves or one of their creatures.

"Get behind me," Gevaudan told Neap and the other two, and moved forward, still crouching, the knives in his hands.

How many of them were there? A dozen, twenty? Gevaudan was still trying to count them when they tore the last of the webs between them and him down. He heard Neap gasp as the Catchmen were revealed in full. A dull grey leathery hide covered their bodies and their mouths were lipless, bloodless slits, so their faces looked mouthless until they smiled, the grins stretching impossibly wide, up to where their ears should have been, huge and red and full of serrated teeth.

And then they rushed at him.

Gevaudan summoned the Fury.

He leapt and everything was fast. A Catchman leapt for him; he sprang aside, slashed it with a knife, spun to avoid another as it screamed. Drove the knife into the second attacker's back, spitted a third with the second blade as it lunged at him

Another Catchman took its moment, clawed thumbs aimed at his eyes – Gevaudan kicked it in the chest, flipping it back. His knives slid free of the Catchmen he'd killed – they were just sacks of leather hide now, the soft tissues frothing out of them in a bubbling pink slurry.

Gevaudan went for the Catchman he'd kicked but claws raked down his back. He cried out; more claws raked his stomach.

He kicked slashed stabbed, but they were as quick as him. Quicker. Then one had his arm, another his leg. He stabbed the one pinning his arm – it screamed but wouldn't let go. As it fell the one he'd kicked came to take its place. Gevaudan smashed his other blade through its right eye, deep into the skull – the blade stuck fast, wouldn't come free.

Behind him, screams – he twisted, trying to get loose, saw Neap and the other two vanish under the other Catchmen. Screams, then silence; the Catchmen rose from their kills, grinning mouths dripping red.

They ran at him, piled on. He stayed on his feet, didn't stop fighting- but then his legs buckled under the weight and he went down. The weight of them smashed into the tunnel floor's mire and filth; he couldn't breathe.

Before the black descended, he thought of Helen in the garden, the candlelight reflected in her eyes.

*

It was a long time before the tunnel was quiet again. Pin pressed herself against the foot of the bus' stairwell, teeth gritted and lips pressed together as cobwebs brushed her face and tangled in her hair. One of the corpses had slipped partly from its seat; its grinning face was an inch from hers.

The bus' door had been ajar, just enough for Pin to squirm inside.

She'd never seen a Catchman for herself, but she'd heard of them; heard how just one, had almost killed Gevaudan. And how many were there here?

She'd heard Neap scream, as well; heard him scream and she'd done nothing. She screwed her eyes shut, she mustn't cry, mustn't sob. There must be no sound.

Blood trickled from her leg wound. Her rifle lay on the tunnel floor; she pulled her machine pistol out from under her jacket, eased the Stemp's bolt back very very slowly, so the click as it engaged was so soft, with luck no-one would hear.

The Catchmen's snarling subsided, leaving only muffled grunting noises, till at last an officer spoke. "All right. Get him out of here. Don't damage him any more than he already is. They want him alive."

Something tickled Pin's hair; a light, feathery touch. Then another, and another, and another, like little thin fingers.

Or legs.

She held her breath, kept still, as the spider crawled across her scalp, her forehead, down over her face. One of its legs wavered a fingertip's breadth from her eye, then settled on her cheek instead.

Down it crawled, down, then landed on the floor and scuttled across to another set of webbing.

Pin huffed out a relieved breath, crawled to the front of the bus and peered out through the main window. She couldn't see much through the grime, but she made out a half-dozen grey, steel-helmeted figures, clutching a tall, black-clad man between them. Gevaudan. She saw him move weakly; then they bore him off down the tunnel.

445

Footsteps; she ducked again, peering out through the crack of the door. Reapers filed past – the ones who'd been up the tunnel, waiting for them at the start, following the others, following Gevaudan back towards Liverpool.

Bastards. They'd been watching. They'd known the rebels were coming. Some had been waiting in the tunnel, others in the city, watching them go in and then following.

We never had a chance. Neap; it had been Neap's first time. So eager to show what he could do. Pin clenched her teeth and shook. Wait. She had to wait.

The last echoes of the footsteps died away. Pin stayed there, crouching, till at last the lights snapped off. She stood, putting her weight on her good leg, and wiped her face, then glanced back down the bus. Spiders hung in their webs, black blots amid the white and grey; she was sure they all watched her, but they didn't move. Pin turned away and squeezed out through the door, hissing to herself as pain shot through her wounded leg.

A couple of fallen candle-lanterns still burned. She picked one up and looked around, as much as she dared. Bodies were scattered across the tunnel, or pieces of them. Blood, still glistening and black, painted the cars.

Had to keep control. Had to stay calm. Had to find someone to tell. Pin peered under the bus and pulled her rifle out, then put on the safety catch and tucked the stock into her armpit, leaning on the barrel as a crutch. She looped the lantern's handle around her wrist and gripped the machine pistol in her other hand.

She wondered how far across they'd got before the ambush, how far she still had to go. Pin took a deep breath, and began limping down the tunnel.

Itching for the next instalment?
Not ready to leave *The Black Road* behind?

To find out more, and keep up to date about *The Black Road*, follow Simon Bestwick here:

🐦 @GevaudanShoal

ℹ️ http://simon-bestwick.blogspot.co.uk/

To find out more about Snowbooks, take a look over here:

🐦 @Snowbooks

❄️ http://snowbooks.com/

📘 Snowbooks